THE ROPE

THE ROPE

—•—

KANAN MAKIYA

PANTHEON BOOKS · NEW YORK

All rights reserved. Published in the United States by Pantheon Books, a division of Penguin Random House LLC, New York, and distributed in Canada by Random House of Canada, a division of Penguin Random House Canada Ltd., Toronto.

Pantheon Books and colophon are registered trademarks of Penguin Random House LLC.

Grateful acknowledgment is made to the following for permission to reprint previously published material:

HarperCollins Publishers: Excerpts from "Emperor" and "When the World Stands Still" from *The Collected Poems: 1956–1998* by Zbigniew Herbert, translated and edited by Alissa Valles. Copyright © 2007 by The Estate of Zbigniew Herbert. Translation copyright © 2007 by HarperCollins Publishers LLC. Reprinted by permission of HarperCollins Publishers.

Random House: Excerpt from "September 1, 1939" from *W. H. Auden Collected Poems* by W. H. Auden, copyright © 1940 and renewed 1968 by W. H. Auden. Reprinted by permission of Random House, an imprint and division of Penguin Random House LLC. All rights reserved.

The Wylie Agency LLC: "Mounds of human heads are wandering into the distance" by Osip Mandelstam, translated by Clarence Brown and W. S. Merwin. Translation copyright © 1973 by The Estate of Clarence Brown and W. S. Merwin. Reprinted by permission of The Wylie Agency LLC.

Library of Congress Cataloging-in-Publication Data
Makiya, Kanan.
The rope : a novel / Kanan Makiya.
pages ; cm
ISBN 978-1-101-87047-1 (hardcover). ISBN 978-1-101-87048-8 (eBook).
1. Iraq—Politics and government—2003—Fiction. 2. Iraq—Social conditions—
21st century—Fiction. I. Title.
PS3613.A357R67 2016 813'.6—dc23 2015026187

www.pantheonbooks.com

Jacket art: From the series "Dark Interludes" 2001, by Walid Siti
Jacket design by Kelly Blair
Book design by Maggie Hinders

Printed in the United States of America
First Edition
2 4 6 8 9 7 5 3 1

For Wallada and Mustafa

Contents

PART ONE **DECEMBER 30, 2006**

The Hanging: Morning · 3

The Rope: Evening · 16

PART TWO **APRIL 2003–NOVEMBER 2006**

2003

Najaf: April 10 · 27

Man in the Alley · 31

March on Karbala · 33

Mother · 37

An Execution in Baghdad · 43

Car Bomb · 45

Uncle · 50

Inauspicious Birds · 53

The Letter · 59

Minarets and Kalashnikovs · 67

Painful Slap · 71

Black Boots · 75

2004

Bad Blood · 83

Foreigner Iraqis · 89

The Cabal of Thirteen · 94

Love of Self · 100

Three Houses · 107

The Sayyid · 115

The Arrest Warrant · 119

War in Najaf · 124

Cease-fire · 128

The Quiet Ayatollah · 131

2005

Betrayal · 143

An Intimate Killing · 151

The Meeting · 159

Aftermath · 167

Grandfather · 170

The Second Conversation · 177

2006

Justice · 185

The Awaited One · 191

Names of Things · 197

The Importance of Being Umar · 203

Abu Muntassir · 209

Haider · 213

Haider and Muntassir · 217

Baghdad · 222

The File · 230

Before the Hanging · 244

PART THREE **WHEN THE WORLD STANDS STILL**

December 30, 2006: Early Morning · 255

AFTERWORD **BAGHDAD TODAY** · 285

Acknowledgments · 293
A Personal Note · 297

PART ONE

DECEMBER 30, 2006

Once upon a time there was an Emperor. He had yellow eyes and a predatory jaw. He lived in a palace full of statuary and policemen. Alone. At night he would wake up and scream. Nobody loved him. Most of all he liked hunting game and terror. But he posed for photographs with children and flowers. When he died, nobody dared to remove his portraits. Take a look, perhaps still you have his mask at home.

ZBIGNIEW HERBERT

The Hanging

Morning

I checked my watch, over and over again, determined to catch the precise moment when the lever would be released. I still almost missed it, the trapdoor clanging open before he had finished reciting his prayers.

"The Tyrant was hanged on Saturday, December 30, 2006, at 6:09 a.m.," I wrote in the evening of that day in a blue-ruled school notebook, whose cardboard covers Mother, God rest her soul, had lovingly wrapped in pink paper decorated with white carnations. She never let me throw away those old notebooks, mandatory in my secondary school in Najaf. The notes I recorded in them between 2003 and 2006 form the backbone of this account.

Three hours and ten minutes earlier, at 2:59 a.m. precisely, he had been transferred to Iraqi sovereignty for the first time since his capture, proof of our independence from the American invaders.

His transfer came on the heels of "a bitter struggle between us and the Occupier," my uncle and mentor said.

"Did the Occupier agree to the transfer?" I asked Uncle.

"Not at first; they fought hard to delay it. But they caved in," Uncle replied, "like they always do."

The prime minister wanted the hanging to coincide with the day Sunni Muslims celebrated the first of the four-day Great Feast, and he wanted it to coincide with the day of his son's marriage. All in the government agreed a higher authority had to rule. And so it was.

After the Sunni Grand Mufti decreed the first day of the Great Feast to be December 30, 2006, our Shi'a clerics ruled that a hanging on the day before the Great Feast was permissible, but not on its first day. And so the prime minister settled on the earliest hour of the morning of the Great Feast, minutes before sunrise and the start of the Great Feast, as the day of the hanging. Technically, the Tyrant would be hanged and the prime minister's son married the day before our Great Feast started.

Sunni clerics saw through the prime minister's ruse. They said the Tyrant, a Sunni, was in fact being executed on a day Sunni Muslims consider a celebration, thus spoiling their Feast; meanwhile, we Shi'a got to celebrate the day our bitterest enemy had been executed, thus enhancing our celebrations.

Thus was the order of the firmament set by the timing of the rising of the sun; it permitted us to execute one of theirs on the first day of their Feast, but not them to execute one of ours on the same day; and this even though all are Believers of the one true faith. It has always been thus.

The body of the Tyrant was flown by helicopter to the prime minister's house, where the wedding celebrations were under way. Accompanied by a chanting, delirious crowd waving Kalashnikovs in the air, the corpse was carried from the helicopter's landing pad to the front door of the house, vacated for the prime minister's use by twelve American lieutenant colonels. At the door of the house in which the wedding party was being held, the shroud was peeled back from the Tyrant's face in his coffin, exposing his bruised and broken neck to the frenzied delight of the chanting mob.

Our new rulers, including the prime minister, are former exiles, returning from cities like London, Tehran, and Damascus. I do not know whether revenge, or blood libel, or communal solidarity was behind the timing of the hanging; perhaps all of them. There are no written records to support one view or the other. On the contrary, the government and the court were at pains to stress their desire to apply the rule of law, to rob the insurgency of its titular head and prime symbol.

The hanging took place in the oldest Shi'a district of Baghdad, in a former intelligence compound, circled by the winding Tigris on three sides and walled off from the populace by a forbidding concrete wall on the city side, recently topped with bales of barbed wire. Government officials, flanked by the personal guard of which I was a member, met the Black Hawk helicopter transporting the Tyrant to the compound he had built for the purposes of interrogation, torture, and execution.

I had visited the compound before in the company of Uncle and his friends during the summer of 2003. "You are an expert on the compound," the turbaned commander who appointed me said. "We might need you in case something goes wrong." And so he decided I should be on the detail assigned to guard the prisoner from the time of his transfer into Iraqi custody to the moment of his execution.

The Tyrant slowly descended the folding steps released from the helicopter, pausing at the top to look around him as though to take advantage of the view stretching to the sinuous bends of the Tigris and the Golden Dome beyond. Looking down, he would have seen the dilapidated complex that had, under him, known better days. His feet touching the tarmac, he paused again, and then walked at an exaggeratedly leisurely pace, past flanking rows of American guards, medics, and other Occupier officials. Stiff and unbending, his back straight as a ramrod, the occasional flicker of a smile across thin lips, he thanked and bade farewell to each and every American, some of whose names he seemed to know. They in turn treated him with equally exaggerated respect, as though he were still a head of state. Walking him to a three-story concrete pillbox of a building with no identifiable entrance canopy, the party moved toward the hole in the wall that passed for a door. Papers were exchanged among officials, including a nervous, balding, mustachioed man to whom my eye was drawn, because his stomach rippled like jelly over a tight belt.

This completed the formalities of the Tyrant's transfer into our custody. My comrades and I, all in freshly minted uniforms of the New Army, took over from the American escort.

I had grown up with his images, wall-size on the street, or framed in glass in every office and living room of the Republic. The Tyrant would appear dressed as an Arab or as a Kurd, as an officer in battle fatigues or as a peasant carrying his spade, kissing children or leading men into battle. For the first time, I was able to observe the man himself.

He was dressed in a black camel hair overcoat made by his favorite Turkish tailor. Freshly dyed, his hair was signature black; his face, calm and impassive, the Stalin-like mustache copied by Iraqi males for a quarter of a century recently trimmed. At the point of handover, his features turned scornful, though he did not say a word, not even to the ministers and government officials present. They did not or could not look him in the eye and were constantly shifting their weight and shuffling their feet. He stood like one of his statues, looking past them when they addressed him, reading from one of their papers; it was as though they were not even there. Wordlessly and motionlessly, the Tyrant humiliated his new jailers.

This man once possessed absolute power; now he had none. Our government officials, on the other hand, never had power and would not recognize it if they had. To be sure they were seekers of it, but to them power was the chauffeured bulletproof vehicle, the size of their security escort, and the amount of noise and disruption the screeching wheels of their convoy could make scattering ordinary people about in the streets, people who would then turn back to look at them with what the officials misconstrued as awe. The Tyrant knew better. He knew that the true politician is one who plays the game, perfects gestures and facial expressions, not some of the time, but every second of every day. He also knew that there is no escape from power like his, no exit, no way out of the predicament that being always onstage creates; there is only death.

Sharply detailed pictures of that Saturday before the Great Feast, like the Tyrant's descent from an American Black Hawk helicopter, come to me frequently; they come in dreams and nightmares, and have been doing so for many years since the hanging, years in which this account was formless fragments, nothing more. I spent them floundering in doubt, dragging my notebooks around in a battered suitcase to a variety of anonymous locations in the urban desert that is today's Baghdad. I carried them with me wherever I went, because on the evening of the day of the hanging, I took a vow before God and His Prophet, Peace Be Upon Him, to record the truth as I began to see it on that day. I understood then what I had to do, no matter how it made me look to others, many of whom I counted as friends. At first they crossed to the other side of the street when they saw me coming; then they began speaking ill of me behind my back; finally they started to persecute me. I knew then I had to sever all ties with the city of my birth, Najaf, and lose myself in a city of ghosts, Baghdad. Nothing else could be done, not after the Tyrant dropped through the trapdoor to the end of the 120-centimeter slack in his rope.

I don't have to be asleep to see him drop; all the pictures can be summoned at will, as I am doing now, years later, sitting at a desk. At a moment's notice, they can materialize one by one like hallucinatory flashes, or take the form of a tightly focused clip of film relentlessly rotating inside my head, easy to summon but impossible to erase. The sharpest and most richly detailed of these images always date back to December 30, 2006.

I see the Tyrant's descent from the helicopter. I see him drop on his rope, in slow motion; then I see the rag doll shape of what was left of him swinging gently as though touched by a breeze, but actually from the spent force of his tightly trussed bucking feet traveling through the rope to the crudely fixed metal pulley attached to the concrete ceiling from which it swung.

The pulley, the type used for hauling building materials, came from a nearby construction site; the execution room, a hastily modified former conference room, contained plastic chairs and a Formica table at one end, and a raised hanging platform made of unpainted crude metal bars with a makeshift balustrade at the other. Above the trapdoor in the center of the platform the pulley had been screwed, askew, to the ceiling.

They had brought us here earlier, Saddam's final escort guard, for an inspection, and to memorize the precise route to this room from the windowless room where the Tyrant had waited for several hours before being marched to the hangman's rope.

I see him climb the podium deliberately, slowly, holding the Holy Book in his manacled hands. As he climbed the steps, I remember the room turning deathly silent, held in a paralytic grip as though by the sheer presence of the man. Never was there such a silence, until he reached the platform. Three guards wearing black ski masks that concealed their features, and mismatching beige and brown motorcycle jackets, were on the platform waiting for him. They started to manhandle him, trying to force a hood over his head, which he refused with a sharp gesture of his head. The same official in the receiving delegation, the one with the rippling stomach, was on the platform; he stopped the guards from forcing the issue. The Tyrant would remain unhooded. At this point one of the thwarted guards spat on the condemned man, shouting an insult. The Tyrant did not flinch, the spittle slowly running down his face. But the stillness in the room came to an abrupt end; it was as though an electric shock had jolted every person, releasing them from a trance.

People started to shout and jeer, some even throwing things, the shouting growing in volume and mysteriously coalescing into a single loud, pulsating throb. The well-intentioned official, his stomach heaving, did not know what to do; he started gesticulating anxiously with his hands to silence the crowd. No one paid attention. The collection of two hundred or so men assembled below the hanging platform were turning into a frenzied mob, hurling the occasional insult at the Tyrant that would break through the steady beat of "Oh, Sayyid. Oh, Sayyid."

That was our Sayyid, my Sayyid, they were calling out for—the Sayyid upon whose instructions I had exchanged my hodgepodge militiaman's garb for a freshly pressed uniform of the New Army.

Now I see the Tyrant grow ever more erect and stiff amid the deafening roar, his eyes boring defiantly into the baiting pack, his lips curled into a snarl. The governor said something to the hangman, and the noose—knotted in the British tradition of making such ropes—was slipped over his head. At that moment, speaking into the formless void above the heads of the crowd, the Tyrant called out, his voice like a foghorn booming into a sea of noise:

"God is great. The nation will be victorious. Palestine is Arab."

Extraordinary last words: extraordinary because they were in such conformity with a whole life. Had he chosen the words beforehand? Had he thought about what his final words would be, whiling away the time thinking them through in his cell?

Consider: "The nation will be victorious."

What nation do you think the Tyrant had in mind standing up there on the platform looking down at his countrymen? The one that was, or the one that is, or, perhaps, the one that has yet to be? The nation was clearly no longer He. Perhaps he could not be expected to acknowledge this fact. The only nation he could see was in that room, ranting and raving. And if it was to be "victorious," the question is over whom? Weren't the Americans who had so meekly handed him over to us supposedly the victorious ones? But the tense is future. So he recognized the nation of the present had been defeated; he meant, presumably, it would be victorious eventually. So whom did he have in mind? The insurgency, perhaps, the nation-in-waiting, which was daily gathering steam.

During his incarceration the Tyrant repeatedly told his American interrogators that he could stop the fighting in a week. What was he thinking? That he could cast a spell and the insurgents would come to their senses and strike a deal through him, symbol of a people who had been wronged, struggling against the Occupation.

"I am the president" were his first words, spoken in English, when the Occupier's soldiers dragged him out of his spider hole on a small farm just outside the city of his birth. "I want to negotiate."

He wanted to negotiate!

Imagine his humiliation, then, at what the Occupier did to him. "Caught like a rat," a delighted American general said. The Tyrant was displayed on CNN with foreign doctors poking at his teeth, pulling his hair, pretending all the while that they were looking for lice.

What a perfectly executed move—perhaps the only public relations success of their short tenure, reluctant and spoiled men that they were, men who no longer had the stomach for anything called sacrifice. The pictures resonated across the breadth of our Arab Muslim world. But it was the last victory the Tyrant's enemies would enjoy.

Now imagine this original humiliation being compounded by the chief of the Occupation bringing a cluster of Iraqi politicians, all of whom he had created, all wealthy gold-watch-wearing exiles returned from London, all gawking at the former Iraqi leader the day following his capture. One of them, smartly dressed with slickly oiled black hair dropping to his shoulders like a movie star, shouted: "You are cursed by God! How will you meet your Creator?"

"With a clear conscience and as a Believer," the Great Dictator replied.

"Why didn't you have the courage to fight or at least die trying? At least your sons fought before they were killed."

This was a logic that the Tyrant understood well.

What foreign ditch did they dig him out of? I can imagine him saying to himself while the apoplectic would-be politician with the black hair, who had done so well for himself in London, paced up and down the room, muttering "He's learned nothing . . . nothing!" and all the while the Tyrant was silently watching him, seated on his prison cot in his pajamas, his dirt-encrusted toenails showing through the cheap gray plastic slippers supplied by the U.S. Department of Defense.

I cannot see what learning has to do with it. Or cowardice with the Tyrant's surrender on December 13, 2003. It certainly is not why he allowed himself to be dragged out "like a rat," as Iraqi television reported, repeating what the American general had said.

The only imperative he obeyed was to live, to live in order to go on and fight another day. That is why in the months since the fall of Baghdad he switched locations daily, "organizing the insurgents," in the words of his lawyer. This craving for danger was not going to be satisfied by charging out of his spider hole with guns blazing. He needed the deaths of large numbers of men, combatants under his command, to sate his cravings and immense appetites. The insurgency against the Occupier was his creation, and could not be otherwise. He made it; he owned it; it was his to deploy in negotiations. The thought that it might take on a life of its own never crossed his mind. It is said they caught him with documents that corroborate his early preparations for the insurgency, dating back to the months before the invasion. I don't doubt it.

His first court appearance showed that he fully grasped the drama of his new situation. In the dreams and nightmares, which never go away, I always see him standing there, his eyes flashing, shouting: "This is all theater," with a dismissive wave to the cameras.

I see him tell the chief judge: "I am not going to answer to this so-called court, out of respect for the truth and the will of the Iraqi people." And he believed it too; he believed he alone had "respect for the truth and the will of the Iraqi people."

And then he said, "I always held the people's interests first . . .

Even today, I can go and sleep peacefully in any town in the country. Can you?" he asked his judges.

The chief judge—a Kurd, incidentally—was at a loss, not knowing how to handle the disintegration of his courtroom. He was dismissed for being too polite. Seriously! Every Iraqi upstart appointed by the Occupier was beginning to realize that, polite or not, there was more authority and self-assurance in the Great Tyrant's posture and delivery than in any of the judges, prosecutors, or attorneys arrayed before him! And they panicked, blaming a judge for saying "Mr. Saddam Hussein," instead of "the accused" or "the Tyrant"!

The Tyrant held on to the idea that he represented the nation, believing, not hoping, it was true, while at the same time knowing it was the only card left for him to play in a game now controlled by his captors. The court before which he stood, trained and nudged along at every step by the Occupier, did not know whom it represented, or by what law it was to judge this man who had in fact made all the laws, laws these very same judges had spent entire lifetimes studying and applying.

The world outside added to the mix an entirely new set of words— "universal justice," "international law," "human rights," "crimes against humanity," and the list goes on—honeyed words dished out on a pillow of empty promises that meant nothing to anyone inside the country; only the Tyrant's words, illusory or not, meant something to the people watching.

It was a moment that could not be predicted or planned for; it could only unfold.

Think of it as theater staged on the grandest of platforms; a play improvised, embellished, written, and revised constantly by none other than its prime subject, actor extraordinaire Saddam Hussein.

At the point of his transfer into Iraqi custody, on December 30, 2006, then and only then, the Tyrant would have realized the play had come to a stop; he would have given up on the idea that the Americans might take him up on his offer to negotiate.

But Iraqi custody was not the same as the nation's custody, and so the Tyrant did not, even at this late stage, surrender. Here lies the true measure of the man, the real leader he always knew himself to be, the proof that false hopes were not what had brought the Tyrant to such a point, nor were they a guarantee of success in order for him to persevere.

The Tyrant chose his moment, and switched course whenever necessary; he had done this again and again throughout his career. When the Occupier was in charge of his fate, the whole point of his life had been to live, to fight another day, by arms or through negotiations. Now that the Occupier had handed him over to his loosely cobbled native allies, the point of his remaining few hours remained as always: to save the nation, only this time by dying for it. He would therefore choose to die in such a way as to turn the tables on death itself. The final act was at hand, and for this too, as always, he had come well prepared.

Consider "Palestine is Arab," the next thing the Tyrant trumpeted out to the jeering mob.

Of course Palestine is Arab. What else could Palestine be? He meant the nation "will be victorious" because "Palestine is Arab." Everyone in that room understood that, which is why it struck a chord in that room on that day. What he was also saying was that every person in that room, all of whom believed Palestine is Arab, were in truth hypocrites, traitors to the fundamental principle of the Arabness of Palestine, which they all said they believed in, but which he alone was prepared to die for. Your Arabness passed muster only if you truly believed, deep in your heart of hearts, that Palestine was Arab; waver over it, as the Kurds might, or approach it less than enthusiastically, as we Shi'a did (for fear of Sunni dominion), and you were instantly suspect.

Palestine is the litmus test; it always has been.

The quality of being an Arab to Saddam meant that he and the jeering mob still had many things in common, what he and his party liked to call the nation's "eternal message." Blood, language, territory, religion, history were useful but not essential attributes;

the nation, first and foremost, was Spirit. And so, in that execution chamber on December 30, 2006, everyone was potentially an Arab, but only Saddam was the genuine article.

Would the crowd in the room understand him? Think about it differently: replace the word "Spirit" with "Belief," and instantly all Muslims in that room understood what the Tyrant was saying. As I said: of course Palestine is Arab. What is Islam but a Community of Believers? What is Arabism but a Community of Believers in the same Spirit?

The Tyrant wanted to follow up the words "Palestine is Arab" with the Muslim profession of faith, first pronounced by our patron saint, the Sayyid of all Sayyids, 'Ali son of Abu Talib, Prince of the Faithful, when he prayed with the Prophet as a ten-year-old boy in Mecca—words pronounced since by every Muslim multiple times a day.

To profess one's faith in God is a right given to every man, woman, and child without exception, a right that cannot be denied to infidels and unbelievers, nor even to those accused of apostasy. Moreover, it followed with iron logic from the Arab nature of Palestine, a land that became Muslim and Arab only after the conquest of Jerusalem in the year 634. By ending his eleven-word speech thus, the Tyrant was bearing witness to his dying adherence to Islam.

Decades of finely tuned instinct and experience had been honed into that last performance, which some imbecile captured on a videophone. The Great Tyrant, perhaps the greatest who ever ruled an Arab and Muslim land, never lost his composure, not even when the trapdoor clanged open while he was halfway through reciting his prayers.

Why was the Tyrant cut off in the middle of bearing witness to his faith? It had to be deliberate, a final insult, the instinct of small men trying to goad an ogre, not the measured and calculated mistake of one following orders. Inside that chamber, no one was any longer in control of anything. Why did the hangman flip the lever in the middle of the holiest set of words that a Muslim can utter, words that remain holy even if the speaker is a barbarous infidel? I don't think he was instructed. The government had wanted to showcase their execution, to highlight to the world their achievement in bringing the great Tyrant to justice. At the same time they wanted to stick it to their Sunni citizens, the ones whose first day of the Feast they were deliberately spoiling. The two impulses were at odds with one another, perhaps, but the latter won out because the government that wanted to achieve all those things was no longer in the room, just as it was absent in the country.

The Tyrant, on the other hand, was there. Solidly, his cloaked presence like some grim harbinger of death filled the room. I see his expensive black camel hair overcoat smoothing out the awkward bumps and shapes of his aging form to create a massive and immovable rock of blackness. He was standing for death itself, everyone's death, not only his own. Yes, he was there. Always he has been there. Only him, his hands bound, the rope around his neck, forever and for all time he will be there, even if around him swirled a vulgar mob, drunk with excitement and thirsty for blood.

The mob was not going to be cheated of its blood. Here were the dregs of the nation the Tyrant had tried to remind us of, my nation, all summed up in eleven words, words that they had heard repeated a hundred times, every day of their miserable lives. In their eyes, as I stood up there on the platform looking down at them, I could see the frenzy of frightened and blind men, men who are blindest when they think they can see, and most frightened when they think they are not frightened at all. The greater their victim, the bigger their fear, even when the object of that fear is tied and bound and a breath away from his demise.

The Rope

Evening

I was not alone in my unease that Saturday; others had misgivings, not that they will admit to them today. For example, my best friend, Haider, who used to live up the street from me in Najaf and with whom I shared an apartment in the Cairo district of Baghdad in the months before the hanging. He was tall and heavy-boned for an Arab of Bedouin stock from Najaf; his lean muscles gave him a grace in motion that was beautiful to watch, qualities I envied, being clumsy as a young boy. Inseparable since childhood, we shared a friendship of opposites, not equals, athlete and scholar, each taking and giving something different to the other. In combination, we felt invincible toward whatever obstacles fate tossed our way. The boy in me saw in my friend the attributes he pined for, and he, I believe, admired to the point of excess my facility with numbers and words. Unfortunately, Haider's mother did the same, a subject she tirelessly badgered him about. Together we joined the ranks of the Army of the Awaited One in 2003, and fought the Occupier shoulder to shoulder in Najaf in that unforgettable summer of 2004. You could not ask for a truer friend and braver comrade in arms.

Haider was there, in the crowd that watched the Tyrant hang that day. But he was chafing because he had not been chosen for the detail and was not up on the platform with me. Still, he was eager to talk when we found time to be together that evening.

"You didn't approve, I take it," he said, noticing how shaken I was by the events of the morning.

"Of what?" I answered, not wanting to talk.

"The Tyrant's execution, of course."

"Approval has nothing to do with it," I replied, avoiding him with my eyes by choosing to busy myself folding my still freshly pressed uniform in readiness to be returned the following day.

"Why so glum, then?"

"I don't want to talk about it, Haider," I said. "My feelings are still raw. I don't understand them myself."

"The affair lacked decorum, no doubt about it," Haider went on, ignoring my request, "and that is bad, very bad. But don't read too much into it. With time, men will learn to behave better. We have never hanged a tyrant before!" he said with a laugh. "The important thing is he is dead. You agree he had to die, don't you? You are not changing your mind about that."

"Of course not! I wanted him executed as much as the next man," I snapped back. "But men in ski masks, I ask you! A platform not large enough to fit everyone! A pulley yanked out of a building site the day before, and incompetently fitted to boot! A mob in place of witnesses! I hope it was not you jeering from the floor! Do you want me to go on? It was an embarrassment from start to finish, a disgrace, not an execution but a lynching . . ."

"Don't confuse the appearance of a thing with the thing itself," Haider replied, in a quiet tone of voice designed to calm me down.

"Executions are all about appearance; that is the whole point."

"But we are, after all, no different from animals, for whom the kill is the end of it. Accept that, my friend, and move on. He is dead; it is finished. Get over it."

"You are being unjust to animals; they kill neither to humiliate nor to insult; they kill out of necessity. And they go about it with a kind of . . . what you call decorum," I replied, calming myself down and sitting beside him on the carpet.

"Okay. Put decorum aside. That was a bad choice of words. It doesn't matter how we die, nor for that matter how we are born; neither lasts very long in the general span of things. But between the two lies the true meaning of our lives; how we choose to live the years between the natural facts of our birth and our death is all that matters. The Tyrant launched wars, killed millions, and tortured countless thousands; he left our country in ruins. These things count."

"True . . . ," I started to say, but Haider would not let up.

"My point is, bigger problems going to the heart of what is happening to this land confront us daily. We are in a war, for God's sake. And he even claimed to be leading the killers blowing up our mosques and markets and neighborhoods."

"He never said he was waging war on us Shi'a; that is what the Wahhabi, Haters of the Family of the Prophet, say they are doing. He claimed to be leading a war against the Occupier, the same war our Sayyid waged in the first two years of the Occupation."

"Words, mere words. The Tyrant was the serpent's head; it had to be cut off quickly to get on with what needs to be done. The Occupier dragged the wretched trial out for three years under the hallowed name of procedure. We humored them, and went along with it, until we understood how ineffectual and weak-willed they are. Now the Tyrant is dead. We can breathe a sigh of relief, and move on."

"Are you saying the terror will end?"

"Our enemies will never find another leader like him; he is irreplaceable; they will be in disarray. Tomorrow no one will remember how we botched his execution. All that will count is the fact that he is no longer there."

"Ahh, Haider . . . Haider, my dear Haider. Is the fact of our beloved Imam Husain's death on the plains of Karbala centuries ago all that counted at the time? Any fool can snuff the life out of a man. You and I have done it enough times to know. Killing is easy; it doesn't require intelligence."

That was a mistake; I should not have made a comparison with the Imam, whose life story was more precious and meaningful to the both of us than anything else. But it was too late. Haider lost his temper:

"Your words border on blasphemy! For God's sake, man, don't let others hear you speak like that! The Imam martyred himself for Justice; Saddam was hanged for his sins. Therein lies the chasm between Heaven and Hell!"

"Yes, yes, of course. But I am talking about how men die, and how they go on living because of how they have died. Our Imam was betrayed, and then martyred by his enemies. Our forefathers called upon him to cross the desert and save them from their Tyrant. When he did, they abandoned him to die alone in the desert, his throat parched, his wives and children dying with him of thirst and scorching heat. If we remember the blessed Imam every year, in the month of his martyrdom," I pressed on, "it is because of our guilt and shame at how he died, his faith intact, ours in tatters—"

"The Tyrant died well," interrupted Haider, "I grant you that. But what else did you expect of him! What would it say about us that we allowed ourselves to be ruled for three decades by a man who was a weakling, lacking in courage and self-respect? Think instead that he died in the way that he lived: violently, cruelly. There is justice of a sort in that."

"Are we like him? And what does it say of us that we allowed the blessed Imam to die alone? What do both deaths say about us? That is the question we should be asking ourselves."

"You are doing it again . . . you are putting the Tyrant on the same plane as the blessed Imam. The devil has taken charge of your tongue!"

"Bah! Stop this posturing, Haider . . . When men die, be they saints or devils, a chapter in the book of lives is not simply thrown out; it is translated into a new language. I fear the new chapter of the Tyrant's life that is about to replace the old one we have just closed."

Haider took to pacing the room, and looking at me strangely. I had seen him agitated before . . . but it was too late for either of us to back down.

"I revere the blessed Imam as much as you do . . . and would exchange my life for his if I could, as I know you would," I continued, "and do I need to tell you of all people how much I hate the Tyrant; he took my father to a horrible end, for God's sake. But what happened today in that execution hall is not an ending; it is a dreadful beginning."

"What are you so afraid of?" asked Haider, who was genuinely puzzled.

"I fear the Tyrant will continue to rule over us, even in death. Dragons' teeth have been sowed by the manner of his death. So he died well. And we expected it of him . . . all the more reason to execute him more impressively than he was able to die. In the name of all that we Shi'a have to lose, you and I and all the poor broken-down people of this country, I ask you, why did we give him the last word?"

"My rope," Haider suddenly said, trying to change the subject. "Did you get me the piece of rope you promised?"

The rope . . . the wretched rope! I was hoping he had forgotten the damn thing. How I wish I had never promised him a piece of it.

The day before the execution, filled with a sense of my own self-importance, I made a rash bargain with those less fortunate among my comrades in the Army of the Awaited One: I promised them a piece of the hangman's rope, which I was sure I could spirit out of the execution hall. The deal was that I would sell whatever length I could obtain for so many thousand dinars per centimeter. Naturally there was no question of charging Haider for his piece; it would be a gift in honor of our lifelong friendship.

Selling the rope had been my idea to start with, but I soon became aware others were doing it. If ten thousand was the going price before the hanging, God knows what it became after. When I left the compound the haggling was still in full swing. Even ministers and high-ranking officials were caught up in it. Everyone wanted a memento to show that they had been there.

All around us the new politicians—"Foreigner Iraqis," Haider called them, the ones who rode into office on the tanks of the Occupier—were establishing new ideas of right and wrong; they thought about position and money, devising ingenious ways of stealing the one through the other. And we, young soldiers and activists, learned from them. Why, only the other day I read in the paper that members of Parliament had voted into law a motion to quadruple their salaries. The worst offenders were those who'd returned from lives abroad, caring only to line their pockets and then rush back to whatever country was left doling out welfare checks to the wives and children they'd left behind.

That is how it all started—the affair of the rope, I mean.

A handful of hours separated the "before" of the hanging from its "after." Before, I bragged about the rope; after, I saw nothing to brag about. Instead I felt ashamed. Mercifully, my parents were no longer of this world to witness my shame in 2006. I don't know what Father would have done; I never knew him. I grew up with the fact of his disappearance in 1991. His body was never found. Not a trace of it anywhere; I know, I searched frenziedly in the summer of 2003 and couldn't find it. Still, I know it is out there somewhere. A fact that is also a non-fact never entirely goes away; it is like the dust that Mother battled with daily. Knowing that is not knowing continues to hang around in the air like dust, in the little nooks and crannies of our minds.

Mother would not have said a word about the rope. She who had drilled into me the desire to excel, to be top of my class, along with the idea that the world outside her purview was dirty, polluting, and to be shunned at all costs . . . all she had to do was look. Her eyes would have bored into my very depths. She was only doing what all good mothers do in lands ruled by tyrants and revolutions and wars. For all those mothers, politics is betrayal, soldiers are brutal, and politicians liars.

But we children of the Great Tyrant were behaving as though it was the physical and literal world that was real and permanent. It was not freedom and the end of war and tyranny that were real; it was the rope that was real. And I was cashing in on that new reality. A world-changing thing—the end of tyranny—had atrophied to one of its artifacts. Too late did I awake; too late did I realize that we had been prostrating ourselves before new idols, like a piece of the hangman's rope.

When the Tyrant dropped through the trapdoor, wildly bucking his bound feet, fighting to the very last millisecond of his life, I saw myself as though for the first time, with my entire being. Something in me had rotted, and neither my friend Haider, nor Uncle, to whom I owed everything, nor the Sayyid, in whom I had so fervently believed, could reverse the stench I now emitted. I was too far gone, marooned, directionless, lost to myself and to others, knowing neither who I was nor where I had come from nor where I was going. This is the moment when I no longer wanted to have anything to do with the rope.

PART TWO

APRIL 2003–NOVEMBER 2006

—•—

Accurate scholarship can
Unearth the whole offence
From Luther until now
That has driven a culture mad,
Find what occurred at Linz,
What huge imago made
A psychopathic god:
I and the public know
What all schoolchildren learn,
Those to whom evil is done
Do evil in return.

W. H. AUDEN

| 2003 |

Najaf: April 10

T here is no God but the One God"; again ten seconds later, "There is no God but the One God"; and again for the last time, "There is no God but the One God"; that is how long it takes for the procession of mourners to carry a coffin past the second-story wooden lattice window of the room in Uncle's house in Najaf, which my mother and I used as a bedroom.

The projecting screened window may have kept the street shaded and cool, and the house private and discreet, but it did nothing to the noise outside my window; if anything it reinforced it, as if the sound waves wormed their way in through the holes in the wooden screen and bounced about wildly between the four inside walls.

Growing up in Najaf, I played, laughed, and dreamed on streets and alleyways filled with sounds of mourning and dead people: the famous dead of centuries past, and the unknown newly dead, whose coffins streamed into the city daily through my neighborhood, carried by wailing mourners from the four corners of the earth, all shouting "There is no God but the One God" so that normal passersby would jump out of their way. Every Shi'a male and female in the world desires to be buried in the city in which I was born, irrespective of where he or she dies; it is the last obligation imposed by the dying on their descendants, and my mother and I paid the price.

Our house was located in the city's Mishraq quarter, in the north-eastern quadrant, a quarter that houses the tomb of the great scholar and Grand Master of our sect, Abu Ja'far al-Tusi, from whom all schools of Shi'ism are descended. Tusi left Baghdad for Najaf in the eleventh century to found his college of theology; a line of teachers stretches continuously from this original college to the well-known scholarly families of our times—the Houses of Sadr, Hakim, and Khoei.

Many other tombs of distinguished personages are located in my neighborhood, as well as houses for pilgrims and Servants of the Shrine of the Imam, a monument that sits at the city's geographical center and is magnificently crowned with a golden dome covering the silver tomb of our first Imam, 'Ali ibn Abi Talib, cousin and son-in-law of the Prophet, and father of Imam Husain, martyred nearby. Pilgrims are told the story of how the city was founded: When the first Imam was stabbed to death in Kufa, his body was put on a camel, which was released to wander into the desert. The place where it stopped is where the Imam was buried, and the holy city of Najaf grew up around his tomb.

The number of people buried in Najaf far exceeds the number who live there—no one knows by how much—and our city's cemetery, named the Valley of Peace, where I often played, is where we made a stand against the Occupier in 2004, and stood our ground for months; it reaches into the Shrine and is the largest cemetery in the world. Pilgrims in the hundreds of thousands, second only in number to those who perform the hajj in Mecca, come annually to the Shrine of the Imam to lament his death, which is the death of Justice in this world; they do so in the hope that they will be able to find both in the next life. Those of them who enter the Shrine from the north do so through the Tusi gate, named after the great teacher and a ten-minute walk from my house.

All of these newcomers to our city need to be fed, housed, washed, buried, told tall stories, and sold false trinkets. Add to that what we Shi'a call the "portion of the Imam," the one-fifth of their income owed by the Shi'a to their clerics in the absence of the twelfth Imam, and it is fair to say that my city's economy rests on the dead and the dying.

The residents of Najaf are famously clever, hurtfully witty, and notoriously deceitful and cantankerous with strangers, whom they treat as prey to be fleeced; they particularly loathe the seminary students who come to study, reserving their most bitter invective for those who come from Iran. There is nothing like a holy city, and pious visitors, to make a city's normal residents mostly unholy and consistently impious.

Death is the only ruler Najaf has known, which is why my mother called it the "City of the Dead," and would exhort me, even as a child, to promise that I would never bring up my children in a place of such ill omen, something that upset her sister to no end, who said her words were disrespectful to the Imam if not bordering on blasphemy.

She, of course, was never given a choice in the matter, having a thirteen-year-old boy on her hands when my father disappeared in the year of the Uprising Against Tyranny. But he was by her bedside at my birth, in the year of the Tyrant's ascension to power, holding me in his arms for hours, I am told, before being swallowed up to serve in the Great War with Iran. We hardly saw him for the next eight years. Uncle, who is married to my mother's older sister, came to the rescue, and I was raised in what became his house, the house of my grandparents on my father's side, and their parents before them.

The house nestles between three other houses, two to the north and south of us, and one to the east sharing our back wall; the only entrance to and exit from the house is through the courtyard on its western side, at whose center grows my uncle's pride and joy, an ancient pomegranate tree eight meters high with a thicket of spiny curling branches spreading overhead that had been there since Grandfather was a child; he grew up watering the sapling daily, in the early evening. From the courtyard an opening through a short corridor takes you to the gate leading to a twisting alleyway that passes by a college of theology founded by the Sadr family in the direction of the Tusi gate, the northern entrance to the Imam's tomb.

This orientation, and the rumor that a huge commotion was going on in the courtyard of the Imam's Shrine, is the only reason that I saw what I saw on that fine sunny Thursday in April, the day of the fall of Baghdad and my country's Occupation by foreign armies.

Man in the Alley

Turning into the alley toward the Tusi gate, I ran toward the Shrine only to find my way blocked by a huddled group of wide-eyed, morose-looking men from the neighborhood. There were twenty or thirty of them staring silently at a crumpled-up heap of clothing on the ground, soiled and encrusted with dirt. Between their white robes, I could see that the clothing dressed the body of a man.

"Who is he?" I asked Uncle, who was looking grimly at the scene.

"An American agent," he said. "They are everywhere. Baghdad fell to the Americans today. We must be vigilant."

"Where is Saddam?"

"He was seen this morning in the Abu Hanifa Mosque in 'Adhamiyah. His Special Guard fought some skirmishes with the advancing American forces and then he disappeared with his men, into hiding. He will lead a resistance to the Occupier. You can be sure of it."

I pushed my head between him and the fellow on his right, and squeezed my way through to the front, where I now had a clear view.

"He looks like one of us. How can you tell he is an agent?"

"He was carrying dollars, lots of them."

The corpse was lying on its side, limbs twisted like pretzels, the fingers scrabbling in the dust, clutching at rubble, blood everywhere soaking into what had been a shirt. Sixteen stab wounds I tallied before losing count; I later found out there had been over a hundred. There were no dollars.

Returning home, I discovered my mother already knew what had been found in the alley. Her face was drained and pale, as though she had seen a ghost, and she didn't want to talk to me about it, barely suppressing her anger that I had lingered at the scene. She would not hear me out and seemed to know a surprising amount about what had happened.

"He was an American agent," I said, trying to get her to take me seriously.

"What makes you think that?" she asked tersely.

"Because the Americans entered Baghdad yesterday and he was carrying dollars," I said lamely.

"A man has been butchered in broad daylight by large numbers of men in front of thousands of witnesses. You hurl accusations at him; he cannot talk back. Why did my son and the son of his father not see a victim, of whom we have more than enough in Iraq? Did you see the dollars?"

"No. But Uncle said—"

"People say many things."

"Why would he say it if it were not true?"

"The things people say come from the sufferings inflicted upon them, which in turn they inflict on others."

It was the sharpest criticism I had heard her make of my father's older brother, on whose protection and generosity she and I relied. I did not understand what was going on.

"So you know who he was."

She would not answer. Nothing I said would persuade her otherwise.

March on Karbala

The next day, I secretly joined Uncle and his friends on the three-day walk to Karbala called for by the Sayyid, a son of the House of Sadr, in his first Friday sermon delivered from his father's mosque in Kufa on April 11. The Tyrant's agents had assassinated his father in broad daylight four years earlier, and everyone attended the son's first sermon to hear what he had to say.

He did not call on us to celebrate the fall of the Tyrant on April 10; he called on us to undertake a pilgrimage with him on foot to the neighboring city of Karbala, Shrine of our Imam Husain son of 'Ali, to honor the fortieth day of his martyrdom on the banks of the Euphrates in the year 680.

I saw pilgrims mourn that day as if our Imam had died yesterday; they would pummel their chests, wail and slap their faces, then whip their backs with chains until the blood was streaming down their white shirts, all practices denounced by the traditionalists. It was so overwhelming; I could see that even Uncle was getting upset.

"They are taught there is great virtue in heaven in shedding tears and blood over the death of the Imam," he said, angry with himself for showing emotion and pulling me away. "They wake up to miracles in the middle of the night, dreaming that they have seen the Imam, his wounds healed by their tears. Fools! Simpletons! How are we to prevail with such supporters?"

Did he really mean it? Or was he covering up for his own feelings? I assumed the Sayyid had hidden intentions in mind in calling this march, meanings that only he could read connecting two cataclysmic events: the fall of the Great Tyrant and the cruel death of our Imam 1,323 years earlier at the hands of his ancient counterpart, Yazid son of Mu'awiyya. What were they?

Walking alongside Uncle, in the midst of the million or so men, women, and children who heeded the Sayyid's call, American helicopters hovering over us like black insects, my heart was bursting with pride as I carried a flag of mourning for the death of my Imam all those centuries ago. Indeed, the past was present; the Truth of the Imam was Justice for us; like a grain of salt in a vast ocean, my own person dissolved into the slow-moving waves of people wailing and crying to its rhythms. Or was it the crowd that was for the first time in my hitherto insignificant life finding itself in me?

The Sayyid was making me feel the way I was supposed to feel all the time, especially during the rituals in which we Shi'a mourn the death of Imam Husain but which Mother would never let me join. She worried. Too much politics, she said. "Cry for the Imam alone," she used to say. "Then he is in your heart." But we young men of the Shi'a were no longer cautious in the way we used to be before the fall of the Tyrant; our Imam was being reborn; it was a moment of celebration. I had been granted the privilege of walking alongside him, side by side with the poor and the oppressed, with whom I could now for the first time feel wholly and completely at one; it was not a mourning; it was a crusade.

Alongside me walked emaciated, filth-encrusted children, men and women of every walk of life, the crippled and the blind, all of them wailing and sobbing and tearing their clothes, tears pouring down their cheeks, not caring who saw them, some beating their chests with fists, a few grabbing and pulling tufts of hair from their heads. It was too overpowering. Their tears were infectious; I too ended up crying, not knowing why or for whom.

Softer now, perhaps because I was crying, or perhaps because he had been harsh earlier, Uncle pulled my face to his, palms on both my cheeks, and looked me up close in the eyes.

"It is all right to cry, son," he said. "Cry because of the injustice and cruelty of the Imam's death. Cry for how he died. Cry for how he was denied water, and how brutally he was cut down with his family by an army ten times their number. That story is the history of the oppressed; it tells what they feel, and its truth is the truth of the poor and the afflicted wherever they may be in the world. They have no names, they have no graves, and they have no nationality. Cry for them nonetheless. But when you cry, remember to cry also because we pledged allegiance to the Son of 'Ali. We asked him to come to us hundreds of miles across the desert. And when he came, we abandoned him; we let the grandson of the Prophet and his family perish at the hands of our enemies. Cry to repent for all that, my son. Cry out of remorse. Cry because that is our Shi'a inheritance. Cry because he died for us, and we were born laden with guilt." And suddenly he let go of my face and grabbed my arm, pointing to the sidewalk farther down the road.

"Look over there! You see that barefooted old man sitting by the side of the road weeping inconsolably . . . and, over there, that old woman in black tearing at her clothes, beseeching Husain, looking up at the sky . . . her tears flowing! They cry for him . . . and they cry for their miserable lot in this unjust world. Cry with them to be sure, but above all cry for them . . . and then ask yourself what you are going to do about it!"

The Tyrant's downfall primed a whole people for change; all that was missing was a trigger, and the Sayyid's march had just provided it.

Still, there was a body in my alley. I had seen it only yesterday . . . stabbed repeatedly, and lying a stone's throw from the holiest shrine of our most blessed Shi'a faith. Whose body was it? Surely he was a person, with a name, someone with a family and a lineage of some sort? I asked everyone. "I don't know," people whispered—always they whispered, always they did not know; they might as well have said, "I don't want to know. Don't ask!"

But Uncle knew. Mother knew. Many people seemed to know . . . and no one would speak to me of what had happened. It was as though nothing had happened; it was all a figment of my imagination. And being a young man, who believed like everyone else in his neighborhood that four thousand Jews were warned to absent themselves from work in New York on September 11 by the true engineers of the fall of the Twin Towers—the Israeli Mossad—because no Arab was capable of such an act, for such a young man . . . it was enough to be told by his uncle that the dead man in the alley was an American agent.

Mother

Mother had rules about what should and should not be said to others. I got into trouble as a young boy overhearing her talking late at night, knowing as she instinctively did that I had parked myself behind a door, or at the top of the stairs. No one in my family talked in a normal voice about important things; they whispered. In fact, if you saw or heard someone whispering in the house, it was safe to assume the subject was important. I learned more about her loneliness from such whisperings than I ever did from normal conversation. She said we Iraqis were made up of two kinds of whisperers, the ones who whisper out of fear of being overheard—the good ones—and the ones who whisper behind people's backs to the authorities. I was taught never to indulge in the second kind of whispering, and not to intrude upon the first. She trusted no one, not even Uncle or her sister. I had to be sheltered from the world, not thrust into it. Not knowing was my shelter. That was the rule Mother would not break about the dead body in the alley.

She had other rules. Saturday, for instance, was the only day of the week on which clothing could be washed; Mondays, no travel was permitted outside the city; Tuesday afternoons, nothing new could be purchased; Wednesdays, she had to prepare fish, even if the dictates of economy meant it had to be a tiny piece; Friday was the only day of the week on which the cutting of fingernails and toenails was permitted, the cuttings then collected and carefully buried in the garden. "Why bury them, Mother?" I asked, wanting to just throw them in the trash and rid myself of the silly task. "Because it is a part of your body which your Creator made from that earth, to which it must return, as a sign of respect to Him."

Her rules were practical, born of hardship and pain, giving structure to her days.

She was the kind of person who made sacrifices on other people's behalf, but never let on that she was doing so, and even denied it. It turned her melancholy into bitterness, and then into cynicism. The mere perception of a slight, or well-intentioned stupidity, gave rise to artfully aimed barbs. She was a self-educated woman, but had a way with words.

Fighting petty battles with her sister in a building whose walls leaked noise didn't help matters. The lack of privacy was the greatest source of tension; our second-floor bedroom doubled as a study during my adolescence, or when the kitchen was occupied. It was a place to sleep, do homework, or receive friends and was equipped with a mini washroom and kitchenette where Mother kept several jugs of water and had assembled two makeshift shelves to store biscuits and tea. The communal kitchen, by contrast, was the setting for arguments, which if they turned into a major conflagration Uncle would have to resolve. He ended up making everyone unhappy. He tried where Mother was concerned, but she never seemed to forgive him. For what, was a mystery.

The hardest part about my mother's life was losing my father, her husband, her first cousin, and her childhood sweetheart; she lost him after too few years of marriage. If survival is a matter of learning to forget, Mother was incapable of it; her memories kept her caged.

Legion were the things that she did not know about Father since his disappearance. She did not know if he was dead, or languishing in some camp; she did not know why he had disappeared if he was alive, or where he was being incarcerated; she did not know the crime he was accused of. And knowing such things was important, because to each type of disappearance and crime there corresponded a different way of living out the rest of your life. She did not know what to tell me, because the less I knew the easier it was to live; she did not know what others knew, if anything, because no one talked about such things; and she did not have a body to bury and mourn— all of these things my mother did not, indeed could not, know.

She wore black from the day after he disappeared until her own death. If she bought a new item of clothing, not only would its color be black, but she would also wait until the period of mourning for our Imam Husain came around to wear it for the first time. She would continue to do that, she said, until either my father or his body was found.

The only way I knew to make her happy was through neat handwriting, perfectly executed sums, and being at the top of my class at school. With Father gone, there was no one who might extend to her a gesture, or a kindness. She needed the small and the trivial and the inconsequential to live. But no one gave it to her. All was work and duty and obligation. I regret not doing more for her. I bought her something practical once—a teapot to replace the one I broke— but never something pretty and perfectly useless, which would have made her face light up.

She approved of my best friend, Haider, knowing that we had a great deal in common: neighborhood, street, mosque. Most important, we were both born in the year of the Tyrant's Great Purge and ascension to power, and, because of him and the Great War that followed his ascension, we both grew up without fathers. If she was wary of Haider, it was because she sensed a lack of centeredness about him that troubled her. But not when we were still boys, when she would wake me up for dawn prayers and see me rush off to the mosque, knowing that Haider would be there, and to breakfast afterward at the teahouse nearby, where we'd eat coarse bread dipped in smoked water buffalo cream from neighboring Hillah. Her greatest joy was to receive the extra eighth of a kilo of smoked cream and fresh hot bread, which I would carry back for her own breakfast.

As I got older, books were a kind of consolation. I remember reading *Notes from Underground* by Dostoevsky because Mother said Father was fond of Russian writers and an old teacher, who had studied in the Soviet Union, found an Arabic translation. It lay around the house for months, but I only finished reading it after going on the march to Karbala, which I kept a secret from Mother.

Perhaps to assuage the guilt I felt at giving her the slip and lying about the march, I asked if she would like me to read the opening lines from *Notes from Underground*. She was delighted at first, but then I began: "I am a sick man . . . I am a spiteful man. I am an unattractive man."

"Enough!" she shouted. "Why do you want to read about such a man?"

"Because it is a great book. I want to write like the underground man; I want to sound like him."

"Your father loved him," she said, "but then again he liked all things Russian. I have kept other of his books safe all these years; it is time you started to read them."

"I want to know who the dead man in the alley was," I said to her, taking advantage of the pleasant mood and closeness that had grown up between us talking about my father and his books. It was a question I returned to with Mother over and over again; Uncle would brook no further discussion of it. But Mother was more pliable where I was concerned. Nonetheless, she did not rise to the bait, not then, not ever, answering me every time the same way:

"There are things it is better not to know."

Worn down by my persistence, she reached out for the top shelf of the kitchen cupboard, which was lined with Father's books, books I had not known were his. Unerringly, her hand picked out a slim volume from the middle of the shelf. It was as if its precise location had been implanted in her mind.

"Read this, and perhaps we will talk," she said, handing it to me. "I bought this book for him during one of his furloughs; it meant the world to him. He used to read and reread it to his friends in the trenches."

Dog-eared and worn, the volume she handed me was more like a pamphlet than a book. The author was Egyptian, and the book was entitled *The Tragedy of al-Hallaj*. On the blank inside front page, in clear and precise letters, the name of my father was inked, and underneath it the phrase "Najaf, 1988."

"Why 1988?" I asked.

"It is the date your father was released from the army after serving eight years in the war with Iran. We were elated that year, thinking all good things were beginning. He destroyed his military clothing and anything that reminded him of those eight years, with the exception of this book that you now have between your hands."

"Were good things beginning?"

"The good times were short-lived; they called him back to army service the following month."

"Why didn't Haider's father return in 1988?"

"We heard he had been captured. Some said he deserted during the war. All I know is that he ended up in Iran. He returned briefly in 1991, and fled again after the Uprising . . . Do you remember your father?"

"Images, snippets of conversation . . . I can picture him sitting on the chair in your bedroom smoking for hours on end, just looking out of the window. It was as though he were in some other place."

"War is a terrible thing."

"But then he just disappeared again . . ."

"He went into hiding after they called him up for service a second time . . . He said he would not fight for the Tyrant anymore, even though they gave him medals for bravery. Didn't you know that?"

"I did not. Where did he hide?"

"Here, in Najaf, in the basements of houses in the Old City. There is an entire labyrinth of them under our feet. He would not say exactly where he was hiding, for our own protection. But he and

I met secretly from time to time. He would stand on corners and watch you go to school, you know . . ."

"I never saw him . . ."

"We couldn't risk you seeing him. Something could have been said by mistake."

"But I remember him after the Kuwait invasion."

"Yes, things changed. The regime had bigger problems to deal with after the Tyrant invaded Kuwait and once the American armada began to gather in Arabia. He started to come home unexpectedly, and spend hours at a time with you."

"And during the Uprising in 1991? I remember him then."

"He was home for three weeks," she said, the tears welling up. "That was the longest stretch I had with him under one roof. And then he disappeared . . ."

"What happened?"

She would not answer.

An Execution in Baghdad

The seventy-five wrinkled, yellowing, and poorly assembled pages of the book my mother gave me fell apart when I first opened them, and had to be pasted back together after reading. They told an ancient story, one a thousand years old: the story of the arrest, trial, and public crucifixion for heresy of a teacher and mystic known as Hallaj. He was mutilated, then hung while still alive on a tree in a public square in Baghdad, and finally decapitated, his head put on display on a wall of the prison before being dispatched to the provinces to convince his supporters he was dead. His torso was burned, its ashes cast into the Tigris to subdue the rising waters, which in outrage at the crucifixion threatened to flood Baghdad. When the waters subsided, as some of the great teachers tell it, Hallaj's ashes surfaced, writing on the clean glass-like surface of the water "I am the Absolute Truth," the words for which he was crucified.

The first reading of my father's book confused me, but I was drawn to strange statements attributed to Hallaj, the ones underlined by Father in light pencil, such as "He who kills me would have fashioned from my dust a story and an ideal." There were other sentences on love. Hallaj loved God so much he could barely put up with living, and would cry inconsolably. Did the good Hallaj love

God too much, to the point of wanting to lose himself in Him? Was that his heresy? Strangely, he said he loved God as hard as he did to escape death, but the moment he perfected his ability to love Him that much, he would die anyway. Trying to understand that conundrum filled me with excitement.

I imagined Father sitting in the trenches of the Fao Peninsula, fighting off waves of young Iranians, fellow Shi'a, intent on martyrdom. In between bouts of fighting he would read passages from this tattered old book, which would then get rolled up and slipped into his army fatigues as he prepared for the next onslaught. Snatches of verse on love were underlined, not once but twice, with a pressure on the pencil so heavy its tip started to rip through the pages. I imagine Father reading, perhaps crying alongside Hallaj at night when he was alone. And then I saw the faces of the men and women among whom I had walked, in rags, wailing and beating their chests for Husain on the road to his shrine in Karbala. Were they the same people whom Hallaj had cried for all those centuries ago? I had cried. Everyone had cried. So many people . . . so much time passed . . . all crying at the injustice of their patrimony.

But in spite of all the tears, the story of Hallaj would have lifted Father's spirit out of its mud-splattered attachment to the terrible trenches of that never-ending war. Just as mine had been uplifted during the march to Karbala. How wonderful it must have been to look into the soul of such a man!

I missed my father at times like this. I turned to look into the face of the young man in the wedding photograph standing in its imitation silver frame on Mother's dressing table. The distance separating us, father and son, slipped away. The photograph had been there for as long as I could remember: he looking at her in a smart tailored suit, crisply pressed tie, stiff black leather shoes; she looking at him in her embroidered bright white wedding dress; the secret was in their eyes.

Car Bomb

The explosion came on the hottest Friday of an already scorching August. The walls of our house swayed and shook from the force. Mother leapt to the swaying kitchen cupboard. A teapot fell to the ground and shattered.

Tearing myself away, I ran toward the smoke and sound, fifteen minutes from our house. It was like scenes from Hell: brick facades sheared away; the stalls of hawkers of drinks, sandwiches, and trinkets splintered into firewood; sidewalks streaked with grime and blood; burned, mangled, and dismembered bodies littering the streets; people running about aimlessly, or sitting in the road weeping inconsolably—no human being can forget such sights.

Loudspeakers wailed, *To God we do belong, and to Him we do return.*

Prayers had ended at 5:00 p.m.; it was shortly afterward, at a moment teeming with departing worshippers and pilgrims, that a car packed with explosives had detonated meters from the entrance to the Shrine of the Imam, instantly killing the most senior Sayyid of the House of Hakim and 125 people who had come to pray behind him; it was the Sayyid's own car, and the bomb had been placed under his seat. Who was capable of such a deed?

The Sayyid, ranked an Ayatollah by some, was newly arrived from exile in Iran. He had led the prayers that day. It was his first sermon in Najaf since his escape from the Tyrant's clutches twenty-three years ago. Two weeks before, also in August, a car bomb had been set off at the Jordanian embassy, and then another massive blast had shredded the headquarters of the United Nations offices, killing at least sixteen people and wounding one hundred others. But that was in Baghdad; no one expected the same hands to be capable of reaching into the holiest city of Shi'ism and plucking out a returning exile, at that time the most well-guarded symbol of clerical authority in Iraq.

To pave the way for the Sayyid's return, Haider's father, Abu Haider, had returned earlier from Iran, to which he had fled twice before: first as a deserter during the Great War with Iran; and second in 1991, after the Uprising that followed the humiliating defeat of the Tyrant in the first Gulf War, when thousands of men of the House of Hakim carrying portraits of Ayatollah Khomeini snuck back into cities in the south to participate. Haider remembers a home in turmoil and a swarthy bearded fellow wrestling with him on the sofa . . . him squealing in delight. But it lasted three weeks, and Abu Haider was gone, fleeing back to Iran just as the tanks of Saddam's Republican Guard rolled into Najaf, blasting at everything in sight.

Haider and I had that in common, the disappearances of our fathers; only his returned, whereas mine never would. The second return of Abu Haider in 2003 was very different: a huge, much heralded occasion. Now a senior commander of the Brigades of the Full Moon, Abu Haider was in charge of security in Najaf, only he had just failed in his duty to the House to which he was so devoted.

The Ayatollah's body vaporized. A single stone from his prayer beads was found; proof, someone exclaimed loudly, that he had died in the explosion. The House of Sadr insisted the death be confirmed. Supporters of the House of Hakim, on the other hand, all returning exiles from Iran like the Ayatollah himself, were convinced that he did not die. They said he had been seen speeding away from the scene with two bodyguards in a light blue sport utility vehicle. They said he would return when the time was right, like the long-awaited Rightly Guided One on the eve of the Day of Judgment.

Mother taught me to see the world as it really was, to look a fact in the eye and face up to its consequences, whomever it offended. I saw evil that day, the day of the car bomb. I saw right walled off from wrong, leaving no room for doubt. I saw the kind of evil that replicates itself in the hearts of others; victims or perpetrators, all would be touched. I knew that in my neighborhood there would be boys, friends of mine, who would say the Ayatollah didn't die, and there would be others who would say he deserved to die, having worked with an enemy during wartime, and then acquiesced in a foreign Occupation for power and personal gain. To me, on that day, none of it mattered. But it would.

I remembered the bloodied corpse I had seen in the alley a stone's throw away from where the epicenter of the bomb had struck. I recall wondering about the difference between a man whose leg had been blown clean off at the thigh and one whose torso had been punctured a hundred times with knives. I was seeing things I had not seen before. A part of me was undergoing burial while another was assimilating into the chaos all around.

Uncle and some of the same men who were with him in the alley on April 10 were at the scene of the explosion, off to a side to avoid getting in the way of the rescue effort but not participating in it. They were exchanging stories. I remember being taken aback because there was no shock in their faces, no sense of outrage. I pretended to be doing something else while I sidled closer, straining to listen.

There were stories of men who had just been released from Saddam's prisons; stories of boys who had heeded the call to arms by our Sayyid; stories of other young men who had refused to join and were being viewed as traitors because they were selling their services as laborers or translators to the Occupier; there were stories of martyrs and informers, of new aspiring politicians strutting about like peacocks, of leaders who were secret agents or collaborators, and lots of stories about the Occupation itself, how powerful or how weak it was, and why it had been imposed on us, was it about oil or revenge.

A story that caught my attention told of a love-besotted local

Romeo from Najaf who had eloped to Baghdad with a young girl because her parents disapproved of him. The group was plotting to pick up his trail by way of relatives in the capital, and speaking of what they would do to the pair once they got hold of them.

Another told of a mysterious Egyptian who offered a young taxi driver from the city of Kut three hundred American dollars to toss a hand grenade at any passing Humvee and then run away and get lost in the market. That is all he had to do. Three hundred dollars for tossing a grenade and running away! The discussion centered on the ethics of doing this, given that the would-be grenade thrower was motivated solely by greed, and in the case in question, the young man had enthusiastically embraced the American army upon its entry into Baghdad. "What does that say of his moral character?" said one man who was having a heated exchange with Uncle, who knew the man. "How can you trust him in a fight?"

"Trust has nothing to do with it," replied Uncle. "You now know what it takes for that man to fight for you."

By far the most important story the men kept on returning to was the disappearance of my father during the Great 1991 Uprising. He had last been seen on a Friday in March in the courtyard of the Imam ʿAli Shrine, Uncle said, just as the tanks of the Republican Guard, with the words "No More Shiʿa After Today" painted on them, rolled in from all directions, firing indiscriminately. The golden dome took a hit that day. I was barely twelve years old at the time. That was the last time Father was seen, Uncle said.

But hadn't he been seen on every one of the last thirteen anniversaries of the intifada in the holy city of Qum, Iran? interjected a member of the group. "That is what I heard."

Not possible, replied another; "he wasn't a Believer."

"He wouldn't go to Iran," replied a third.

"He died a martyr, blown to smithereens by a tank he was trying to destroy," said a fourth. "I know a man who saw it happen."

That was the first time I heard any of these stories. I looked up to Uncle to see how he would react. But he was quiet, smiling as though barely interested, neither confirming nor contradicting, turning toward the growing crowd of onlookers gathered at the scene of the explosion.

His friends kept on bandying theories as to what had happened to his brother, with the misguided expectation of drawing him out. But he wouldn't be drawn, maintaining an inscrutable silence that slowly turned him into the center of the gathering.

Suddenly Uncle turned to me. "Are you a patriot, son?" he said.

"Of course," I replied, taken aback. I couldn't see what being a patriot had to do with the evisceration of an Ayatollah.

"The House of Hakim you see scurrying about over there sided with our enemy, Iran, during the Great War. Your father, may he rest in peace, fought Hakim's Brigade during the battles over the Fao Peninsula in the last year of the war. Those people," he said with a dismissive nod of his head in the direction of the wreckage and frenzy and blaring ambulance sirens, "could have killed him."

"Who wanted the Ayatollah dead and organized such a terrible way of killing him?"

"Only the Iranians," he said. "No Iraqi has the required skills."

"But why would they want to kill him? He depended on them; his organization wants to extend the Islamic revolution into Iraq."

"The Ayatollah was distancing himself from Iran in his sermons and becoming an ally of the Occupier. They did not like that."

"So was he a patriot?" I asked Uncle, confused by all the combinations of friend and foe that were surfacing.

"Of course not!" he said. "But your father was. He fought for Iraq, not Saddam."

"Wasn't it Saddam who attacked the Islamic Republic?"

"Your father had no choice in the matter. He had to fight for his country; that was the patriotic thing to do."

"What if he had refused to fight on either side?"

"He would be a coward—a disgrace to country and God."

Uncle

In a variety of roles and guises, Uncle runs like a tangled skein through my life; it is impossible to keep track of all of them: guardian, provider, teacher, and in the end commander. The uncle in whose house I was raised, the one who intervened on my behalf over and over again, the real father who stood in for the one I entertained in my imagination, the mentor that took me in hand during my activist years, this extraordinary man lived a life of secrets. So many, even he could no longer pick them apart, separating fact from fiction. How then can I be expected to do so? Uncle not only had secrets but also loved to stock up on them, his and especially other people's, deploying them like clues, which he would drop like breadcrumbs, because he knew that if you put the secret together in your own mind you'd be more convinced by it than if he told you the whole story, only you never really could put it all together because there were never enough clues, a fact he relished greatly.

Behind his back, his enemies accused him of arrogance bordering on spitefulness. I remember him taking his sweet time pulling out of his parking space at the city's municipal office. He had noticed another car waiting for the space, and wanted to show the other driver who was boss, knowing that he was wasting his own time as well as that of the other driver.

Uncle's reputation meant that he never had any real friends, but then he never seemed to want to have them either. After I began working for him, I realized that much of what Uncle appeared to be outside the house was based on what others around him said he was; he never had to say it. He surrounded himself with minions at work, whom he could abuse one moment and shower with gifts the next. In company he was a joy to watch: rollicking, jovial, and gesticulating wildly at one moment, dripping with erudition the next.

No doubt I was the son Aunt had never been able to give him. But even I was never sure of the extent of his feelings toward me. Did they stand in a category apart from all the others? For years I thought so. Or was I sometimes a pawn in a complicated piece of intrigue whose purpose only he understood? I look back, for instance, at how he won me over to the Sayyid's army, working his way around my mother's objections by persistence and persuasion. He favored me throughout my service, making me privy to tidbits of insider information, which he liked to toss my way and I liked to catch.

During my first few years in the Army of the Awaited One, I didn't even consider the question of whether or not I was being used, for no activist was as fortunate as I to have been blessed with such a mentor. Even after everything fell apart on that terrible day of the hanging in December 2006, when Uncle was forced to disown me because it was he who had vouched for me in the first place, even denounce me as a traitor to the Sayyid's cause, he did so gently, just enough, as the expression goes, to whiten his face among his comrades in the Sayyid's inner circle, but not enough to expose him as an opportunist or toady, not even to the Sayyid he stood by and served so well. Uncle was a staunch Iraqi patriot, and if there were matters he hid from me, or did not want to disclose, perhaps it was for a good reason, I said to myself, for a higher purpose that I would in due course come to understand. In those years I trusted him implicitly in a way that had nothing to do with ideology but often in politics ends up so doing.

Uncle didn't much care for virtue. He valued intelligence akin to his own—cunning, calculating, and street-smart—and was contemptuous of people who were not quick-witted or well-read. There was nothing Uncle hadn't read, or at least read enough of to make you think he had read it all. Often I would find a book or two chosen to impress—a work of philosophy, or a biography of some Iraqi politician whom he admired—left open to a certain page when I went to visit him in his office. I would leave the room on such days in awe of the man: What other politician would know about, much less read, such books?

Later, I took to wondering if they had been left there for my benefit; even so, I would say to myself, what difference did it make? The books were in good taste, and knowing which ones to leave out for this person, or remove entirely for another, showed good judgment and a highly attuned sense of character. Haider, for instance, never stumbled upon books when he went to Uncle's office; he was regaled with tales of bravery and chivalry from days long gone instead. Once in my presence, speaking to Uncle, Haider said that he thought Iraqis were much nicer than other people, especially Iranians, whom he particularly despised after the scandal surrounding his father erupted.

"Of course we are nicer," Uncle said with a twinkle in his eyes. "But we are nicer because we have no rules. That is how we get things done."

Inauspicious Birds

Perched on top of the roof of the balcony of our second-floor bed-room, my aunt saw a flock of crows, the foulest and most inaus-picious creatures on the face of the earth, she wailed, beating her chest with her fists.

"But very intelligent," said my mother calmly, "and they outlive us," trying to dampen the hue and cry that her sister was creating because of the ill omen that had descended on her balcony. "Does not the crow seek the most excellent of fruit such as can only be found in a house as richly endowed as yours?" she said to her sister.

"I saw two of them fly away, circle the whole neighborhood, and return to the rest of the flock a few minutes later," my aunt cried. "They chose us! Woe upon our house! Woe to us! What have we done to deserve this?"

Next morning, a crisp, cold winter day, Mother did not feel well, waking up with a different kind of headache that told her something was unusually wrong. All day, until the doctor and an acquaintance from the neighborhood passed by, her sister and neighbors fussed over her, arguing over which of the six different flavors of pome-granate juice available in Najaf would best relieve her symptoms: the sweet kind that relaxes the bowels, or the sour kind that has the opposite effect. Aunt won the argument by opting for the juice from the tree in our courtyard, because it was between sweet and sour, and, she said, it was good for inflammation of all organs of the body.

I was sitting on my bed, on the other side of our shared room, watching as the doctor conducted a perfunctory examination that uncovered strange bruises on my mother's back that she could not explain, and which the doctor instantly dismissed, assuring her that there was nothing seriously wrong, nothing that a good rest and a glass of boiled milk would not cure by the morning.

The bruises grew in the course of the week and then disappeared, leaving strange configurations on her skin; then, remarkably, they returned. Her gums turned white, and she was soon too exhausted to stand up, having to crawl on all fours to move around. Still she would not go to the hospital. It was filthy, she said, and would kill her for sure; anyway, they had no medicines, and whatever they had had been doctored on the black market and couldn't be trusted. On this, for once, she and Uncle were in agreement.

By the end of the week I am certain she knew she was dying. The dying know before anyone else.

"Your grandfather, son . . ."

"Yes, Mother. What about him?"

"Talk to him. Know him better. He was good to me . . . he worshipped your father."

I had never really been close to Grandfather. He was truculent with everyone in the house except her, especially Uncle. But why did Mother mention him now of all times? "Of course, Mother," I told her. "Don't worry about such things. I will talk to him."

"Your uncle . . ."

"Yes, Mother?"

But she couldn't bring herself to say whatever it was she wanted to say.

"Yes?" I said, egging her on as gently as I knew how.

"He . . . is a complicated man."

I tried to brush it off. "I know, Mother," I said with a laugh. "He is all politics. Half the time I never know what is on his mind. Why, only the other day, he pressed me about my patriotism and was worrying about Iranian infiltrations in the country."

She didn't like to hear that. I could have kicked myself. No politics; that was the rule. Her face turned anxious. She must have been puzzling through Uncle's reasons for bringing up the subject.

"Your father loved God, son," she said.

"Of course he did."

"Don't let anyone tell you otherwise."

"Why should they do such a thing?"

"Because his God was not that of other men. His God was not your uncle's God."

"Mother! There is only the One God. Your fever is speaking."

"Your father was different."

"Different from whom?"

"Other men. Talk to your grandfather . . ." And that was the last thing she said before drifting into sleep.

The next night, she called me over to her side and asked me to remove a chain from around her neck. Attached to the chain was a small key, the key to the top drawer of her chest next to her bed.

"This now belongs to you. You will open that drawer after I am gone," she said. "There are a few trinkets of mine that I would like you to have—perhaps your wife in the future may like them—and there is a letter that has been waiting for you to read for thirteen years." Of course I wanted to open the drawer right away, but she would not allow it.

We talked late into the night. She said that we people of Iraq belonged to an unfortunate race, a people who had missed out on love. In love's place, she said, fear ruled. Every crisis, no matter how big or small, was an occasion for a new fear. A deep, impassable chasm, she used to say, walled off those who were afraid from those who were loved.

She herself was afraid. She understood tyranny, and how to live in its shadow; she had learned to cope with pain and sorrow; she had even found a way to manage loss and uncertainty. But anarchy posing as freedom was something alien and terrifying to her; it obeyed no rules and, she said, released the beast lurking in men. The war, the fall of Baghdad, the escape of the Tyrant, the insurgency, but above all the emergence of a bewildering number of parties contending for the hearts of the young and the impressionable—men like me—all this terrified her.

Fear is why she cooked a piece of fish on Wednesdays. Fish, and only on Wednesdays, she used to say, blessed the entire household. Before sunset, also only on Wednesdays, to further ward off the evil eye, she would put three pieces of red-hot coal into an aluminum bowl and sprinkle a handful of dry harmel seeds over them, until a gentle popping sound could be heard. As the smoky aroma filled the room, the bowl would be turned in circles around my head three times, the smoke gently blowing into my face while she slowly recited a verse from the Quran.

> In the name of God, the Compassionate, the Merciful.
> Say: "I take refuge with Thee,
> Lord of Creation,
> From the evil of the slandering whisperer,
> Who whispers in the hearts of all,
> Be they jinn or men."

Everyone in Uncle's household, and the stream of visitors from the neighborhood who came to pay their respects to him—because they were not coming for Mother's sake—treated what was happening to her as a temporary affliction, mere unpleasantness, repeating the bland reassurances of the doctor, who visited two or three times a week, taking her temperature, checking her pulse, measuring her blood pressure, even as her sister, Uncle's wife, and the neighbors continued fussing over her.

Everyone was living a lie: the lie that Mother would get better if only she kept on being told she would get better. Her sister, the neighbors, other visitors, even Grandfather, needed to keep on repeating this lie, which they knew was a lie; it was as though they too had an obligation to keep up the pretense of normalcy. I was miserable and angry with all of them. Family life in our world was governed by a strict set of unwritten rules; speaking the truth to the sick and the dying was not among them. Lying was. But there were times and ways of lying, rules even in lying that had to be adhered to.

The doctor must have confided the truth of Mother's condition to Uncle—that was a rule—and it was understood between them that no one else needed to know. I was the next man in line after Uncle, and should also have been told. But wasn't. Everyone else could be lied to. All anyone knew was that everything was going to be all right. That way, when she died, the doctor could say he knew all along she was going to die, but was trying to make her feel better and put her mind at peace. If by some miracle she lived, he would boast about how he had been right all along. Did it even cross that stupid doctor's mind to order a simple blood test, or draw her blood himself and send it to the laboratory? Perhaps it did, but he knew her case was hopeless; why waste Uncle's money?

Mother died late on a Thursday afternoon, a month after the headache had made its first appearance; the attending physician at the morgue diagnosed her with acute leukemia.

I continue to see her every day, even after she passed away. It is the same dream. Her hair is going gray, although she is still young. She is seated in the bedroom we shared in Uncle's house, on a rickety old chair that she refused to discard even though it was barely capable of supporting her slim frame. It belonged to Father—that and his library and some old clothes that she kept clean and well pressed were all that he had left her.

In the dream, she never sees me. Her face is heavy, lined with sorrow. I am calling out, "Mother . . . Mother . . . Mother," but she does not hear. I keep on calling, my anxiety mounting, and my voice getting louder and louder until it seems the whole house must wake up. On a bad night, the walls of the room begin to tremble and sway as if some terrible beast had grabbed the house by its foundations and were shaking it to and fro. *If only she would look in my direction,* I say to myself in the dream. But she does not hear, and she does not turn her tired face toward me.

When, finally, I awake in terror, she is there beside me on the same frail chair, stroking my hair, telling me it was just a nightmare. And there she stays until I fall back asleep. But then she is gone, and there is only the darkness of the night to wake up to.

I often wonder how it was when she died, when she drew her last few breaths lying in pain on her bed. What is it like knowing your very last breath is just about to be drawn? Could death at that singular moment in the span of our lives be pleasurable—not that the causes of it ever are pleasurable, but rather the moment itself, perhaps only milliseconds long, the moment or moments immediately preceding death, when you know for sure you are going to die, and including, of course, the actual tiny sliver of time in which death itself consists, since it has to occupy some space of time—could pleasure, or call it happiness, finally have visited Mother in that minuscule little sliver of time?

I like to think so. I like to imagine she lost her fears, and all the bitterness and anger of late. I like to think she finally accepted that her fear, like all our fears, was very down-to-earth—the knock on the door, the barbed piece of gossip, the inquisitive questioning of a neighbor; it certainly never had the face of the dead man she took so gently with her to bed every night, and whom she slept with in her dreams; I like to think all of those things, and to know Mother finally had a taste of what it meant to live.

Whatever happens in the final moments of our lives, I hope I can meet death the way she did, with the sort of self-assurance and inner calmness in which is hidden a kind of immortality.

Goodbye, Mother. Goodbye.

The Letter

I opened the locked drawer in my mother's chest late that evening, after her body had been ritually washed, wrapped, placed in a simple coffin, and returned home to await burial the following day; she was downstairs in the living room, wrapped in the same white shroud Uncle had carried with him during his pilgrimage to Mecca to be blessed. The female mourners, who had spent the late afternoon by her side reading from the Holy Book, had left, and the house was quiet, not a sound to be heard except the scraping of wood as I gently pulled the drawer open. Tomorrow we would carry her in a procession of mourners, headed by Uncle and myself, to visit the Imam one last time in his Shrine, after which she would be taken to the cemetery to be buried, a journey that Mother and I had watched from our second-story balcony window hundreds of times.

The letter was from my father, and written from the camp in which he had been incarcerated after being captured. The paper looked like it had been intended for rolling cigarettes; the handwriting, tiny and neat—a lot of care has to go into calligraphy that small. Beside its manila envelope was a fountain pen whose cylinder had been gutted. So this was how it had been smuggled out; tightly rolled up inside the barrel of the fountain pen. Mother must have lightly

ironed the sheets, because I found them crisp and flat, folded once
lengthwise to fit in the envelope I had removed them from. The top
sheet was dated April 1991; I would have been twelve at the time he
wrote them. I fondled the thin sheets, turning them around in my
hands gently; they were as fragile as dry onion leaves. It took me a
while to gather up the courage to read the words.

MY DEAR WIFE,

I scratched your name on my fingernail last night with a nail;
my pencil I spare for this letter, which I will use until its lead
is finished. The writing by itself brings you closer to me.
How strange? It is as though you are next to me even now,
and we are talking. Do you remember when I would return
on furlough, hold you in my arms, and you would talk, and
talk and talk . . . sweet nothings just to calm me down, all the
while running your fingers in my hair? To be honest I cannot
recall the words; the sounds I do remember, rippling and
bubbling like a mountain stream. Nothing can replace those
times.

I will not ask questions you cannot answer— How are you?
How is our son? Has he returned to school yet? How are you
coping? Is my brother treating you right? How is my father
coping with his rheumatism? Know that I think about them
endlessly instead. I write against all odds, but in the hope
that these words do by some miracle find you. God willing,
they will. I want to believe that they will. Care has been
taken to avoid clues that could lead my jailors to you. And yet
the messenger, who bears it, is one of them. Trust him if he
chooses to reveal himself; he may not. We served together on
the front, and bonded like brothers. Still, writing is foolhardy;
I know it, but I can't help myself. Hallaj says, "Love, so long
as it hides, feels itself in great danger, and is only reassured by
exposing itself to risk."

Know, my dear, that by the time this letter reaches you,

I will be gone to a better place. I do not want you to be sad, but even less do I want you to entertain false hopes. My last remaining pleasure in this world is to believe you will receive this letter and be safe. Then I can go to my Maker in peace, your name etched on my fingernail.

Everything about this wretched country of ours has let me down, everything except you; you are the only good thing that happened in my otherwise wasted life. Ours is a nation of sick and spite-filled men, of selfish men, of hollow men, of treacherous men who would whisper ill of their fathers and brothers, and sell them to the devil for a pittance.

Know, my dear, that I was betrayed, my location revealed to the police; it beggars the imagination to think they would have found me on their own. But I have no proof. Who could have betrayed me? I do not know, but he had to know me well. The two good men I was with escaped ten minutes before they came bursting through the door; thank God for little mercies; they were looking for them too. How did they know we were three? I had to have been betrayed. Trust no one, my love. Too many Iraqi souls have withered and fallen from the tree; the rest were poisoned from the well.

In the darkest days of our war against Iran, you would not have found me saying such things, but what I have seen and experienced in these last three weeks exceeds all the horror I lived through for eight years on the front; I am in the darkest corner of hell, and it is called Radwaniyya, a prison, if you can call it that, just outside Baghdad's airport. I wish that you did not have to know such a place existed. But there are things that must not be forgotten. It pains me to have to relate them to you, but I have no one else. Years from now, at the right time, you will know what to do with this knowledge. Use it, my love, only when it is safe for you to do so; and when our son is of age allow him to read this letter; he will want to know how his father died.

We were brought here by the busload, from Najaf, Basra, Amarah, Kut, and other towns and villages. As we left the prison bus, we were faced with a dozen or so starving dogs. There was no way to exit the bus without running the gauntlet of these terrible dogs, followed then by prison guards standing behind them wielding wooden truncheons a meter long. Just imagine the mad rush of prisoners to the doors of the entry hall. No one escaped an injury of some kind: a broken rib, a cracked skull, and one or two dog bites at least. But it was the horror of it that I was left with! One woman who was on the bus with me lost an eye.

This greeting is what the prisoners inside called our "entry tax" into Radwaniyya. The real tax, our formal "reception," as the guards called it, consisted of a dozen or so of them inside, all armed with truncheons, herding us into a corner and flailing out in all directions at the huddled, cowering, and screaming prisoners. To slip away meant to make it to a different corner of the same locked hall, only to be followed by guards and a still more concentrated beating, from which there was not even the relative protection provided by the huddled mass of bodies. They beat us this way for thirty minutes or so, until their arms were too tired to raise the truncheons.

When I say "guards," perhaps you think I am talking of men; I am not. They are all boys, teenagers, not one of them in his twenties. Imagine what happens to a boy who spends a year or so of his most formative years doing this kind of work? He is changed forever. Think of these boys—I see them now in the distance—and keep our son away from such evil, even if you have to send him away from you.

On that first day, I saw something worse: the face of a man, desperately thirsty, asking for water. The guard takes a hosepipe and shakes out a few drops. In his desperation for more, the man reaches out to hold the hose so as to suck in a bit more; it is as though he has organized a rebellion, or cursed Saddam Hussein to his face. In the blink of an eye, five of these teenage guards descended on him, beating him all over. When he fell to the ground, he was kicked in his ribs, on the liver, around his testicles, on the head . . . until finally he lay prostrate, barely alive. I thought this was the end of his sufferings, only I was wrong. The sick minds of these teenagers endlessly innovate; in fact, they are rewarded for innovation in the delivery of pain. One of them took the hose and stuffed it into the mouth of the prostrate man; he shoved it deep, very deep, so that the force of the water would not push it out. I witnessed this terrifying scene and all I could think was, what place was this that I had entered? Where was I? Was this really happening in Iraq? Did anybody know what was being done? The hose was turned on full blast, and water poured into the poor man's stomach, which inflated until it started emptying out of every orifice—nose, ears, and mouth. Ten minutes later his limbs fluttered, and he went still.

Once again, my dearest, I apologize for inflicting these stories on you. But somebody must know what happened here; the world must know; it is my only way of fighting back. How could those Americans who came halfway across the world to push him out of Kuwait stand by and let him do these things to our people? That is where we were headed, the three of us, before they caught me: to the American lines, less than a kilometer away from the house in which they caught me, to ask for help, or at the very least access to the regime's ammunition warehouse, which they were standing guard over.

Upon arrival in Radwaniyya, I befriended a man—call him Qassim. He is a professor at one of our prestigious universities, better not to mention which one. Four of his relatives had been executed by the regime, and for this reason alone they arrested him in his house. Yesterday we were all

paraded before the Tyrant's cousin, who was in charge of
the southern sector, dragging our heavy shackles behind us.
After he left, the heavy interrogation began. They started
on poor Qassim, with all of us watching, accusing him of
participating in the Uprising. He denied he had anything to do
with it, whereupon they began to beat him with long sticks,
electricity, the whole works.

The chief interrogator, a man of the Shi'a like us, was
perhaps the most brutal man I encountered at Radwaniyya.
He was huge, with a large paunch—terrifying to behold—and
on that day he was wearing an olive green uniform. If you
tried to read the features on his face, you would think some
evil force had deformed it. The man looked like a monster;
there is no other way to put it. That day he approached the
guards softening up poor Qassim; he came with his personal
guard, one aide in particular had been assigned to carry
his own personalized meter-long truncheon, which had an
ornate, bulbous decorated metal head at its end. He asked
how the interrogation was going.

"He is refusing to confess, sir," replied the guard in charge
of Qassim.

"Did he kill?" asked the chief interrogator.

"I suspect he has," replied his junior, "but I have not been
able to extract a confession from him."

"Hand me my stick," the chief said to his aide. He then
shouted at the prisoner, "Are you going to confess?"

Poor Qassim was so far gone I doubt he even heard the
question. He raised the stick with the bulbous metal end on
it and brought it down on the man's head with great force.
"One," shouted his accompanying guard in unison; they had
done this before. Again, he struck; "two," they shouted; and
finally a third time. "He's dead," they all cried out for our
benefit. Qassim lay prostrate on the concrete floor. Blood was
everywhere, on the chief interrogator's shirt, on my face, all
over the guards standing by.

Tomorrow it will begin again. Perhaps it will be my turn, perhaps not. At any rate, you must assume I am dead. Nor will you ever find my corpse. The rule in Radwaniyya is that you do not lift a corpse and carry it away; it has to be dragged by the ankles to the main door, and then left to pile up, two, four, six, and sometimes even ten in a big heap. At the end of the day, a garbage truck circles around and men toss the bodies into it. Then, with all the prisoners looking on, because the barred windows are so low, the truck drives up to a hill, a hill of corpses, and cans of white powder are sprinkled over each fresh load of corpses tossed on top. The hill grows higher and higher by the day.

As God is my witness, I saw these things.

Radwaniyya means death, but the strange thing about the way we are dying here is that it makes me think about things I did not think about before. I always thought of myself as an Iraqi, but every prisoner here is from among us Shi'a, and was brought here because he was a Shi'a. Amid the danger all around me, I feel safe with my fellow prisoners; there are several thousand of us. I feel relieved to be among them, to be in a group I can call my own and whose fate I am about to share. I find myself overwhelmed with tenderness toward them. As you know better than anyone, these are not feelings I ever had before.

But, among our guards are some Shi'a, not many, like that chief interrogator brute, senior aide to the Tyrant's cousin; they are, would you believe it, without exception the most brutal men in the prison. Isn't that strange? Are they trying to prove something to their Sunni lords and masters? I don't know. I just know this is not the Iraq I used to know. Then there are Sunni guards, like the man bringing this letter to you, who secretly do us little kindnesses, in tiny doses, when nobody is looking. Such is life in Radwaniyya Prison.

Our people have changed; the violence all around and for so long has changed them. They were not like that before;

those who rule have turned them into brutes. Forgive them, my dear, and teach our son to forgive them. Teach him not to seek revenge for what was done to his father; teach him never to act out of hate. A brighter day will come, and he will live to see it. Hope is not something that is logical or reasonable. But I am filled with it for him in spite of everything. You too must live for it, my dearest. Survive for it! A Russian poet wrote:

Mounds of human heads are wandering into the distance.
I dwindle among them. Nobody sees me. But in books
much loved, and in children's games I shall rise
from the dead to say the sun is shining.

Now, my piece of pencil is all used up, I surrender this letter to fate; its messenger beckons. Still, I am left with your name, scratched on my fingernail; it is enough.

Minarets and Kalashnikovs

As we drove to Baghdad in a ten-year-old tan-colored Toyota sedan, Uncle at the wheel and two Kalashnikov-wielding guards in the backseat, the car would every so often have to veer off the tarmac onto rubble shoulders a few feet wide. The pink-faced soldiers on the end vehicle of a convoy of huge American army trucks were still not as trigger-happy as they would become, and happily waved Uncle on to their left if the coast was clear; the problem was, no one could really see what was barreling down at one hundred kilometers per hour in the opposite direction.

"Sons of whores," Uncle would mumble to himself every so often as he flattened the accelerator, driving past them, one set of wheels on the tarmac and the other on the soft shoulder.

The sun was harsh by late morning, the land barren, relieved every now and then by clumps of barely clad children and scrawny dogs, staring in amazement as cars whizzed by. No trees or bushes, and if you passed one, it was never green—its leaves would have turned brown from the dust and ceaseless punishment endured at the hands of the sun. Two materials defined the human contribution to the landscape—concrete block and corrugated iron—along with the transfiguring consequences of a quarter of a century of war with all its attendant debris. It would be an exaggeration to call the structures by the road buildings; more like shacks or crude half-finished built events, with perhaps a piece of canvas stretched over uneven and irregular walls held in place by a concrete block or two. No design. No landscaping. No fields. We drove past scattered groupings of such structures, stopping once for sweet black tea; it was a refreshingly clean place, decked out with a few tables and chairs and pleasantly cool, having just been hosed down.

I was accompanying Uncle to search for my father's file, which we were hoping to find in a former intelligence compound in Baghdad built on a bend in the river Tigris—and the very same location in which the Tyrant would be executed three years later.

Before driving to the compound, however, Uncle had an important and confidential assignment from the Sayyid—to meet and discuss strategy with a senior cleric, head of the Islamic Scholars Association, a man deemed by the Americans to be a formerly high-ranking Ba'thi, currently leading the insurgency against them, and the spiritual head of its militantly Sunni Iraqi wing. The meeting was to explore avenues of military cooperation against the Occupier, should it come to that.

The Islamic Scholars Association had taken over a mosque built by Saddam after the 1991 Gulf War called the Mother of All Battles Mosque, renamed after the 2003 war the Mother of All Villages Mosque—a reference to Mecca, the Mother of All Cities. We entered Baghdad from the south, driving past the nondescript townships of Mahmoodiya, Latifiya, and Yusufiya—later to become the sites of heavy fighting and community cleansing campaigns—and ending up on the highway north, which took us uninterruptedly to our destination sandwiched between two Sunni suburbs of Baghdad, also sites of much killing after 2005. But in November 2003 there was not a hint of the cleansing campaigns to come, and we arrived uneventfully at what was my first introduction to Baghdad, the fabled city of the Abbasid Caliphs, where Hallaj preached and had been crucified, the City of Peace, as the politicians loved to remind us.

I still think of the building as the Mother of All Battles Mosque, perhaps because of its design, and the memories of its being built as an act of defiance toward the armies that left the Tyrant in power. There had been much fanfare surrounding the construction, coinciding with the years of my childhood, years of sanctions and privation. I had never seen anything so lavish before. Money was not spared; the whole was clad in gleaming white limestone of the finest quality, enriched here and there with blue mosaic. The Tyrant, it is said, had personally overseen every detail. All this would have been enough to impress anyone, but here is the odd thing: the outer four minarets, each the height of a ten-story building, were built in the shape of barrels of Kalashnikov rifles aimed at the sky; the inner four, only slightly lower, were built to look like the Scud missiles that the Tyrant had fired at Israel in 1991, during the Mother of All Battles—none of which hit their mark (and one of which fell on a Palestinian neighborhood). The red, white, and black flag from the Tyrant's era still fluttered from the peaks of these minarets, and a reflecting pool in the shape of a map of the Arab world encircled the mosque. In the blue water was an island in blue mosaic in the shape of the Tyrant's thumb. Perhaps this is why it is hard to think of this mosque as anything other than the Mother of All Battles Mosque.

A sumptuous lunch rich in meat and rice followed Uncle's meeting, and we took the road again to the intelligence headquarters complex in Kadhimain, the oldest Shiʻa district in the heart of Baghdad, where another of our twelve Imams is buried.

The afternoon had turned hot and windless by the time we got out of the car, the heat made worse by asphalt, concrete, and the packed crowds of people on foot. I remember pushing through the throngs gathered outside the gates of the compound, following slowly in Uncle's wake, a big man barreling through as though it was his God-given right.

Suddenly I came face-to-face with an old woman cloaked in black, whose expression I shall not forget to my dying day. She pressed a photo of her missing son into my hands at the gates of the compound, just as Uncle had successfully broken through the crowds. She was not being allowed in; Uncle, on the other hand, was the Sayyid's man, which was as good as if he owned the place.

I looked at her son's photo and saw that the face was blank, like those white oval images of the Prophet in an illustrated book in my father's library. The silver on the old woman's photo had been wiped off from years of touching and stroking. I turned my eyes from his non-face to her wrinkled anxiousness, not able to say anything. A young man accompanying her spoke instead:

"Ignore her. She comes every day." And then he made a gesture with his hand to indicate she was not right in the head.

How I hated the Tyrant at that moment—more even than I hated him for killing my father.

Mother's passing had released me. I could now come all the way from Najaf to search this battered collection of filth-encrusted buildings for a file, my father's file, in the hope that it would tell me what had happened to him and where he was buried. I searched in a frenzy, under obligation to no one, a man possessed, allowing himself to be consumed with anger, oblivious to everything and everyone around him, throwing chairs and smashing tables without rhyme or reason, even though they belonged to Iraq, no longer to the Tyrant.

I looked in every broken room of every decrepit building in the compound. But there were no files, no paperwork of any sort; if there had been, they were now gone, looted by professionals in the first days after the Tyrant's fall, perhaps by the Americans, but more likely by one of the militias that had slipped in the moment the slow-witted Occupier had cleared all obstacles from their way.

Painful Slap

Following our return to Najaf, I joined the Army of the Awaited One, serving the Sayyid, whose father and two brothers had been murdered by Saddam in 1999, and who is the cousin and son-in-law of Muhammad Baqir al-Sadr, a leading Shi'a scholar of the 1970s and founder of our movement, whom we called "the First Martyr" after he was tortured and killed by the Tyrant in 1980.

"You will not be a soldier," my mother had said in a tone that brooked no discussion. Uncle had not contradicted her. In the months following the Sayyid's call to arms, Uncle broached the subject again, saying she would think differently now that she was in heaven with Father at her side; they would both smile down on me, he said, serving my country the way Father had done. Truth be told, I didn't need him to say anything; I longed to be swept up in the storms of change rolling up young men like me all over Iraq.

I was standing in line outside a local recruitment center when the news of the Tyrant's capture in a hideout fifteen kilometers south of Tikrit was announced. There was jubilation in the streets, with men dancing and firing into the air. In front of me, waiting in line to register his membership, was a man a few years older than myself, also following through on the Sayyid's call to arms. He had a peculiar name, al-Muntassir, the Victorious One, which was one of the things that drew him to my attention, because he asked the registering officer to change it to Muntassir, or Victorious. Men like him had been pouring into recruitment centers during the last few weeks in such numbers that many had to be turned away. But Muntassir, as he preferred to be called, had received the blessings of the Sheikh of his local mosque—whose name as a sponsor was recorded in a big ledger, alongside his.

My recommendation had come from Uncle, whose name triggered so much deferential treatment that it embarrassed me before the other recruits. There was no question of the center's head asking me questions. Haider and I had finished our military training with the army's First Battalion in Basra three weeks earlier, and our unit had been sent back to Najaf, where I was to be stationed. Training in those days consisted of rising before dawn for early morning prayers followed by a breakfast of dried dates. The next few hours were spent learning to use, dismantle, and reassemble weapons, such as the Chinese version of the Russian Kalashnikov. Lunch, a single piece of flat bread and chickpeas, was followed by two hours of live-fire training on the empty hillside. Occasionally we practiced throwing live hand grenades, more often painted stones the size and weight of a hand grenade. The standard day ended with ball games and wrestling followed by dinner. This went on for two weeks. A few recruits were then chosen for more intensive training, including learning how to wire explosives and blow up buildings and bridges. Our registration in Najaf was a pure formality.

Muntassir had come to the Sayyid's center in Najaf to complete the registration procedure, which in his case included answering questions confirming his commitment to the cause. What distinguished this scrawny young man in a dirty dishdasha from everyone else in the line that day were his black leather boots; they were worn down at an angle on both heels, with a very badly scuffed right toe. Muntassir didn't seem to realize how inappropriate his footwear was, given the rest of his attire; he was expecting a uniform but did not get it. He had worn his boots so as to be prepared for the sol-dier's uniform he was expecting. His face beamed pride in his life's new mission; at least he still had a soldier's attendant footwear, even though the boots were not the right size and were laced up wrongly, having their tongues pulled out of the bottom lace and hanging for-ward, as though lapping at the leather.

The registering officer was a white-turbaned Sheikh, the black tur-ban being restricted to Sayyids who are descendants of the Prophet. He was doubling up as cleric and head of the recruitment center located in a neighborhood of the Old City adjoining ours. The Sheikh looked Muntassir up and down carefully, and then advised him that he had to answer all questions put to him truthfully on pain of com-mitting a grave sin that the Sayyid would not forgive.

Muntassir nodded his assent vigorously.

"Who are your parents?"

"They run a stand on the Najaf-Karbala road selling soft drinks and candy," Muntassir replied.

"Do you pray regularly?"

"Of course, my Sheikh. I have never once missed a prayer."

"Never? It is a terrible sin to lie to the Sayyid."

"Never. Never. I swear it."

"And do you fast at the prescribed times?"

"Yes, most certainly, my Sayyid. Every Ramadan. I have never missed once."

"Why did you want to join our army?"

"I wanted to be a fighter on the first day of the Occupation, after I heard the Sayyid say, 'The smaller devil has gone, but the bigger devil has come.'"

"And what did you understand these words to mean?"

"I realized that the Sayyid's love of Iraq was very great, and I wanted to fight for my homeland against the Occupier."

"Yes, but who is the smaller devil?"

"Saddam."

"Are you happy he was caught?"

"Of course. I only wish we had gotten to him before the Occupier."

The Sheikh nodded in approval, then looked up at Muntassir and said, "And the bigger devil. Who is he?"

"The American Occupier, who was dealt a painful slap by the destruction of the World Trade Center."

"A painful slap?"

"Yes."

"Both painful and a slap?"

"Of course, because it has not destroyed America, not yet, but America was hurt, and the cowboys who rule it seek revenge by stealing our oil."

That was all it took for Muntassir to become a member of the Army of the Awaited One.

Black Boots

S hortly after he had completed his two-week training course, Muntassir's unit, on orders from our Sayyid, was assigned to occupy the Shrine of the Imam Husain in Karbala. This meant wresting control of it by force from the House of Hakim, in favor of the House of Sadr. We were going to humiliate them; that was the idea behind this opening shot in the war between our two Houses, the first in a succession of such wars that would go on for the next three years.

Muntassir and his unit were ill prepared for the fight, meeting fierce resistance from experienced fighters, among them veterans of the Great War holed up inside who had just returned from Iran and were much better equipped and trained. The attack was easily repulsed, leaving dozens of our comrades dead and wounded. The repercussions of our failure spread to Najaf, and our newly formed army was in no time being denounced by traditionalist clerics and the Shi'a militias allied to Iran.

One circular posted by militiamen of the House of Hakim on a wall near my house the next day read, "The Army of the Awaited One is composed of suspicious elements, including elements from the extinct regime. Its security officers are Ba'th Party members who have wrapped their heads with white and black rags to mislead people into believing that they are men of religion when in truth they are emissaries of the devil. We, the people of Najaf, do not need this false army, which they have slanderously called the Army of the Awaited One. Our Awaited Imam is in no need of an army made up of thieves, robbers, and perverts under the leadership of a one-eyed charlatan."

Uncle thought it wise that Haider and I disappear for a while. So I decided to stay with Muntassir, who had been wounded in the fighting and taken for treatment to a mosque outside the city, loyal to our Sayyid.

Muntassir was in much worse shape than I had been led to believe; his left side had been shredded by shrapnel from a grenade, and the thigh had become infected; there were no medications to relieve the pain or deal with the infection. A young man in a white coat, probably a medical student, was examining him and cracking sunflower seeds between his teeth at the same time. Muntassir's hoarse breathing was all that there was to shoo the flies away from his mouth; otherwise they were all over him. Still, he managed a smile when he saw me; I could see he was dying.

The student stood up, saying to me in a loud voice, "There is nothing anyone can do for the man, and therefore no point in my going on with this examination." I glowered at him, hoping he would choke on his sunflower seeds, until he hurriedly pocketed his stethoscope and went away, leaving behind what remained of the seeds.

Settling down beside Muntassir, with a bowl of cold water, some cloth, a piece of cardboard to shoo away the flies, and a plastic cup of pomegranate juice that I had bought on the way in to cheer him up, I started wiping the sweat from his brow, squeezing drops of water into his mouth, and generally trying to create small talk that might help get him through the ordeal.

"What's with the pomegranate juice?" he asked, taking a sip for my sake even though swallowing was clearly painful.

"All good things come from the sweetness of pomegranate juice, my mother used to say. The fruit is blessed, being mentioned in all the Holy Books numerous times. Drink up; it will do you good." And he obliged.

Men who are most in need of compassion from others, especially those who think they are deserving of it, whose own lives have been filled with suffering, are often least able to extend the same outward. It is as if we human beings are endowed with a fixed amount of compassion, and if we use it all up feeling sorry for ourselves, there is nothing left to share with other people.

Not so with Muntassir. All my friend wanted to do in the last hours of his life was inquire about those of his comrades who had been hurt, and would I please send them his greetings, his wishes for their speedy recovery, even though none of them was wounded as grievously as he. He asked me to distribute among them the paltry one hundred dollars in salary that was due to him. Meanwhile, he kept on sipping his pomegranate juice to please me, even though the effort of it clearly pained him. I took the cup away from him after a while.

Muntassir told me what had happened in Karbala: He and two comrades found themselves trapped behind a corner stump of a wall, while a group of militiamen from the opposing side were lobbing hand grenades at them. After the first grenade went wide, he decided their situation was hopeless and that the next grenade, or the one after that, was bound to land on target. So he made a mad rush to a wall on the side to try to get around the enemy, and succeeded. But when he raised his head to unload a magazine clip into the group lobbing grenades, barely ten meters away, he found himself staring at the face of a man younger than himself, with scared black eyes that were looking right at him; Muntassir was paralyzed by the fear he saw in his enemy's eyes, and hesitated, just enough to give the other fellow time to toss the grenade right at him, not missing this time. That was all he remembered until he found himself here.

I asked if he had any regrets.

"What future did I have selling soft drinks on the road to Karbala? My dream was to be a part of something bigger, to serve Muslims as poor as my parents. My father was a soldier in the war with Iran;

those are his boots. I wore them on the day of the battle," he said, pointing limply but with pride at them sitting on the floor in the corner of the room, neatly placed side by side.

"My father fought for his country against Iran during the Great War, and that is why he named me al-Muntassir, the Victorious One, after our great victory."

"Why did you ask to shorten it to Muntassir?"

"It was pompous; it was my father's victory, not mine."

"And the fighting in Karbala . . . was it worth it?"

"I was not going to let the Iran my father had fought and defeated occupy our mosques. I wanted to feel that my life was worth something."

"And did you succeed?"

"No doubt about it," he said. "My comrades made it out safely, you know. I managed to divert attention away from them. I am proud of that."

"Why didn't you pull the trigger?"

"I had a strange thought when the grenades were being tossed."

"What?"

"The pomegranate juice you brought reminded me of it just now. I remember thinking it was not right to call a hand grenade a 'pomegranate,' the way we Iraqis do in Arabic. A thing that takes life should not be confused with one that grows in Paradise and is in the Holy Book as a giver of life and sweetness."

"How true! I never thought of that before."

He should never have been there. He had the spirit but not the heart for killing. How many men like Muntassir were there among us? I wondered. Perhaps better training would have deadened a part of his heart; then at least he might have survived.

I stayed up with him all night watching as his face changed color; his breathing got more ragged until by the end he was struggling for air. But he never lost control, and told me at some point toward the end that he had seen death. I asked him if he was frightened. "No," he said. "I think I will be going to a better place." I told him I was sure of it, and that I would never forget him.

His eyes kept turning to the worn-out boots on the floor. His heart, I thought, was like those boots: worn down from proximity to death; that brought his death and his boots into some kind of alignment. Perhaps that is what it means to die. The last thing he said was, "I want you to have my boots."

Muntassir died of asphyxiation; his blood replacing air in his lungs. My impotent face was the last thing he saw of this world. The Sheikh read the opening verses of the Holy Book over him in the small hours of the morning, and said, "He wanted you to have these," handing me a plastic bag with Muntassir's black leather boots. I asked him how he knew. He said Muntassir had told him, before my arrival.

It is hard to live rightly in circumstances of war and violence, but, for reasons I do not claim to understand, I feel Muntassir succeeded. I was humbled by his death, not shocked, as I had been back in April when I stumbled upon the corpse near our house, nor angered, as I had been when I saw the carnage that accompanied the car bomb that killed the Sayyid from the House of Hakim in Najaf. There was no glamour or drama in death this time around, no desire for revenge, no spirit for the good fight; death passed us by that night, leaving only emptiness behind.

I took the plastic bag of personal effects from the Sheikh, including my friend's oversize black leather boots. It did not matter that I did not know how to put them to good use. They would remain his boots, and those of his father before him: the wearing down, the scuffing on the leather, and the endless replacement of heels . . . these actions no longer belonged to specific times and places, separated by the different wars of a father and his son; they summed up the only tiny little shreds of dignity and honor attached to the story of Iraq. That was reason enough to keep Muntassir's boots. In time, I would need them more than he did; but not for battle: I needed them to cling to, the way a drowning man needs a piece of driftwood.

| 2004 |

Bad Blood

Muntassir died because of a rivalry gone sour between two great clerical families of Iraq: the House of Hakim, which fled to Iran, and the House of Sadr, which stayed in Iraq. In Najaf, the rivalry was made worse with the return of Abu Haider from Tehran.

This second return from exile in Iran of Haider's father, in May 2003—the first had been during the Great Uprising of 1991—was the subject of much gossip in the neighborhood. Haider was delighted at first, and proudly retold stories of his father's feats abroad, his rise in the ranks of the Brigades of the Full Moon, which was in those days the armed wing of the Supreme Council for Islamic Revolution in Iraq, an organization established by the House of Hakim in Tehran and blessed by Ayatollah Khomeini himself.

But in the winter of 2004, word reached Haider's mother from a most unlikely source that there was another family in Tehran, and two children by Abu Haider's new, considerably younger Iranian wife, about whom nothing had been said in the preceding months.

The source of the startling news was my grandfather on my father's side, Uncle's father, who lived with us in our house in the Mishraq quarter, and to whom Mother had been devoted. I had not, I am ashamed to say, made good on my promise to Mother, lying on her deathbed, to talk to Grandfather. His crinkled leathery face, like an illegible old map, put me off; I was afraid I would be rudely turned away. How did this surly old man find out about Abu Haider's second wife? I don't know to this day, but it was certainly he who told our local Sheikh, who in turn visited Haider's mother, who in turn let her brothers know, and they all lost no time spreading it around the neighborhood, something Grandfather knew would happen.

Abu Haider did not deny the story—a useless exercise, as it was supported by considerable evidence. On the contrary, he vigorously defended his God-given right to marry again, the right of any good Muslim Believer in conditions of hardship and exile, to whom adultery is forbidden, but who is, thanks be to God, still endowed with a healthy sexual appetite, as Abu Haider most certainly was. Anyway, had not the Prophet allowed a man four wives? All of this poured salt onto wounds that were opening up inside Haider's household.

Rapidly the halo surrounding Abu Haider after his return dimmed, until through his refusal to concede any measure of indiscretion on his side it was extinguished forever. Family tensions became woven into political ones, coming to a head during the fighting over Karbala's shrine, when dear Muntassir lost his life. Thus did the tensions in Haider's household escalate to the point of threatening the fragile balance between the two main houses of Iraqi Shi'ism in Najaf: the Houses of Hakim and Sadr.

Abu Haider had high expectations upon his return from Iran, which were not shared by his wife, Haider's mother, or her family, who owned the house they all lived in a few doors away from our own. He had expected to be received as the conquering hero, the man whose self-sacrificing efforts on behalf of the "struggling downtrodden Shi'a," as he liked to put it, had brought about the fall of the Tyrant in Baghdad. In the euphoria of his return, he was given the benefit of the doubt.

It did not last for long. Abu Haider, it began to be said, had not lived through the hardship of life in Iraq under the dual weight of tyranny and sanctions; he had not lost a loved one during the eight-year war with Iran, the country he had taken refuge in. There was no way

Haider's mother and her family were going to let Abu Haider lord it over them now, and in their own household, after finding out he had spent twelve years getting married, siring new heirs, and living the good life as a high-ranking member of an organization funded by an enemy of Iraq, Iran, whose people said of Arabs that they were "eaters of locusts while the dogs of Isfahan drank cold water." Our whole street bristled with talk like that, and sided with Haider's mother, turning their backs on Abu Haider, even walking out of whatever shop or teahouse he happened to be in.

Both Uncle, whose allegiance was only to the House of Sadr, and my grandfather hated Abu Haider. The two leading Sayyids from the Houses of Sadr and Hakim, the most learned clerical families in our city, hated one another, even though—or perhaps it was because—they both came from Najaf, but, whereas our Sayyid had stayed and suffered in Iraq as his father had done—only assuming his father's mantle after the latter was murdered by the Tyrant—the Sayyid from the House of Hakim had fled to Iran to establish an organization that would spread the tenets of a revolution started in Iran and led by an Iranian. The rivalry between the two Houses had evolved into a major conflagration between two deeply divergent conceptions of the nation itself: one indigenous, familiar, and indubitably Iraqi, the other imported and foreign, which in practice would mean the permanent rule of foreign jurists over Iraqi ones.

Grandfather's hatred was a mystery to me, made deeper after I found out that he had gone out of his way to spread the news about Abu Haider's second marriage. Grandfather had never been a pious man, rarely visiting the local mosque, not even for Friday prayers, and was forever denouncing clerics for being thieves and charlatans, refusing on principle, he said, to give them alms or donations of any sort. What moved my toothless and withered grandfather, whom I had never seen do anything other than glower from his regular perch in the living room, to actively seek to undermine the position of my best friend's father in the neighborhood?

·　　·　　·

The week following the outbreak of the scandal, Haider and I visited the Sheikh of the local mosque we attended, a man aligned to the House of Sadr and with whom we had studied the Quran throughout our adolescence. He had played a role in the dissemination of the story; perhaps he could shed light on the matter.

We found him sitting cross-legged on a pile of cushions in his usual alcove in the mosque, chain-smoking as usual, and eating from a bowl of sugared almonds, which he gestured to us to share. What did Grandfather have against Abu Haider? we asked him.

"Bad blood," he said. "There is much bad blood between your two grandfathers. It began long before Abu Haider's return. Your grandfather," he said, looking at me, "knew I was under an obligation to let Haider's mother's family know." Then, turning to Haider, he apologized if he had been the cause of any distress. But, he said, he was under an obligation that had to be fulfilled.

This was the first time either Haider or I had heard of "bad blood" between our respective households.

"Tell us the story, O Sheikh; as God is my witness I never heard about it before," said Haider, who had taken the news that he had siblings in Tehran very badly.

"Your grandfathers were both Communists as young men, and the best of friends. Between them, they ran our neighborhood."

Ran the neighborhood . . . and Communists to boot? I wondered. How long ago? I wanted to know.

"Oh . . . let's see. It must have been at least thirty, forty years ago. They were in their twenties; I was a few years older, a student at the seminary at the time. So it must have been in the 1960s. I remember them both stirring things up, especially after the most senior Ayatollah of those days from the House of Hakim issued his famous ruling, in the late 1960s, saying that all Communists were atheists, and to be shunned. He was trying to diminish the influence the Communists then had among most of our young men. He ruled it a sin to work with them. That Ayatollah was the father of the Sayyid who, you both no doubt remember, was blown up last August in a car bomb."

"Do you mean the Sayyid who returned from Iran last summer just after my father did?" Haider asked.

"Yes. Your father always worked with the House of Hakim, most of whom fled to Iran in the early 1980s—those who remained, that is, after Saddam executed about eighty members of their family."

"Are you sure my grandfather was a member of the Communist Party?" I asked, still unable to imagine him in that light; not that I had any idea what a Communist was, but I had read in a history book that after the overthrow of the monarchy there had been a party called the Iraqi Communist Party.

"Card-carrying," replied the Sheikh, picking up the bowl of sugared almonds and insisting we each take another, "along with your grandfather, may God rest his soul," he said, nodding in Haider's direction. "Both were very committed to social justice and the poor, and excellent organizers, as well as being inseparable."

"So what happened?" Haider asked, crunching on a particularly noisy almond; it is impossible to eat the sugarcoated variety without making a noise.

"Saddam happened! That's what happened. May he rot in hell! He ran the secret police in those days, the 'Instrument of Yearning,' I think they used to call it."

"What a strange name," I said in a low voice.

"He coined that name during their years in the wilderness, before the Ba'th came to power in 1968."

"What were they yearning after?" I asked, now completely distracted by the strangeness of the name.

"Power, of course—what else? And that was the problem with Communists in those days, including both of your grandfathers. They did not understand power; Saddam did. His Ba'th Party was a small organization, whereas the Communists could mount demonstrations in the hundreds of thousands. Yet it was the Ba'th, not the Communists, who seized power and captured the state."

"How did my grandfather die?" asked Haider.

"Your grandfather," he replied, "was killed fighting the Ba'th in the marshes near 'Amarah. You see, as soon as the Ba'th engineered their coup, they offered the Communists a deal: enter our government and we will give you a few ministers; refuse to do so and we will cut you down, every last one of you. The condition included the Communists accepting the leadership of the Ba'th Party, something the Soviet Union was pressing them to do, but it was hard for them to do so. They fought bitterly about it inside their party; I remember your grandfathers going at it tooth and nail in a teahouse not far from here. It ended badly, with your grandfather and his group denouncing their comrades as fascist appeasers and traitors to the cause, and splitting off from the party and disappearing from the cities, where they knew the police would hunt them down. That ended everything between them.

"Meanwhile, your grandfather," the Sheikh said, looking at me, "accepted the condition and entered the civil service, working for one of the new Communist ministers."

"And mine hid out in the marshes?" asked Haider.

"He didn't just hide out; he and his comrades took up arms, modeling their struggle after Mao Tse-tung and going to live among the peasants."

"Are you saying that my grandfather still bears a grudge about all that to this day?" I asked, unable to picture the old man caring about anything other than himself.

"He went further. He forced his sister to break off her betrothal to his former best friend, making her deeply unhappy for the rest of her days. I know because my father oversaw the original marriage contract. Bad blood feeds on itself; it never goes away."

We thanked the Sheikh profusely for being so forthright; he in turn insisted on pressing into both of our hands little bags of sugared almonds, of which he seemed to have an endless supply. "It has been a happy week," he said by way of explanation. "Many marriages; lots of bags of sugared almonds . . . But, my sons, don't let this news spoil your day. There is no virtue in going down the road your grandfathers took."

Foreigner Iraqis

Haider returned yesterday from a trip to Baghdad with a strange story: in the office of the Iraqi national security advisor, an educated man who had lived and worked in London for decades, he had seen an enormous bust of Saddam Hussein wearing a helmet such as British officers stationed in Iraq wore during World War One. This gigantic object had been carefully placed in a corner, so that its dull, vacant eyes, sphinxlike with no irises, stared at the face behind the desk.

"There are Iraqis like us," Haider said, "and in Baghdad there are Foreigner Iraqis."

"What do you mean?" I asked, intrigued.

"They hate Saddam differently."

"You are not making sense."

"We had his picture on our walls because we had to: a nosy neighbor, gossip reaching the ears of the police, that sort of thing. We wouldn't dream of having it around otherwise."

"So . . ."

"Saddam was our whole life; he was our world. We didn't need his face to be reminded of that. We hate his pictures and his statues, like we hated him and his regime. Our hatred is natural. As soon as he is gone, we want nothing around that reminds us of him."

"And how do they hate Saddam?"

"He lives not in their hearts but in their heads as an idea, a fixation they cannot rid themselves of, even though he has nothing to do with their lives. They say they love us, their 'people,' the Shi'a, but that is only because they lived far away, not among us. Do we look at one another and marvel at how wonderful we Shi'a are? That would be stupid. We are who we are and move on. While we look forward to the future, they look backward to their ideas."

"Hmm . . . I see. But why call them 'Foreigner Iraqis'?"

"Because they are simultaneously foreigners and Iraqis, and yet they are neither at the same time. They look like us, because they were born among us, but they no longer feel or think like us. They no longer dress, or eat, or have the same habits we do."

"You are describing hybrid beings."

"I am," Haider said excitedly. "That is a good way to put it. They arrive with the Occupier; live in Baghdad in heavily guarded compounds; they remember a fairy tale of life as it 'used to be' outside of their offices; they avoid us ordinary Iraqis, whom they appear to fear, never once showing up at the scene of a terror attack."

"Come to think of it, I have never seen them visiting victims in a hospital or assisting their stricken families."

"They are revolutionaries in words alone, men whose lack of standing in the community has to be compensated for by the equally foreign thugs they hire to protect them."

"You are saying a Foreigner Iraqi is a deeply unsatisfied person; he has an inextinguishable longing to be somewhere else, longing to escape where he is, wherever that may be in the world, and never belonging to the place that he goes to."

"Probably it is even simpler than that; he is escaping the dullness of life in the well-ordered societies that gave him refuge and opportunity."

The citadel of Foreigner Iraqis in the new Iraq was something the Occupier called the Governing Council: twenty-five men and women not picked by the Occupier for their character or leadership abilities, or for their standing in the community, but by virtue of the tribe, sect, religion, sex, ethnicity, and foreign country whose interests they were deemed most likely to represent. What Uncle called "the politics of pretty pictures" determined why thirteen out of the twenty-five members of the Governing Council were Shi'a.

Of all the politicians of Iraq, only our Sayyid had denounced the Council right from the outset, in the summer of 2003, calling its members "infidels" and "lackeys of the Occupier." At the time, Uncle managed to convince him of the wisdom of moderating his hostility, better still concealing it, realizing that these Foreigner Iraqis had to be contended with and could be useful, particularly the thirteen members who now took to calling themselves the House of the Shi'a.

This new House was established in secret to give de facto control of the Occupier's Council to its Shi'a members, all of whom had been carefully selected by the Occupier; the Thirteen would meet secretly before each crucial decision in the Council and present a united front—to thwart its Sunni Arab members.

Uncle's moderation was purely tactical, however.

"They wear their Shi'ism like an ill-fitted suit," he said to me, "too tight in some places and too loose in others." To further divisiveness of this kind in politics, he said, "a man must be well-rooted among his own kind first," which none of the Foreigner Iraqis were.

He was in the room with them one day when a secular Sunni Arab Council member from London, a close personal friend of his Shi'a Council members, also from London—they all went to the same clubs—realized his Shi'a friends were up to something. Following a succession of speeches made by members of the House of the Shi'a to cover up how they had secretly decided to vote, it suddenly dawned on this Sunni Council member that a hidden agenda was being advanced under his nose, and by his London Shi'a pals. His face turned ashen in utter disbelief. In the deathly silence that filled the normally noisy room, sectarian politics was born.

From that moment until the end of the Occupier's experiment

with the Governing Council, Shi'a agendas pitted against Sunni agendas were all that were on anyone's mind in the plush gold-trimmed offices of the Council in the Green Zone. The citadel of Foreigner Iraqis misnamed the Governing Council had given up on governing themselves, much less a country called Iraq.

No one talked about sectarianism, thought like a sectarian, justified ideas in the name of sectarianism, argued like a sectarian, and then denied that they were sectarian more than the thirteen members of the House of the Shi'a in the Governing Council—certainly no one from the House of Sadr or in the Army of the Awaited One.

Later, once sectarianism had been established as the way of doing politics in the new Iraq, our movement would champion it, and we would prove to be a thousand times better at being sectarian than any Foreigner Iraqi had ever been. But not in those first two years when Foreigner Iraqis were setting the tone and laying down the rules of the game. These appointees of the Occupier taught the Shi'a of Iraq how to whine about their victimization under Sunni rule, which they equated with Saddam's rule; they behaved as though all Ba'this were Sunnis, and all Sunnis were Ba'this, and therefore equally suspect. In the only institution that Foreigner Iraqis dreamed up and controlled, the De-Ba'thification Commission, they practiced sectarianism like no Iraqi in the history of the country had practiced it before.

"In a contest between them and Saddam over who is more sectarian," Uncle asked me, "who do you think would win?"

"I couldn't say," I said.

"I will tell you," he said, his big round face breaking out in a smile. "Saddam was less sectarian."

"He didn't have to shout it from the rooftops," I said. "That doesn't mean he wasn't sectarian."

"Politicians turn sectarian when they are weak."

"Do you think it was by design?" I asked Uncle. "Is this what the Occupier wanted?"

"Divide and rule is the Occupier's way of doing things. Only the

Americans call it democracy. But there is another explanation for what these Foreigner Iraqis brought to Iraq."

"Which is?"

"Rootlessness. When you are without standing among your own, you need to invent enemies and spread fear, trick people in effect into thinking they need you for their own security. The Tyrant used this tactic all the time."

"But the Ba'th were in power at the time; the Governing Council isn't."

"It is only about power. What these fools don't realize is that you can only be truly sectarian when you have it, not if you merely appear to have it."

The Cabal of Thirteen

A few weeks later, I found myself with Uncle and a small group of his colleagues seated cross-legged on the thickly carpeted floor of a room adjoining his office. They were Persian carpets of the finest quality—Uncle was a collector—laid one on top of the other, making the floor soft and rich. You were intended to feel Uncle's station under your feet as you entered the room.

An old servant who had been with him for as long as I could remember was serving tea. Carrying a heavily decorated ceramic teapot in one hand, and a kettle of boiling water in the other, he topped each man's glass teacup on its gold-laced saucer. Bowls of sugar and glasses of water were scattered around on silver trays within easy reach. A decision had been made before my arrival regarding an Iranian proposition that had come to Uncle by way of one of the thirteen members of the House of the Shi'a in the Governing Council. It was the first I heard of it.

"So we are agreed," Uncle was saying, "we will never get a better price for the arms and grenades than what they are asking for. We will tell this toad arriving any minute that we are going to make the purchase. But what should we do about these newfangled mines with shaped charges the Iranians want to try out on us? I hear they are designed in Iran."

"I don't see why we should not accept a few hundred of them," an old colleague of Uncle's named Hassan said. He had been at Uncle's side for at least a decade, from the days of Sayyid Sadiq, our Sayyid's father. "After all, they are giving them away at the moment. We can tell the Iranians we will pay for the next batch if we like them."

"I don't like it," said an older man in spectacles sporting an immaculately trimmed graying short beard and dressed in shirt and trousers. "Why are they giving us weapons free of charge, sworn enemies of their closest allies, the House of Hakim?"

"It suits them that we fight one another," Uncle replied, looking down at his tea before taking a very noisy slurp.

"The mines are useless in the battles to come with the House of Hakim," said Hassan.

"It suits them even more for us to fight the Americans," Uncle replied morosely. "They were specifically designed to penetrate their armored vehicles. The House of Hakim isn't going to use them while they are in bed with the Americans in the Governing Council. The Iranians want us to test them out. Think of it as an Iranian investment in us, in our Iraqi future," he said with a bitter laugh.

"Aren't we putting too dark a spin on this?" I piped up. "There are weapons on offer from fellow Shi'a in Iran. Why not assume they want us to be able to protect ourselves even if they don't like our Sayyid? Perhaps they are trying to reach out. We are all Shi'a after all. What proof do we have that it is Iranian manipulation? Maybe the House of the Shi'a in the Governing Council negotiated the deal on our behalf. They are eager to improve relations. I hear they press the Americans daily to bring our Sayyid into the Council."

Uncle paused, his glass of tea suspended in midair for a moment before it continued on its way for another especially loud slurp. Then he turned and looked irritably at me. "Don't call them that! The last thing they represent are the Shi'a of Iraq. They are not a house but a cabal. I call them the Cabal of Thirteen."

"How the Sayyid laughed," Hassan chuckled, "when you coined that name. Now he refuses to call them by any other—"

"Sorry, Uncle . . . ," I said, interrupting Hassan because I was worried that I might have offended Uncle by contradicting him in front of his friends. "Why shouldn't the Shi'a set themselves up as a caucus inside the Governing Council?"

"Because Iraq is the prize, not just its Shi'a community. Anyway, there is no such thing as a House of the Shi'a. Just look around you! Only outsiders can come up with such a lie. The Cabal of Thirteen, by contrast, is real; that is what they are; it is how they behave inside the Governing Council, a name, incidentally, they insisted upon."

"How so?" I asked.

"The Occupier wanted to call them an Advisory Council; they waged a fight to change the name. The Tyrant had just fallen, the ground was moving under everyone's feet, and they squabbled for weeks over their name! They thought it made them important to be referred to as 'Governing,' even though they don't govern anybody. In life as in politics, son, when you meet a man who is more concerned with how things look than with what they really are, it is a sign of weakness. Soon you are about to meet one of them, and you can judge for yourself. Incidentally, he is acting alone, without the knowledge of his fellow Council members."

"No . . . ," I said, taken aback.

"Yes," Uncle replied. "The man is a viper, one in a nest of thirteen. The Iranians like him because he is incapable of having an independent idea. He is coming in order to gain leverage with the Iranians over his friends. Can you imagine our Sayyid sitting in a council with such a man? You will find no Shi'a solidarity in him."

I remained unconvinced, turning to the tea to gather my thoughts, my spoon tinkling pleasantly against the sides of my glass as I stirred.

"But surely, Uncle," I said after a pause, speaking as politely as I knew how, "the Shi'a in the Governing Council, while being weak as you say, are seeking to defend Shi'a interests. What is wrong with that? Do we Shi'a not have the right, even the obligation, to respond to injustice? If I am attacked for being a Shi'a, then am I not justified in defending myself by asserting I am the very thing I am attacked for being? Perhaps this commendable sentiment lies at the root of their sectarianism."

"Why should anyone believe what these people say?" Hassan now interjected, looking toward me with affection. He had known me all my life and was trying to head off the irritation he sensed rising in Uncle. "Nobody attacked these men from London and Tehran," he said; "they all live very well, thank you. And why are they conceding to the Kurds what they are unwilling to give to their Arab brothers?"

"You have lost me, Hassan. What are you talking about?"

"Federalism, of course. They are maneuvering even as we speak to find a formula in the interim constitution that will allow the Kurds to declare a federal region but not Sunni Arabs who come from the same tribes as they do."

"Sunni Arabs don't even want Federalism."

"Now they don't. But the House of the Shi'a in the Governing Council is making sure that even if they change their minds at any time in the future, the constitution will be worded so as to preclude their ever being able to. That is why our Sayyid has opposed the whole idea of Federalism as a camouflage for dividing up Iraq."

Hassan's intervention had the desired effect. Uncle picked up the argument. "Son," he said, "there is nothing commendable in reserving the quality of being a victim only to oneself. If you want to rule Iraq, you must start from the fact that all Iraqis were under attack by Saddam, not just the Shi'a."

"I am not denying that, Uncle."

"Moreover, we Shi'a are really a majority in the land. Inside the Governing Council we are a majority. So why are we behaving like an embattled minority?"

"Perhaps because we are a minority among Muslims worldwide."

"But we don't live in the whole world. We live in Iraq."

Now the bearded older man, who was not a military commander but, as I later found out, a statesman and theoretician of our movement, decided to enter the conversation.

"We Shi'a," he said, "see ourselves as history's victims. Victimhood defined who we are. We have adapted over the centuries to venting our bitterness at this condition on those around us. Sometimes we convince ourselves of what we in effect imagine, and almost need to be true. It has been so since the death of the Imam, whom we pledged our allegiance to and then abandoned. Since that time we Shi'a have perfected the art of feeling guilty, and directing it outward, away from ourselves."

"Are you saying that to be a Shi'a is to be by nature discontented?" I said loudly, feeling under attack.

"Discontent arises from feeling yourself a victim combined with guilt at the conditions that made you one. That is what our learned comrade Abu Ammar is trying to tell you," Uncle replied firmly, displeased at my tone of voice. "Hear him out."

"You were right, young man," Abu Ammar went on to say, "to surmise that we Shi'a have been shaped by our minority status among Muslims worldwide. It has made us prickly and defensive, constantly trying to prove ourselves to other Muslims, to prove that we are good Muslims who only wanted authority to reside in the House of the Prophet. Combine those feelings with the many waves of persecution to which Caliphs have subjected adherents of our faith in times past, and you have all the ingredients for understanding that which shapes our worldview to this day."

I turned toward Abu Ammar during this speech with a newfound respect. He looked back at me earnestly. With his folded hands resting on his crossed knees, he continued:

"We entered the world both as victims and as betrayers of the Imam, God's Blessings Be Upon Him. Both are constitutive of who we are, and, perhaps, we were obliged to turn both into means of survival as a community. Do we not annually reenact our victimhood and his betrayal as a pageantry of mourning and theater in every city in which we have a presence? Guilt tortures a man, makes him unhappy, and breeds discontent in his heart. What is true of one man is true of all men. Ideas of rebellion, expectations of Absolute Justice, and exaltation of our victimhood come easily to us. It follows that we Shi'a will tend to hold those who govern us responsible for our woes, irrespective of whether it is true or not."

Concluding his lecture, Abu Ammar said: "I think what your

uncle is trying to tell you is that to govern well requires an entirely different set of gifts from the ones we have inherited in our culture and our faith; it requires not the gift of great feeling, but the gift of flexibility and clear-headed reason. We have an ingenuity for feeling, but not the wisdom or flexibility that comes from experience of the world; it is why we Shi'a turn out great artists and poets, but never great leaders or statesmen."

The whole gathering was silent, held spellbound by Abu Ammar. I was unsure if that meant they agreed with him or not. The spell was broken when Uncle's trusty old servant entered the room, bent over Uncle, and whispered into his ear.

"It seems our messenger boy has arrived. I will leave him to your good offices," Uncle said to his colleagues. "My presence will only give him ideas above his station . . . Thank you, Abu Ammar. You have given us a lot to think about. What say you, my son?" he said, now looking at me.

"Hassan, make sure you tell the toad we want two hundred of those shaped charges at least, and don't agree to pay anything for them, not now or anytime in the future. We will not be beholden to the Iranians. Make sure he understands that we are doing them a favor, not the other way around."

Love of Self

U ncle turned to me after we were left alone in the room; he could see how upset I was. Abu Ammar's erudition made me feel like a fool in front of Uncle and his friends.

"Son, don't take any of this to heart . . . it is just words and talk."

"All these complex forces of the past and assumptions of current duplicity confuse me," I blurted out. "I don't know what to think anymore."

"When that happens, just turn things around in your head and look at them from a different angle. Go back to where we started from: Iraq; it is the prize everyone seeks. Can we Shi'a rule this land alone or do we need the support of our Sunni Arab brothers? What say you?"

"It goes without saying we need to rule together."

"Then it also stands to reason that we should keep our Sunni brothers close to our chests, not push them into the arms of their worst fears. They have fears at the moment, justifiably so. The Tyrant was one of theirs. Everyone is blaming them for his excesses. Should we fan the flames of their fears, as does the Cabal of Thirteen, or should we dampen them?"

"Dampen them, of course! We are all Muslims. Why, we even descend from the same Arab tribes and intermarry all the time."

"True. And in that truth good governance lies. But suppose we are not capable of it—and that remains to be seen. Then there are only two courses of action left for us Shi'a now that the Tyrant has fallen: either desist from government altogether, as we have done for centuries, but go on to flourish in our neighborhoods, cities, seminaries, in culture, trade, and the free professions . . . flourish like we never flourished before. Or, be prepared to wage all-out war in the name of our sole right to rule, accepting that we will be hated for all time even if we win."

I stared at him in astonishment, trying to imagine that stark choice.

"I take it you think the House of the Shi'a—"

"The Cabal of Thirteen . . . yes, they have already made the latter choice," he said, completing my sentence for me, "which is bad for Iraq."

"How about the Kurds? They caucus separately. Why is that all right, but when we do it you say we are being vindictive? Are the Kurds being vindictive too?"

"They are a minority and think like one, never seeking power over the whole of Iraq, only autonomy in a small corner of it. And they are pure victims."

"Pure victims? What is that?"

"The kind of victimhood that is untainted by the blood and tears it took to make this country, to hold it together. Even when we used them as soldiers, they were sacrificial lambs, necessary casualties, not collaborators in the project of building this Arab Iraq of ours. We Shi'a, on the other hand, are an integral part of the whole bloody enterprise, implicated in its every twist and turn. Men like your father fought Iran to a standstill in the 1980s; they were on the front lines, not the Tyrant. The blood spilled willingly in defense of Iraq was theirs. We took pride in their sacrifice. The Tyrant gave your father a medal, you know, for courage and gallantry."

"I didn't know . . . I still don't understand . . ."

.   .   .

We remained in Uncle's office, lying back on the cushions he had strewn all around. His trusty retainer returned with a fresh pot of tea and replenished our glasses. Uncle seemed lost in thought. Having apparently reached some kind of decision, he rose from the cushioned floor and took to pacing up and down on his soft carpets in his socks, his chin lowered, almost touching his chest. He stopped and squatted to lift the corners of one of his Persian carpets, reminding himself of the colors and design of the one below. "Once a month I move the carpets around. Some on the bottom rise to the top; others stay where they are, or change location in the room. The sunlight then hits them from a different angle and they wear down evenly. Every time I do this my guests remark on how new and fresh everything looks. The cloth merchant down the street makes a point of visiting me just to see the new arrangement." And then he dropped the carpet and returned to pacing.

"It is with carpets as it is in life. We need to change perspective to be fully alive.

"Consider love of self," he suddenly said after a pause. "It is a perfectly natural impulse, wouldn't you say?"

"That is quite a change of perspective, Uncle," I said, smiling a little. "Where would merchants be if they did not look out for their interests?"

"Or love of God; it too is an extension of our desire to be in His good graces on the Day of Judgment, to enter Paradise and shun Hell. All God's creatures start loving and looking out for themselves; it is normal and good."

"I suppose so."

"By extension, love of self is love of the family and local community into which one is born."

"Of course," I said, puzzled.

He was starting to talk to himself rather than to me; it was as though I was not in the room.

"But that love has to be extended further; it has to reach out to others, in order to become true virtue. I mean, by itself there is nothing virtuous in loving oneself; it is just God's way. How much further do you think it should reach out, son? What do you say?"

"Uhh . . . I don't really know, Uncle. I never looked at things that way before."

"It must embrace our neighborhoods, our cities, and our whole Shi'a community. That goes without saying. But is that enough? We live in a world of nations and states. These are as necessary to our public lives as breathing is to our personal lives. Are we Shi'a a nation? I don't think so. Should self-love be extended as far as the whole country? The Prophet, Peace Be Upon Him, said, 'Love of the homeland is of faith.' It follows that love of self should be extended to the boundaries of one's country and that this love is a virtue esteemed by faith. All men should aspire to this virtue. But can one extend self-love too far? The great danger is that it becomes unreal and unrealizable. The Tyrant did that in his early years, when he forced us to love all Arab countries, treating them as if they were our own, belittling our own smaller Iraq for the sake of a pipe dream he called the Arab nation."

Uncle stopped now, and looked strangely at me as though unsure of himself.

"Worse than the Tyrant, however, son—and please hear me out before you react—worse than him is the case of someone like your father: his communist beliefs entailed extending self-love to embrace all countries and cultures of the world, to embrace foreigners spread across all four corners of the earth; to all of them he wanted to extend love . . . love of the world, he called it . . . the whole world, a kind of universal love that included other nations and cultures and all living creatures in God's creation . . . a far bigger fantasy than the Tyrant's pan-Arab nation."

"Father believed that?" I asked, astonished.

"Indeed he did. He subordinated love of self to love of the world, and that God never asked us to do; it is abnormal. But I could not convince him of it. We used to argue about these things; those stormy discussions remain some of the most memorable moments of my life . . . By God how he could talk, your father! . . . He lit up the room; everyone turned to listen. He had a way about him . . ."

Were those tears welling up in Uncle's eyes? He turned his face away from me before I could be sure. It had come so suddenly. I stood as still as a stone, not a flicker of movement apart from my eyes, which were following his lips opening and shutting like a fish out of water. I looked into the dark space between his lips, lost in the immensity of his and Father's past opening and closing before me.

"Understand, son! I loved him dearly; we all did. Your grandfather doted on him; everyone loves a dreamer . . . He was my little brother . . . ," he said, almost choking on these last words. "Perhaps his ideas and way with words made him a beautiful person, something I never claimed to be. But it also made him a poor judge of human nature."

He collected himself and turned to look at me; it was as though a veil had slipped from his face, opening up to my gaze a man who normally did everything in secret.

"The smart thing to do," Uncle said, "is to couple love of one's nation to hatred of the foreigner, something your father also did not know how to do . . . I mean, how can you hate if you love everything equally . . . but it is what our leader, the Sayyid, is doing . . . and what his father, Sayyid Sadiq, did before him."

"Is that what you did, Uncle? Is that why you became an Islamist?"

"I sought to belong to those I was born among. That impulse burned in me like a red-hot coal when I was young. All those people who walk the streets of your neighborhood, and go to the same mosques and teahouses that you frequent, live by the same ideas of right and wrong that we call Islam. When I walked among them, in the souk or in the Great Shrine, I sucked in the smell of their sweat and the smoke of their cheap cigarettes, and I fell in love with them; their tears were my tears. How you cried on that march to Karbala! Remember? Like you on that day, I yearned to be at one with them, to feel their pain even when I had not fully experienced it. I learned from them, not from books or clever men like Abu Ammar, that when they hurt, they find a language to express their pain. These languages may be wanting in precision, because they take the form of stories. Our rituals and stories of heroism and self-sacrifice, our tears and lamentations, these are my people's language; it is the only one they have with which to ward off the evil there is in the world.

"I wanted a politics in which we Muslims could see ourselves without outsider help in the shape of intellectuals and their foreign ideas. Only then would I find my roots and become at one with their hopes and desires. These feelings drew me to Sayyid Sadiq, our Sayyid's father. He was a cleric of the common man; he hated the ivory tower cleric. In his teachings I found a home such as my father, your grandfather, was never able to give me, a sense of belonging to a thing bigger than myself, but not one that was so big you got lost in it, like my brother did, God rest his soul."

"So you are a Believer?"

"I don't practice as much as I like to, I admit . . . that is not for talking about in front of others! However, I gladly do what is expected of me, like pray in public. Praying in private feels too much like hypocrisy. I am not personally committed to ritual. But you cannot get total immersion in a people whose politics is so sensual without conforming to what they cherish. When I follow the crowd in prayer, I take pleasure in being at one with them. Islam gives us that breathing space; it does not make excessive demands on a man's soul; it simply asks him to conform. And so, yes, I am a Believer."

"If Islam comes first, and derives from love of self, what follows?"

"Hatred of the one who is not you, the infidel or the foreigner who wishes to occupy or steal from you. Think of the Occupier in our land today as that distant foreigner, toward whose culture and values our self-love cannot be extended, as your father would have us do. We should not even try."

"But hate is such a vile thing, Uncle! . . . Mother would never have approved." And then I remembered what my father wrote to Mother in his letter: "Teach him never to act out of hate." But I didn't say anything. Uncle was replying.

"Look at the skin on your hands, son; it is turning brown and dark from all that training in the desert sun. I see a new leanness and hardness in you. You are no longer a boy ... That is a good thing! It is the man you are becoming who must learn to hate, not the boy your mother kept hidden from the world. Without skin like that you will never be able to fight the foreigner, whether he comes from America or from Iran. The members of the Cabal of Thirteen are incapable of hating, much less fighting, the foreigner to whom they owe everything. They turn hate inward, onto their own, but in the name of their own. They occupy the space of that contradiction. Couple these two things together, hatred of the foreigner with love of self extended to your community and your state, and you have the foundation of a well-ordered and virtuous society."

"You can count on me, Uncle. You know that. Always." And then, I don't know why, I added: "You are the father I never had. Know that I am with you until the end."

I felt myself coming alive as I said those words; I felt the doubts that had beset me following the death of Muntassir lifting, filling me with a new sense of discovery and purpose. The words touched him; I read it in his face, but he made no acknowledgment.

Three Houses

In a sermon, our Sayyid had described the September 11 attacks as "a miracle and a blessing from God," words that infuriated the Occupier. Our papers and publications were closed down. Uncle went into hiding, moving to a well-guarded secret basement in Najaf. Then he called for me. I was not told where he was, but taken to him.

Armed men were hanging about, doing nothing for the most part, but tension and anxiety lined their faces. I was ushered in to see him. He ordered the door closed and, after a few pleasantries, seated me across from his desk.

There was tea on a kettle by his side. After pouring me a glass, he leaned forward, his elbows on the table, his heavy jowls resting on the interlaced fingers of his big hands, his eyes boring into mine like daggers. The expression on his round face was gentle, yet I felt uncomfortable and did not know which way to direct my gaze.

"Look at me, son," he said quietly, settling the question.

"We are now at war with the Occupier. You will be stationed in Najaf, with Haider and your unit. Our forces will shortly be reinforced from other parts of the country. Understood?"

"Yes, Uncle."

"I have information that an arrest warrant is about to be issued for the Sayyid. You must move carefully, even inside Najaf."

"Arrest warrant!" I said, shocked. "How dare they? On what charges?"

"Do you remember that corpse of an American agent that you saw on April tenth of last year, the day after the regime fell?"

"Yes, of course. How could I forget?"

"The Occupier is trying to pin his death on the Sayyid."

"Who was he?"

"I told you, he was an American agent."

"What was his name?"

"Khoei."

"The same as the Ayatollah who died in 1992?"

"His son, Majid."

"And did the Sayyid have anything to do with his death?"

"Of course not!" he said, his face turning grim. "The man was seen by worshippers in the Shrine of the Imam in the company of the Kelidar, the most hated man in the city, the Custodian of the Shrine and holder of its keys, a well-known Ba'thi who boasted photographs with the Tyrant in his office in the Shrine. The two were seen entering the office. Worshippers gathered outside, demanding that this much-hated man, the Custodian, be handed over to them. Shots were fired from inside, killing a man in the crowd. When people saw this, they rushed the office, and in the altercation that followed both men were knifed to death. The Sayyid had nothing to do with it. Some of his followers tried to protect Majid, but failed to get to him in time."

Images of that first corpse in the alley near our house in Mishraq, of the stab wounds and the dried blood and the shredded clothes, had been fading, smothered by the daily assault of thousands of similarly terrible images—until Uncle's words, like a bolt of lightning, brought them back into focus.

I had been living in the eye of the storm for twelve months, but now I was yanked back to the beginning, to the day of the fall of the Tyrant, April 10, 2003. Uncle did this by simply dropping a name. I had cajoled him into it, to be sure, and succeeded where I had not succeeded twelve months earlier with Mother, but still I had succeeded; he had spoken the name Mother had not wanted me to hear, the name no one would utter in public although everyone knew it was out there: Sayyid Majid, scion of Ayatollah Khoei, Shi'ism's Supreme Source of Emulation and most senior religious authority until his death in 1992.

I thought Muntassir had fallen victim to a great feud between the Houses of Hakim and Sadr, but a third great clerical House was in the mix, the House of Khoei, about which I knew little. Could Majid's death be about clerics who had collaborated with Saddam and others who hadn't? The father of our Sayyid, Sayyid Sadiq, had made that accusation, saying that Ayatollah Khoei collaborated with the regime in the 1980s to marginalize him, Sayyid Sadiq, in the clerical establishment of the Holy City. The same accusation was leveled at Sayyid Sadiq after 1992, because whisperings from both the House of Hakim and the House of Khoei said he owed his elevated position after the death of Ayatollah Khoei to the Tyrant, who entrusted the rebuilding of the destroyed city of Najaf to him, providing him with funds. Was that true? Were both allegations true?

Perhaps the feuding was not about collaboration with the regime at all, but collaboration with the Americans, which made sense, as Uncle said the murdered Majid was an American spy. But it couldn't have been about his collaboration after the fall of the regime, because our Imams in their sermons after the Tyrant's fall were blasting moderate clerics for this every Friday and they never mentioned Sayyid Majid's name. What held them back? The Occupier was not in Najaf during April 2003, and the Occupation had not even begun when Majid arrived nearly two weeks before the fall of Baghdad. Therefore the collaboration, if true, had to have been with the Occupier before the Occupation, at a time of sanctions and great hardship for the people, when the Occupier was still only a would-be invader. If that were true, the charge of collaboration would apply to the whole Governing Council and countless others.

The three great clerical houses were always in competition over money, large sums from the contributions of pilgrims and wealthy donors. The House of Khoei had controlled the disbursement of the lion's share of contributions. The House of Sadr, beginning with Sayyid Sadiq, our Sayyid's father, wanted a larger share, particularly in view of their growing popularity during the late 1990s. When our Army of the Awaited One took on the House of Hakim in Karbala, in the battle that killed poor Muntassir, the rumor spread that it was all about money from the Shrine of our martyred Imam Husain.

But money was a poor explanation for the murder of Sayyid Majid, seeing as how the House of Khoei had lost its control of revenues arising from the Shrines in Najaf and Karbala after the death of the Ayatollah in 1992. The House of Khoei was not in need of more money, being far better funded from the large Shi'a communities worldwide, especially in India, Africa, and the Far East.

What if the struggle were not about finances or collaboration, but a clash of ideas concerning the role of the clergy, ranging from the activism of the House of Sadr to the passivity and quietism for which the House of Khoei was famous?

Our Sayyid, following in the footsteps of his father, took to heart words attributed to the first Imam, the incomparable 'Ali ibn Abi Talib, who said that in each historical period there were two Imams: one silent and passive, the other vocal and active. The Imam, may God's blessings shower upon him, warned that such a state of affairs could lead to strife in the community. On this basis our Sayyid distinguished between vocal clerics, like himself, and silent ones, like Khoei, whom he despised, as his father had done before him.

The vocal clerics seek an active political role, and openly advocate an Islamic state, while the silent ones reject political involvement by the clerics on the grounds that the realm of politics is bound at all times to corrupt true religious belief, at least until the Infallible Imam, the only true successor to the first Imam, returns. They prefer to talk among themselves in the meantime, one authority to the other, and have disdain for speaking to the masses on all-important matters of governance. Thus was the tumult of war and politics around the fall of the Tyrant matched by a war of ideas both within and among the three great Houses of Shi'ism in Najaf.

The quietists had a very poor view of our movement, considering us vulgar troublemakers, especially after some young men calling themselves followers of the Sayyid—some of whom may have been in the Great Courtyard of the Shrine of the Imam on the day of the murder of Sayyid Majid—surrounded the house of Khoei's successor, Najaf's Grand Ayatollah, demanding he go back to Iran, from whence he had come. The siege was on April 10, 2003, the day of the murder, and was only lifted days later after the Ayatollah called in two thousand Arab tribesmen from the outlying villages to disperse the mob. We Sadrists consider the traditionalists opportunistic collaborators, and said as much every Friday from the pulpits of our mosques. Some of our wilder members even tore down pictures of the Ayatollah on the streets of Najaf, until our leaders put a stop to it.

Poor Haider got sucked into the vortex of this war. I will never forget the day he came to me, visibly upset, and asked me to go with him to the courtyard of the Shrine to talk over something that was troubling him. He is good at feeling the pulse of a situation—a mood on the street or forebodings in the country; then he will perhaps jump unwisely into it, without thinking twice. I am by contrast the kind of a person who looks backward over his shoulder, neither perceiving nor feeling enough before he rationalizes. Haider was my weather vane for the mood of the city, and I assumed that was what was troubling him. I bought a pomegranate to share while we talked, cracked it open, and handed him the biggest seed-laden segment.

"I met this preacher in a small village," he said, "just a few kilometers northeast of Najaf, an extraordinary man, mesmerizing to listen to; he calls himself the Judge of Heaven."

"What?" I said in amazement. "That is not a name!"

"No. It is who he says he is. He was a student and ardent follower of our Sayyid's father, Sayyid Sadiq, and has extended his mentor's ideas concerning the signs that will precede the coming of the Awaited One, and the evidence suggesting his arrival is imminent. Sayyid Sadiq, as you know, is the only clerical authority in Najaf to ground his view of Islamic government on its proper theological foundations, namely the rule of the Rightly Guided One, who he says will return very soon. The preacher I met claims the Messiah is coming even sooner than Sayyid Sadiq thought; moreover, the Messiah actually speaks to him in premonitions and dreams."

"So is he crazy . . ."

"I did not find him crazy at all! Quite the contrary: he speaks softly, is articulate and persuasive, giving reasons and proofs for everything, and he lives more frugally and simply than his followers! There is nothing crazy about him, unless you call the fervor and intensity of his beliefs signs of a deranged mind. I spent two days in a camp with hundreds of his followers, whom he calls Soldiers of Heaven. They are there with their wives and children."

"You are convinced, then, that this preacher is actually the Awaited One, the Rightly Guided Imam after whom our army is named, come to bring Justice and usher in the end of the world?"

"I did not say that; I am confused. The preacher is, after all, one of us."

"No, he is not!" I said, horrified. "I would be careful, my dear Haider, about saying such things in public."

I did not expect Haider to take such nonsense seriously. But he said something that stuck in my mind about Sayyid Sadiq's teachings, something I had not encountered before. A growing number of self-proclaimed Messiahs had been operating out of Najaf in recent years. Haider's experience with that crazy preacher had planted a crucial clue: I should be looking into how the various doctrines dealt with the all-important issue of the Absent Imam, the Awaited One, with whom our Sayyid was so enamored.

The most fundamental theological difference among the three

great clerical Houses of Shi'ism—Khoei, Hakim, and Sadr—differences that men have killed for in the past, all boiled down to one's interpretation of the meaning of the Absent Imam, the Rightly Guided One, whose appearance would restore Justice and usher in the end of the world.

The more remote in time one interprets the advent of the Imam to be, or the more one sees His Coming as having purely symbolic meaning rather than as a physical, literal Coming, the more separate are going to be the religious and political realms of authority, and the more qualified, mediated, and limited the role of religious authority in the present. This is the quietist extreme.

On the other hand, if the Coming of the Imam is imminent, then, depending on the degree of its imminence, the religious and political realms collapse into one another, entailing the absolute authority of the jurist in all matters personal and political. This is the activist extreme.

The House of Khoei, represented by its youngest scion, Sayyid Majid, lay at the quietest extreme of the spectrum, while the House of Sadr, as represented by its youngest scion, our Sayyid, was at the activist extreme. As for the House of Hakim, they were somewhere in the middle, seeing as how while in theory they advocated an Islamic state like ourselves, in practice they were colluding with the Occupier and did not have the religious authority to establish it. Haider's rogue preacher, by defining himself as the Awaited One, was not even on the scale.

Could such doctrinal differences spill over to bring about the death of Sayyid Majid? Men kill over True Belief; it is in the history of all religions. But I had now gone behind the facade of ideas to the deepest doctrinal differences, the very essences of faith undergirding these ideas—the doctrine of the Hidden Imam. Was that too abstract and unsatisfying as an explanation for murder? The thought of it alone was too terrifying to contemplate. The Shi'a of Iraq had never faced such a conundrum before. But could I rule it out completely as an explanation for what happened in the courtyard of the Imam's Shrine on April 10, 2003? I did not know what to think.

.   .   .

I did not stop feeling uneasy about the murder, perhaps because I could still see my mother's face when I returned from the scene that fine spring day in April. Could the scion of such a great House as the House of Khoei, I kept on asking myself, or of any of the great Houses of Shi'ism, a man only a few years older than our Sayyid, and therefore a man of his own generation—why, they grew up as boys just a few streets from each other; perhaps they even played together in the street—could such a man be an agent of the Central Intelligence Agency?

Uncle claimed Sayyid Majid and about twenty of his friends were transported by plane from London to a spot in the desert a few kilometers from Najaf, landing ten days or so before he was killed. In the desert, they split up, and Sayyid Majid with his closest aides made their way into Najaf, where they started meeting with fellow conspirators. Was that credible? I had heard another story that he had been heading to the house of Najaf's most senior Ayatollah, the Supreme Source of Emulation in the Shi'a world and Ayatollah Khoei's successor, until blocked by a cordon of our men. The Grand Ayatollah, in other words, was unable to leave his house on the day of the murder. The regime's agents were still in control of the city at that time. Was it credible that the son of such an important Ayatollah would allow himself the indignity of having hundreds of thousands of U.S. dollars strapped around his chest under his black clerical robe, as Uncle insisted he had done? Why was he in the Shrine of the Imam in the first place? Why, after all these years, was he in the holiest spot of the holiest city of Shi'a Islam on the first day of the Occupation? What was he doing there?

If it were even remotely possible that our Sayyid had ordered the murder, why would the Occupier choose this moment in time, so long after the fact, to charge him with the offense? It didn't smell right; our relations are at an all-time low with the Occupation, skirmishes between us are breaking out all over southern Iraq, and now they decide they are going to arrest our Sayyid!

The Sayyid

"The Sayyid can never be mistaken," Uncle had said to me on our way to my long-awaited meeting with the Sayyid, a meeting Uncle had organized. "If he is, it is not your place to say so. Are we understood?" Then he told me a story about the Sayyid's father, Sayyid Sadiq, whom Uncle clearly admired.

Uncle and Sayyid Sadiq were seated in the Sayyid's formal quarters, where he received guests, when a man came in to ask the price of tomatoes.

"The question infuriated me," Uncle said. "I rose from my seat with the intention of forcibly ejecting him from the room, and scolding him for his insolence. But the Sayyid grabbed me by the arm and pushed me down next to him on the carpet. Then he astounded everyone by giving the man a detailed answer, going into the price of different kinds of tomatoes, comparing them with their prices last week, and with other vegetables. He seemed to know everything there was to know about the price of tomatoes! I caught up with the man outside as he was leaving and asked him why he had asked that particular question. 'In selecting a Source of Emulation,' he replied, 'I choose the one who knows my problems.' I thanked him and left feeling ashamed of myself."

"That is a nice story," I said.

"Sayyid Sadiq was not one for burying himself under a mountain of books, as other senior clerics do," he said, a barb clearly directed at the House of Khoei, and Khoei's chosen successor, the Grand Ayatollah of Najaf.

I asked Uncle if our Sayyid was as wise as his father had been.

"He is the youngest son of his father, Sayyid Sadiq," he replied, "who originally owed his position to a cousin, the first martyr and founding thinker of our movement, Sayyid Baqir of the House of Sadr. Sayyid Baqir differed from other clerics in that he did not issue rulings on trivia, such as how women must clean themselves and pray after their period or upon giving birth. He chose to think bold new thoughts, for which he died a martyr at the hands of the Tyrant in 1980. All the ideas of our movement go back to him. Sayyid Sadiq carried on the first martyr's legacy. It was he who first returned to the doctrine of the Hidden Imam, whose return would bring Eternal Justice to the world. He wrote prodigiously on the subject and was murdered by the Tyrant in 1999 for doing so, along with his two eldest sons. That left only our Sayyid, the youngest and the last link in the chain of this great activist tradition. Our Army of the Awaited One is named in honor of Sayyid Sadiq's great insights and his revival of the traditions of the Hidden Imam. Remember, also, that our Sayyid is an Arab, unlike the traditionalists, who are Iranians. This is most important. And his focus is the evil of foreign Occupation, which also distinguishes him from the other Houses."

I could not help but notice how circumspect Uncle had been; there was no mention of the Sayyid's personal attributes. Meanwhile, we had arrived at the Sayyid's house, near the Holy Shrine, an alley away from where I had stumbled upon the corpse of Sayyid Majid.

Our Sayyid was a short, plump man in his twenties, with a dark complexion and a dour, round face; he never smiled, unlike his father, who liked a good joke. He looked grim when we were first ushered in, because, I am told, he sees in this facial expression great virtue. He was seated cross-legged on the heavily carpeted floor of a room much like Uncle's office, only smaller. Cushions were spread along the four walls of the room, but he was not using any, hunched forward as he was, playing with his worry beads when Uncle and I entered. He rose in a single motion to greet Uncle, and then proffered his hand to me, which I bent down and kissed, the large turquoise and silver signet ring feeling cold against my cheek. After exchanging pleasantries with Uncle, who was exceedingly casual with him, he seated himself and turned to look at me.

"So this is the young man you have been telling me about! I hear you are doing important work for us and are highly educated. Well done, son."

I blushed at that and lowered my eyes out of respect.

"Do you have any hobbies, my son?"

"Football."

"Hmm . . . The law generally forbids this kind of activity, which distracts people from their duties to God."

"I did not know, Your Eminence."

"The West, you see, created in us certain needs that cut short our completeness as good Muslims. Football is a case in point. What is the meaning of a big strong man running after a ball? What happens, I ask you, to his manliness? Instead of shooting a ball into a silly net, he might as well aspire to a goal that is noble and devout, one that facilitates a man's arrival at God's feet. I ask you, do the Jews waste their time playing such silly games? No, of course they don't. They leave such distractions to us. Did America or Israel ever win a World Cup? They spend their time on science and bettering their lives by inventing things like satellite television, leaving the silly games for us to get worked up about."

"Are there games beloved by religion, my Sayyid?"

"Of course there are! Sword fighting, for instance . . . good horsemanship . . . Do you ride a horse?"

"No, my Sayyid."

"Well, you should. If you need to learn dexterity or strengthen yourself, do so in a morally uplifting manner. You can exercise your muscles at the same time. Running is good, and comes in handy. Swimming is okay. Do you swim?"

"No, my Sayyid."

"Why not?"

"Mother discouraged it; she said the Euphrates, which is nearby, had been polluted by Saddam."

"Hmm . . . Right she is, right she is . . . God puts obstacles to test our faith . . . I must go and pray now . . . Obey your uncle in all things. He has spoken of your mission?"

"He has, my Sayyid."

"Go with God's blessings, my son."

The Arrest Warrant

The events following my meeting with the Sayyid proved Uncle right and exposed the perfidy of the Occupier: our newspapers were closed and high-ranking leaders of our movement arrested, including a dear friend of Uncle's. An American helicopter tore off an Islamic flag from a pylon, triggering fury among the people. But above all the arrest warrant issued for the Sayyid, which Uncle had predicted was on the way, signaled we were at war with the Occupier.

In the summer of 2004, Haider and I were in awe of the Sayyid, holding him to be the embodiment of the religious idea on earth, a man blessed with a special relationship to God, one that devotees like Haider and myself could not hope to fathom. However, I never went as far as some of my more featherbrained comrades in the Army of the Awaited One, who said of our Sayyid that he was the true Redeemer, the long-awaited Rightly Guided One for whose return we Shi'a prayed.

I believed our Sayyid, scion of a great line of martyrs of the House of Sadr, was being set up by the Occupation authority, accused of being the prime instigator of the mob attack on his archrival, the collaborator Sayyid Majid. To pin the murder on him was the Occupier's way of weakening his standing among the Shi'a, and avenging the murder of their friend Sayyid Majid.

The Sayyid took to dressing in a white burial shroud instead of the dark robes he was accustomed to wearing, a sign that he was embracing his martyrdom, just as his father had done in 1999. "Continue the resistance," he said to his supporters in a sermon. "Do not use my death or arrest as an excuse not to finish what you have started." Having launched the war, he went into hiding.

A flurry of meetings began with the government to negotiate the rescinding of the arrest warrant and arrange a cease-fire. The national security advisor, a former supporter of our House who had returned from a quarter century in exile, represented the government. But he was as mistrusted by the government he represented as he was by us. He was also a member of the Cabal of Thirteen, which was the intermediary in the negotiations even though its interests were not those of the government, which it tried to undermine at every opportunity. The House of the Shi'a pressed hardest for a cease-fire, and was represented by its architect, the president of the Governing Council, a long-standing and formidable foe of Saddam Hussein, who had done more perhaps than all the Foreigner Iraqis put together to bring about the downfall of the Tyrant. Uncle led our delegation and brought me along as an aide.

The national security advisor and the Cabal of Thirteen had the same overriding goal: to get the Occupier's arrest warrant rescinded, a precondition of ending the war. One might have thought that, being appointees of the Occupier, and friends of Sayyid Majid from their days in exile, they would believe there was merit to the case against our Sayyid. But it was not so. Uncle was surprised to discover that the members of the Cabal of Thirteen were drooling at the prospect of being able to do our Sayyid a favor. They would, Uncle said, have kissed the Sayyid's shoes to be granted the kind of audience I had with him the previous month.

We met at the president's home, away from the prying eyes of Occupier and government officials. Chairs and softly cushioned sofas lined all the walls; in the middle was a large, formless expanse of marble tiles, with a few Persian carpets scattered about like lost souls. It was not a room to be enjoyed, but to leave an impression.

Upon our arrival, the president sprang up from his seat in the center of the wall farthest from the doorway, where the chairs were higher, fuller, and more spacious. "You are doing God's work" was the first thing our host said to Uncle as he shook his hand. "The Sayyid is leading a genuine Uprising against the American Occupier, one as important to the Shi'a of Iraq as that led by his great-grandfather against the British Occupier. It is God's work, God's work. Welcome to my house!

"Did you know," he went on, still standing, "there were eleven thousand of the brave men of Najaf, a number twice that of the Ottoman army, fighting a well-armed British force many times their number in April 1915? Did you know that? They were led by the brave scholar Muhammad al-Haboobi of Najaf, whose family was a great friend of ours. Haboobi fought like a lion for three days, repeatedly repelling the much larger and more well-equipped forces of the British Empire, before falling in battle on the banks of the Euphrates. The Ottoman commander committed suicide out of shame at his soldiers' performance. But there was only glory in the fighting spirit of our men of Najaf—a spirit we see once again bright and alive in the shape of our Sayyid from the noble and illustrious House of Sadr . . ." And then suddenly in an aside, he said, "The Holy Shrine in Najaf has just fallen to your forces, has it not?"

The president was in the habit of displaying his knowledge, down to the details of who said what and when, and then shifting gears to pry out an apparently innocuous piece of information. Uncle knew he was dealing "with a fox," as he later put it, prone to spellbinding digressions designed to elicit information; he knew he had to be mindful to steer the conversation back to the repeal of the arrest warrant, the subject that was uppermost in his mind.

"The Shrine and the city have both fallen, with barely a shot," Uncle replied, his bearing and tone of voice displaying more than a hint of pride in this achievement. "Your police and soldiers just dropped their guns, shed their uniforms, and fled. We are now in total control of the city."

"They are not my police and soldiers," the president replied with a show of disdain. "Don't confuse me with this caricature of a government headed, incidentally, by a former Ba'thi."

Thus did these Foreigner Iraqis talk about each other.

There was no mention of the arrest warrant the entire evening, until, in a whispered aside, the president let drop an assurance that the Sayyid would get everything he wanted. All members of the Cabal of Thirteen, it turned out, had put their names to a letter, demanding from the Occupier a "suspension" of the arrest warrant, followed by a cease-fire. They even demanded that the Occupier integrate our Army of the Awaited One into the political process unfolding in Baghdad. All our army had to do was withdraw from the Holy City, ending its occupation of the Holy Shrine in Najaf. The letter, a copy of which was given to Uncle for the Sayyid's approval, was later read out to the Occupier in a secret meeting presenting the "demands" of the Cabal of Thirteen upon the Occupier!

The Occupier's army did not trust our Sayyid and his army; neither trusted what was left of the Governing Council, which in turn was so divided upon itself it could not agree on anything. The Occupier-appointed Iraqi government did not trust its own national security advisor, because he was a member of the Cabal of Thirteen, which in turn was the least trustworthy of the lot because it was permanently on the verge of breakdown through backstabbing and rumormongering.

The most interesting word in the letter—which the Occupier read but was refused a copy of—was "suspension." This was a sop to the Occupier, demanded by its legal advisors, who objected that since the Sayyid was charged with a crime, a crime based upon an elaborate investigation by an Iraqi judge, the Occupier could not be seen to be dealing with him, or put him on the Governing Council, or integrate his army into the New Army of the government. "Suspending" the arrest warrant meant putting aside the file the judge had opened, not closing it forever, a compromise a member of the Cabal had conjured up to resolve the impasse. In practice it meant that the Occupation Authority would toss the crown of thorns of the arrest warrant into the hands of a duly elected future Shi'a-dominated government, which, Uncle was privately assured, would immediately rescind that which they were now merely pretending to "suspend." On the basis of these reassurances, Uncle agreed to the word "suspension." That is the only concession he made in this affair.

War in Najaf

The following week in August 2004, the Iraqi government, disregarding the recommendations of its national security advisor and the Cabal of Thirteen, sent its American-trained, Iraqi-officered New Army into the Holy City. This would be their first major engagement. The troops began by opening fire on a demonstration of unarmed pilgrims marching peacefully in support of our Sayyid. Eighteen people were killed, our men were incensed, and the fighting intensified. Overnight Najaf turned into a city of ghosts.

American tanks, planes, and Apache helicopter gunships bombarded our positions around the Shrine. Marines attacked a building in the inner ring of the Old City, reaching a few meters from the Shrine. Only this time they dug in and held their ground, not just attacking and leaving as they had done before. Our commanders ordered us to fall back into the Holy Shrine, which Americans would not fire upon. Several thousand of us poured in, turning the Shrine and its Great Courtyard from a sanctuary and place of worship into a city, with hospitals, canteens, and stacks of coffins for our dead and dying.

Meanwhile, units of the new Iraqi government's army continued parading about in the areas captured by the American marines. We were safe inside the Holy Shrine, but the city had been reduced to crumbling buildings, blackened storefronts, cars crumpled like tin cans, and dead goats and dogs littering the sidewalks. Najaf looked like its sister city, the Sunni stronghold of Fallujah, after the Occupier had pounded it into submission back in April.

Our army, which had started out five thousand strong, had by the summer's end reached twenty thousand fighters.

We began coordinating with Sunni jihadi insurgents from Fallujah and Ramadi, forcing the Occupier to fight on two fronts at once. Uncle's continuing relations with the Islamic Scholars Association that had taken over the Mother of All Battles Mosque, which I visited with him back in 2003, were paying off. Fighters from the Sunni triangle were being bussed in to augment our forces. Even the Muslim Brotherhood, the wellspring of all militant Sunni organizations, was issuing statements in support of our Sayyid.

Haider and I had been moved into the Shrine and paired up as a sniper unit. He was the shooter and I the spotter in charge of communications with base via a prized satellite phone, of which our several thousand fighters in the Shrine had fewer than a dozen. Our training took place on the first three dusk-to-dawn missions into the Old City, when we were accompanied by a professional sniper from Fallujah, an older man of great renown as a shooter who had trained under the Tyrant but who could still scramble up rubble and falling walls like a goat, and who handled his rifle as though it were his third arm. I saw him splatter the brains of a soldier on the run at three hundred meters. The art, he taught Haider, was one of patience and concealment. We learned from him the value of spending hours choosing a location, and setting up meticulously until both the weapon and its handlers were perfectly concealed; then followed the wait—the hardest part.

The killing that counted in this August war was done by snipers; the rest was mindless mayhem and destruction caused by planes,

Apache helicopters, and tanks, none of which we had. The Occupier had better equipment, and snipers who had trained longer and harder than we; the terrain was a problem. Our enemy's snipers, whom we feared more than his tanks, had to keep close to their front lines; venturing out was risky; they had been known to lose their way in the rabbit warren of alleys that made up our Old City. We knew those alleys.

Haider and I ended up going through houses as well as around them, traveling over rooftops and hiding in old mosques and new ruins; we knew every alley, every rooftop, and which remains of each partially gutted building had better vantage points. Taking out soldiers and officers of the New Army was child's play; killing Americans was harder, not because we could not get close enough, but because they reacted instantly, their tanks like wounded elephants obliterating within seconds the building we were concealed in. Or, if we had not been spotted from the flash of Haider's rifle, a tank would plow through the whole alleyway, bringing down everything on either side. And yet the only Americans to die in the war over Najaf were killed by snipers like Haider and spotters like me.

Haider excelled at his work, and he was in rapture over his semiautomatic Soviet-made Dragunov sniper rifle, standard issue to sniper squads in the days of the Tyrant. He took to saying there was something akin to a religious experience in a meticulously prepared, patiently hunted, and perfectly executed kill. First, he said, there was the near ecstatic awareness of the proximity of death, your own and, you hoped, someone else's; second, there was total focus on body, self, and task, to the total exclusion of the world; third came the higher value you placed on your comrade's life over your own; fourth was the warm feeling of being part of something bigger than yourself and full of meaning, like our presence inside the Holy Shrine; and finally, the exhilarating explosion of happiness and relief at being able to distill all these components of an authentic religious experience into the perfect killer shot.

There is a savage joy in a good killing. Perhaps all our fighters who had occupied the Shrine felt it. I felt it. Perhaps our Sayyid felt it as well, catapulted as he now was out of the shadow of his mar-tyred father and brothers to near mythic status by the boldness of his takeover of the Holy Shrine, and yet knowing, as he must have, the terrible consequences on his beloved Najaf.

I remember marveling at the way the experience of war changed the men around me. Haider's mind had been unhinged by a crazy preacher awaiting the apocalypse; his home life, destroyed by the revelations about his father. But for those four weeks we were holed up and at war in Najaf, Haider's mind and body were in harmony with one another, pitched to perform one singular task perfectly.

I look back in amazement at those feelings and memories from the scorching hot August days of 2004 fighting the Occupier. Perhaps there is more than one person inside us: one who thrills in destruc-tion, and the other who recoils from the fact. Or perhaps it is a mat-ter of those despised parts of our natures that are normally frittered away as harmless foibles giving rise in times of war to monsters.

One incident I will never forget: I was sneaking back into the Shrine, carrying a wounded comrade, when an old man called out just as I approached the alley's end and was preparing to sprint across the open space to the tall wooden doors. "Look," he said, pointing at a dead donkey that had been pulling a cart laden with blocks of ice. "Help me. My donkey was shot by a sniper." The cart, tilted for-ward, was on the verge of spilling its contents over the dead animal. "Those bloody Americans," I shouted back, and pointed to my bleed-ing comrade by way of explaining why I could not tarry to help.

An hour later, Haider, his Dragunov, and I, carrying the rest of our kit, snuck back out of the Shrine from the same doorway to take up a position west of the Old City. Near the dead donkey, lying face-down in the dirt, was the old man, a hole centered in the back of his head.

"Good shot," remarked Haider.

I looked at him aghast. "Why . . . who?"

"Who knows? Probably just a practice shot."

Cease-fire

The war with the Occupier did not end because the Occupier "suspended" the arrest warrant for the Sayyid; it did not end because of the maneuverings of the Cabal of Thirteen; it did not end because our Army of the Awaited One obeyed the terms of the deal that had been struck with the Occupier-appointed Iraqi government. It ended because a ninety-year-old recluse forced himself out of his sickbed and, against his doctor's orders, led a march for peace from the city of Basra all through the southern provinces into Najaf. It ended because one million Shi'a men and women walked with him, not weeping and wailing and beating their chests, as they had done on the march to Karbala in 2003, but calling for peace and an end to all gunmen in the Holy City.

There was nothing our Sayyid could do after that except meet with the old man, and strike the best possible deal that would allow us to withdraw with dignity from the Holy Shrine.

The meeting with the Grand Ayatollah of the Shi'a world took place as the great march was ending in Najaf; it took place on the last Thursday in August. Crowds of people were still on the streets. The Sayyid entered the Ayatollah's house and found him sitting cross-legged on the floor of his small reception room. It was the Sayyid's turn to bow low from the waist and kiss the old man's hand. The Ayatollah did not wear large turquoise and silver rings on his fingers as our Sayyid did, so the Sayyid kissed the wrinkled skin on the back of the old man's hand. Did the Ayatollah withdraw his hand, as he was wont to do with esteemed visitors whom he wished to put at ease? We don't know. Uncle doubted it. Did the old man for that matter rise from the floor out of respect for his guest? "Definitely not," Uncle said angrily. There was no equality in that room on that extraordinary day.

The meeting with the old man lasted fifteen minutes, but our Sayyid had to stay in the room longer, alone, while the Ayatollah's aides obtained assurances of safe passage for him. The old man had drafted a statement, which he wanted our Sayyid to copy out in his own handwriting, sign, and affix his House's seal onto. Our Sayyid agreed with the text after it was read out to him, but tried to avoid signing it. The old man would have none of it. He had to have the words copied out in our Sayyid's hand, and then signed, sealed, and read out loud by the Sayyid into a tape recorder provided by the Ayatollah's aide. There was neither equality nor trust in that room on that extraordinary day.

The Sayyid squeezed one concession out of the old man during the fifteen minutes. He wanted us, his fighters, to exit the Shrine with heads held high, not as an act of surrender. The Ayatollah agreed, "for your fighters' sake," he said, but on the condition we turned in our guns. Our Sayyid then said he feared his fighters would be photographed as we filed out of the mosque and punished later by the Occupier; he asked for assurances in the shape of ten thousand unarmed worshippers mingling with us, his soldiers in the Army of the Awaited One, as we left the Shrine. The Ayatollah agreed the fear was warranted, and conceded two thousand.

Filing out of the tall wooden doors of the Shrine, my comrades and I threw our Kalashnikovs and RPGs into a cart standing outside. The voice of our Sayyid, which the old man had insisted be recorded on tape, came crackling out of the loudspeakers of the Shrine: "In the name of God, my brothers in arms of the Army of the Awaited One. You defended yourselves. You fought for your Imam bravely and unflinchingly. Now I ask you, and the Ayatollah of this blessed city asks you, mingle with the peaceful unarmed pilgrims from Kufa and Najaf who are among you, and depart from the Holy Shrine."

Neither the Americans nor the Iraqi Army and police, whom we had fought in Najaf for a month, were to be seen as we walked out. We threw our arms into two carts that had been placed outside the gates. It looked like we were disarming; in fact, the carts were driven to a warehouse outside the city, where we later collected the same weapons we had discarded. When American trucks showed up to collect the weapons they were told were waiting for them in the carts, nothing was there.

Exhausted and hungry, carrying our dead and wounded, but with our dignity and honor intact, we walked out mingling with thousands of ordinary pilgrims, dispersing ourselves in the alleyways of the Old City.

As I left, in the distance I could see a crowd of reporters and camera crews milling around the house of the old man. The Holy City's Supreme Source of Emulation had said how it was to be, and everything was as he said. A press conference was under way announcing the terms of the cease-fire to journalists from all over the world. The Ayatollah's aide was standing on a raised platform. As I walked toward the reporters to see what was going on, out of the corner of my eye I spied our Sayyid, flanked by two of his aides, slip out of a side door of the Ayatollah's house and make a dash for his car, black robes flowing.

The Quiet Ayatollah

A few days later, Uncle was obliged to follow up on details of the cease-fire agreement with the Grand Ayatollah's aide. I accompanied him, and was instructed to wait in the courtyard of the house where the meeting was taking place. A young man my age had organized refreshments, and he sat down with me out of politeness. He was a student of the Ayatollah's studying jurisprudence and ethics. I asked him what kind of a man his teacher was. He began with a story about the Ayatollah when he was a young seminary student in the Holy City of Qum in Iran.

At that age, the seminarian said, the Ayatollah was known for two things: good looks and love of philosophy. One day he seated himself in a circle of the most esteemed teachers of his college, who were discoursing on issues of predestination and free will. After a while the oldest in the group, and clearly its leading scholar, noticed the young cleric and said: "Have you a question you would like to put to us?"

"How may we know the difference," the young cleric asked, "between the acquired character of a person and his or her true heavenly essence?"

"That question is pretentious, young man," the scholar replied abrasively. "Why not say what is really on your mind, like how can

I use my good looks to become superior to my contemporaries? Isn't that what young men like you think about?"

The young cleric was silent, thinking about what his elder had said. He then thanked his interlocutor most courteously and took leave from the company.

"Why did he thank a man who was so rude to him?" I asked the seminarian.

"Because the scholar's answer made him reexamine his reasons for asking the question in the first place."

"He wasn't offended?"

"No."

"Does the Ayatollah speak in Arabic or in Farsi?"

"That depends."

"But he is an Iranian."

"No."

"I don't understand. He was born in Qum."

"His is the Community of Believers in Him, none other."

"Does he think of himself as an Iraqi?"

"No."

"How then does he think of himself?"

"As a subject of our Lord, frail and prone to error, as are all His creatures."

"But we call him our most Supreme Source of Emulation!"

"He is not responsible for what others call him."

"Does he love Iraq at least?"

"Of course."

"Does he love Iran?"

"Naturally."

"Equally?"

"Equally."

"Doesn't he love any one place more than another?"

"He reveres the Holy City, Najaf, above all other places. Here he has lived for half a century."

"That long! Is that why he intervened to resolve the standoff in Najaf?"

"He intervened because the Holy City faced destruction; it called out to him."

"Leading a march into Najaf is an unusual intervention for a man who despises politics."

"The crowds who flocked around him did not think so."

"Why did he not intervene on other occasions, when there was fighting in Sadr City, in Karbala, or in Fallujah, for instance?"

"Loss of any Believer's blood, Sunni or Shi'a, is like a dagger in his heart. But he will not intervene in situations where he can achieve nothing."

"He lives, it seems to me, in an altogether different, unreal world."

"What is real? Are not all worlds contained in this one?"

"Hmm . . . Who was his teacher?"

"Ayatollah Abu'l Qassim al-Khoei."

"The Ayatollah who died in 1992?"

"The very same, and our Supreme Source of Emulation for a quarter of a century. On his deathbed, Khoei nominated him to be his successor."

"Ayatollah Khoei had a son who lived in London, did he not?"

"Sayyid Majid, who escaped the Tyrant in 1991. His older brother was killed by the Tyrant because of it."

"I did not know. What did the Ayatollah think of the death of Sayyid Majid?"

"He excused himself from his classes that day and went into mourning."

"Did he meet with Sayyid Majid when he returned to Najaf in April?"

"No."

"Why not?"

"He was prevented by your Sayyid's followers. They cordoned off his house, demanded he return to Iran, and would not let Sayyid Majid through."

"I don't believe it!"

"You asked a question; I answered."

"I am sorry. I did not mean to offend. I was surprised. I did not know . . . perhaps it was some overzealous followers. I am sure our Sayyid would not have approved."

"Perhaps."

"What is he like as a teacher?"

"Kind and tolerant, impatient of fuss and pomp. All he asks of us, his students, is that we learn to ask good questions of him."

"Does he not teach you what to think?"

"He teaches us how to think."

"Kind, you said. Many people are kind. It doesn't mean anything."

"Perhaps, but few are tolerant."

"What do you mean?"

"Accepting of difference. Looking into one's own heart before judging that of another."

"Including infidels?"

"Including infidels."

"Did he support the Occupation?"

"No."

"Did he oppose the Occupation?"

"No."

"Why does he not speak up on public affairs?"

"He does not pretend to be qualified and prefers the company of his books to that of politicians."

"What is wrong with politicians?"

"He sees the practice of politics as damaging to the soul."

"The souls of Shi'a politicians as much as the Sunni ones?"

"Especially those of Shi'a politicians."

"Why especially?"

"Because their responsibility is greater."

"Greater?"

"The future of the country and all its many communities is in their hands."

"But the suffering they must redress is greater."

"Can suffering be measured? In any case, Shi'a hearts have to be more forgiving than other hearts."

"And you are saying at the moment they are not."

"It is not for me to say."

"I am glad he met with our Sayyid."

"He would work with the devil to save Najaf."

"Are you saying our Sayyid is the devil?" I said, getting angry.

"God forbid, no! He is a politician."

"But the Ayatollah is also doing politics."

"He rose out of his sickbed unwillingly, and only because the Holy City was in dire straits."

"A reluctant politician, then?"

"Reluctant, but never a politician, which is why he is loved."

I spent the month after the cease-fire lying on my bed in Uncle's house in the Mishraq quarter gazing dumbly at the bare walls of the second-story room I had shared with Mother for so many years. In the corner was the rickety old chair and the chest that had contained Father's letter; I carried it in a leather pouch around my neck these days. The room seemed to belong to another life, one I was growing distant from. My thoughts wandered from memories of camping out in the open courtyard of the Shrine between ever more dangerous forays into the Old City, to our movement's now declining status in Najaf. The old man had done what neither the Americans nor the Iraqi government, and least of all the House of the Shi'a, had been able to do. But he was leaning on our old enemies to do it, the House of Hakim, whose intent was to supplant us in Najaf. How did he do it? I wondered. What was the secret that had suddenly materialized into a million people swarming around his car and pouring into the city marching for peace? He was too feeble to walk, but not too feeble, it seems, to engineer miracles.

My mind turned to the exhausted and hollowed-out faces of the thousands of young men camped out with Haider and myself in the courtyard. I could see them fidgeting about to find a better position to sleep on the hard ceramic floor, or having their wounds cleaned and dressed before foraging for a bite to eat. We knew hunger that month. Days would pass on dry bread and water alone until fresh supplies were smuggled in. Then a dozen of us at a time would sit around a huge vat of warm rice and vegetables, the melted lard floating to the surface hiding the absence of meat. Eager hands wiped clean on soiled shirts would dig in from all sides as an outer ring of lads waited their turn, cracking jokes and slinging epithets at this or that politician. Only the Grand Ayatollah they did not joke about; they asked, instead, when he was going to deliver them; they asked like little boys who knew they had misbehaved.

I was prepared to die in Najaf, but only for them, for their frightened faces and dirty humor and smelly bodies. In the blink of an eye, they too would have died for me. When shrapnel or gunfire mauled one of us, we ruffians-turned-angels carefully washed and dressed our fallen comrade's wounds. The dead we washed again, carefully, all over, lovingly wrapping a corpse before placing it in a simple wooden casket to await burial in the unknowable future. I was in charge of storing these temporary caskets and the erection of a timber scaffold to enable us to layer them, to store one on top of the other on a smaller footprint. Space was at a premium in the Holy Shrine that August. My monument stood impassively in the courtyard as a reminder, a giant ever-growing wooden tomb built up of many perfectly aligned discrete caskets, a stone's throw from the silver mausoleum of the blessed Imam himself.

Life quickly went back to normal in Najaf. The Ayatollah was very much in command. Roads and sidewalks were cleared, and hopelessly damaged structures pulled down; new construction sprouted up everywhere. I felt myself changing along with my city—the city that no longer felt like mine. Those who were not present in the courtyard during those blistering hot August days no longer counted the way they used to. Our movement was still a formidable force in Baghdad. Perhaps I could move there, team up with Haider in an apartment in Sadr City. My band of brothers had dispersed after the month of fighting holed up in the Shrine; I would never see them again; it had been a moment, not to be repeated. Worse, as the days passed, and I would get up from my bed in the evenings to climb up to the flat roof and gaze at the star-studded sky, my comrades' features began to dim. By the end of the month I was struggling to remember their names.

Late summer nights in Najaf, when it is still hot and dry during the day but cool and quiet in the early evening with a gentle breeze wafting across from the Euphrates River, these are times to be alone on the roof of Uncle's house. I would stretch out on the summer beds prepared by Aunt, and gaze up at the incompleteness of the moon surrounded by mysterious flickering needle points of light organized into lines and orbits immeasurable distances away. These had meaning and structure, our Sheikh taught, forming shapes and constellations as mysterious as the workings of the mind of that old man. The Sheikh had taught Haider and me to trace out of those lines a handful of shapes. I remembered the stars that connected to outline a horse, an Arabian stallion, he said, in whom are gathered the traits of courage, purity of intent, and nobility of character.

I needed to be alone to think about such things. Haider checked up on me from time to time, but he was distracted by tasks like resupplying under Uncle's direction, finding secret new warehouses for ammunition and weapons, and preparing for future battles. My mind was elsewhere.

Defeat had factionalized us, with Uncle at the head of an "Iraqist" faction calling for increased collaboration with the Sunnis, and other leaders calling for a "Shi'ification" of our movement and a greater collaboration with Iran. Our Sayyid absented himself from answering such difficult questions. He went into retreat, biding his time before taking sides in the divisions that were everywhere opening up. But to the old man, such preoccupations were entirely foreign, or so I dimly discerned while lying on my back looking up at the stars. And then I remembered my comrades in the Shrine, who seemed to fall back on the old man for succor when the going got rough. Fall back on him, not on our Sayyid! What did that mean?

What kind of a Shi'a was the Ayatollah? I wondered. That is a stupid question, I thought to myself. Why, he is the incarnation of the meaning of the word. He is the purest embodiment of who we all were and all the traditions we came from. But why did he not seem to need to brandish his Shi'aness about, like the members of the Cabal of Thirteen did, or like some of our own members in the Army of the Awaited One nowadays did?

I recalled Uncle's remark that the members of the Cabal of Thirteen wore their newfound Shi'a identity like an ill-fitted suit. But not the Ayatollah. He seemed to wear it like it was his skin, unselfconsciously; he took it for granted, never thinking twice about it, and certainly not with every passing day as all the rest of us Shi'a of Iraq were doing since the fall of the Tyrant. We were all talking about what it meant to be a Shi'a. Should we join this House or that House? Which had the better interpretation of an Islamic state? Was the Imam's return imminent or not? Should one be Shi'a first and Iraqi second, or vice versa? Was it permitted to pray in a Sunni mosque?

Such questions bedeviled us. But not him. Oh no! The old man had no problem being the incarnation of the quality of being a Shi'a on the one hand and praying in a Sunni mosque on the other. Born in Iran but loyal to Najaf, a quietist compelled to activism, neither an Iraqi patriot nor an Iranian one, a man who abhorred the public eye but was adored by the public. He loved Iraq and Iran, and probably many other places too, like one loves the birds and the flowers and the trees. Equally. There are differences, I imagined him saying, but no hierarchy, no competing loyalties—the Holy City excepted, of course.

Under that glorious dome of the night sky, I envied one who could know himself, and be known, like that; a man with no divided loyalties, who saw no contradiction between being himself and the rest of the world; all he seemed to ask for was the solitude of his books. I wonder why? To know himself even more, no doubt. Could we all be like that? I wondered. Was it imaginable? Or was there only one of such a man?

I began to wonder if he was a bit like Father. Did the old man, like Father, extend self-love to embrace all countries and religions of the world, including unbelievers and infidels, to all of whom he extended love, not hate? Uncle had said it was necessary to hate the foreigner. I couldn't imagine the old man hating anybody. But then I couldn't imagine him agreeing with Father either. What did that say about being him? During that month of recuperation at home in Najaf, his enigma, I concluded, was as dizzying and incomprehensible as the immensity of the stars and the galaxies above.

¦ **2005** ¦

Betrayal

The story of Sayyid Majid continued to haunt me. Who was this threatening figure who had appeared out of nowhere? Why was a collaborator, the son of a Grand Ayatollah, seeking an audience with his father's student, another Grand Ayatollah? I could no longer accept things the way everyone—Uncle, the Sayyid, the Iraqi government, the Occupier, the Governing Council, and the Cabal of Thirteen—wanted them to be accepted. There had to be more to his story than anyone had led me to believe. Even though I did not believe in our Sayyid's responsibility for Sayyid Majid's death, I felt a growing obligation to know what happened on April 10, 2003.

What was in this so-called file of evidence the judge had collected against our Sayyid? Who was this man who had started deposing witnesses immediately after the murder, before there were any foreign troops in the city? Should our movement worry about the file the judge had assembled? Might some unscrupulous politician leak it to discredit us in the upcoming elections for the Constituent Assembly, which our Sayyid had reluctantly agreed to participate in following the resolution of last summer's fighting in Najaf? The arrest warrant had after all been suspended, not rescinded.

Could one man have been responsible for the murder, stabbing frenziedly over one hundred times? Or were the killers a collective of a hundred or so separate men? More likely they were a handful of conspirators, each striking multiple times. It had to be a group killing, I concluded, with many parties at once intent on the deed. Did the perpetrators know whom they were killing? Was there prior intent to kill a Grand Ayatollah's son? Not if it had taken place in a back alley, at night in some dark Godforsaken corner of the city. But Sayyid Majid was cut down on a glorious spring afternoon, and first assaulted in the Shrine, while speaking before a crowd many hundreds strong. People said he spoke for thirty minutes before the crowd turned into a mob. How can a man stand for thirty minutes listening to a speech without asking his neighbor who it is that is speaking?

They knew who he was.

Not a single member of the Cabal of Thirteen seemed troubled by the fact that they had covered up the killing of a man who had been their friend. They had worked with this man closely in London during the years of opposition in exile. They knew his family, and had accepted his hospitality. They had kissed his hand out of respect for his father, the Grand Ayatollah of his time, Sayyid Abu'l Qassim al-Khoei, the most revered religious scholar of our age. This was no ordinary man. Sayyid Majid was an illustrious member of our own Shi'a community. Had not these friends of his set out to defend the interests of the Shi'a inside the Governing Council? Was that not what the Cabal of Thirteen, or the House of the Shi'a—whatever you want to call them—was all about? During all the meetings the Thirteen had in July and August 2004, drafting the language of the secret letter designed to cover up his killing, didn't at least one of them remember those days in London, and ask himself: "So who killed my friend and colleague at whose house we often pondered such weighty issues as the fall of the Tyrant and what to do the day after he fell?"

Did the Cabal of Thirteen agree with Uncle that their friend was a collaborator? Is that why they were so willing to gloss over his murder? But if he had collaborated during those days of exiled opposition, which he undoubtedly had, then so had they; they had done the same a thousandfold, and were no doubt handsomely rewarded for it.

The Cabal of Thirteen betrayed Sayyid Majid, not caring a fig whether or not he had been a collaborator.

This, it seemed to me then and it seems to me today, was not a case of one sect betraying the other; nor a case of one political party or leader jockeying for position and betraying the other. It was the worst kind of betrayal: the kind that happens inside the same family, among men of the same sect all bound by the idea of their victimized sect's right to power, men who had worked decades to bring about the fall of the Tyrant . . . and then the day he falls, the one takes to stabbing the other in the back! If our new would-be Shiʻa rulers found it that easy to betray so illustrious a one of their own, then who was there among the rest of us ordinary Shiʻa, not to mention other Iraqis, whom they would not betray?

I can understand betraying your country for the sake of your community, fighting alongside your kin even when you know they have done wrong, fighting simply because you are of them and not to stand by your own is unthinkable. There is honor of a kind in that. The only person you will have then betrayed is yourself: what you stand for, and the kind of man you aspire to be. When I lie to protect my friend, I am that kind of a betrayer. I can live with that. But I cannot live with betraying my own. So it was with Cain's betrayal of his brother Abel, and Yusuf's betrayal at the hands of his brothers, who were so jealous, they planned to kill Yusuf to keep their father's love all to themselves. That kind of betrayal is beyond the pale.

Was the Cabal of Thirteen jealous of Sayyid Majid? Did they fear he would suck all the glory out of toppling the Tyrant for himself? Did it matter that Sayyid Majid had been cut down on the day of the fall of the Tyrant, and in the holiest site of the holiest city of our Shiʻa world? Did it matter that he had appealed to his friends on the day of the murder?

No one seemed to give a damn as to who the real murderer of Sayyid Majid was. The Cabal of Thirteen did not want to talk about it; above all they did not want anyone in the outside world to even know that such a murder had happened. The more secular ones among them had plans, Uncle said, to use our movement and our Sayyid to split the Islamist camp, not only across sectarian lines, but also within our own Shiʻa sect, to bring the House of Sadr into the Governing Council in order to weaken the House of Hakim and the prime minister's Party of the Call. They told the Occupier that all his problems would disappear once our Sayyid was brought into the tent, instead of left to piss on it from outside.

I found myself gradually turning against the very people whose ideas about the Shiʻa I had once admired: ideas like the singular place of our Shiʻa victimhood under Saddam, or ideas about the sectarian all-Sunni state he had set up, and our God-given right as Shiʻa to take back from Sunnis by guile or by force that which was our due, and then rub their faces in the dirt after we took it. Not for them was the warning of our incomparable First Imam: an eye for an eye turns the whole world blind.

These Foreigner Iraqis did not understand us; nor did the Occupier. All they cared about was that the house of straw they had so elaborately erected did not go up in flames over the killing of Sayyid Majid.

As for Uncle, sphinxlike, impenetrable, and ever so frustrating to deal with though he remained, I grew closer to him in the months that followed. But I no longer shared with him my every thought as I used to do. I learned caution, sensing that in this business of the death of Sayyid Majid lurked dangers and pitfalls that I had only barely begun to discern. I agonized in private, not even drawing dear Haider into my confidence.

·　　·　　·

Betrayal matters. It casts a dark pall of suspicion and mistrust inside a community. Because it matters the Cabal of Thirteen kept the letter they had signed a secret, agreeing to participate in a cover-up and wash their hands of responsibility for their friend's spilled blood, on the condition that no one, not even their American friends, got hold of the proof of it. They lifted the letter up in the air so that the American political advisor meeting with them could read it and report to his superiors that he had seen it, and then each member of the Thirteen tucked his copy safely away to use against his fellow Shi'a members of the Cabal in the event that he too was one day betrayed.

That letter is their mark of shame, just as the Tyrant's rope is mine.

The "suspension" of the arrest warrant was engineered to give the Occupier a face-saving way out of the corner we had boxed him into by occupying the Holy Shrine. The Thirteen had no intention of reopening an investigation into the murder once they came to power; Uncle received assurances to that effect, which he followed up on, looking each man in the eye to hold him to his word. One by one they promised they would make the whole affair go away after they took power, legally of course, by way of fair and free elections, only not now while they were still so beholden to the Occupier.

In April 2005, after a Shi'a-led government took office in Iraq, the first in Arab history, the original file of investigation into the murder of Sayyid Majid disappeared. Two followers of our Sayyid who had confessed and were convicted of the crime were released. The original file was replaced with a new one, and new witnesses came crawling out of the woodwork, the old ones not being found, or having left the country, or disappeared, or worse.

No one believed in the new file, not even the new prime minister who had commissioned it—he of the slippery tongue and interminable sermons. I didn't believe in the new file either, not for a second. Not a soul believed in the new file, assuming, of course, they knew it existed, which the government tried to ensure they didn't. Anyway, what kind of a file is it in which everybody says, "I saw nothing" or

"I don't remember" or "I was not there"? Nothing was specific in the new file. Everything was shrouded in ambiguity. All understood it was a sham. But the case could now be closed, and everyone's complicity covered up.

The new file held no one responsible. Sayyid Majid was cut down in plain sight of a few hundred people, and no one was responsible. Because no one was responsible, it followed that no one could be held accountable. The Thirteen had turned the world upside down: because it did not *suit* them to hold anyone accountable, therefore no one *was* responsible.

The new file went a step further: it blamed Sayyid Majid for having inflamed the crowd with an inappropriate speech in the Great Courtyard of the Shrine. The worshippers, being poor, simple, God-fearing folk, who were only there to cry over the Imam and give alms, were upset. One thing led to another, as it so often does in life—this is how the new file read—and a mob jumped upon him, doubly offended by the words he spoke and the bullets his entourage had ostensibly started firing into their midst for no apparent reason. Or so the file claimed . . . And the knives just started slipping in and out of his belly and back and sides, by themselves, as it were; it was all the fault of the Sayyid's poor choice of words.

The 2005 duly elected Shi'a government, untainted by the Occupier, now turned on the hapless judge who had caused the problem in the first place by opening a case without authority—unless it was the Tyrant's authority.

They launched a witch hunt into his original appointment, using their array of commissions—the De-Ba'thification Commission, the Ethics and Integrity Commission—to hound him out of office and declare him incompetent. Sayyid Majid's friends in the Cabal of Thirteen controlled both commissions. That is the kind of friends they were. The judge was a closet Ba'thi, the two commissions concluded. He must have been working for the Tyrant, even though the Tyrant was on the run at the time. And still the judge continued to be hounded across the length and breadth of the country, until finally the Kurds put a stop to it.

"This man is under my protection. Back off!" said the Kurdish president of the republic, or words to that effect. Only then did the new prime minister desist, at least on the surface.

Still, they had gotten away with rewriting the official version of events. We were supposed to forget about Sayyid Majid's murder, but not forget the terrible things the Tyrant had done. We couldn't afford to let Sunni Arabs off the hook. The Thirteen were not responsible for anything . . . only Saddam was responsible . . . even when he wasn't. Let bygones be bygones, they said, when it was their excesses that were being covered up—this was the spirit of the first big lie with which the first duly elected Shi'a government in the history of our country began its first term of office.

"Betrayal" is an ugly word. Abandonment is the core event behind all types of betrayal. We hate the heretic but tolerate the Unbeliever and the skeptic. Why? Because the heretic abandoned God *after* believing in Him, while the Unbeliever who was always an Unbeliever did not abandon anybody; he can be bound to a community by oath, truce, or pledge of allegiance; abandonment doesn't even arise as an issue. But it does in the case of the heretic or the traitor to the nation, both of whom accept *and then abandon* their community; we punish them harshly because they are the archetypal betrayers, the Princes of Betrayal, so to speak.

In their defense the Cabal of Thirteen will say they were driven to betrayal, forced into it against their wishes by a "higher" sense of mission that filled their hearts, an obligation to the community of all the Shi'a that demanded sacrificing the justice due to their friend Sayyid Majid in order to save the lives of thousands in the city of Najaf during the August 2004 war, along with countless millions in the country at large, had the fighting extended into the Holy Shrine itself. He was, after all, only one man, they will say, and they had millions to save. What their enemies describe as betrayal, they see as loyalty; they are the saviors of the Shi'a, not the betrayers of Sayyid Majid. Who am I to say otherwise? Can they be both things at once?

In the world that the Tyrant built in Iraq, everyone betrayed some-one, sometime. In such a world, betrayal of friends and neighbors, or of other members of your own sect, was the norm. Was that the norm that the Cabal of Thirteen were still obeying, as though out of habit, the Tyrant's henchmen having long since disappeared? Did they remain locked into the imperatives of the Tyrant's world, not the new world they claimed they were building in Iraq?

I want to believe that the members of the Cabal of Thirteen are honorable people. I want to take them at their word and give them the benefit of the doubt. Many Shi'a lives, Haider's and mine included, were saved from a battle over Najaf. Perhaps the secret let-ter, and the betrayal of Sayyid Majid, who was after all dead, was a small price to pay for the saving so many Shi'a lives.

Suppose this is so. I ask: How many lives need to be saved to jus-tify the sacrifice of one man? And who in the end really saved us: the shameless Thirteen, or the old man rising from his sickbed to do what he hated doing, what he knew was wrong in principle for him to have to do, but knew he was obligated before God and his conscience to do?

An Intimate Killing

On a Friday, one cold winter's day in 2005, Haider showed up at my house in a frightful state. His speech was barely coherent and his thoughts surfaced in scrambled fragments, spat out into the air staccato-like.

"I must speak to you . . . dear friend . . . I need you . . . I need you now . . . Terrible things are happening," he said in a shrill, near hysterical voice. "Terrible . . . beyond belief . . . terrible, I tell you! You won't believe me, I know . . . They are killing good men . . . Come with me. You must meet him."

"Calm yourself, my friend. You are not making any sense. What on earth are you talking about?"

"They are killing Iraqi Air Force pilots and officers! Secretly assassinating them in the dark," he said, his voice rising to a shout. "It is outrageous! We must do something."

"Slow down. Take a deep breath. Who is 'they'?"

"Iranians, secret agents in our midst . . ."

"I don't follow you. Who is this person you want me to meet?"

"His name is Abbas; he is waiting for us in a teahouse only a few minutes away. Come . . . come . . . let's go now. I promised him you would come. He asked for you . . . specifically. I want you to witness what he has to say."

On the way, I tried to lighten Haider's heightened anxiety with what I thought was a joke. "Why would MiG-25 Foxbat planes buried in the sand need fighter pilots and officers?" I said with a slight laugh, reminding him of the time we had watched Americans dig out Iraqi fighter planes buried by the Tyrant in the desert outside Najaf less than two years ago. "I doubt there are any fighter pilots around for Iranian agents to want to assassinate."

But he took it seriously: "*Former* pilots and air force officers. Former . . . not current. They are hunting them down . . . picking them off one by one . . ."

"But why?"

"To settle accounts . . . to rid this country of its talent . . . How should I know why?"

"That's crazy! Those kinds of men would be too old and out of practice, unable to fly anything today; not that we have anything left in the army that flies."

But my friend was not listening. His world was coming apart, and there seemed to be nothing that I could do to stem the bitterness mounting within him. Once the cease-fire in Najaf set in, relations between him and his father broke down completely, aggravated by the fighting because the two were on opposite sides. He had overreacted to what his father had done when he abandoned one family in Najaf for another in Tehran. His delight at his father's return, his pride in his father's exploits in exile, turned into anger at the underlying deceit. It was not so much the infidelity toward his mother as the duplicity toward him, the shame before his friends, that undid him. Red lines were drawn inside the family, as they had been in the city. From mother to family to city, the hatred expanded outward like ripples in a pond to embrace family, sect, country, and nation.

In Haider's eyes, his father was now a traitor to the idea of Iraq, as well as its Shi'a community. I heard him say that his father's infidelity, if that is what it was, turned him into a betrayer of the family of the Prophet. The more vigorously Abu Haider tried to defend himself, on the grounds of his God-given Muslim right to marry over his wife, the more unreasonable grew his son's sense of betrayal.

A particular source of aggravation at home was a young atten-dant in his twenties named Najmaldin. He had returned with Abu Haider from Iran. Najmaldin's Arabic was thickly laced with shades of Farsi and figures of speech not used by us. Still, he claimed to be a full-blooded Iraqi Arab from the city of Karbala. Haider natu-rally made inquiries, but no one could track down the man's family, and he decided Najmaldin was lying. Moreover, Najmaldin slept in a spare room near Abu Haider, closer to him than his own son, even though Haider's room was much nicer, a fact I was at pains to con-sole Haider with. But the strange thing, which neither Haider nor his mother could tolerate, was Najmaldin's disappearances, often for days on end.

No one knew the reasons for Najmaldin's comings and goings, or what the precise nature of his job was. Abu Haider called him an "assistant," assigned to him because of the importance of his work in the local Najaf office of the House of Hakim. Every so often Najmal-din and Abu Haider would closet themselves in a room and talk for hours in Farsi, a language neither Haider nor his mother spoke. It was usually after such meetings that Najmaldin would disappear, to return who knows when.

Arriving at the teahouse, Haider pointed to the farthest corner, where a man sat with his back to the wall supposedly reading a newspaper. I could see his eyes upon us the moment we came into view.

Abbas was a stocky man in his middle to late forties with short, cropped hair and a thin, neatly trimmed mustache; he was wear-ing pants and a white shirt, signs of a middle-class professional. An untouched glass of tea sat on the table in front of him. Pleasantries were exchanged; I ordered tea; Haider was too worked up to drink anything. "Tell him what you told me," he said breathlessly, "tell him, tell him"; the words could not tumble out of his mouth fast enough.

"I want to join the Sayyid's army and serve his movement," said Abbas in a calm and collected tone of voice, suddenly cognizant of the fact that his cause might no longer be well served by anything Haider had to say. "I was hoping you could vouch for me with your uncle. I have technical skills and can be of great service. I was told you are the man to talk to."

"Respectfully, my brother Abbas, I hardly know you. What are these skills you talk about?"

"I served in the Iraqi Air Force all through the 1980s, flying emergency search and rescue missions on the front lines; there is nothing mechanical that moves or flies which I cannot repair or improvise upon when spare parts are nowhere to be found—"

"Yes, yes, yes," interrupted Haider, "but tell him *why* you want to join our movement. That is what is important."

I looked directly into Abbas's face, my quizzical expression reiterating Haider's interjection.

"I need protection," he said, returning my gaze.

"From whom?"

"It is not for me to make accusations. I only know that friends and colleagues of mine, who served with me during the Great War with Iran, are being found in alleys, shot through the head, usually at night or when no one is around. The killings are professional executions, with no witnesses, signs of torture, or vindictiveness of any kind showing on the corpse. All means of identification are removed, and the body is often concealed and covered with trash so as to delay its discovery and complicate the task of identifying the assassins."

"Professional! . . . You heard that, my dear friend . . . he said 'professional,'" interjected Haider, beside himself with outrage. "This is organized; only a state intelligence organization can pull it off . . . and who would that be but the Iranian Revolutionary Guard! No Iraqi lone gunman would work like that."

"But why would the Iranian Revolutionary Guard want to indulge in such senseless killings?" I exclaimed, turning to look at Abbas: "What do you think?"

"There is no obvious explanation, but there is a pattern; they are targeting former officers in the air force. We have formed a network of our own retired servicemen to keep one another informed, and provide protection if the circumstances allow it. We also investigate the facts after each killing, the extent to which they conform to a pattern, and so on. From all of this information it is clear to us that the killer or killers are working to a set modus operandi. If not an openly political agenda, the only other motive is revenge."

I liked his methodical way of reasoning. "Go on," I said.

"From here onward it is pure speculation. Memories of the Great War run very deep here and in Iran; they lost three men, often young boys, for every one of ours, suffering casualties of a million people. The war ended only sixteen years ago. That is not long enough to erase the wounds of those eight years of bloodletting. Whether the killings are state-organized or run by vigilante groups and veteran organizations in Iran—which exist; we have checked up on that— I do not know. Revenge is the only explanation I can think of. The Sayyid and his movement are patriots and lovers of the idea of Iraq, as am I. That is why I come to you."

"Do these mystery killings target both Shi'a officers and Sunni ones?"

"They do not discriminate. Two of the men killed, a pilot and a maintenance man, were close friends of mine, both Shi'a from the city of Kut, where I was born. The people behind this appear to hate all things Iraqi and don't care what sect or nationality their victims belong to."

"So why target only the air force? Why not officers in general?"

"Perhaps they do. I only know that my friends and comrades who were in the air force are being cut down. I cannot speak for the other services."

I told Abbas that I would speak to Uncle, and that Haider and I looked favorably on his joining our movement. We shook hands and parted company. Uncle took an inordinate interest in the case and met privately with Abbas, who became a bona fide member of our army within the week. The word then went out to the House of Hakim—deemed closest to Iran in those days: Abbas was now under the protection of the House of Sadr, and if anything untoward were to happen to him, there would be an account with us to settle.

But Haider would not let the matter rest there. A few weeks after Abbas's safety had been secured, Haider approached me again. We met in the same teahouse. I gathered he had become a stranger to his house, to the great consternation of his mother, renting a hovel of some kind close to the latrines of a larger adjoining house, a far cry from the immaculately tidy room, smelling of orange blossoms, that his mother always kept ready for him.

Haider was unshaven and looked disheveled, his eyes bloodshot from lack of sleep; they darted from table to table seeking out dangers that he saw lurking around. The upshot of our meeting was that he wanted me to embark on a most senseless and dangerous undertaking.

He had taken to tailing Najmaldin, following him twice to Sadr City in Baghdad for several days at a time, and once to Karbala. He was convinced that Najmaldin was an Iranian hit man, attached to his father, who engaged in the kind of killings described by Abbas. He had rifled his room and found a revolver, an unusual weapon for an Iraqi male to possess, whose weapon of choice was invariably a Kalashnikov because these had been distributed freely by the Tyrant to every household during the 1990s, and had been widely available ever since.

Haider had not actually witnessed Najmaldin kill someone, he reluctantly admitted, "because at the very last moment he always managed to give me the slip." On the other hand, the killings Abbas and his friends had tracked were all done furtively with revolvers at close quarters, proof, Haider said, that Najmaldin (and others like him) were behind them.

My friend's imagination had then leapt to wild accusations regarding Najmaldin's killings of "Iraqi patriots," as he now took to calling the victims. I tried different ways of reasoning with him, pointing out that he needed proof before taking any kind of irreversible action.

"What if the killings had nothing to do with Iraqi patriotism," I said to him, "or serving in the Great War with Iran, but were motivated by past activity and membership in the Ba'th Party? These men, who just happened to be officers, were being killed for being former Ba'this."

"Nonsense!" Haider shouted. "Why would your uncle have signed on and protected Abbas if he had been a Ba'thi? He had him checked out, didn't he! Nobody is as thorough in these matters as your uncle."

Accounts were being settled all over Iraq. The Tyrant had killed dozens of people from the Hakim family, just as he had done from the Sadr family. It was certain the surviving family members would seek revenge. Perhaps that is what was going on, in which case an Iranian vendetta against Iraq, focusing on former officers, was most unlikely, and Haider should not feel compelled to precipitate action.

But such arguments did not impress Haider. Nothing I could say would convince him otherwise. He had grown so self-absorbed, and estranged from his father, that he even turned irritable toward his mother, whose concerns for the deteriorating state of her son now exceeded her anger at Abu Haider's marital infidelities, a fact that incensed Haider even further.

Sensing all this, I asked my friend what was on his mind. Why had he called this meeting?

"I want you to interrogate Najmaldin."

"What!" I exclaimed in shock. "What do you expect me to ask him? Why would he even want to talk to me?"

"He is waiting for us not far from here," Haider said. "You are better with words than I am and can approach the subject indirectly. Just get him to confess that he is working for Iran. I have a little tape recorder we can use to record his confession . . . Here, see," he said, pulling the small device out of the plastic bag he was carrying.

"You say he is waiting for us?"

"Yes, hurry," my friend replied, grabbing me by the arm and leading me out of the teahouse. After a convoluted fifteen-minute walk, we came to an abandoned, partially destroyed building. Climbing over the rubble and through what used to be a courtyard, Haider led me into the last remaining intact room, newly boarded up, where I found Najmaldin. He had been shackled to some pipes coming out of the concrete, his face beaten to a pulp, both eyes swollen shut. I looked for a pulse in his neck; there was none, although the body was warm.

"He is gone, dead. Oh, Haider, what have you done!"

"I left him alive . . . I swear it . . . I just knocked him around a bit . . . He admitted everything . . . and then I went for the tape recorder . . . I had to find someone to borrow it from . . . and then I came looking for you."

The Meeting

Najmaldin's body took several weeks to locate and identify, during which Haider was nowhere to be found. I searched all over Najaf and Sadr City in Baghdad looking for him, but to no avail. In the meantime, the House of Hakim was once again ascendant in the city, its offices mushrooming, eclipsing ours, and its Brigades, not our army, deployed to protect the Holy Shrine.

Shortly after the first elected Shi'a-led government took office in the spring, Uncle received a request from a very highly placed cleric in the House of Hakim suggesting that it would be in "the common interest"—by which was meant the interest of the Shi'a alone—for Uncle and Abu Haider to have a meeting attended by a neutral "higher" authority trusted by both. The intermediary was an aide of considerable standing in the Grand Ayatollah's office. At this time Uncle did not know the fate of Najmaldin, and I did not know his body had been found in the abandoned building where I had last seen it.

We Arabs have a saying, "My cousin and I against the stranger; my brother and I against my cousin." Haider was like a brother to me. And so I did not breathe a word about Najmaldin, complicit in what my brother had done, all the time hoping that the affair would just go away, with everyone thinking that Najmaldin had decided to return to where he had come from in Tehran.

Uncle simply assumed the meeting had been called to discuss the new strategy of the Sadrist movement, described by our Sayyid as "political resistance," designed to replace the old one of "armed resistance" that had culminated in last August's showdown in Najaf. Our army had taken a terrible punishment during the fighting without disintegrating. Uncle thought the House of Hakim was calculating that although our fortunes in Najaf were in decline, now was not the time to strike a deathblow, because our standing in the country at large was soaring, especially in Baghdad. So there was room for maneuver, Uncle must have thought, and he welcomed the visit, which he insisted take place at his house.

A war of wits was about to commence, and its first move was where to meet; when all parties unhesitatingly agreed to meet at Uncle's house, he thought he had won the first round. In the meantime, our movement's rhetoric against Iran had softened, and to Uncle's great consternation, Iranian military aid, which he had taken in 2004 with head held high, as though he were doing them a favor, was now flooding into our movement at our request and coming in the shape of better weapons, communication systems, and, worst of all from Uncle's point of view, "advisors" attached to our Army of the Awaited One. All this was happening around the time of the meeting—another reason, Uncle surmised, why the House of Hakim, which was even more heavily indebted to Iran, might have called it.

Uncle was at the forefront of those senior leaders of our movement who opposed the new orientation toward Iran, and it is said our Sayyid sided with him—his father having held Iranian-born clerics in contempt. But the lure of Iranian money, Iranian guns, Iranian personnel, and Iranian mines specially designed to penetrate American armor lulled our Sayyid, Uncle said, into accepting the devil in our midst. Our priority was now the tidal wave of suicide-bombing attacks by Sunni haters of the family of the Prophet, followers of the austere eighteenth-century preacher Muhammad Abdul Wahhab, targeting our Shi'a community in their neighborhoods, mosques, markets, and sites of pilgrimage. As these precursors to the all-out war that was about to erupt increased in number and ferocity, the opportunity for Sunni-Shi'a collaboration, something Uncle and our Sayyid always stood for, narrowed sharply.

The delegation arrived at Uncle's house in the late afternoon of the first Thursday in July. The intermediary was a black-turbaned cleric of impeccable credentials about Uncle's age; a younger white-turbaned man, who I gathered was an assistant of some kind, accompanied him. Abu Haider was in his black robes, a sign of mourning. The two men with him were also wearing black.

Uncle was dressed informally in his favorite white silk gown, freshly pressed and cleaned; in a deliberate provocation, he had chosen to invite the Sheikh of our local mosque, the gossip whom Haider and I had shared sugared almonds with, and who had brought such grief to Abu Haider's household; the Sheikh looked even smarter than Uncle in his all-white flowing robes, which matched nicely with his carefully arranged white turban. Grandfather, looking no different than he always did in a white dishdasha that should have gone to the laundry, was also in attendance, which was unusual. He seated himself next to Uncle, which was even more unusual. I was there bringing up the rear, and sat in the least conspicuous place I could find.

The party of black sat on one side of the room, and two empty seats away, on the other side, our very own party of white. Uncle's heavy frame sprawled on the plushest armchair in the house; everyone else was seated on a sofa (the room had been rearranged for the occasion). The three Sheikhs, two in black, one in white, were leaning forward like boxers getting ready to jump up at the sound of the bell. Abu Haider, stiff and bolt upright, exuded calm. Only Grandfather was his usual devil-may-care self, moving his body around his seat until it reached the desired level of comfort, not giving a damn about anyone else in the room.

The first hour of such meetings is always a waste of time. This one was no different, with talk about the rampant corruption in Baghdad, differing evaluations of the new crop of ministers in the first elected government of the Shi'a, the threat to our community posed by al-Qaeda and its Iraqi allies, the poor state of Najaf's infrastructure, and so on. Glasses of cold water and tea, followed by biscuits and Arabic coffee, followed by towering platters of every kind of fruit imaginable, were served by a young boy who was brought in for the occasion. My aunt never appeared; she organized it all cloistered in her kitchen quarters.

Finally, when the high-ranking intermediary chose to break the ice, as was his prerogative, it took the highly surprising form of addressing Uncle by praising me for my erudition, my outstanding reputation for integrity in the community, and finally my loyalty to my friends.

You could have knocked me down with a feather; something was afoot. Even Uncle was taken aback. Everyone realized the preliminaries were over, and the business at hand was about to commence. The intermediary concluded this peroration suddenly, with a question to Uncle:

"We were wondering if your esteemed nephew could shed any light on the fate of poor Najmaldin."

"Najmaldin?" asked my Uncle. "I am afraid I don't know whom you are referring to."

"My brother-in-law," Abu Haider interjected.

Najmaldin was the brother of Abu Haider's second wife! Did Haider know all along? Or had Abu Haider hidden the fact from his family in Najaf, even after the disclosure of his second marriage, not wanting to complicate his life in Najaf further, adding insult to injury by revealing the identity of his assistant?

"We are all brothers," Abu Haider continued, looking straight into Uncle's eyes without blinking, as though there were no one else in the room. Both men kept marking time fingering their worry beads. "Why, my very own son is like one of your own, committed to the cause of your Sayyid and your House of Sadr," he said, speaking clearly, softly, enunciating every word slowly, in a room that had gone deathly silent apart from the beads clinking into place like a metronome.

"Please understand, I respect my son for such independence of mind," he continued, "and hold no grudges. But he is young and brash, inclined to act before thinking, unlike your nephew, news of whose abiding friendship and wise counsel to my son reached me even in Tehran during the difficult years of my exile. For this I am most grateful."

"Thanks are due only to God," said my Uncle politely, still puzzled and biding his time until he could fathom what this wall of praise was intended to entrap.

"Thanks be to God," replied Abu Haider, nodding his head gently. Everyone fingered his worry beads faster now. A few moments later, he went on. "Yes, my son was blessed by the bonds of friendship that the pair of them have enjoyed since childhood. I only hope he proves worthy of them."

Pausing again, looking at Uncle, he continued, "My son has dropped out of sight and taken to not visiting his family, including his poor mother, who is beside herself with worry. We need to save him from himself. Najmaldin was last seen in Haider's company, heading from my house toward the market. An hour or two later your nephew," he said, looking in my direction, gently smiling in acknowledgment, "was seen with him in a teahouse in the vicinity of the market. Najmaldin was not there, but customers sitting nearby say Haider appeared agitated, and your nephew was reasoning with him, trying to calm him down, apparently to no avail."

Abu Haider stopped here, indicating he had come to the end of what he had to say for the time being by reaching out for his tea and taking a long and very noisy slurp—the custom in Najaf to indicate appreciation for the hospitality on offer. He had not stated the main point; it was all by way of inference.

Uncle was now obliged to indicate that he understood what

needed to be done. He began by singing the praises of Haider, speaking eloquently of Haider's "dedication to Islam and commitment to service," especially toward his fellow Shi'a coreligionists; he spoke of our long friendship, during the "most formative" years—an indirect jibe pointing at Abu Haider's absence—during which he had tried to the best of his "limited abilities" to be a "father" to both boys, both of whom had been robbed of their biological fathers by the "cruelty of the Tyrant."

Uncle concluded by praising Haider's "excellence in sports and bravery and prowess as a soldier on the battlefield of Najaf the previous August" (which would have stung Abu Haider deeply, because his men had fought alongside the government and might have been engaged by Haider directly), contrasting these with my "excellence in academic pursuits," and speaking of how the pair of us so perfectly complemented one another. "Theirs is a most remarkable and unusual friendship, like magnets bonded to one another through their opposing polarities." On that high note of superfluous elegance, he ended his paean of praise by turning to me.

"Did you see Haider in the teahouse on the day of his disappearance?"

"I did, Uncle," I replied.

"Have you seen him since?"

"I have not."

"Go on then, son, don't dawdle. Tell his father what he needs to hear. I want the truth, and nothing but a full and comprehensive account. This is not a time—"

At that moment Grandfather interjected, clearly disapproving of Uncle's gentle rebuke, which he did not realize was not intended as a rebuke but as a signal to the intermediaries that Uncle took seriously the possibility, however remote, that his nephew might be involved in Najmaldin's terrible fate.

"Leave the boy alone!" he said sharply to his son. "He is the model of rectitude and honesty. Everyone knows that!"

I appreciated his interruption, which gave me the moments I

needed to shape my response. I turned my head slowly and looked at Abu Haider, whose eyes were now fixed on me. "He was, sir, as you say, very anxious and unhappy. Deeply unsettled. I was doing my best to calm him down."

"What was he unhappy about?" Abu Haider asked in a low voice, feeling compelled to ask because I was not being forthcoming enough. Realizing my mistake, I went into a little peroration of my own.

"Everything, sir. He had recently met this preacher, a student of Sayyid Sadiq, and was reading his book, a biography called *Judge of Heaven*. He visited the small community that the preacher established in an orchard just north of Najaf. Haider, I know, stayed there and was taken by the simple communal life these families live, awaiting the End of Time, which they believe is around the corner. Haider, I could see, was deeply moved by the gentle ways and manners that prevail in that community, in such stark contrast with the tumult and turmoil going on everywhere else in the country. We talked about that. The real problem was the claims of their preacher, who sees himself as having a direct link to the Absent and Awaited Imam, on the basis of which he claims His Coming is also imminent. His followers have put themselves on hold, as it were, waiting in this beautiful orchard for his arrival—"

"Did he say anything about Najmaldin?" Abu Haider interrupted.

"Haider was very confused, agitated, looking to settle his turbulent mind. Najmaldin's presence, the fact that his bedroom was closer to yours than his own, bothered him. I tried to tell him it didn't matter, that his room was after all so much nicer . . . but Haider is stubborn, as I am sure you know, sir. When he gets something stuck in his mind, it takes time to dislodge. Deep down all he really desires, although he does not know how to say it, is your respect and to be taken into your confidence."

"Did he mention being with my brother-in-law when the two of you were at the teahouse, the last day he was seen alive?"

"No, sir."

"Are you sure, son? This is very important."

"I am absolutely sure."

"Would you swear on the Quran to that?"

"I would, sir."

"Thank you . . . Do you know where my son is?"

"I don't, sir, as God is my witness." This time I could take refuge in God's name up front without having to be pressured into it, because I had no idea where Haider was.

"I have searched high and low for him for days to no avail," I continued. "I was told he had been seen in Baghdad, and traveled there, staying overnight. But nobody had heard from him. I cannot even vouch for the witness who claimed to have seen him."

"Do you think he was capable in his state of mind that day of killing Najmaldin?"

"Shame on you, Abu Haider!" shouted Grandfather from his couch. "How can you ask his best friend a question like that? Are you asking him to betray a man he loves, your son no less?"

Abu Haider contained his fury, but his contempt for Grandfather was hardly concealed in the protracted withering glare he directed at him, before turning finally to me, expecting an answer as though Grandfather had not even spoken.

"No, sir. Absolutely not," I lied. "Your son is not capable of such a reprehensible deed."

Aftermath

So I lied. I had to. How simple it was; so authentic and natural, I almost believed in it myself. It seemed to me at the time there was more shame in telling the truth. I would not abandon my friend; I would not betray him. I lied not only because the consequences of telling the truth were so grave for Haider, but also because my honor as his brother in arms, and in life, was at stake. Grandfather understood, which is why he intervened, incurring Abu Haider's wrath. Perhaps that is why he insisted on being there. This was a new side of Grandfather, one I did not then understand. He, after all, had lost his best friend, Haider's grandfather, over a political dispute—how trifling in retrospect! That was Grandfather's irredeemable moment, all those decades of hate and bitterness Saddam brought upon two best friends, both sworn enemies of the Ba'th. Perhaps it bothered him, and he did not wish it upon Haider and myself.

Abu Haider had arrived looking for answers, convinced that our House contained them. Answers were not forthcoming; there was bitterness in that. Najmaldin was a kinsman, not by blood to be sure, but his kinsman all the same. Worse, he had lived in Abu Haider's house, under his protection. Therein lay a whole other set of obligations. Abu Haider's home, Najmaldin's sanctuary, was his bond, and the seat of his honor; all had been violated. There was shame for Abu

Haider in that, as there would have been for me had I betrayed my friend. The world had contracted to the sharper of two choices: his shame or mine. It was no choice at all.

Blood calls for new blood. Those are the rules, as the poet sang:

> *With the sword will I wash my shame away,*
> *Let God's doom bring on me what it may!*

So, where would Abu Haider lay the blame? Since he had no specifics, Abu Haider chose to place it all on the House of Sadr.

Shortly after the meeting, information reached our security officers that Abu Haider was the hidden hand who had organized a provocation in the shape of demonstrations outside our offices in Najaf, claiming that they were full of closet Ba'this, and that the Ba'th Party had infiltrated our movement from as far back as the days of Sayyid Sadiq; militiamen from the Hakim Brigades then ransacked our offices, beat up members of our staff, and demanded that we be banned from opening new offices in Najaf. Abu Haider had played his first hand.

Uncle, after consulting the Sayyid, responded vigorously. He ordered the mobilization of thousands of our militiamen across southern Iraq; overnight, they sacked more than three hundred offices of the Hakim Brigades, leaving them in ruins. And Haider was spotted in Baghdad throwing himself recklessly into the fray against his father's Brigades. Had Uncle pulled out all the stops and found him after the meeting, thrusting him into the fray? I don't know, but Uncle was involved, of that I am sure. Uncle's decisive riposte to Abu Haider's pathetic demonstrations was a masterstroke: settling the score for the old wounds of 2004, tilting the scales of the war of Shi'a against Shi'a back in our favor, and laying the grounds for our ascendancy in the coming battles over Baghdad.

Two weeks later, word reached Uncle that Abu Haider had a copy of the original investigator's file that had been the basis of the Occupier's arrest warrant, now rescinded by the first elected Shi'a government.

Uncle called me into his office.

"Abu Haider is threatening us with a file, the one concerning the death of Sayyid Majid. It seems to have been prepared by a judge, who started deposing witnesses shortly after the body was buried. I want you to find that wretched man. Consider it a top priority. I want the original file; I want to know who has copies, and I want to know the names of everyone who spoke to the judge and whose name appears in the file. Do I need to tell you how much is at stake in all this?"

Grandfather

Two of the three Houses of Iraqi Shi'ism met at Uncle's house, but the ghost of a third, the House of Khoei, was also present. If Abu Haider was going to seek other ways of obtaining satisfaction for the murder of his brother-in-law, the file on Sayyid Majid's killing was his best bet. He knew of its existence, but did he have a copy? Uncle thought not; regardless, it was imperative that I find the file quickly.

No one in the prime minister's office or at the Ministry of Justice could locate the original or a copy of it. Once the new file had been generated in the spring of 2005—the one in which no one could remember anything and no one was responsible, and the death of Sayyid Majid was deemed an unfortunate accident caused by his own rash behavior—the old file "must have been inadvertently destroyed or mislaid," in the words of the filing clerk in the Ministry of Justice. I searched the shelves myself, and found nothing.

I was given access to the office of the prime minister, whose files were in such a state of disorganization that nothing could be found. That office seemed not to have been introduced to the concept of filing, to the point that no one was in charge of the place where all the inactive files got dumped, just outside a foul-smelling toilet. That "archive" I spent hours rummaging about in, finding nothing (I did find correspondence with the United Nations spilling over into the toilet, amid other stacks sitting alongside unopened cartons of toilet paper). There was no question of going to the Americans, who had to have a copy. My only recourse was to find the judge who had generated the file in the first place. I had a larger purpose than what Uncle had in mind: I needed to know the truth of what had happened to Sayyid Majid.

But finding a man who does not want to be found, especially in Baghdad, to which he had been transferred, is a big undertaking. I extended feelers everywhere, trying to gather as much information about the man as I could, while I waited.

A few months after the meeting, Grandfather's health began to decline. There was nothing catastrophic or abrupt like organ failure or a major fall. He just wasted away. In Mother's case the person remained, whether as memories or as illusion; in Grandfather's case, toward the end, the person that he must have been, that Mother wanted me to get to know, was annihilated.

He not only stopped struggling to live, but toward the end he also stopped believing in himself, collapsing inwardly and distancing himself from his previous life and beliefs; it was as though dying slowly disfigured his self-image to the point that even his loved ones no longer knew him. I saw Uncle turn away in disgust from his father on the few occasions that he did show up; Grandfather was beyond noticing such things.

Strangely, I learned to appreciate him during flashes of lucidity in the course of his deterioration, and began to understand why Mother had been keen on my getting to know him. But even the little I gained in love while he withered toward the grave was gone by the time he passed away. I could handle the sunken cheeks, the hollow eyes, and a skeletal frame that was more bone than flesh. But the foul language, childish behavior, and barrage of insults that accompanied any attempt by Aunt to help him were insufferable. Toward the end he was a man without taste for either happiness or food, which he would spit into my aunt's face as she tried to spoon it into his mouth. I had to turn my face or leave the room. Poor woman: childless and therefore powerless, with a husband who despised and used her as one would a servant, she took refuge, after Mother passed away, in caring for and doting on me.

I visited Grandfather after he was taken ill, but not from noble motives. I did so because it finally dawned on me that Grandfather knew things that mattered a great deal to me.

The first conversation came early in his decline and followed my telling him about Father's letter to Mother, which he knew all about.

"Your mother read it to me the day after she received it. I told her to hide it."

"Why?" I asked, but he would not answer, turning his face away.

"Does Uncle know about the letter?" I pressed.

"No. And don't tell him!"

"Why not?"

"It is better that way!" he said, and refused to discuss the matter further. "No one except your mother and I, and now you, knows the letter exists. Keep it that way."

"I don't understand, Grandfather. You and Mother have always been so close; you even gang up against Uncle. I have never heard you criticize her or say a harsh word, not once."

"Your mother, God rest her soul, was an angel, an angel . . . you hear me. She didn't just love your father; she was his rock, his backbone. You know what it was like to serve in that wretched war, and always be out there on the front, not in some cushy desk job? And all because you are a Shi'a and your paperwork has Najaf listed as your city of birth! He was a shambles each time they gave him a few days' leave. She stitched him back together again after each furlough. He would never have made it without her. And she always gave him a book to take back with him to the front. I remember one of them, which she went down to Baghdad to find. *The Tragedy of Hallaj*, I think it was called . . ."

"She gave me that to read, months before she died. She said it was Father's; I read it carefully . . ."

"It was your father's . . . but only because she bought it for him. She used to say it was the job of Iraqi mothers to bring back the love that was absent in the lives of their children. Did you know that?"

"I did, Grandfather. She talked to me about it."

"Why do you think she said it?"

"I just took it for granted. Isn't it something all mothers say?"

"Nonsense! All mothers are not like yours. Never take her for granted. She understood things your father was unable to understand: that Iraq is a land where there is no trust, a land where the norm is to expect to be stabbed in the back. And when there is no trust, there is no love." He seemed to drift off at this point, leaning back in his pillows and closing his eyes.

"Grandfather, are you okay?" I asked worriedly, leaning forward toward his craggy, bony face. He opened his eyes and turned toward me.

"Your father, God rest his soul, had his eyes permanently lifted up, looking always to the horizon, and beyond. He never remembered an insult, believing in the essential goodness of all men, who are driven to live up to that goodness. He could not think an ill thought about a person and excused his behavior, no matter how atrocious. Your mother loved him for that, but she knew when to turn her eyes down into the mud . . . the stones . . . yes, and the filth that lay strewn under both their feet. She was his eyes, son; with him it was like leading a blind man through a house filled with snakes . . . And he would follow her, wherever she led . . ."

He fell silent. I was embarrassed. Grandfather was not a man one associated with tenderness. And then I blurted out:

"Did you love her?"

But he would not answer; it was as though he was pretending he had not heard my question.

"Without her," Grandfather went on, "your father would have perished long before his time . . ."

"Was Father betrayed in 1991?"

"Of course he was . . . It was someone he knew . . . It had to be. And from Najaf, because no one else could describe the location of the house he was holed up in accurately enough for Saddam's security men to find."

"What was Father doing there? Why did they go to such efforts looking for him?"

"He was helping Sayyid Majid al-Khoei escape, of course."

"Sayyid Majid! The man who was killed in the Shrine of the Imam on the day of the fall of the Tyrant!"

"Who else do you think I am talking about, boy? Don't you know anything?"

"Are you sure, Grandfather?"

"I am sure. They grew up together and were the best of friends, going to the same schools, parting only when your father went to university and Majid to the seminary. But during those terrible two or three weeks of the Uprising, they were like brothers again, inseparable . . . the brother your father never had."

"What do you mean, the brother my father never had? What is Uncle?"

"Your uncle says nothing; he shares nothing . . . he has an infinite capacity for intrigue and suspicion. It drove your father crazy. Always he has been like that! I don't know where he got it. Not from me!"

Then he fell silent, and would not explain. But as he spoke to himself, mumbling most of the time, sometimes too softly for me to follow his train of thought, I caught this sentence:

"Your father was tormented by lies."

"Lies? What lies, Grandfather?"

"Any lies, white lies, the ordinary lies that people need to get through the day. Not so your uncle . . . or me. In that your uncle definitely took after me, I am sorry to say. Will God forgive me?"

"Of course he will, Grandfather . . . Do you believe in God?"

He wouldn't reply, just looked at me with incomprehension.

Then he abruptly said: "Do you think Haider believes in God?"

"I am sure he does, Grandfather . . . It goes without saying."

"Think about Haider, what he has done or might have done, and then think about what you just said, son. Now don't talk to me anymore." And he turned his head and fell silent, a signal for me to leave. I bowed my head and stayed, not moving a muscle, and was rewarded a few minutes later when he started mumbling again.

"Neither one of us resembled your father . . . such a gentle man . . . too gentle . . . He was obstinate and not made for this world. God, how obstinate that man was!"

He was getting all worked up at this point, his head turning sharply and rapidly side to side, as though he wanted to bang his cheeks on the soft pillow. The open palm of his right hand started beating the sheet. Even his yellowing eyes, sunk deep in their sockets, were moistening. I reached out and put my hand on the wrist of his left arm, and squeezed just enough for him to realize I was still there. Then he abruptly turned toward my side of the bed, seizing me tightly by the shoulders. His face had gone pale, his eyes glistening with intent, the irises yellower than ever. But he couldn't speak. It was as though he was choking on the words. I put my arms around him to calm him down. After a short while he sunk back into his pillows, exhausted. I stayed by his side until he fell asleep minutes later.

There was so much that I did not know. What had gone on in the past between Uncle and Grandfather? Why, I was now bold enough to start thinking, had Uncle been standing by the body as I came careening down the alley nearly three years ago? Was he involved in the murder in some way? Why all this secrecy and subterfuge whenever the subject of what happened to Sayyid Majid came up? Why not tell me Sayyid Majid had been Father's best friend?

And what of Uncle's relationship with his brother? True, he was six years older and had no education beyond high school, being largely self-taught. He had stayed on in Najaf, becoming very successful in business, owning three shops in the Great Souk opposite Maidan Square. Meanwhile, my father left for Baghdad to study at the university and then was conscripted into the army the year I was born, deserting nine years later when he was called back to service even though the Great War had ended. Did the brothers have a falling-out?

Uncle had spoken of Father as a dreamer whose heart was brimming over with "love of the world." But his defenses had been lowered when he said that. "Feelings are a weakness in men," he always said; if so, he had weakened that day, letting his emotions run away with him. Perhaps he was thinking of me. It was the only time I had seen him exhibit emotion. I even thought I saw tears . . . as I had seen them in Grandfather's eyes; I still see them in my mind's eye today, recalling the exact words Uncle ended upon all those years ago.

"Perhaps his ideas and way with words made him a beautiful human being, something I never claimed to be. But it also made him a poor judge of human nature." They are the words of someone who loves somebody, very much, but is also angry with him about something.

The Second Conversation

The second conversation came a couple of weeks later, during a lucid interval in the course of Grandfather's decline, and followed my asking him what Father and Sayyid Majid had been doing in Najaf during the Uprising of 1991.

"You have to understand there were bodies all over the place . . . on rubbish heaps, in the alleyways . . . of Ba'this, of the young rebels who had stormed the police stations and party offices, of bystanders . . . all Shi'a bodies, often innocent men or women killed to settle a score. Some of them must have been wounded and crawled into a dark corner to die. Sayyid Majid and your father scoured the city collecting whatever bodies they could find, identifying them where possible, and giving them a proper burial. This was after Ayatollah Khoei issued his ruling on the third day of the Uprising, March 5, 1991, I think it was, in which he urged everyone to do their duty and bury the dead with dignity, according to proper rites and to refrain from maiming corpses or stealing anything."

"You saw this, Grandfather, with your own eyes?"

"Yes, I saw it. I went out in the afternoon of the first day, until your Uncle locked the house down, put a guard inside, and arranged for someone to scrounge for groceries. He ordered us all indoors. There was no going out after that."

"What did you see?"

"I saw young men—boys younger than yourself they were—hundreds of them at first, swelling to a few thousand. They couldn't have been older than eighteen ... They came pouring out of the alleyways and backstreets to storm the police stations and party centers around the Great Courtyard of the Imam's Shrine. They were armed with clubs, swords, and pistols at first, rifles and automatic weapons by the end of the day. By sunset the Shrine and its courtyard had fallen and the rebels were running mock trials for their prisoners, slitting people's throats or shooting them left, right, and center."

"And Father?"

"At first he and Sayyid Majid had to go looking for a child of eight, a neighbor's son ... Ahmed, I think, was his name ... Anyway, his mother had sent him to the shops just before the whole thing began. She was hysterical, tearing her hair and clothes. Although they had many other things to do, the Sayyid and your father went in search of him."

"Did they find him?"

"Several hours later. The local greengrocer had taken Ahmed in when he came to buy onions in his shop; it was shuttered down to protect against the looters ... He took a long time to find."

"I had not imagined Sayyid Majid as that kind of man," I said, speaking to myself, but Grandfather perked up.

"What kind of man did you think he was?"

"I don't know. An American agent, Uncle said."

"Hah!" his voice rasped back, and then he made a big effort to pull himself onto his elbows and with piercing eyes hollowed out in their sockets he struggled to say, "He was a gentleman, a man of honor, his father's son in every respect. Ask Ahmed and his mother!" And he fell back onto the pillow from the effort.

I did not know what to say after that, torn between my feelings for Uncle and Grandfather's emotion. In a different situation I might have dismissed what he said as the rantings of an old man, but that no longer felt right. The things I did not know, and might never know, were just too much. Then Grandfather said:

"I saw your father one last time after that."

"What was he doing? What did he say . . ."

"Just before leaving, he came to tell me he thought his brother was right to lock down the house and made me swear on the Holy Book that I would make sure that neither your mother nor you went out looking for him. He was going to meet Sayyid Majid, who was as appalled by the behavior of the rebels as your father was. Both men thought the violence would be the Uprising's undoing. Youths, sometimes led by clerics, were storming every public building. They would kill every official in sight, steal everything they could carry, spread a can of kerosene around, light a match, and get the hell out of there fast. He saw good friends of mine killed, old comrades or sometimes merely fellow travelers of the Communist Party—Falah Askar, Ridha al-Faham, Kareem al-'Iraqi, and Hasan al-Najafi."

"Why would the rebels kill aging Communists? They probably don't even know what communism is. It doesn't make sense."

"They were not being killed for that, boy! Don't be stupid! These were broken men, talented artists and poets from the good old days; the Ba'th courted them after they crushed communism in Iraq, and forced them to pen songs praising Saddam and the Ba'th. We had the whole intelligentsia in the palm of our hands in the old days, all through the 1970s. Did you not know that, son? Have I not told you the story of my good friend Hassan al-Najafi?"

"No. But tell me about Father."

"Hassan was his friend as well. I used to organize poetry evenings in which Hassan always ended up as the star. He would recite to us some of his old compositions. Your father never missed a recital. Hassan, you see, didn't believe in anything anymore and had never been a real card-carrying Communist . . . He just loved his work, which others abused for political ends. You know how it all started? No, of course you don't! Ba'athi goons, you see, had broken up his wedding day; they beat up his wife, mauled her father, and smashed everything. The next day poor Hassan got a call directly from the Tyrant. That was in . . . let me see . . . 1978! Yes, 1978, just before Saddam became president. He said he was very sorry to hear what had happened, and if only Hassan would compose a few verses on the achievements of the great Ba'athi revolution in Iraq, he would personally guarantee the culprits would be found and punished. It was an offer poor Hassan could not refuse . . ."

Grandfather fell silent.

"Well, what happened, Grandfather? You must tell me now."

"They slit poor Hassan's throat in the courtyard of the Shrine. They said he was a collaborator, and called it justice."

We both fell silent. I was trying to imagine the scene with Grandfather's poetry evenings, but it would run into images of old Hassan bleeding to death in front of the Shrine of the Imam, of Sayyid Majid being stabbed in the very same location twelve years later, and of Father running around like a chicken with its head cut off trying to save somebody. I was trying but not succeeding to make sense of it all.

"Poor Hassan," Grandfather suddenly said, starting to cry and mumbling softly to himself, his drained face looking like it was already touched by the earth to which it would soon return.

"He spent his best years in pursuit of art and high ideals; the realization of either would have satisfied him. But in the end both got drenched in the blood that pumped out of his throat in the Great Courtyard . . . Shame on them . . . Shame on us. What are we? Animals to be slaughtered and carved up?"

"We are victims, Grandfather . . . we have always been victims. But rest assured, we are fighting back now."

"There is nothing reassuring about that, boy!" he suddenly snapped back. "In 1991, I saw so-called victims inflict more pain than was ever inflicted upon them . . . Those were not good men to be," he said, speaking to himself rather than to me. "Better to retain one's honor and self-respect, even as a victim . . ."

I was horrified! Was the honor in the deplorable and servile state of being a victim, or in the overcoming of it? I had joined the Army of the Awaited One to fight back. He was now saying that if in that fight the victim went too far, slitting poor Hassan's throat, for example, his excesses under those circumstances were not justified. To be sure vengeance was not justified; God's law is clear on that. But the Tyrant left us with no choice but to fight fire with fire. Surely violence in the service of one's own self-affirmation and that of his community was right, consequences be damned! Am I to tell a man driven by pain and humiliation to obey rules in the life-and-death struggle he is waging to survive and remake himself into a new kind of man? We didn't obey rules either in Najaf in August 2004. Nor did the Occupier. Why should the insurgents against the Tyrant have been expected to do so in 1991?

┆   2006   ┆

Justice

My past, Haider's past, the past of all of us who leapt into the future with our eyes shut in 2003, is the rule of the Great Tyrant. It lasted longer than the age of three-quarters of the population. Two Iraqi generations knew nothing but him. Grandfather's past was much larger than ours. He had seen many Iraqs come and go. There was no war or revolution or cruelty or form of human degradation that he had not lived through. Or so I thought, until the bulwarks of Shi'a pain burst on the day we put him in the ground, the twenty-second of February to be exact, the day the Wahhabi, Haters of the Family of the Prophet, attacked a site sacred to us Shi'a—the Askari Shrine in Samarra. They tied up the guards and blew up the Shrine, filming themselves doing so—an act of pure provocation. The pictures spread like wildfire. We were incensed; the Sayyid was enraged; Uncle threw up his hands in despair. A tidal wave of rage swept over the land.

Hitherto, we Shi'a had patiently endured the violence directed at us; we stood by when 270 pilgrims were killed during their pilgrimage, and when suicide bombers targeted us, in our mosques and marketplaces, or at our weddings, or wherever we might assemble.

Hitherto, the war between Iranian and Iraqi Shi'ism, between the House of Hakim and the House of Sadr, was fought in the background; we conducted it with vigor among ourselves, and poor Muntassir and Najmaldin died because of it.

Hitherto we had listened to the words of restraint of the Grand Ayatollah, words that so resembled those of his teacher and mentor during the 1991 Uprising . . . We'd listened and obeyed, confining ourselves to fighting the Occupier. Again he was urging restraint, asking that the sanctity of all Muslim mosques and homes be respected. This time we did not listen, and the pent-up rage of the Shi'a ripped through even his words of restraint.

The government issued denunciations and decried "foreign" sedition. The Parliament disintegrated amid recriminations and shouting matches. And the House of Hakim redoubled their dirty war of assassinations-by-night of regime loyalists, or people denounced as such. The Tyrant's outlawed party, they said, was responsible for the dastardly deeds.

Only our Sayyid tapped into the street's pulse, and felt its force, unleashing us upon the city. A new war of Shi'a against Sunni commenced in Baghdad, less than six months after the old one with the Occupier in Najaf had ended. It was a war whose language had been foreshadowed by the Cabal of Thirteen, but it was ours to wage on the ground.

No sooner had it begun than a strange thing happened, something no one had expected at the outset: the once frightened ordinary Shi'a of Baghdad, who had never warmed to the Cabal of Thirteen, turned to us as their saviors, to our Army of the Awaited One, and even when it was not our own men wreaking havoc on Sunni neighborhoods—exacting retribution, forcing Sunnis out of their homes, gunning them down at checkpoints, and robbing them of all their possessions—people said it was.

Our movement and its army, hailed by all for its gallant fight against the Occupier in the summer of 2004, now struck terror in Sunni hearts. We were the great bogeyman, dubbed the Frankenstein of Baghdad by some, stalking the streets of the city at night

while unspeakable horrors were being committed. Policemen doubled up as death squads, switching over to our uniforms at night—no
one else's—and claimed to be fighting for our Sayyid, manning unau-
thorized roadblocks at random, robbing innocent passersby, and killing every male with a Sunni name or from a Sunni neighborhood.

Black was the color of our uniforms, pitch-black from head to toe
with a black ski mask. Thus did we dress our killer squads, and chill-
ing they were to behold, even when they were not bursting open
your door and dragging out your menfolk. Pictures of our Sayyid
were pasted onto each and every Sunni house, and woe to any man,
woman, or child who tried to take them down.

These things continued to happen in our name all through the
year. How had a war against foreign Occupation come to this?
Uncle tried to stop it; the Sayyid, taken aback by the furies he had
unleashed, and losing control of his own men, also tried to put an
end to it—to no avail. I was rushed from one flashpoint to the next,
urging restraint, but it was like dousing an inferno with teacups.

Haider had metamorphosed during this war from the anxious,
wild-eyed man who had beaten Najmaldin to a pulp into a leader of
men, as famous for his ruthlessness and ferocity against Sunni foes as
he had been against Iranian "agents" like Najmaldin. Fighting Sunni
terror transformed him.

His name popped up whenever a new pile of Sunni corpses was
found with holes drilled into their hands and feet, and especially
when the coup de grace took the form of a hole drilled all the way
through the victim's skull. Rumor said that the electric drill was
Haider's trademark. Sunni killers preferred the knife—the Prophet's
Companions used knives, they said—beheading their foes, not cru-
cifying them. The Sunni knife was pitted against the Shi'a drill all
through the battle for Baghdad. The men under Haider's command,
and eventually throughout the ranks of our army, took to calling
him Dhu'l Fiqar, the Sword of Justice that had belonged to the First
Imam; his enemies called him 'Azra'il, the hideous-looking, avenging Grim Reaper.

I looked for Haider everywhere, but did not run into him during the worst of it. One moment he was there; the next he was gone; the only traces of his work were rotting corpses and rumors swarming around them like flies. Perhaps that was a good thing; it might have ended badly between us. We were in the same army, but on opposing sides of this new war.

He had cooled down by the time we finally met in the summer. Or perhaps I needed to believe that, and it was not really the same Haider, just another changeling fathered by the country's demons, mirroring in his person the twists and turns of so many young Iraqi men—killing Americans one day and fellow Shi'a the next; hating Iranians on the third day, and playing electoral politics on the fourth; and now cleansing the city of its Sunni Arabs. We switched enemies and alliances with dizzying speed all through that year. By the end of the Battle of Baghdad we controlled half the city, had ejected one-third of its former Sunni residents, and controlled 80 percent of the Shi'a areas within it.

I write "we," but, I now asked myself, who was "we"? I had pushed the question to one side before, until Grandfather, in a moment of lucidity during my vigil by his side, forced it out into the open.

"And you!" he snapped nastily. "What are you doing in that ragtag army? Some army! Your father and mother are turning in their graves. The 'Awaited One,' my ass! I thought you were smarter than that!"

"Grandfather! You are insulting a great Sayyid, descendant of the Prophet and son of a line of martyrs, all of whom died fighting for Justice!"

"Justice!" he screamed in my face. "They slit poor Hassan's throat for that, you know! And your father died for it. As did a hundred thousand other good men by his side. And my old friend, Haider's grandfather, died for it, thirty years before them."

"I thought you two had a falling-out . . ."

He collapsed back into the bed, exhausted by his outburst. Even the hollows in his cheeks seemed to sink deeper into his face.

"You think because we disagreed over how to fight the fascists, I didn't know how he died, or for what. Perhaps his courage made me look small; perhaps that is why I bore him a grudge. Have you thought about that? Oh yes, he died for a good cause, for justice in this world . . . they all died for that, long before your Sayyid was born. Did your Sayyid raise so much as his little finger against fascist dictatorship? Never. Did your Sayyid, or for that matter his father, rise to the defense of those who did? Not once. Did they at least say that all those Iraqis before them also died for justice? No, they didn't. Instead they called them heathen-loving atheists, who had to be crushed in the name of God Almighty."

And then his voice picked up strength and he started shouting again. "Where is the justice in that, I ask you? Where? . . . Go on, tell me! I am sick and tired of all the noble things men say they want to die for. Give me reasons to live, not die!"

"Grandfather, please . . . take it easy. Shouting is not good for your health . . . To live . . . I agree with you. That is what it is all about. I live for justice, or at least strive to . . . Is there something wrong with that?"

"Don't! Don't live for justice. That is a stupid thing to do," he said scathingly, but quieting down. "We have been put on this earth to live. Life is a gift with but one purpose in mind, and that is in the living of it."

"But do we not live for a purpose?"

"Live for the light in a lover's eyes and the beauty of a flock of birds in the ebbing light . . . Live for the shape of the crescent moon and the taste of a juicy pomegranate. Justice is but a means to go on living for these things; it is not a substitute for them . . . The moment justice is pursued with the same zest as life, it turns into a monster capable of indescribable cruelties, and therefore itself a crime. God save us from impassioned men burning with zeal to be just! Their justice is a harbinger of death. Never go looking for it, son, because when you look too hard, you will find it in every infraction; why, you will even find it where there is none. That is how things are . . ."

"Should we Shi'a not seek to right the wrongs done to us in the past?"

"How can we? The past is but a camouflage for memories that are forged and reforged in a world that is daily being made anew. The past lives only in our imagination and dreams. What is wrong with you? . . . Look into yourself, son. A fighter in an army that awaits some magical being's descent from the heavens to deliver . . . what? Justice? And the moment it arrives, the moment He makes His appearance, this is supposed to mark the end of the world. What is the point of that kind of Justice if we are to perish at precisely the moment it appears?"

The Awaited One

I joined the Army of the Awaited One in a fever for Justice. I had not been brought up a particularly observant Muslim in Uncle's household, but I became one after I joined.

Our Sheikh taught that Islam was a religion of justice, not love as Christians believed; justice for the poor and the oppressed whom I had marched and cried with on the road to Karbala three years ago; justice for Palestine, which the Jews had snuffed out. Going to the mosque, listening to Friday sermons, fasting and learning to say certain phrases in praise of the Lord, forged a sense of brotherhood among my fellow soldiers. Fighting for Iraq was fighting for justice, as it had been for my father before me. Justice for Iraq meant fighting the foreigners who coveted it, and other Muslim lands, as the Jews had coveted Palestine.

None of this changed because we were now soldiers for Islam in the Army of the Awaited One. Islam was in and of itself justice for Muslims wherever they may be in the world. Nor was I alone in this; all the sons of my neighborhood were like Haider and myself, fired by justice and less observant of ritual and literal readings of the Quran. Growing up in a Holy City has that effect, especially when you have to put up with the idiocy of pilgrims and simple souls from the provinces, who when they joined the Army of the Awaited One did so with very different expectations.

Over the years I mixed with many kinds of comrades in the Army of the Sayyid. I envied someone like Muntassir at first the ordinariness of and simplicity of his world, to which he was still deeply attached. One needs to live in the trivial and the commonplace at times, in the watching of Mother tending to our room, or the fussing of Aunt over what she needed to shop for. That aspect of my life had disappeared after the fall of the Tyrant. But once the war of Iraqi against Iraqi broke out in February 2006, and was heralded as soul-cleansing Justice for us Shi'a, the simple and the ordinary ended, and the fantastical arrived, filling the heads of these same simple souls I had once envied with strange new beliefs that stamped out old-fashioned notions of fighting for justice for Palestine or Iraq, or old-fashioned notions of loyalty to family and country.

"The downfall of the Tyrant is a sign," one such zealous recruit said to me. "The arrival of the Occupier is a sign!"

"Of what?"

"The Coming of the End of Time and the return of the Imam."

"Has He come out of Occultation?"

"Yes."

"Who is He?"

"He has come in the guise of our Sayyid . . . come to deliver Justice. We are His avenging arm; we are His sword and the rock upon which He will stand to establish the reign of Absolute Justice."

"It can't be; he would have told us so."

"It has to be. Why else are the Sunnis blowing up our Shrines and killing our pilgrims? They seek to kill Him. We need to root them out . . . There are more signs . . ."

"Such as?"

"Chaos, suicide bombers . . . why, even the electricity cuts. Our Shi'a dead are piling up in the streets. Sunnis are hiding the Haters of the Family of the Prophet in their neighborhoods and homes . . .

We must root them out . . . The government is more corrupt than Saddam ever was . . . They steal openly. The Great Imposter is coming . . ."

"Who?"

"The Great Imposter, the Antichrist. Our Sayyid's father, Sayyid Sadiq, predicted it."

It was young men, boys really, with thoughts like these in their heads who were the shock troops for the killing done in the summer and fall of 2006. The Sheikh of our neighborhood, the one who had told me about Grandfather's Communist past, counseled me that it is not always wise to reason with such men.

"If you question everything, my son, if you demand a rational explanation for everything, you will drive yourself mad."

"But I must know what I believe in; I must be able to explain it to myself. My whole life has been one of asking questions that I never find answers to."

"Like what?"

"Like knowing the full story behind my father's disappearance. I just found out, for example, that my father was a very good friend of Sayyid Majid's; they were almost brothers, it turns out. That complicates everything all over again. Did you know about their friendship, my Sheikh?"

"Of course I did. Two good men, your father and Sayyid Majid, are now dead. They were friends. What of it? Why torture yourself looking into worlds of darkness that are forever closed to us?"

"I don't know, my Sheikh," I replied, looking at the ground, my eyes beginning to moisten. "I don't know. Perhaps I still live in that darkness and ask questions to find a way past the demons that nightly visit in my dreams."

We were eating in an orchard of palm trees on the outskirts of Najaf. I was trying to bring the turmoil I was feeling under control, and looked up at the tree fronds above so as not to embarrass myself further; the ghostly crescent of the early evening moon was filtering light through them.

"Does our Sayyid believe he is the Awaited One come to bring everlasting Justice to earth?" I blurted out.

"He does not," replied the Sheikh, beginning to sense what was going on. He took the first bite out of the wrap of bread and cheese he had brought with him, and motioned with his eyes for me to do the same.

"Why doesn't he say so loud and clear then?" I asked, relaxing through the act of slowly chewing at the bread and cheese.

"He has to be discreet; in learned circles he refutes the claim of his more enthusiastic supporters."

"He is discreet because of the short term?"

"Yes."

"But isn't that a bit opportunistic?"

"Look at that palm tree above your head. It is not just a tree. It is a symbol of rest and hospitality; God tells us such trees have been privileged to adorn Paradise, and in the next life the Dome of the Rock will stand on a tree just like that one, issuing from one of the rivers of Paradise. The Prophet covered his home with palm fronds, and raised the first mosque as merely a roof placed atop palm trees. See how many meanings are in such a simple thing as a palm tree. Do not underestimate a symbol's power. Symbols are what lead volunteers to join our army in the belief that they will form the vanguard upon which the Imam will rely when he reappears. To electrify the masses, to make their hearts burst with faith, not just understand something through reason, our movement must always return to the power latent in the idea of the Awaited Imam."

"Will we ever achieve our goals?"

"Do not confuse us with the other militias; we are an army of ideas that give structure and moral purpose to the dispossessed. Man's need for general ideas to justify himself and his causes is one of the noblest qualities God has endowed him with."

"So we will never disband?"

"Not until Absolute Justice rules the land; to do otherwise is to admit failure. Our mission is a historical one; it goes beyond the mundane interests of even our own Shi'a selves. It is a divinely commanded mission of purification that must not be soiled by compromises and half measures. The House of Hakim will disband their militia once they have merged with the state's security apparatus. But not us. Never us. We await the Rightly Guided One; we are His soldiers, no one else's. It is a beautiful thing if you dwell on it."

"Still, you say . . . there is politics?"

"Always there is politics. But we are uncompromising when it comes to resistance to injustice, as was our beloved Imam Hussein."

"So wherein lies the politics?"

"In winning, pure and simple. Your uncle is the master of that. You want to win, right?"

"Of course . . . but I did not think power for its own sake was a cherished value of ours."

"It is not; Absolute Justice is. And winning is."

"And what are the long-term dangers in believing the Sayyid is divine?"

"Consider what would happen if, God forbid, the Sayyid were to die, which you and I know he must one day. The simpleminded among his supporters will be devastated; they won't be able to accept it. We face a huge problem because our supporters lack education. That is where the handful of exceptional men like you come into the picture."

"You honor me too much, my Sheikh. I think I see your point, but—"

"What is the source of your Sayyid's strength, my son?" he interrupted. And then he went on to answer his own question.

"The idea of the Imam's return, His Coming, holds the promise of the people's revenge against the rich and the unjust; it is the earthly promise the Awaited One makes to the dispossessed. Through Him they will be redeemed. Even though our Sayyid is not the actual Imam, he is nonetheless the herald of His reemergence."

"Have we not returned to where we started from?"

"Not if you think with your heart, my son. Let your head rest."

"You said revenge . . . I thought we were speaking of justice?"

"You cannot, alas, have the one without the other."

Names of Things

Although we were the first militia to appear after the Tyrant's fall, many armed groups followed us. So many, I took to keeping a notebook to track all the names, at first because it was in the nature of my work to know what was going on—Uncle expected it—but later because my own curiosity propelled me to understand what was happening.

I begin for no good reason with my own Army of the Awaited One, known by some of our detractors as the Pink Army, because of the pink pills, said to be amphetamines, steadily supplied by Iran to our soldiers since 2006. Splinter groups from our army have gone on to operate independently. Most important among these is the Party of Virtue, a Basra-based group whose members claim to have no links with Iran or any of the formerly exiled opposition groups. Also one must include the Army of the Chosen One, about which I know very little; a women's organization known as Daughters of Grace, which owes allegiance, or so they claim, to the House of Sadr; and the League of Truth, which is almost totally Iranian funded and trained (the salaries of their fighters are consistently higher than ours).

The Soldiers of Heaven were a group convinced the End of the World was imminent; it may or may not be deemed a splinter group from our Sadrist movement, but that is moot today, as the whole organization was wiped out in air strikes conducted by the American army in coordination with units of the New Iraqi Army on the ground shortly after the Tyrant was hanged in 2006. A great mystery surrounds this operation, but it later transpired that the Americans were acting on false information supplied by the House of Hakim. Uncle believed the villain was Abu Haider; he had fabricated a claim, backed by his friend the governor of Najaf, a man also from the House of Hakim, that the Soldiers of Heaven were a Shiʻa offshoot of al-Qaeda; and the credulous Americans believed him, even though everyone else in Najaf knew this was nonsense. Why the Occupier did not know these things, and was so wasteful of his own military resources, is a mystery known only to God. Mercifully, Haider, who was in the habit of relaxing and unwinding in their company, was not visiting the camp at the time of the air strikes. Several hundred harmless innocents were killed in a matter of hours—men, women, and children. Afterward, everyone—the Americans, the House of Hakim, and the government—colluded to cover up the outrage. Only Abu Haider was pleased, having finally gotten his revenge for the murder of Najmaldin.

In working up the list, I started with the following distinctions: Shiʻi or Sunni; Islamic or Patriotic; Arab or Iraqi or Kurdish; Political or Criminal. But that was too general to be useful. So I added ideological criteria for classification, using known or knowable political inclinations based on proclamations and public statements. That was also unsatisfactory. In yet a third system of classification, I tried to organize armed groups by type of operation: car bombing, armed attack, secret assassinations, personal vendetta, suicide bombing, and so forth. In a fourth I used targets: attacks on a street, in a mosque, in a hospital or public building; attacks on pilgrims versus those on employees, or officials (including police), and so on.

For all of these lists, irrespective of how they were classified, I discovered I needed a column for the completely random violent event, about which no reasonable inference from place or purpose, stated or unstated, could be made. Often nothing about such incidents could be correlated to intent. Once I realized that "random" and "unknown" and "unidentified" and "miscellaneous" were outstripping in numbers all the other categories, I gave up altogether trying to classify the armed groups waging violent operations in the land.

To continue with the list of names: two small organizations about which very little is known are the Movement of God's Revenge and the Party of God–Iraq Branch (more than one organization with such a name exists in southern Iraq, not to be confused with the Lebanese organization that carries the same name).

Then there is the oldest Shi'a armed group in Iraq, which emerged like ourselves and the Party of Virtue from the House of Sadr, and has provided two prime ministers since 2003: the Party of the Call, by which is meant the Call to True Shi'a Belief. The Party of the Call is not one group but many, all claiming the same name, as the old guard and collective leadership were shunted aside once the party took office in 2005 and a new Party of the Call, based on government patronage and largesse dominated by the prime minister, came into being (itself possibly two or three organizations, all sharing that name). The oldest militia belonging to the original Party of the Call is the Forces of the Martyr Sadr. I have often wondered if the rapidity with which the Tyrant had to be hung in December did not have something to do with the fallout inside the Party of the Call at the time, with the prime minister's faction seeking to gain credibility for itself because it executed Saddam Hussein. God alone knows.

Aside from the policing and military institutions of the state, which the Party of the Call in government controls, it is in the process of forming many separate well-funded militias, each linked to the prime minister, and operating clandestinely. These are known to run secret prisons and torture centers.

The Supreme Council for Islamic Revolution in Iraq was formed in 1982 in Tehran to extend the Iranian Revolution into Iraq. The House of Hakim founded it, in contrast with the previous Shi'a militias, all of which in one way or another pay allegiance to the House of Sadr. Later the Council changed its name to the Islamic Council, removing both "Supreme" and "Revolution" in order to show its democratic nature (no longer "Supreme") and to distance itself from Iran (no longer promoting a "Revolution"); it is not an easy thing to change people's perceptions by changing one's name, but a necessary one in Iraq, given how unpopular the Iranian connection makes anyone who tries to flaunt it. In 2005, the Supreme Council for Islamic Revolution in Iraq nominally agreed to demobilize its armed militia and turn it into an "Organization for Development and Reconstruction," but no one took that very seriously, not even the Occupier, whom they were trying to make happy with all these name changes.

The Brigades of the Full Moon are an independent and formidable militia controlled by the House of Hakim. Abu Haider served as one of its senior commanders. This is the militia that killed Muntassir in 2003, when our Sayyid tried to wrest control of the Shrine in Karbala from them, and that provided the Occupation forces with false information that led to the decimation of their fellow Shi'a organization the Soldiers of Heaven. The Brigades fought the Iraqi Army during the Iraq-Iran War, and may very well have been on the wrong side of the front lines in Fao while my father was defending his country against Iranian aggression; they have a reputation, unproven as far as I know, of having executed Iraqi prisoners of war who did not transfer their allegiance to them after having surrendered. After 2003 the Brigades of the Full Moon specialized in carrying out revenge killings against Ba'this, former regime officials and army officers, taking care to never fire a single shot at the forces of the Occupier.

I must not forget two special cases of fully Iranian-operated militias: the first is the Iraqi extension of the Party of God in Lebanon, headed by Sheikh Nasrallah and funded by Iran. The second is the militia known as the Jerusalem Force: technically it is an extension of the Iranian Revolutionary Guard specializing in overseas operations and working semi-clandestinely inside Iraq, in close cooperation with the Brigades of the Full Moon; in practice, however, it functions on the ground as its own much-feared militia, recruiting fighters and conducting operations as though it were an all-Iraqi organization. It is also in the business of training a whole host of smaller Shi'a militias, approved, funded, and run from Tehran. Starting in 2004 the Jerusalem Force started flooding the country with lethal roadside bombs; these fire a molten copper slug able to penetrate American armor, and wreaked havoc on the Occupier.

Turning now to the Sunni militias, I begin with the Council of Iraqi Religious Scholars, which is run by a former Ba'thi, Harith al-Dharri. They claim not to have a militia, their name chosen to convey academic overtones, but I saw several hundred heavily armed men patrolling the Mother of All Villages Mosque (formerly Mother of All Battles Mosque) when I visited it with Uncle in June 2003. Moreover, they are the only so-to-speak meta-Sunni organization, providing ideological guidance to all and sundry fighting the Occupier or its puppet government. The Base-Iraq was run by a Jordanian, Mus'ab al-Zarqawi, until the Americans killed him in 2006. Now someone runs it under a different name from the city of Samarra in Iraq.

Lesser known but equally deadly Sunni militias go under the names the Army of Muhammad; the United Islamic Front for the Liberation of Iraq; the Victorious Ones; the Front of the Victorious Ones; the Army of the Men of the Naqshabandi Way (a Sufi-based order run nowadays by Izzat al-Douri, the former Iraqi vice president under Saddam); the Soldiers of Islam; the Islamic Army in Iraq; the Islamic State for Iraq and Syria, otherwise known by the acronym ISIS; Partisans of Islamic Law; the Islamic Party; the High One; the Army of the Tribes; the Army of Pride and Dignity; the Soldiers of the Companions of the Prophet (whose claim to fame was blowing up a Shi'i mosque in Saydiyya); the Council of Jihadis; the Islamic

Emirate of Iraq; the Supporters of Islam; the Soldiers of God; the Army of Abu Bakr (the first Caliph of Islam, who ruled after the death of the Prophet); the Lions of al-Baraʻa Son of Malik Suicide Brigade; the Thunder Brigades; Supporters of the People of the Sunna; the Islamic Unity Brigade of the Sword of Truth; the Supporters of Suicide Brigade; the Mother of Believers Brigade; the Islamic Rage Brigade; the Umar Son of Khattab Brigade; the Muslim Youth Brigade; the Assassination Brigade of Supporters of the Sunna; the Lions for Islamic Unity. I have excluded the remnants of the Baʻth Party, like the Martyrs of Saddam, due to their growing insignificance or transformation into organizations with other names, some of which I have identified.

Often organizations from both sects have multiple brigades attached to them, which go under different names. Sometimes a given brigade will change its name, say, when an operation goes wrong and the brigade does not want to acknowledge responsibility for it. I have excluded these duplicates, but I can no more claim perfect accuracy than I can count the blades of grass in a field.

Many armed groups exist, or existed at some point in time, about whom I know nothing except their names: the Trustees of the Awakening, the Sons of Islam, the Supporters of Jihad in Iraq, the Supporters of the Sunna, the Supporters of Ibn Taymiyya, the Organization of Unity and Jihad, the Forces of His Truth Set Forth, the Brigades of His Just Retribution, the Party of Enthusiasm for God.

This list is incomplete. There are other groups about which I know nothing, not even their names.

The Importance of Being Umar

A good man I befriended in Baghdad in 2006 was named Umar—a name hated by the Shi'a—even though his father was named 'Ali and his uncle Abbas, both names venerated by us Shi'a. This was the cause of many problems. His father and uncle had no trouble walking the streets of Baghdad that we controlled in 2006, but poor Umar was kept at home out of fear that he would be killed simply because of his name. In other words, Umar was apparently not who he really was; it was who he was mistaken for being. When a soldier in our army saw this name, Umar, say on a random inspection at one of the hundreds of checkpoints we set up across Baghdad, a real human being was not there; certainly not my friend. Only his name, which belonged originally to the Second Caliph after the Prophet, God Bless His Name, whom this soldier's Sheikh had taught him to hate and curse as many times as he could in a day, for the higher the number of times he cursed the name Umar, the greater blessings there were to be found.

And so it seems that once a name has fixed itself in our minds, every other thing or person that bears the name, no matter how beautiful and God-fearing, is seen as conforming to the original type. There is no justice in this, as is attested by the case of poor

Umar, who would have holes drilled into him were he to be caught at one of our checkpoints, or showered with endless cups of tea if he were inspected at one of theirs; all this is simply a testament to the importance of how things are named.

When I first joined the Army of the Awaited One, I paid no attention to our name, much less anyone else's. I said dismissively, "It's just a name! What is in a name anyway?" Following my discussion with the Sheikh about our army, and observing how some of our members read our name as a sign of the Coming of the End of Time, I started to think more carefully about names. What did they mean? Was a name a clue pointing to the nature of a thing, or merely an unimportant symbol or label accidentally or whimsically attached to it?

I remember, as a child, picturing a person by his or her name. The attributes of that person thus became attached to the name. Saddam, for instance, means the one who confronts, who smashes up obstacles. I was often struck by how well the Great Tyrant fitted the name bestowed on him at birth. Surely no father knows the kind of a son he will beget. How then did the inner core of the Tyrant's personality come to fit his sign, his name from birth, so perfectly? This was a source of great wonder and mystery to me growing up. And so, if another infant of my father's generation were to be called Saddam, I would be hard-pressed not to see in him the cold-blooded killer Saddam was.

A name, the good Sheikh of our neighborhood taught us, is a sign conveying knowledge of that which the name denotes; it is intended as a mark of distinction. So it troubled me that according to my notebook, there were 268 separate armed organizations operating in post-Saddam Iraq between 2003 and 2006. And all carried the name of the Lord, of which He has 99, or of His Prophet and His Companions. And these 268 names accounted among them for an average of 106 violent attacks a day in 2005, according to my calculations.

The good Sheikh would go on to say that past, present, and future are all contained within a name; the name may denote something existent, like religion, or nonexistent, like Justice in our world. When men swear or give an oath according to the saying "in the name of He whose name is in every chapter of the Holy Book," it is because the name of the Lord, and His Prophet, or the name of the much-awaited Rightly Guided One, cannot be repeated often enough and is always filled with beauty, loveliness, and all good things, especially Holiness.

But, I said to myself after I did all my research, this cannot be true of men or organizations that take His name in vain, not just once or twice but over and over again. To inflate and multiply His name, and then maim and kill in His name, has to be a form of blasphemy. Because, our Sheikh said, there always remains a tiny little essence of a thing in its name, perhaps worn thin by time, like the paper-thin vestiges of a memory, so thin at times as to justify the thought that nothing was there—except the name. The mistake these inflators and multipliers of God's name make is to forget there is always something left behind. Taken in vain and repeated in minute variations across the length and breadth of the land, a name necessarily has its connection to that original essence diluted to the point of denial of the very Sublime whom the name is trying to evoke. God, who does not cease to exist if men lose their faith in Him, nonetheless is rejected many times over when men do terrible things in His name, or take in vain the names of His Messengers. Not only, therefore, is the name of a thing important, but its inflation is also a debasement of the Lord Himself.

I presented Uncle with a report of my findings of 268 independently run armed militias operating in post-Saddam Iraq between 2003 and 2006. I accompanied it with many other statistics concerning casualties, armed operations in different districts, collapse of services in Baghdad, and plummeting electricity levels. He corrected and modified a few names here and there and reviewed my methodology, but by and large I could see he was as pleased with my work as he was taken aback at the results.

He then got up from his desk and sat me down on a sofa beside him. There was a bowl of pomegranates in front of us on a coffee table with small plates and a knife. They had come from the tree in our house, he said, picking the reddest and juiciest one he could find, and handing it to me. I cut the sphere in half as my mother had taught me, and then scored the two halves so that I could break it up into manageable pieces. He took one and motioned to me to do the same. Eating a pomegranate is normally a messy business, but not if you are as practiced at it as we all were in Uncle's household. The art is to pick the seeds out of the segment using teeth and tongue, while using your hand to roll the segment from side to side; a matter of hand, eye, teeth, and tongue coordination; Uncle loved eating them that way.

"Excellent work, son . . . excellent. You know, I don't get to see you much these days. We must change that. How is Haider?"

"I can't find him; he is lost in the throes of the war in Baghdad."

"Perhaps he does not want you to find him?"

"I think you are right. I never told you, Uncle, that he did in fact kill Najmaldin. I apologize for not saying so before. He has been avoiding me ever since the meeting with his father."

"I guessed as much. When you do run him down, talk to him; he is becoming too fond of this killing business."

"Certainly. Uncle, can you tell me what you conclude from my findings? They trouble me."

"As they should. You can live with guns and bombs and murder and mayhem . . . Things are bound to get better, you say to yourself. But this, the horror of it . . . ," he said, shuddering and pointing to the sheaf of papers that I had put down before him.

"What does it all mean, Uncle?"

"The end of Iraq, son . . . at least as you and I have known it."

"No! I don't believe it."

"Once Saddam went, Iraq changed. You changed, the Sayyid changed, why, even I changed."

"How . . . changed?"

"Ours is a new world where everyone wants to rule but no one is strong enough to do so."

"Everyone will then want to keep on fighting."

"Exactly, and whoever is left will be king of the ruins. No country to speak of. Only dead people."

"Dead Shi'a or Sunnis?"

"The dead have no sect."

"Is Iraq that fragile?"

"Iraq is just a name, son, no longer even an idea, much less a nation. A name . . . one more to add to the two hundred sixty-eight other names you have just given me. Would that I could say otherwise, but I cannot; I would be wrong. Perhaps its fragility is why it never ceased to require the presence of a strongman to arbitrate between its different factions. But now even the name is fast disappearing. Notice not one of the organizations on your list confers allegiance to something called Iraq. That was never the case in the past."

He was pointing to the many sheets of names scattered on the table before him, and then he looked up at me. "Your heart must now catch up with what your head has uncovered," he said. "We all must now unlearn what we thought we understood but perhaps never did."

"You are speaking in riddles, Uncle. I don't understand."

"To every idea that we adopt, there is a corresponding reality, which explains the hold that that idea has managed to exercise over our imagination. This reality is necessarily of a piece with the idea. Iraq is such an idea. On the eve of the Tyrant's fall the idea was still alive, barely so, but still breathing in spite of the abuse it suffered from being represented by the Tyrant for so long. Think of Iraq, the idea implicit in the name, I mean . . . think of it as a basket of snakes, lifting the lid of which runs the risk of releasing deadly venom into a room full of people. That was the state of the idea on the eve of his fall. And yet still it was there, as a basket, with a lid on it, and in theory at least one could manage those snakes artfully, so as to orchestrate their return into the basket."

"Not their destruction . . . but their return to the basket."

"Those snakes are who we are, son. You, me, and all those people in two hundred sixty-eight militias out there," he said with a wave of his hand in the general direction of the outdoors. "Ours has always been the culture of the tomb and the cleansing of the dead and the concealment of women. Politics was the art of returning us to the fold, to the basket, a good thing. What actually transpired, and what your research has underlined, was our rejection of the basket. We have thrown it away . . . ," he said in an exasperated and tired tone of voice, "torn it to shreds."

"And Iraq?"

"It has turned into a question for itself."

Abu Muntassir

H ad the man said "Abu Ahmed," I would have paid no attention. But he yelled, "Abu Muntassir, more tea! Hurry up!"

I had been summoned to report to our army's central headquarters building in eastern Baghdad. We were a group of about a dozen or so experienced comrades, skilled in different things, milling about in an anteroom adjoining the interview room, where high-ranking officers of our army were selecting candidates to serve on the detail that would guard the Tyrant following his transfer into Iraqi custody. Abu Muntassir's job was the lowliest imaginable, making tea, gallons of it, which he both brewed and served, shuffling back and forth between his kettles and the officers shouting at him.

Muntassir, Victorious, is a unique name among us Shi'a, especially after the fall of the Tyrant, because it could be taken to simply mean what it says, or, in the case of Muntassir's father, it could be taken to be an identification with the goals of the eight-year-long war against Iran, which we had all been happy to identify with under the Tyrant. Things had now changed, and the name Muntassir, like Umar, was a liability, not only because there were Iranian agents everywhere, but also because some of our own could turn nasty at the idea that Iraq had triumphed over an Islamic Republic of the Shi'a.

I turned to the tea maker and asked if he used to have a soft drinks stand on the Karbala-Najaf road, and a son a few years older than myself. He confirmed both things, delighted that someone would know who he was, and added that his son had been killed in 2003. I told him that not only was Muntassir my friend but I was with him when he died. We embraced warmly, tears welling up in his eyes.

When we separated, still holding each other by the shoulders, he lifted a heavily lined and pockmarked face, pain-filled and unashamedly ignorant, the face of human goodness, I thought, now all lit up by his smile and sparkling eyes glistening with tears at meeting a friend of his son's. I asked him what he was doing here and when he had joined our army. He replied that he had done so shortly after the death of his son nearly two years ago.

"Why?" I asked, astounded that a man so advanced in years would even consider, much less be accepted for, membership. "To avenge the spilled blood of my son," he answered, referring, of course, to the House of Hakim, whose men had repulsed our ill-advised assault on their headquarters in the Shrine in Karbala, leading to the death of Muntassir.

We talked about Muntassir, how he died—I hid the worst of it—the great admiration he had for his father, the black boots that he treasured—and, yes, he did show up at the recruiting office wearing them—his patriotism, his spirit of sacrifice, the consideration he would show toward others, especially his comrades in arms; above all we talked of his love of Iraq, something I soon gathered Muntassir absorbed from his father; it was not an abstract, theoretical kind of love, but one that attached itself to a particular street here, the grocer's shop there, his neighborhood, and even the marshes region in the south, which the Tyrant had drained. He talked about the plants Muntassir grew up with, down to the palm grove a short walk away from their old house (now reduced to rubble), and the animals—Muntassir kept a dog, which his father had to hide from the neighbors because they considered dogs unclean. Then it dawned upon me that I needed to give Abu Muntassir the black boots his son had bequeathed to me. I would be returning them to their original owner, to remember his son by. Of course he would not accept at first, saying his son's wishes were that they pass on to me, anyway he was long past fighting age, and did I know they had always been uncomfortable, causing foot sores . . . all excuses, because I could see that he was delighted by the idea.

I insisted that Muntassir had given me the boots not as a gift but as a matter of trust—a lie, but a harmless one—that he had specifically asked me to give them to his father should our paths cross, that anyway my work had turned me into a kind of nomad who could not afford to travel with excess baggage of any kind, my life having become one of hopping from city to city, and from house to house, and that under these complicated circumstances he would in fact be doing me a favor by accepting the boots, which would in turn fulfill my obligation to his son.

After that, he could only thank me, promising that he would let his sister and her family and the Sheikh of his local mosque know, and that it was his and his son's wish that the boots be returned to me upon his passing away. I thanked him, and said I felt doubly honored, first by his son for giving me the boots, and now by him for willing them back to me.

My interview with the selection committee over—it settled my assignment to Saddam's personal guard detail—I asked Abu Muntassir to wait while I bolted off to my lodgings to collect the boots and dash back; he was there waiting for me when I returned, seated now on the concrete steps leading into the decrepit concrete-block building that served as our offices in Sadr City, the interviewing having finished and all work for the day ended.

A few weeks later, I thought I would surprise Abu Muntassir at work. I was in the neighborhood, under no obligation to anyone; it just seemed like a nice thing to do. But he was not there. A barefooted young lad in torn and filthy trousers was making the tea instead, using the same kettles and teacups Abu Muntassir had been using.

I asked after Abu Muntassir, and was told he had gone for a drive two Fridays ago in a twenty-year-old Czech Skoda with his sister and her two small girls; they went for the day to Najaf to pray in the Shrine of the Imam and then picnic with the children in the courtyard. On the way back he ran into a U.S. Army checkpoint. In broad daylight, sunlight glinting off the windshield of their car, he must not have seen the checkpoint soon enough, or more than likely he did not understand—no one did—the system of hand signals and flashing lights invented by the Occupier to order Iraqi vehicles to pull over. The soldiers, marines from Texas younger than myself, opened fire with heavy machine guns, convinced they were being attacked by a suicide bomber (the state of the ancient vehicle did not help matters, old cars being more expendable for suicide bombers than new). The Skoda, which by itself was a death trap, lurched off to the side, hit a concrete barrier, and burst instantly into a ball of fire. The identities of the bodies were tracked down from the car's number plate. An American force of several Humvees duly showed up at Abu Muntassir's sister's house to offer condolences, and a wad of dollars in cash, which, to our shame, the husband of Abu Muntassir's sister accepted.

Haider

In the end it was Haider who sought me out. In three years, he had aged unnaturally; you could see it in the lines on his face.

He fell upon me, hugging and kissing both cheeks. I reciprocated, tears welling, until several minutes later we found ourselves with arms outstretched, holding one another firmly by the shoulders. I said, "God, how I have missed you. Where have you been? Why were you avoiding me?"

He looked at me softly, the aging falling away just for a moment, and said, "I couldn't . . . see you, I mean."

"Couldn't see me? My dear Haider, not me . . . We have walked through fire together."

"I know, my friend, I know. That is why I felt so guilty, you standing up for me the way you did at that wretched meeting . . . May God cast that man's soul into the everlasting fire."

He couldn't even bring himself to name his father. "But of course I would," I said; "what did you think . . ."

"I knew what you would do. That is not it. I was . . . how can I say it . . . ashamed of your judgment, unspoken no doubt. We know one another only too well," he said with a small laugh.

The tears ran down my cheeks, and I put my arms around him, as sorry at that moment for the man I was as he.

Later that evening, after a heavy meal in a kebab kiosk near his house, we turned to politics. I mentioned the cleansing of Sunni neighborhoods that was going on in Baghdad, and the "disgraceful gossip" surrounding his name, which, I said, I did my utmost to repudiate at every opportunity.

"What gossip are you referring to?" he asked me.

"People are exchanging stories about you terrorizing neighborhoods and torturing Sunni prisoners with an electric drill."

I didn't get the angry dismissal of the rumor that I expected.

"I make no apologies, and you shouldn't either, my friend, not on my behalf. The public good demands from us terrible things."

"Haider, I don't understand . . . these are fellow Iraqis we are talking about! Most of them are innocent of the bombings and killings being done in their name."

"The days of lamentation and breast beating have gone. Our innocence is gone. We Shi'a are too often short of steel to stiffen our resolve. But the circumstances are changing us.

"We are Shi'a now, first and foremost!" he said, raising his voice. "Then Iraqi, and only after that Arab! All is the politics of life and death now . . . We must act, as our enemies have always acted, with warlike fervor and force. The struggle over who is to rule is a bloody one. There are no two ways about it. Two communities are at war with one another. The choice not to take sides, to shed crocodile tears over the resort to violence, *is* today the unethical choice; dare I even say it, the seditious choice. Would you have us make a pact with the powers of darkness?"

"But we will lose such a fight, my dear friend," I said loudly, throwing my hands in the air. "Everyone will lose . . . There has to be a plan, a moral underpinning that rules our actions. Surely there are laws to which we are not indifferent . . . There is a constitution, which—"

"Which means nothing," he interrupted equally vigorously, "mere paper and words, if the very core of who you are is under attack. When we joined the Sayyid's army, we washed our hands of those laws you talk about. We obey a higher law now. Anyway, if there are laws and a constitution, where is the state to uphold them? Do laws not require violence to uphold? If there is no state, what are we to do . . . Say it . . . Why do you hesitate? . . . I will say it for you: take the law into our own hands, carry out the violence ourselves, in self-defense if you prefer to put it that way."

"Are you saying we can do anything we want, and conversely, that anything that is done to us is equally legitimate? What will bring it all to an end? Violence never put an end to itself."

"Not for nothing did our Sayyid call us the Army of the Awaited One. We are soldiers with a mission. Our mission is guided by the idea of the Return of the Imam; His realm is Justice. The signs of His Coming are everywhere. Whatever we do under such circumstances entails risk. But risk does not mean we should hesitate, and prevaricate, in the fear that violence might lead to excesses on our part. I embrace gladly the risk that violence entails, and accept the judgment and legitimacy for my actions that only violence can deliver."

"You are saying that violence by itself can succeed in resolving what is good and right."

"The question is not what is good and right—I take it you and I have no disagreement on that—but whether my kind of violence is capable of resolving to our favor the life-and-death struggle now raging in this land. To that question, I do not yet have an answer. Time will tell. But I do know that my actions today, and yours, will decide tomorrow. The Shi'a are remaking who they are through struggle. To win is to be reborn free, rid of the centuries of servility that hung around our necks like a millstone; we are on the cusp of standing proud of who we are, no longer wailing and beating our chests like old women at a funeral. At times such as these, good men like you carry little weight, my dear friend. Only deeds and the relationship of forces on the ground count."

"Listen to you speak, Haider! Violence takes away as much as it creates, and what it creates is sometimes worse than what is lost; it breeds monsters; it doesn't make heroes." I was raising my voice now, and in the back of my mind I could feel Grandfather listening. "You speak of resolving matters in our favor. Who is this 'our' you talk about? We will end up like the snake that eats its own tail. How can you win against the other half of your own self? Did we not fight side by side with Sunnis, when we fought against the Occupier in Najaf two years ago? Did they not stand by us then?"

"That was then, when we had hatred of the Occupier in common. Now we need to be reborn as Shi'a, my friend," Haider replied, lowering his voice but not softening its intent, "if we are to live as Iraqis tomorrow. With the fall of the Tyrant, and the withdrawal of the Occupier, we Shi'a discovered the meaning of our presence on this earth, and the direction we must take to fulfill the promise implicit in the Return of the Imam. Our fight is to realize that meaning; it has less and less to do with the Occupier; necessarily, it is a fight among Iraqis, started by our enemies, haters of the Shi'a; we have no choice but to pursue it to the bitter end. We do not have the luxury to be squeamish or make errors and experiment with talk and diplomacy. Victory will turn our audacity into a new and just order. Then, when it is all ended, I promise you, my friend, you will find me pushing myself to the front of the line, to stand before Him, and be judged for the terror I waged in His name."

There was no moving him. His words were cast in cement. Gone were the questions and uncertainties previously entertained, as when he met that crazy preacher who had carried the ideas of Sayyid Sadiq to such ridiculous extremes.

"So tell me, my friend, you sought me out; you know me; you must have known the things I would say . . . What is it you want of me?"

"I missed you . . . I need you."

Haider and Muntassir

I need you," he had said. The tears come to my eyes when I remember those three words. I longed to be there for him, but another part of me realized that to wean him of impulses grown so outsized was nigh on impossible. Where had they come from, these demons that had wreaked such damage upon my friend? Were they in his head in the shape of new ideas, or in the act of killing over and over again? War not only kills, I thought, lying in bed; it is disfiguring. Haider had not just aged; he had gone to seed. I could see it in his eyes; they had turned cold and forbidding. The conflict with his father had something to do with it. He had been devastated by his role in the slaughter of his friends in the orchard. He had healed by turning hard on the outside, while remaining a man at war with himself on the inside. Candor was his saving grace. If he had turned into a cauldron of turbulent emotions, he had the presence of mind to know that he too had betrayed. His betrayal had exiled him, leaving him with a hole in the place where his heart had been. It was not entirely his father's fault that Najmaldin had accompanied him back to Iraq. Nor was it so outrageous that Abu Haider had married another woman during his years of exile in Tehran. Had not his father tried to reach out to him when he first came back? And had not the son punished the father by joining "the enemy," so to speak, our army, a huge embarrassment for a Brigades Commander of the House of Hakim?

Betrayal brooks little interrogation to he who lives with it. What better way of living with it than to continue to do what you do best—be a warrior, in Haider's case—and do it with a tremendous excess of zeal, focusing like a laser beam on the task at hand, never considering that the future will be forever altered because of it. With zeal in killing as a line of work is bound to come a measure of success, the measure being how much territory one has captured, or how well cleansed a particular neighborhood has become of its former inhabitants, not to mention your continuing to hold that territory and setting up a whole variety of "protection" rackets (on movement, goods, security) to keep your men and your immediate superiors happy, their palms well greased.

But this kind of success came at a price: Haider had turned arrogant, quick to take offense, often at a wholly imagined slight, like the time he knocked one of his men down to the floor in front of me for not giving the proper salute, when it was clear that the poor soldier had not even realized Haider was in the room. Haider was becoming someone for whom the differences between flattery and the truth were impossible to pin down. He could no longer hold friendships, much less make new ones; at least he tried to make an exception in my case.

I could not help but compare Haider with Muntassir. Both were made of the stuff that the Tyrant had left behind; they carried in their hearts that same exaggerated legacy of pain and idealized victimhood; not to mention they were both soldiers of the army that was now focused on doing the exaggerating: my very own Army of the Awaited One.

We were all young Iraqi males who embarked upon our journey to the new world with no occupation other than to become followers of our Sayyid, he who hated the sport Haider excelled in: football. Why did our leader hate such things? Because his father, Sayyid

Sadiq, consumed with fury at the Houses of Hakim and Khoei, had so decreed. No other reason.

Haider had survived because he knew how to adapt to every twist and turn of his rapidly changing times. His soul paid the price for it, not by dying but by living; it was the cost of living in dark times. Muntassir, by contrast, the Victorious One, died horribly, writhing in pain, and yet fundamentally at peace with himself, the same predictable and sociable soul that he had always been. An all-around "good man" who could live on dreams, Mother would have said, something Haider was incapable of. Muntassir's strength lay in his character, his moral nature, you might say, and not in how quick he was to grasp the relativity and transience of all things.

No doubt I exaggerate Muntassir's virtues, seeing in him a lost ideal of an equally lost world that perhaps even never existed. It doesn't matter. Muntassir is what I needed him to be.

Muntassir would never have survived the new Iraq even if he had emerged unscathed from the assault on the Shrine in Karbala. Something else would have felled him. His nature was mysteriously at odds with his times. Between the death of the one and the meteoric rise of the other lay the distance a whole generation of young men had traveled since the fall of the Tyrant.

Haider, now a true solitary, insisted I move into his house in Baghdad. He would not take no for an answer. I began to feel he was forcing me upon himself, perhaps throwing himself a lifeline because he sensed he was drowning. He had no one left who loved him except his mother, and she was out of reach in Najaf, a city too dangerous for him to be seen in. In those days I still thought I could help him. But I was wrong.

The house that was our home for the next three months, until the day after the hanging, when I collected my stuff and left without even saying goodbye, had been "liberated" from a former officer of Saddam Hussein's secret police. Or so Haider said. They must have lived like pigs. Its front door opened onto an alley with an open gutter for sewage running down the middle of it. But the slant of the concrete trough was too slight. The sewage wouldn't move along unless you hosed it downstream, pushing it along to the next group of houses at least twice a day. Otherwise the stench was too unbearable. That passed for the municipal system of waste disposal in my neighborhood, and I daresay it is still like that today.

Directly above the gutter, and bridging the two sides of the alley, was a tangle a meter deep of electrical wires sagging dangerously in the middle directly over the flowing sewage. Everyone was of course pilfering his electricity from someone else; it was impossible for even the most skilled electrician to tell who was stealing from whom and who was paying for what. Not that it made much difference when you had less than two and a half hours of electricity a day, compared with five times that in the days of the Tyrant. Haider had installed a generator to make up the difference, the fuel of which was "donated" as alms to "the Sayyid" by the petrol station two streets over.

My private room, which overlooked the alley and its tangle of wires, had two large dead cockroaches on the floor when I first moved in, and one flitting about when I flipped back the covers on the mattress. Haider chose, for "security reasons," to sleep in a room toward the rear of the house, close to the outdoor toilet, which spewed a smell so foul that no amount of disinfectant could dispel it. In Baghdad, he had become, it seemed, much more acquainted with the seamy side of life than he had been in Najaf. At night, when I wanted to wash my face before going to bed, more often than not the tap wouldn't run, because, Haider pointed out in a rare flash of humor, there was not enough water to go around in Mesopotamia, the land of the Tigris and the Euphrates, the two greatest rivers of antiquity.

Upstairs, through Haider's room, was the armory, which he kept padlocked, the key always hanging on a chain around his neck. It contained a dozen light automatic rifles, mostly Kalashnikovs; three wooden crates of hand grenades; a rocket launcher with a two-case supply of rockets; and a heavy-duty machine gun fitted out for rapid assembly on a pickup truck and designed for service by a crew of three. But there, in pride of place, centered on the white wall facing the door, hung his Dragunov sniper rifle, which he had operated, and I had spotted for, during the Battle of Najaf in 2004. The room, like a polished idol, stood apart from the rest of the house; it was spotlessly clean and free of dust, the weapons gleaming and well oiled, all neatly arranged in purpose-built racks on the walls.

Baghdad

There were no children on the streets in the fall and winter of 2006, when I moved into Haider's house; there would have been trees, but they had been cut down during real estate booms that eliminated the city's parks and gardens of once beautiful upper-middle-class homes. You told the seasons apart by the temperature—whether or not it was possible to fry an egg on the car's hood—or by the kinds of fruits and vegetables found in shops, because there were no more orchards. The prices of everything, not just real estate, rose and fell precipitously, always rising higher than they had fallen, and they did so to the drumbeat of the violence to which the city was being subjected.

The Baghdad I finally settled into was a city of ordinary people turned even more ordinary because they were so afraid; ordinary people scurrying about in despair to get away from streets and public places; ordinary people suspicious of or indifferent to one another, wanting only to burrow themselves in their houses like moles going to ground; it was as if the city was in the early stages of being stricken by a mysterious plague: frightened, but not yet in total panic, a city of barely controlled chaos threatening to implode.

Gone was the desire to stand out and be different, to dress well and look handsome, to see and be seen at a restaurant. Gone was the desire to linger and stare, to window-shop and stroll, or to just sit in a café doing nothing but gaze . . . and be gazed at in return.

By the time I arrived in Baghdad, it had been broken up and radically segmented. Blast walls of concrete meant to keep bombers at bay, decorated at checkpoints with plastic flowers, made an appearance—the Occupier's contribution to urban decor. Did the vast stretches of slums, the piles of uncollected garbage, the broken-down sewage and water delivery systems, the wretched street facades garishly painted in a newly discovered maintenance-free Chinese aluminum paint, did all of these things sit on top of the Caliph Haroun al-Rashid's fabled city of antiquity? I wondered. Perhaps there was an underground city I was not aware of. Haider, a king astride the apathy that had leveled everyone else down, took it upon himself to dispel my misgivings by driving me around to show off the sights.

"Here are the Ceremonial Parade Grounds," he would say; "there is the Unknown Soldier monument"; and then, when I asked him what was left of the architectural wonder of the perfectly symmetrical round city that Abu Ja'far al-Mansur had founded in the eighth century, he took me to a roundabout and said, "See over there . . . that is Abu Ja'far al-Mansur himself. What do you need his city for?"

The eighth-century Caliph had indeed been sculpted in exquisite detail, as though the artist and his model had needed multiple sittings to get everything right—the aquiline nose, a high and protruding brow that was noble-looking, the neatly trimmed beard without a hair out of place. He had been cast in bronze to become the man himself, in the flesh, as it were, frozen in place at the center of a roundabout. Of course, no one knew who the real Abu Ja'far al-Mansur was, much less what he looked like. Still, he had been conjured up to grace traffic jams, his bronze skin turned blotchy with layers of dust impacted into mud, and dead flowers strewn in circles all around as though to decorate a tawdry idol.

Was this city of false memories the same as the one in which my father's hero, the great Sufi mystic Hallaj, had roamed, preaching to thousands on its streets? Where was the square in which he was crucified? Where did the court that tried him sit? Or the palace that exonerated him? How far were these places from the square in which the great man himself was crucified? I don't ask for precision, not even for anything that can be seen, just the evidence that someone cared: a rough sense of place, a marker in the ground maybe, saying this was one such place; over there was another. Perhaps then I can walk from marker to marker, and connect the city's sorry present with its imagined past. But I can do none of those things. No one can, because no one knows.

We lived in the Cairo district of Baghdad, on the eastern side of the Tigris. Our all-Shi'a neighborhood lies between the districts of Kadhimain, west of the Tigris, and Sadr City (previously called the City of the Revolution), the social base of our movement, to the east. Sadr City is not really a district but a twin city to Baghdad, numbering two million people; its size and location made it strategically important to the control of Baghdad. Our movement renamed it in 2003, just after our Sayyid led the million-strong march on Karbala, calling it the City of the Martyr Sadr, in honor of the father of our Sayyid, Sayyid Sadiq, who was gunned down by the Tyrant in 1999.

Haider's house suited me fine because it was a few minutes' walk to the University of Imam Ja'far al-Sadiq at the head of Palestine Street, and a further short walk down Palestine Street would take you to Mustansirriyya University, named after the oldest university in Baghdad, established in the thirteenth century, whose library I often used. It is a short drive from there to the Shrine of the Imam Musa al-Kadhim, after whom the district of Kadhimain is named, by way of the Bridge of the Imams, scene of the stampede last year in which one thousand pilgrims fell to their deaths into the Tigris, fleeing rumors of a suicide bomber in the Shrine of the Imam. The pressure of the one million or so pilgrims escaping the Shrine caused the bridge's iron railings to give way. Some government imbecile had ordered the other end of the bridge closed because of a security alert, and there was nowhere for the crowd to go other than drop nine meters into the Tigris or be crushed to death on the bridge.

To get to this bridge from our house requires driving through the Sunni neighborhood of 'Adhamiyah. The bridge connects the two oldest quarters of Baghdad, one Shi'i, built around the Shrine of the Imam Musa al-Kadhim, and the other Sunni, built around the tomb of the Great Imam Abu Hanifa an-Nu'man, a renowned scholar and founder of the Sunni school of Islamic jurisprudence in Iraq.

Haider's dream was to conquer this Sunni quarter, 'Adhamiyah, bastion of Arab nationalism in modern times, which is why he chose to live close to it in the Cairo district; he wanted men to say in future times that he was the one who had brought 'Adhamiyah to its knees. He never realized this dream; the men of 'Adhamiyah held firm throughout the civil war, walling out men like Haider with concrete, upon which they hung banners with slogans like "No Entry to Police," "No Entry to Iranians," "No Entry to Zoroastrians," and "No Entry to Solaghis," after the name of the minister of the interior from the House of Hakim who ran secret prisons torturing Sunnis and who was responsible for the order that closed the Bridge of the Imams. The banners were signed: "The People of 'Adhamiyah."

In 2006 Haider counted more than 1,500 checkpoints in Baghdad. "The men at these checkpoints supply us with information on decisions taken at the highest level," he told me proudly. "And they depend on me. Do you know that at the entrance of the Hurriya neighborhood, police officers and soldiers often ask me what they should do in the event of a problem? They want to follow my orders, you see . . . I don't even have to pay them. So I tell them to go inspect cars that look suspicious. They ask me, what is suspicious? I tell them whatever pops in my mind or whatever it is I want to know. The important thing is they should have confidence in my judgment. The soldiers of the prime minister's New Army are more loyal to me than they are to their own commanders. Do you know how easy it would be for me to organize a coup?"

"What!" I exclaimed, horrified. "Why would you want to do that?"

"I don't want to do it. I am simply telling you I can do it."

"How?"

"It's easy. I would lock everybody up in the Green Zone by placing a few gun trucks at each entry point, along with a tank or two; then I would deploy my men in the Parliament and buildings attached to the prime minister's cabinet. Outside the Green Zone, I would encircle the Karrada neighborhood, where the House of Hakim have their forces; they, of course, would have to be fought to the finish."

My own experience confirmed Haider's boast; militias and security forces ruled the main roads. Driving a typical twenty-minute distance of a few kilometers along a central artery in a middle-class neighborhood, I had counted at least three checkpoints and nineteen different gun trucks, either on the road or parked along it. Shadowy characters bought the silence or acquiescence of soldiers and police officers for a few dollars and infiltrated these checkpoints, letting trucks loaded with explosives be escorted by "hired" police vehicles, a fact that prevented them from being searched at other checkpoints.

As I drove through the slums that supplied us with a steady flow of fighters—not on the main avenues and highways, but behind middle-class districts, through the side streets of places like Hurriya and Sadr City—scenes of utter desolation greeted the eye: half-finished houses made of bare concrete block, wrecks of cars looking like stripped skeletons crawling with squalid urchins in filthy rags, flies swarming around their faces. If I dared emerge from the car or roll down the window, they swooped on me like vultures, hands outstretched. The beggars I was used to in Najaf were harmless old people, whose resignation to fate I could pity and wish to ameliorate. They would sit in the shade of the gates of our local mosque, and I was always happy to share my lunch with them. But not these snarling, whining hooligans, who pushed each other about to get ahead, knocking down the weak or smacking the sickly with their yellowing, hollowed-out faces, shoving their faces into mine, not asking for money but demanding it, and turning vicious if they did not get it.

Slums like these are warehouses of cruelty that grind out whatever virtue is left in a heart. The borderlines between life and death
to navigate there were different from anywhere else in Baghdad. I
knew of no one, not even the brave and fearless Haider, who could
navigate them at ease; he, like me, would not pass the test of getting
out of a car without an armed escort in the heart of one of these
slums—and yet our whole movement lived and fed upon them.

At night, the random violence of the day gave way to closed streets,
dark corners, lurking shadows, absent electricity, no light of any kind
unless it was a militiaman's two-bar electrical heater at a checkpoint
working on stolen electricity. Sometimes you would not hear a single
pulse of life other than your own breathing, whose loudness made
you anxious. Only a howling dog, a snarling cat, or a burst of gunfire in the distance relieved the deafening silence. The exceptions
were the places where corrupt politicians and businessmen, or party
leaders and Foreigner Iraqis, lived. These places may have had a late-
night restaurant and a shop or two, but always they were filled with
cronies and gray yes-men who hung on someone else's every word
in order to use it against him the next day. Always one could find
supplicants lining up behind corrupt and trigger-happy policemen,
and other colorless go-betweens, outdoing one another in the degree
of their servility.

Haider had spread out on the floor of the armory, which doubled
as his office, a huge map of Baghdad on which he had colored the
various districts and routes of access. He had cardboard cutouts indicating a gun truck or a sniper's position or a checkpoint—his own,
those of the army and police, and those of the enemy; these he played
with, moving them around the map to make a point about the wisdom of attacking here, not there, and with only so much strength
because of what was needed in reserve and why. He studied the city
like a military commander studies his battlefield; I learned much
from him this way.

Our neighborhood, for example, he would say, pointing to it with
his ruler, borders the Grand Army Canal Highway to its west. The
Grand Army Canal Highway cuts Baghdad in a razor-sharp straight

line from the southeast all the way up to the northwest; it is four lanes wide, and the only one of its kind in the city with a wide island in the middle, where the canal, more like a ditch these days, used to run.

The highway was built in the early 1960s at the same time as Sadr City, then called Revolution City, which borders it to the east. But the 1960s was a long time ago, when Baghdad was a city of one million people. Today it is six million and all those planning considerations no longer work as intended, Haider would explain. Originally a barrier to wall off the flood of Marsh Dweller migrants from the south because their sprawling slums were threatening to invade old Baghdad from the east (it was rumored the Ba'th had contingency plans to flood the ditch with oil and light it up in the event of an urban insurrection), today, Haider would point out with his ruler, the Grand Army Canal Highway "is the key to our victory in the war for Baghdad"; it provided gun trucks with rapid access to the whole sprawling eastern side of the river Tigris, including old Baghdad, and linked it to the Shi'a south of the country. He showed me how rapidly his men could zip up and down the highway, dart in and out, striking adjoining Sunni neighborhoods to the west until one by one they fell, and we gained yet more bits of territory to extort, and from which to launch the next cycle of takeovers.

Living in Baghdad, you heard people ask themselves questions like: Which is worse, a car bomb or a suicide bomber? Each sound had an entirely strange and heightened significance, and had to be considered separately and cautiously, whereas in Najaf the sounds blended into one. Eyes behaved differently in Baghdad, constantly darting from left to right, suspecting everybody and everything. Odd forms of dress were viewed with suspicion. Previously women were not the objects of any kind of fear, but as soon as female suicide bombers made an appearance, the heavily veiled, all-black-cloaked females who had been ignored had to be shunned. Men took to doing the shopping; children were barred from the streets. The danger was abstract, but strangely, we tended to adapt to it.

At first the violence changed us Baghdadis in small molecular ways; then we woke up one day to notice everyone had changed and nothing was the same. You could see it grinding us down, pulverizing who we used to be, turning us into helpless atoms of pure solitude, be it my kind of solitude or Haider's. Danger and the new habits that arose from it bequeathed to the people of Baghdad a city in which trust had long since passed the limits of anticipation, and distrust, a means of survival at first, had become the norm. In the abyss of this Baghdad, betrayal metamorphosed into a way of life.

The File

The judge worked out of a building housing the Special Tribunal of the Criminal Court, established by the Occupation Authority in 2003; he had been relocated from Najaf to Baghdad shortly after the Court was set up. His office was across the road from the tomb of Michel 'Aflaq, founder of the Ba'th Party, and was set apart from all the other office buildings in the city by the tall clock tower attached to it. But getting there was an obstacle course through the Green Zone, one that began by joining the throngs of people trying to pass through the multilayered checkpoint and concrete barriers closest to the Bridge of the Republic.

Having failed to get a response from the judge by saying who Uncle was and what organization I belonged to, I tried a new approach on Haider's advice, using my grandfather's name, and explaining how devoted my father had been to Sayyid Majid, how he had died protecting him and facilitating his escape in 1991. This secured the appointment.

Haider had dropped me off in a smart civilian-looking sedan that the unit he commanded used for such purposes. The plan was that once I had penetrated the checkpoint, I would be picked up by a car from the office of the prime minister, which had already supplied me with the necessary paperwork. Looking like a smart civil servant, I was dressed in a clean pair of freshly pressed gray pants, a crisply starched white shirt, and a navy blue jacket. All I carried in my hands was a plastic bag containing six juicy, firm red pomegranates from Uncle's tree, a whole box of which he had passed on to Haider and myself as a housewarming present upon hearing we were living together.

Haider thrust the plastic bag into my hands as we headed to the car, a gift to the judge, he insisted. He had taken the trouble early that morning of seeding one of the pomegranates, by cutting it in half, covering the cut with his cupped palm, and then thumping the hard skin with a wooden ladle to release the seeds into a container. He insisted on my sitting down and having tea while I watched him perform the procedure the way my mother used to. "No point in getting juice on your shirt today," he laughed. And I laughed with him as he bustled about cleaning the container, sealing it in plastic, adding a plastic spoon, and throwing the lot into a plastic bag.

At the checkpoint, a mass of people—cooks, houseboys, gardeners, guards, translators, drivers, nondescript junior "advisors," and employees—were piling up against the first set of obstacles, propelled by the conviction that the sooner they penetrated them the less likely they were to be blown away. As a consequence, they were all being crushed at the entrance and slowly disgorged like so many discarded plastic bottles at a sluice gate on the Tigris; this flotsam and jetsam of Baghdad, believe it or not, were envied because they had jobs when no one else did, but they also knew that so much envy brought danger, and so another reason they wanted to get through the barriers quickly was in order to remain anonymous; they had lied to their families about being employed in the Green Zone and didn't want anyone in the crowd to recognize them and catch them out in the lie.

I jumped into the fray, shouting and elbowing my way through like everyone else until I could show my papers; unlike the others, however, once I had shown my papers, I, a prince of the Sayyid's movement and Uncle's protégé, was ushered in like royalty.

.   .   .

The beginning was awkward, but the pomegranates worked. I put the container and plastic spoon on the desk before the judge. He smiled, tossed a spoonful into his mouth, declared them excellent, as good as anything he had tasted from Karbala, from whence he hailed, and insisted we share the box of pomegranate seeds, miraculously ferreting out another plastic spoon from one of his drawers, which he passed on to me. Then he motioned to the armchair and sofa nearby, suggesting it would be more comfortable to talk and eat over there. The rest was smooth sailing.

"My father tells me he knew your father and grandfather well; he praised them both to the skies."

"Thank you. I am deeply grateful to you for this meeting. I hope I am not inconveniencing you in any way?"

"Not at all," the judge replied. "Our fathers endured difficult times. My condolences for the loss of your grandfather, by the way, belated though they are. So tell me, why are you so interested in this case?"

"Your Honor, I hardly knew my father growing up, but looked upon him as the beacon of my life. I have read the books he left behind many times over. I seek only to know him whom I admire so much. Four years ago, on her deathbed, Mother gave me a letter my father wrote to her, the last thing he did, which told how he and thousands like him were caught and treated and how they would die."

"I am sorry . . . How she must have suffered."

"Thank you, sir. Still there was no mention in the letter of his relationship with Sayyid Majid. He did not explain why Saddam's forces sought him out and wanted him arrested. Perhaps he did not want to give unnecessary detail in case the letter was intercepted."

"I understand."

"And then, on the day of the Tyrant's fall, April 10, 2003, I ran out of our house in Najaf to see what all the commotion in the Shrine was about, and just a few minutes away down an adjoining street I almost stumbled upon a corpse in the street. I had never seen a dead man before, but to see one killed like that left a big impression on me. I did not know whose body it was at first. There were a number of men milling about, some from the neighborhood, but I did not know if they were bystanders or what. For three years I did not connect that body with my father . . . until Grandfather began to tell me stories."

"What kind of stories?"

"Stories about the Uprising in Najaf during 1991, how my father and Sayyid Majid grew up together, and how in the confusion of the Uprising they tried to carry out Sayyid Majid's father's, Ayatollah Khoei's, rulings on bringing order to the city to stop the senseless killing, the leaving of corpses untended in the streets . . . It was toward the end of those tumultuous days, as the regime's tanks were rolling into the city, that both men disappeared, my father forever and Sayyid Majid for a while before reappearing in London, where, I am told, he worked tirelessly for many years against the Tyrant."

"So what do you want to know?"

"I want to see the file of your investigation into his murder."

"There is nothing in the file about 1991 or your father. My investigation concerned the murder of Sayyid Majid on April 10, 2003."

"I want to know who killed him and why."

"There is a government-approved version of what happened, issued by the first elected Shi'i prime minister, a friend and fellow exile of Sayyid Majid's in London; it was adopted by the new government, and all the men we had investigated and put in jail in 2003 were found innocent and released in accordance with the new investigation. That is now the only official version of what happened. I was not in charge of that new investigation and had nothing to do with it. You should read that document, which, alas, I do not have a copy of."

"I have read that file, Your Honor. I don't trust its version of events. I want to compare it with the original file that you prepared."

"I am sorry, son. Even if I had the file, which I don't, I would not be able to show it to you. It would be unethical, not unlike a doctor sharing his patient's notes with a stranger."

"At least give me the background to your investigation. What made you take up the case in the first place?"

"That I can do. It happened by sheer accident, in the course of an entirely separate investigation I was conducting regarding corruption coming out of the governor's office in Najaf."

"You were conducting an investigation after the fall of Saddam?"

"I was. It started shortly after his flight from Baghdad. No one knew who was in charge and to whom to report. The police force was especially demoralized . . . and afraid. Men were afraid for their jobs, afraid of what they might be accused of, afraid of being held accountable for the past . . . afraid of their fellow citizens. In fact, ordinary citizens were stronger than policemen in those days. In this chaos, political parties no one had heard of before began to make an appearance, not real parties, but people who claimed to be in a party coming from abroad, and who claimed to be protected by the Americans . . . These people behaved very arrogantly, as though they owned the place and had nothing to fear. They were in fact stronger than the still-standing institutions of the city of Najaf, most of which had virtually collapsed. I began to receive complaints from citizens showing up at my office and saying that a new governor had been appointed, by whom nobody seemed to know, and he was arresting people indiscriminately, demanding protection money, ransom money, barging into people's houses and taking their goods. He even set up a car-stealing ring, selling cars to Iran. And he did all this in a crude, all-too-obvious way, leaving a trail of evidence sometimes in his own handwriting! The man was a charlatan and stupid to boot! And somehow the police were going along with it, acting under his orders, all under the impression that the Americans had appointed him."

"Had they?"

"No! In fact, they didn't even know who he was! My first contact with an American was with a polite young man who described himself as a military liaison officer; he didn't speak a word of Arabic and had been told he was responsible for the Holy City. I asked him through a translator whether they had appointed this new governor who was riding roughshod across the city. He said he didn't know, and disappeared for a few days to go and check—I have no idea with whom. When he came back, he said the Americans had not appointed anybody and had no idea who the man was. In my capacity as a senior investigating judge, I officially opened an investigation. You have to understand, the situation was strange. This man whom no one had appointed, and whose thugs were now dressed up as police, and whom not a soul in the city knew but whom everybody was obeying because they thought the Americans had appointed him, was actually for a short while in control of the holiest city in Iraq. And this state of affairs went on for a couple of weeks! Bizarre! That is how things were in April and May 2003. At the time, there was no such thing as a Sadrist movement, or an Army of the Awaited One, or a Coalition Provisional Authority, or a Paul Bremer. Nothing of the sort."

"So what did you do?"

"I said to myself, 'You are a judge; you have a job; you are good at what you do; go investigate.' After I compiled a preliminary case, I presented it, with all the supporting paperwork, to this young American liaison officer I mentioned. He took it away, God knows where or to whom, maybe all the way to George Bush in Washington and back—to this day I don't know. At any rate, a decision from high up—Bremer was still not on the scene—came back agreeing that there was a case for serious corruption, and asking me for a recommendation. I said the man should be arrested. They agreed. This time the senior American military commander in charge of Najaf showed up at my office, and said he and his men were at my disposal. We went ahead and arrested the self-appointed governor, just like that. He claimed he was a member of a party that no one had even heard of! I think they came from the north; some people even said they were Kurds. They were crooks, not political; that much I am

sure of. My investigation now became much easier; lots more witnesses were encouraged to appear, and for a week I was taking depositions all day long. One was from a man who during his deposition
said something strange. He blurted out, 'Your Honor, this man"—
meaning the governor—"not only extorted money; he allowed the
killers of Sayyid Majid to escape.' I said, 'Who is Sayyid Majid?'"

"What! You did not know who Sayyid Majid was!"

"No, I didn't. Of course I knew his father, Sayyid Abu'l Qassim al-
Khoei; he was our Grand Ayatollah, our Supreme Source of Emulation; we were all his followers in my family from when I was a child
until his death in 1992. But I had never heard the name of his son
mentioned before the witness in the governor's case brought it up."

"What did you do?"

"As soon as the witness said this, I stopped everything, and asked
everyone in the room to leave except the witness. The Americans,
their translator, the policemen, and my assistants who were taking
down the deposition all filed out and waited in an anteroom. Once
the door was closed and there were only the two of us in the room,
I looked the young man straight in the eye, and told him to forget
the deposition and tell me what he was talking about. I asked him
to speak to me personally, off the record, with no tape recorders or
stenographers present."

"So you realized something important had happened?"

"Not just important, my friend, earth-shattering! This witness
gave me my first account of the whole story . . . He started with
Sayyid Majid's return to Najaf and ended with the killing itself,
which he was, however, not directly a witness to. But he gave me a
list of names of people who had been there who could corroborate
his story. After he had finished, I asked the others to return to the
room. And we returned to the facts of the original case concerning
the corruption of the governor."

"How did you proceed from there?"

"Well, now I had two cases folded into one. I had the story of a
murder wrapped up in a story of corruption. I had to separate the

two. Further investigation showed the corruption case had nothing to do with the murder of Sayyid Majid—the governor, it turned out, had not deliberately let people out; the prison walls themselves were broken into, and they escaped. So the next thing I did was open a new file on the case of the murder of Sayyid Majid. That was the beginning of the whole affair."

"And the governor issue?"

"It went ahead, and he was eventually imprisoned for fifteen years. To the best of my knowledge he is still in prison."

"And the new case concerning Sayyid Majid?"

"One witness led me to another, and the first big discovery was that three people had been killed, not one. A man called the Kelidar, the keeper of the keys of the Shrine, and another man I later found out was from Diwaniyya named Majid. Five or six others had been seriously wounded. I looked into our files for case notes of some sort, an old file, anything. There was nothing. I called the chief of police. He said he heard something had happened on April 10, but he did not investigate; times were chaotic and no one knew what was going on. He did not even know if he still had a job; then he added that it was a 'very sensitive' case and he had been advised to steer clear of it. Sensitive? What does that mean? I asked him about the corpses. Where were they? Who had buried them? Had autopsy reports been filed?"

"What a mess . . . Had autopsy reports been filed?"

"Perfunctory ones. There were no case notes to speak of."

"And the bodies?"

"They had been buried by 'people,' I was told. I soon found out they were members of the victims' families. So I searched them out and took their statements. I asked them if they wanted to press charges—they all did, but some were afraid. I got their permission in writing to exhume the bodies for proper fresh autopsies for purposes of an investigation into the incident."

"Where was Sayyid Majid buried?"

"A distant family relation said Sayyid Majid had been buried in the Green Mosque, inside the Shrine of Imam 'Ali, Peace Be Upon

Him, next to his father, Abu'l Qassim, and his brother, Sayyid Taqi, killed by Saddam in a fake traffic accident shortly after Sayyid Majid escaped. And that is where we found his grave—all three of them lying side by side, opposite the tomb of the Imam, God's Prayers Be Upon Him."

"You had the authority to exhume in this holiest of all holy places? How can that be! I don't believe it."

"Technically, under Saddam's laws, yes, I had the legal authority. But I did not presume to exhume the body on that basis alone. You have to understand there were great difficulties with the place of burial, beginning with the sensitivity of its location, followed by the awkward fact that the Green Mosque itself was a short distance away from the Sayyid's house, and the scene of the crime. There were, in other words, spiritual, social, and, most important, security dimensions to the issue of removing Sayyid Majid's corpse for autopsy. This was not an ordinary exhumation."

"So what did you do?"

"I asked for permission from the office of the Grand Ayatollah himself, God bless him. He replied in his letter to our office, which is also on file, that if an autopsy would help 'reveal the truth,' his phrase, then it had his full support. This is finally what made exhumation of Sayyid Majid's body possible."

"All that is in the file?"

"It is . . . as is the paperwork of the new autopsy, following what must be one of the most thorough and comprehensive autopsies I have seen in all my years as an investigating judge."

"What did the autopsy report conclude?"

"It confirmed to a remarkable extent the things said by the thirty or so witnesses from whom I had obtained depositions. There was an astonishing near one hundred percent conformity between what the autopsy showed and what the witnesses said. The knife wounds, how his hands had been tied, the cutting off of one of his fingers, the broken jawbone, the innumerable cuts all over the body. The knife wounds were varied, some deep, some slight, some fatal, others not."

"I did not know a finger had been cut off. Were the Americans in the picture?"

"Barely . . . One never saw them in Najaf in those days. I did inform the liaison officer that Sayyid Majid's body was going to be exhumed. Bremer still had not been appointed."

"I am surprised you were so fearless in pursuit of this case."

"I was naive at the outset, never really having concerned myself with clerical intrigues in the past. They are a staple of our city, but I had my eyes on a career in Baghdad. You could say I fell into a swamp, because I did not know where I was going. And then it was too late. Once you start a thing like this, there is no going back. You have to go where the evidence takes you. Also, I believed in my profession. Contrary to what the Americans thought when they first arrived, there was a real legal system and competent judges and courts—not everything was tainted by politics. The Americans came with this ridiculous notion that all judges were corrupt Ba'this serving the interests of the party. That is plain ignorance. To be sure there were political courts, and Ba'thi political appointees, and political trials and political prisoners. All that is true. But they accounted for a tiny percentage of the entire legal system. In the meantime, there were still robberies and nonpolitical crimes of every sort and description to contend with. I was part of that system. And I was ambitious and young, aspiring to be an important judge one day."

"Did no one put pressure on you to drop the case?"

"My friends in the police and courts advised me to drop the investigation . . . They said it was dangerous for me personally and my family. They said the House of Sadr was involved, and implicating them could set off an avalanche of unpredictable consequences. But the strange thing is, the more they warned me off, the more I wanted to know what happened. Only after I opened a file and took up the case, after I had deposed more than thirty witnesses, when it was too late to back down, did it become positively dangerous for me to continue. But by then it was too late. I had to see the case through to the bitter end."

"Why dangerous?"

"There were two attempts on my life. The first, a bomb placed outside my office window, which the police defused. The second, an ambush of my car from afar, using a rocket-propelled grenade, which missed."

"When was the first time you heard of the House of Sadr's involvement?"

"Virtually all the witnesses mentioned it. The aged mother of the Kelidar accused them directly, and asked for her son's blood to be avenged. She wanted to bring murder charges herself against the Sayyid. She was too frail to come to court so I deposed her at her house. She could attest to the fact that Sayyid Majid had dropped by, and left the house with her son to go to his office in the Shrine. Then the Kelidar's sister, a most respected highly qualified doctor in the city, also filed a case. Of course, neither had any direct proof the Sayyid was implicated. Over time, however, the families withdrew from the case. I believe they grew afraid or were warned to back off."

"What happened next?"

"I visited the site of the killings, saw all the evidence of bullets and dried blood, had it all photographed and cataloged. We found bullet casings and two of the knives used in the stabbings. Everything is in the file."

"Weren't your colleagues in the coroner's office, in the court administration, and in the police afraid?"

"Very much so, but the chief of the court always stood by me and wanted the investigation to go all the way. I had one investigator who also would not be deterred, and the police, to be honest, were by and large excellent. Very professional. They were all the old police; no new appointments had been made."

"Tell me about the witnesses."

"They lie at the heart of the case. The initial net I cast led us to an outer circle of about fifty names. These were people who were at the scene, potential witnesses of one sort or another. Gradually we winnowed this number down to around twenty very crucial witnesses, among whom two were decisive because they had been as close to the murder as I am to you in this room. Moreover, their testimonies confirmed one another and established in no uncertain terms who ordered the killing and who delivered the fatal wound."

"What about arrests? Did you arrest anybody?"

"We started arresting early in July, right after the first attempt on my life in June. The end of my involvement in the whole case was in August, when Bremer, who had finally shown up, assigned me to Baghdad. All in all, just over thirty depositions are in the final file. Arrest warrants were issued for everyone whose involvement had come up in the depositions, including unwilling witnesses. Many of those we arrested immediately began to confess. We have their statements. The moment they were brought into the police station for a preliminary hearing, the words started to pour out of them, implicating more and more people. We continued arresting and getting more confessions. It became clear that the crowd milling about in the courtyard of the Shrine, outside the Kelidar's room, had been a strange mix, some individuals with light criminal backgrounds like robbery, but also some who'd committed murder. Young men with no ideology, no profession even, who had nothing personal against Sayyid Majid, only they had police records. Then there were ordinary citizens who got caught up in the melee. We let them go right away. Most important were a number of key personnel from the office of the Sayyid, who seem to have been giving the orders and running the show. But even these individuals started to confess, some of them telling the story in great detail, how Sayyid Majid had been captured, then tied up, who gave the orders, and what exactly was said."

"They tied him up?"

"Yes, with his hands behind his back, after which the rope was wound around his torso several times. He was left completely defenseless. I found that strange, so I asked who gave the orders to tie his hands. The witnesses all said it was the Sayyid's people. When I asked them why they had done this, I was told, 'Those were our orders.' Everyone agreed there were orders."

"What were those orders exactly?" I asked, getting excited. "That is very important to know. After all, they may have been trying to protect Sayyid Majid."

"True, and that is precisely what one of the men claimed. All the accused agreed that they had orders to bring Sayyid Majid to the office of the Sayyid. But one of them suddenly blurted out, 'We were trying to defend him from the crowd.'"

"You see!" I said. "I knew it! Surely that casts an entirely different light on the meaning of events?"

"Not really, not after you start to carefully piece through the sequence of events," replied the judge. "I challenged this witness at the time, asking him, if defending Sayyid Majid was the purpose, why then did they tie his hands? And why tie them to his rear, not to the front, where he could at least have used his arms to block the blows that were hailing down on him from every direction? And why run the rope round and round his torso with men pulling front and back, rendering him totally immobile? And why let people go on beating him and jabbing at his body with knives during the entire length of the walk to the Sayyid's office? Why do all or any of those things if you wanted to protect Sayyid Majid?"

"What did the man say?" I asked, crestfallen.

"He fell silent and stared sullenly at the floor."

"I was just hoping . . . ," I said softly. "Damn it! I don't know what I was hoping." I was muttering to myself and then fell silent as my own lingering illusions began to dissipate. The judge came to the rescue by getting up to serve us both glasses of water from the jug that was on his desk.

"By the way," he then said, looking at the glass as he poured, "all of the men we arrested were afraid. I mean really afraid. They knew they had landed in a hornet's nest but did not know if anyone was going to come to their rescue. I will never forget one man who wore a turban; he must have been a Sheikh. He said something in the antiquated language these clerics use, which I didn't understand at the time. He said the Sayyid had asked them to bring Sayyid Majid to him in order to 'say his word on him.' I did not understand that expression, which I gather is common in medieval texts. I found out later it meant the Sayyid wanted him brought to him to pronounce judgment on his fate."

"What was the condition of Sayyid Majid by the time they reached the door of the Sayyid's office?"

"He was upright and conscious, barely so, but strong enough to speak, and, in that same formal Arabic that these Sayyids use, he asked for protection from the House of Sadr. You understand this is a very powerful thing to ask for. An Arab of true nobility and character cannot refuse the protection and hospitality of his home when asked, not even by a murderer. Two men were already dead. Sayyid Majid and two more of his group, also bound, had made it alive to the door of the Sayyid. Now came the moment of reckoning. What was the Sayyid going to say?"

"A truly remarkable moment," I said in amazement.

"A historic one, if you think about it," replied the judge. "I mean, here are two sons of Grand Ayatollahs, the most venerated men of their age, leaders of two of the greatest Houses of the Shi'a, the one son having come with the Americans supposedly to liberate Iraq, the other having stayed and lived all his life under Saddam; both have lost brothers or fathers to the great Tyrant; they meet on the day of the fall of Baghdad, at the door of a house bordering the Great Shrine, the holiest site of the Shi'a world, and the one asks for the protection of the other."

Before the Hanging

The judge and I fell silent after that. I was over my moment of weakness. Nudging away at the back of my mind was the feeling that something important had just happened. The time for prevarication and searching was past. I was at the end of a journey.

Meanwhile, it was getting late. I couldn't expect the judge to stay much longer with me. He had duties to perform. I had to squeeze out of the moment every little detail I could. "What happened next, Your Honor?" I asked.

He woke up as if from a reverie, and snapped back quickly into his former rhythm: "It is at this point that two versions of why all of this was happening appear: One version has it that all along the Sayyid wanted to protect Sayyid Majid. But that did not make sense. The door would have been opened if that were the case, and Sayyid Majid would have been taken into the house, his wounds tended to. That did not happen. Two other witnesses within earshot provide an entirely different version. They actually heard the Sayyid say from inside the house, 'Take him out of here and dispose of him.' At which point an unidentified person opened the door of the Sayyid's office and passed on the message. You have to understand there was no more than a meter or two between the people standing inside the office and the crowd milling about on the other side of the door.

Upon hearing this, Sayyid Majid was struck a fatal blow with a long knife plunged deep from the rear and through his left side; this is the blow that actually killed him. He fell, dying but not yet quite dead. Seconds later another man appeared at the door—there must have been quite a crowd inside the office whispering and talking to one another all at the same time. This new man, less than a minute after his predecessor, said, 'The Sayyid says, keep him close, until he chooses to say his word on him.' But it was too late. Sayyid Majid had already been delivered the fatal blow, and his body was convulsing and twitching on the ground at the time this other man opened the door."

"How do you explain what was going on?"

"If true—remember, these are people's testimonies we are talking about—I think it means the Sayyid for whatever reason changed his mind at the last minute, but it was too late: Majid was already dying or dead."

"What happened to the body?"

"It was tossed out like a bag of garbage into the street, which is where you saw it. Family and friends later, when it was safe, collected and buried the Sayyid in the Holy Shrine."

"No one opposed them?"

"No one. He was a Sayyid, after all, a descendant of the Prophet. Holy law forbids it."

"I suppose it does." I don't know why I said that. It seemed so out of place. I needed all this to soak in and so took my time reaching out for a glass of water, topping it up, and settling back on the edge of the sofa. The judge answered the telephone. I drank and took a few deep breaths. A thousand more questions came to mind, along with the strange sensation that everything had already been said. I prepared to leave. As I reached the door, I paused and turned to look at the judge, somewhat embarrassed.

"My apologies, Your Honor . . . something personal. I will not rest until I know it . . . I am sorry. This is the last question, I promise . . . Ah, let me see . . . My uncle is—"

"I know who your uncle is, young man," he replied, interrupting and looking me straight in the eye, sparing me the discomfort of having to stumble on further. "He was not there. No one brought up his name in any context whatsoever during the entire investigation. You have my word of honor on that."

"Thank you, sir. This country is blessed to have such an honorable man serving it."

I left the judge's office, and exited the thicket of concrete barriers out of the Green Zone, walking past the Ministry of Planning across the Bridge of the Republic, to Liberation Square. I continued walking, heading northwest across the square, vaguely in the direction of our neighborhood, perhaps with my apartment and Haider in mind. I can't remember. I just walked the streets that day, shoulders drooped and head hung low as though staring at something interesting in the dirt or concrete sidewalks. But I was not looking at anything. Bits and pieces of the last four years, in pictures and snatches of conversation, were washing over my conversation with the judge, seeking to find some sort of foothold in my brain.

Why had Uncle said Sayyid Majid was an American agent? He knew he was buried in the Holy Shrine, next to his father, two meters away from our patron saint, the Imam 'Ali. How could he allow an American agent to be buried in such a holy location? After talking with Grandfather, I had to conclude Uncle never really believed Majid was an agent. All Uncle was trying to do was besmirch his character so as to lessen the offense, hoping to dismiss the whole affair, concealing from me in particular the enormity of what had happened.

Mother knew Sayyid Majid personally. She knew the kind of a man he was. Had word reached her of his return before I stumbled upon his body? Did she know it was he, lying in the alley? On that fateful day, April 10, 2003, she already suspected Uncle of something. But of what? The judge said Uncle had nothing to do with the murder. Still, Mother could have suspected him of the deed. She never trusted Uncle. And why did she not tell me Sayyid Majid was a dear friend of Father's? Perhaps he officiated over her engagement. Perhaps he was the Sayyid who signed their marriage contract.

Mother did not want me to know these things because she too was thinking of me, and of my relation with Uncle. Whatever her own feelings, she did not want to disturb an arrangement that had served us—she and I—well since Father's death. I can see her telling herself that . . .

Grandfather thought Sayyid Majid was an honorable man. But did he know who killed him? No doubt he suspected the House of Sadr, as did many people in Najaf, all of whom kept quiet. Talking about it might have soured his relationship with Uncle, which was already bad.

As for Haider, who knew what I knew, when I knew it, he didn't think twice about Uncle's being on the scene, or for that matter about who killed Sayyid Majid or why. Deep down I don't think he cared; if he gave the appearance of caring, it was to humor me, out of friendship. Certainly my other friends and comrades in the Army of the Awaited One, and in our neighborhood, didn't care.

No one cared.

The Governing Council had Kurds and Sunnis and Turcomans and Christians among its twenty-five members. None of its thirteen Shi'a members wanted to wash their dirty laundry in front of the others. So they did not allow the subject of the killing to be discussed inside the Governing Council. "A private affair," the non-Shi'a members would have said. "True, we all knew Sayyid Majid to be a good man, but what business is it of ours if they don't want to hold anyone accountable for the murder of one of their own?" More important matters of state were at stake.

All twenty-five would have known who killed Sayyid Majid.

The Cabal of Thirteen knew much more than the rest of the Governing Council. They knew that all the little details in the file prepared by the judge were true, as did the national security advisor, the prime minister, and the former president of the Governing Council, all of whom had personally negotiated the suspension of the arrest warrant and were the architects of its later quashing. When they came to power the following year, they concocted a new file, a file they knew to be a pack of lies designed to obfuscate and hide what had happened. They did these things because they had deals to make with our Sayyid that involved stabbing each other in the back in the Governing Council. They needed our Sayyid to approve of their way of handling the cover-up; it would make them look good in his eyes. If only they knew the contempt he held them in! Perhaps they did, and it did not matter.

In the wake of the American war, which they benefited from the most, they worried about the consequences for their right to rule if the truth about Sayyid Majid should become known. Disgrace would fall upon them if the world knew one of their own had butchered the other and tossed his body into the street. They could not afford to lose credibility in the eyes of the Occupier, or in the eyes of the world, which was following everything like a hawk. How could the Occupier hand power to men who had so blatantly disregarded the rule of the law that they had called for while the Tyrant was still in power? And so the Thirteen conspired to cover up the murder, to prepare a phony file in order to pretend to the world that their house was in control of itself, even when it wasn't.

The original file the judge had prepared remained dangerous. In the hands of the House of Hakim, it could be used to blackmail and discredit the House of Sadr, which had denied them the influence over Iraq's Shi'a that they had taken for granted. That is why Uncle had to have the judge's file; he needed to deal with the evidence it provided before it fell into the wrong hands. I never reported back to Uncle on my visit to the judge, and did not tell him the things I now knew. I did not want what he might have done to be on my conscience. That is also why the judge would never have given me a copy of the file even if he had one.

The Cabal of Thirteen, the Governing Council, and every formerly exiled minister and advisor in the Shi'a-led Iraqi governments that followed the war knew who Sayyid Majid was, held him in the highest esteem, counted themselves among his friends, but nonetheless chose to cover up his murder. Forced to confront the evidence, they would no doubt have appealed to lofty ideals, which they were compelled to place first, ahead of their personal morality and their obligation to Sayyid Majid and his family. It was after all a "noble lie," they would say, undertaken on behalf of all Iraq's Shi'a. They would point to us, to men like Haider and myself, and say: "See, they are alive. We lied and we covered up in order to save them; it was all for them, only for them."

Everyone went along with that.

Of course, the Occupier always knew who killed Sayyid Majid, issuing an arrest warrant because of it, and then "suspending" it after the Cabal of Thirteen clamored for it. The American military commander of the Holy City knew who killed Sayyid Majid. Paul Bremer knew. Presumably even George Bush, Tony Blair, Donald Rumsfeld, and Colin Powell knew. Sayyid Majid had put his trust in them as well; they were his allies too.

Why was everybody conspiring to pretend that a dead person did not exist, and a murder in the Shrine of the Imam on the day of the fall of the Tyrant did not happen? Did they think the judge was naive and old-fashioned because he, like myself, did not know what was going on and thought it his duty to find out?

The judge did not realize the enormity of what he was uncovering even as he was uncovering it. Truth is like that: often uncovered by those who are least aware of what they are uncovering. His colleagues at work in Najaf had a better sense of what was going on. They were the only other honorable men in this affair because they respected their colleague, and wished him well, and if they too did not want him to dig deeper, it was because they were afraid for him.

All this evasion and fear began with a killing; one that boiled down to the hatred our Sayyid bore toward his peer from the House of Khoei. As the judge said, here were two sons of greatly revered lineage, meeting in the Holy City on a most auspicious day for both their country and their community. Their respective Houses had shaped the spiritual life of the Shi'a, not only in Najaf, but wherever there were Shi'a walking the globe. Was it the decades of competition over funding for students, or the petty quarrels over who had sold out to the Tyrant, or the spiteful jealousies between Arab and Iranian that came between them?

No doubt the ideas of the fathers had poisoned the minds of the sons. Why was that not compensated for by the fact that both Houses had lost loved ones to the Great Tyrant? One stayed, grieving for his murdered father and brothers; the other fled, his brother killed in retaliation the year following. So much hurt. So much pain. Why was all that pain not directed outward at the Tyrant? Why did it not bring the two grieving men together, instead of tearing them apart?

Even here there were secrets that no one wanted to talk about.

Our Sayyid's men had milled about, blocking access to the Grand Ayatollah, stopping Sayyid Majid from speaking to his father's most illustrious student. Why go one terrible step further, and disrupt Sayyid Majid's speech . . . and with guns and knives, inside the holiest of holy sanctuaries? Why have him bound and tied, pricked like a hog, then dragged as though he were a common criminal to the front door of our Sayyid's house? How can a descendant of the Prophet do that to another descendant of the Prophet? First he orders the killing, and then he changes his mind! How shameful! And I served him for four years! If I was in denial during those years, the sordid truth now stared me in the face. And now that it had been laid bare, what did I have to turn to in its place? What was there left worth believing in?

Nothing.

Look too deeply into the awfulness of the world, and one must reject it, turn his back on it, and walk away. But where to? Nowhere. There is no exit from the world.

Everyone behaved as they did because they were afraid. Just as in the time of the great Tyrant, fear had returned to become the common denominator uniting the actions of all the people in the story of Sayyid Majid. We Shi'a who set out to build a new Iraq in 2003 did so on a foundation of fear, fear nurtured by pain and fed by lies, fear concealed by hypocrisy, and crowned by murder, more and more lies.

What was so frightening about Sayyid Majid? He had no armies, no militia, no armed men; he was an honorable man. Was that it? Had he become the lightning rod of men's fears because he was too honorable? Men who have known only the Tyrant's rod don't understand those who live by different rules. They look up to the next man with a rod; him they always understand.

Perhaps, however, it was not the person of Sayyid Majid that was frightening; it was his story, without which his death would be lost in the ocean of dead that this benighted land of ours has offered up. The deaths of men mean nothing; their stories mean everything. We need more stories about how my people died and why. I was meant to be Sayyid Majid's storyteller. Father would have wanted it that way.

Meticulously collected and minutely organized, the fabric of little facts that the judge had assembled is the stuff of my ordinary Iraqi story, as ordinary as the millions of other untold stories of how my people died. But in its ordinariness, in the littleness of all its facts added up—yes, even in their sordidness—the outline of something grander is revealed, a different kind of truth, the kind that even good men turn their eyes away from, a truth that is terrifying and yet sublime, a truth far greater than the mystery surrounding the death of one honorable man.

It is the kind of truth that threatens the powerful and the small-minded, the kind that can force the hands of courts and be manipulated for good or despicable ends; it can topple governments or enrage millions, bringing them out onto the streets peacefully for justice, or as avenging angels tearing down and ripping out everything in their way. Its harsh light is undiscriminating; it illuminates the darkest corners of men's souls: those who wield power over others, or those who will do anything to do so, both willing to sacrifice everything in their way. Such men fear its scrutiny; they need to rule, either not knowing or deliberately concealing how small and insincere and treacherous they really are. These are the men who in the name of all of us Shi'a of Iraq have since the fall of the Great Tyrant wrought such evil upon this poor blood-soaked land.

If all this were so, I began to ask myself, walking through the detritus of Baghdad in the winter of 2006, who was Sayyid Majid really? Who was this man whose death could stand in for so much?

He is not just one specific man who met an untimely death like many others. He is everyman. He is all of us. He is me.

PART THREE

WHEN THE WORLD STANDS STILL

—•—

It happens very rarely. The earth's axis screeches and comes to a stop. Everything stands still then: storms, ships and clouds grazing in the valleys. Everything. Even horses in a meadow become immobile as if in an unfinished game of chess.

And after a while the world moves on. The ocean swallows and regurgitates, valleys send off steam and the horses pass from the black field into the white field. There is also heard the resounding clash of air against air.

ZBIGNIEW HERBERT

December 30, 2006

Early Morning

In between the hanging at 6:09 a.m. and the Tyrant's transfer into our custody, three hours and ten minutes passed. Subtracting the fifty-five minutes it took for all the senior government officials—from the prime minister's office, the judiciary, and others whom I did not recognize—to play with their paperwork, look important, and talk loudly to one another, and then the five minutes to walk him through a poorly lit corridor to the room in which he would await execution, left two hours and ten minutes before the trap door would clang open. Subtract another five minutes for his last walk from the waiting room to the execution chamber, and the remaining two hours and five minutes is precisely the time the Tyrant spent in the sole custody of our handpicked detail of escort guards.

Groups of soldiers were all over the building, but only four of us were assigned to his person, two outside the only door into the room, rotating with two inside.

The waiting room was windowless and small, and had been supplied with a chair centered along the length of a rectangular table, upon which was placed a plastic water bottle and one glass. We had been instructed to treat the prisoner with respect, and supply him with tea if requested—nothing else; it did not occur to anyone to say we could not talk to him. I am not saying our superiors approved of talking with him; I am saying the circumstance did not cross anyone's mind, least of all ours.

The floor was bare concrete, with cracks running between walls that had been whitewashed recently but with no attempt to repair the crumbling plaster underneath. A naked lightbulb hung from its cable, which disappeared into the ceiling without a fitting. He might have been assigned a room that, in another life, had been intended for a more sinister purpose.

Saddam sat, stretching his long limbs under the table; two of my comrades left the room, standing guard outside; 'Ali, an older, poorly shaved man who looked shabby in spite of his new uniform, and I took the first watch, standing stiffly to attention at the outset in the two corners of the room facing the table. We were positioned to cover every eventuality, including suicide or something worse. I did not see the point, but those were our orders.

No sooner had 'Ali and I been left alone in the room with him than the Tyrant began to stare at us with those eyes about which so much has been said: large, round, pitch-black, but above all unblinking and piercing.

"You," he said, pointing to 'Ali, whose shirt had no collar. "Yes, you, the one fidgeting with his Kalashnikov in the corner, and rolling his eyes all over the room. Be still! I am talking to you. You are wearing sandals. Where do you think you are, son?"

I hadn't noticed until he mentioned it. 'Ali had replaced his brand-new government-issue boots with sandals because the boots gave him blisters.

"Look at the filth encrusted on your toes," he went on quietly. "I warrant your skin has not touched water for a month. Perhaps you have not worn shoes before?"

'Ali snapped to attention, not knowing what to do or say.

"Ah . . . of course. You are a liberated man . . . I forget.

"A pox on your liberation!" he suddenly shouted. "Degradation, I call it, not liberation."

He continued, his black eyes roving from Ali's face to mine.

"No soldier of mine was ever allowed to present himself like this. I taught them love of order, respect for authority. I gave men like you shoes . . . the whole lot of you! To wear shoes was both a right and an obligation, and I made sure you followed through. A soldier who is forced to be clean and disciplined, to follow exacting exercises on a daily basis, to stand in the sun with his weapon unflinchingly for hours on end, this kind of a soldier will, when asked to confront an imperialist offensive, do so unthinkingly . . .

"Are you capable of standing up to an imperialist offensive?"

He was looking straight at us. Large eyes in dusty climes like ours were supposed to blink all the time, but not his. Perhaps that was why men flinched when he stared at them. Unblinking is unsettling. Once it became clear 'Ali was not going to answer, he answered on his behalf.

"No, of course not . . .

"It takes generations of hard work to convert discipline and love of order into instincts; thirty years I labored on people like you, and it wasn't enough. Look at the speed with which all my hard work evaporated! Skin-deep those instincts remained, even among my very best, my own Republican Guard. But it was not from want of trying . . . and not from want of caring . . . I just needed time, much more time . . .

"The way you all crumbled in 2003 . . . Had an officer of mine even dared to suggest the possibility of it beforehand, I would have had him shot; it is not a matter of right and wrong, you understand; it was his duty to tell me the truth as he honestly saw it. But I had the morale of a nation to hold firm; necessity is unforgiving. She it was who made me withdraw from the company of others, not even choosing the company of my family lest it breed weakness of will and resolve."

He looked away now, as though right through the dirty white walls surrounding the forlorn lightbulb dangling uselessly on its cable. I thought I detected a note of regret when next he spoke in a voice so low I had to strain to hear:

"He would have been right, of course, to warn me. Baghdad should have held out longer . . . It should have . . . Seeing it fall like that to foreigners, and looted by its own citizens was the worst day of my life . . ."

Folding his hands over his elbows, he rested them on the surface of the table, to which his gaze was now directed as though in deep contemplation of its wooden grain. "What difference does it make now," he said to himself.

Minutes passed. 'Ali and I looked at one another in bewilderment tinged with relief that the pressure had lifted. Then, as though in unison, we stood rigidly to attention, looking straight ahead, locking our knees, straightening our Kalashnikovs, hoping to distance ourselves from what was turning into a dangerously private moment.

Leaning back in his chair, his face in profile, Saddam resumed talking, still to no one in particular.

"The queasiness, the acidity in the stomach, the rising bile . . . it all started that day," he said, the volume of his voice dropping, the tone almost conversational. "April 10, 2003, the day Iraqi sovereignty snapped like a twig, the day my army fled like dogs, their tails between their legs . . . So what if it threw my bodily fluids out of equilibrium. I am an old man. But no, it is not age. It is the thought of all the things that might have been; that is what does a man in.

"Bah! Why dwell on it!" he suddenly said, lifting up his head, raising his voice, and snapping back into his more feisty self.

"The blame does not lie with you," he said, looking at 'Ali. His face was lined, and I noticed wrinkles of weariness around those big black eyes, which he had tried to conceal with powder of some sort. "Dirty though you may be, at least you are trying to be a soldier. It is not your fault. You are poorly served. Liberated lost souls . . . free to regress daily, accountable to no one," he said, looking down at Ali's dirty sandaled feet.

"You imagine you are moving forward but actually you are going backward, sucked by the undertow of your unformed nature into the ways of yesteryear, your great-grandfathers' ways. Back, back, back . . . to sandals and pissing and shitting in the outdoors, no running water, no electricity, the way it used to be in my youth. I see it all coming back . . . When did you last have four continuous hours of electricity, or a street that didn't smell like a sewer?

"Mark my words! Foreigners already overrun your unguarded cities.

"Think of me, my sons, as the last piece of something called Iraq that you will know. You were born into this world with bits of me wedged in to hold up the ramparts of your characters. You have known no one but me. What will you do when I am no longer there?"

Still seated, he took a long pause. I think he was enjoying himself; at least the eyes were no longer intent on skewering us.

"Did you notice what happened less than an hour ago? Perhaps not . . . no reason why you should. I will tell you: one of the escorting judges forgot himself at the doorway; he referred to me as 'Mr. President.'

"'Mr. President,' can you believe it! Oh, how I relish such moments. Your new leaders forget they are supposed to lead, in spite of themselves. The reasoning part of their brain concedes to instinct! This particular judge knows me well. I appointed him; we unearthed many a conspiracy together, and each time he compromised himself a little more than the last time . . . Now he no longer knows who he is.

"The old fool instantly checked himself . . . but it was too late. I turned and looked his way, as if to say I was grateful for the courtesy. He turned red as a beet; I understood his position perfectly; in fact, I was counting on it. Needing to save face before his colleagues, he barked out an order, and said—much too loudly—that today was the happiest day of his life. Why? Because I was about to get my just deserts for ordering his brother's execution.

"Poor stupid man, and fat to boot! What a combination. Did you know I put my fat officers and government officials on diets during the Great War with Iran, that judge included? Had their weight measured regularly, and salaries docked if they did not meet our guidelines. Probably you did not know; it was long before your time.

"Of course I ordered his brother shot, along with sixteen others if I recall. It was just after the 1991 Mother of All Battles, that most treacherous page in our country's history. How his brother groveled! I remember him well, even as he informed on six of his friends; there were only ten of them at first, and then my men broke him down, helped him see the light, you might say, which brought the number up to sixteen. More fuss was made of that creature dead than ever was made of him alive.

"I despise informers! . . . Still, one cannot do without them . . . to the point of needing to create them. I could not have ruled without informers. Pain, sometimes just the threat of it, is the only way to make a truly gifted informer. The true mettle of a man is always revealed during torture; the sad thing is that in the very nature of the operation you lose the good and are saddled with the bad. I had that judge's brother shot anyway.

"We shot the lot on a suspicion that they were plotting against me. No arms, nothing in writing, no logistical planning—nothing! Just a lot of talk . . . not that talk is to be belittled.

"You would think that your new leaders wanted to hang me for something like that, in view of the hundreds of times I have resorted to it . . . Hmm, that is probably an underestimate. I should have had a count made.

"Think about it! Countless thousands like that judge's brother died in my torture chambers, and at the top of the list sits your very own revered Imam, your Sayyid's uncle and the founder of your movement, Sayyid Muhammad Baqir of the House of Sadr. I had him tortured and killed along with his sister in 1980. Now that was a real man—especially seeing him withstand all the things we threw at him. But his death was forced upon me. I needed him to confess and turn on his comrades, only he wouldn't. I handled it personally, you know, attending to him in his cell. None of it worked. He broke eventually—they all break down—after I had his sister raped in front of him . . . A last resort; it couldn't be helped . . . Sometimes one has to resort to this kind of nastiness.

"Cruelty is a lesser fault, you know, than weakness or stupidity. One has to do whatever it takes. Think of me, my sons, as you would a surgeon, operating on the body of a man riddled with tumors, cutting and manipulating tissue as needed . . . Why? Because the nation is in need of saving. I am my country's doctor. And your Sayyid Baqir was my patient. In those days he stood with Khomeini; the fate of Iraq was at stake. He had to be broken. And his death was necessary, however horrible. None of this has anything to do with the undiminished respect I carried for him all through his ordeal."

He stopped talking, and after a few moments rose from his seat and started pacing up and down the room.

"Even the best break; the braver they are, the more pathetic the breakdown. There he was, the leader of Iraq's Shi'a, the would-be Khomeini of our Iraq, drooling, in tears, entreating me, making promises, all the while mouthing the same primal sounds we all make, whatever civilization we come from: grunts, groans, babblings, screams . . . We are all the same when we are broken down to the basics of biology.

"Pain is a great leveler, my sons, reducing men to that which they share with everyone else; it destroys language and culture and ideas, and has the whole world collapse into a bundle of sensations and feelings; it is world-destroying. That is when the names come tumbling out . . . and we pick them up one by one. Did your leaders tell you any of this? Of course not. They don't want you to know how like the rest of us your great hero turned out to be. But I know. Oh, yes, I know . . .

"Now I ask you, why am I not being tried for all the terrible things that I did to Sayyid Baqir and his sister?"

It was a good question. I never forgot it, and I still have no answer. I don't think anyone knew with certainty, before the day of the hanging, what had happened to Sayyid Muhammad Baqir back in 1980.

Whatever horrors we surmised he had endured were rooted in gossip, the kind the regime encouraged because it instilled fear.

"I was willing to provide the evidence, and take full responsibility for Sayyid Baqir's death . . . The bigger the victim, presumably, the better for them. I told the investigating judges this a hundred times. But your leaders were not willing to go down that road. Why? Could it be because they knew I would tell the world not only why it was necessary for Sayyid Baqir to die, but how he died, whimpering at my feet? His halo would not be worth a pot to piss in after that. Meanwhile, my own would grow, as the arch-monster of our times perhaps, but also as the one who always did what it took to stave off the barbarians at the gates.

"I defeated the country that humiliated America. I annexed Kuwait, in Arabism's name. I gassed and crushed the Kurds, coming closer than any Arab leader before me to a final solution of the Kurdish question. All these things I did while never stooping to body counts to judge whether I was right or wrong. If I set the oil fields on fire in 1991, it was in order to teach those Gulf rulers a lesson. Shame on them for paying foreign armies to do their fighting! And if I taught you Shi'a a harsh lesson in 1991, it was so you would not forget who you were. Rising up against your nation at a time of war is gross treachery! And did I not build a nuclear capability, not once but over and over again each time it was destroyed? Why should the Arabs not have that which Israel and the West do not deny themselves? I did these things disregarding the cost in the short term, mindful only of the glory passed on to future generations.

"How the peoples of Palestine and the Arab world cheered me on when I did these things! They at least understood. Is that why the Occupier's minions did not try me for them? They knew I wanted to be remembered for those deeds! I had earned the right to be tried for them. And so they had to execute me before such trials could be held. They were afraid to look small by comparison with me. And you know what? They were right.

"What am I being hanged for in the end? For punishing men from a defeated little terrorist organization who organized an ambush at a time of war, firing upon their head of state's motorcade—only to botch the job? By God! Their country was under attack; 1982 was our worst year; the Iranians were pushing back and had taken territory inside Iraq! And botch it where? . . . In a Godforsaken village called Dujail! I mean, really . . . no one had heard of the wretched place before! . . . What a fuss over nothing. Kings have killed for less since the beginning of time, and had their praises sung to the skies because of it."

He had a point. The Tyrant ordered indiscriminate mass killings to crush the Uprising of 1991. Tens of thousands were killed or buried alive in prison camps like Radwaniyya, where my father met his end; others were shoveled into mass graves with bulldozers like the ones being uncovered near Hilla. My father was in one of them. Why was the Tyrant not being punished for what he did to my father?

Could it be because he had executed followers of the prime minister's own party in Dujail, and the prime minister wanted the small wrong done to his party to go down in history, instead of the enormous wrongs done to the whole nation? If the Great Tyrant is hanged only for the 142 dead of Dujail, instead of the millions of others he had killed, his band of failed conspirators look more important than they actually were. The Tyrant admitted to the executions at his trial. He always took responsibility for his handiwork, dismissing as irrelevant the names in official correspondence. His judges were delighted, thinking that they had nailed him with his "confession," as he expected them to.

Meanwhile, he had started talking again.

"Do you really think the Americans came halfway across the world with hundreds of thousands of soldiers to punish me for Dujail? Three years of incarceration, endless interrogations, mountains of documents, truckloads of depositions, billions of American dollars spent . . . and Dujail is the best they can do! Pathetic.

"It took character and leadership to order those people shot. You were both too young to remember," he said, turning from 'Ali to me.

"We were in retreat and taking heavy casualties; Iranian saboteurs were crawling all over the country. No doubt some of the people I executed in Dujail were innocent. But could I afford to waste time ferreting them out when Iraq's fate was hanging in the balance?

"Shooting the lot in Dujail bolstered the authority of your state, which was under attack. Do not imagine I cared two figs about my own personal authority; it was your future that was on the line . . . It was war! Your fellow citizens were dying. Should I have put their lives in danger as I counted out the one or two who might be innocent? And what if the murderous sons of bitches in Dujail had succeeded? The Iranians would be inside Baghdad within the week, their clerics cutting off your heads for not wearing the right clothes!

"Men pay for their beliefs in blood. It has always been so. The willingness to die, the ability to do it well, like the judgment to kill in Dujail, and be seen doing it with absolute conviction, is a gift only a handful possess: the gift of leadership. This quality is not present in the carpetbaggers whom the Americans put in that courtroom, men like that judge, who wants to be seen by his colleagues getting revenge for a brother who informed upon his friends, some of whose relatives were sitting on the court's benches judging me.

"You are not like them . . . are you? . . . Yes, I am talking about both of you. Don't be alarmed. I don't bite.

"It's the Americans I don't understand," he suddenly said, not waiting for an answer and rising from his chair to pace up and down the tiny room. He walked slowly, in carefully measured steps, his age showing through the badly powdered wrinkles of his face.

"Did they not have a plan for the day after?" he went on, talking to himself. "How can you defend your interests as an Occupier with such people in command? There was a time when nations sought to surpass one another, to defeat each other in battle, and then to the victors went all the spoils. The rules were simple; I applied them in Kuwait. Gut the place; take everything; teach the bastards a lesson.

But these Americans are different; it is not spoils they are after—those are anyway going to their enemy Iran.

"They seem to have come with this strange idea of wanting a whole country to love them and be in their own image. It is like the English and their dogs: they are never so proud as when they think they have succeeded in making their dogs love them, and never so disappointed as when they realize that not all dogs want to love their masters."

He stopped abruptly and thumped the wooden surface of the table with his fist, turning his gaze right at us; his eyes now held ours in thrall, like a snake fixating on a bird.

"Tell me, what glory is to be had from a competition between things that are all the same? It is the differences between nations that are interesting. Strangely, inside America it is the opposite; each person is a nation unto himself. And yet they are all the same in that they have no other love or idol but for themselves. Pure egoism binds their men and women to the world . . . the opposite of our own Arab experience.

"On the outside we Arabs are composed of a great variety of countries and communities. But deep down, where it matters the most, and when the nation is at its most glorious and at one with itself, which happens from time to time . . . we are as one, everybody coming together in a common cause, all parts striking as one fist. I live for such moments!

"Tell me, young man," he said, looking straight at me, "do you love America? Or you," he said, turning to 'Ali, "do you wish you were an American?"

We said nothing. Poor 'Ali seemed to be fading away into a trance, staring grimly at the cracks running through the floor slab. He looked sick. There was nothing in the rulebook that we had not been given to tell us what to do in circumstances like this. I began to worry 'Ali might do something stupid.

"I thought so," he said.

"Then again," he said in a lower voice but still boring right through us, clearly coming to a conclusion of some sort, "perhaps I have got the Americans all wrong. Perhaps they never intended to turn Iraq into America, but were seeking revenge for their defeat in the Mother of All Battles in 1991! . . . Perhaps they want the descent into the anarchy and chaos that now engulfs us. Perhaps that is why they never took me up on my offers to negotiate and went along with that charade of a trial."

He returned to pacing up and down the bare concrete floor of the room, carefully avoiding the cracks, his hands clasped behind his back, calibrating each step, adjusting its length, working things out. Minutes passed in silence, until he seemed to arrive at a decision. The private portion of his musings had come to an end. He looked up, and asked us to relax and be at ease—not an easy thing to do under the circumstances.

He, Saddam, "President of Iraq," had something important to set before us; it was his testament, he said, which had already been given to his lawyer. He had a copy in the pocket of his overcoat, intended as notes for a final speech "to posterity," as he put it. He hoped to deliver the speech in the execution hall. But that was before the handover; Iraqis were now going to execute him, not Americans. He knew he was not going to get the opportunity to deliver it. He reached into the pocket of his overcoat and pulled out several pieces of neatly folded paper, which he spread out on the table in front of him.

"What shall I do with these?" he said in a conversational tone of voice and with a smile on his lips as he looked at us.

'Ali was looking as if his mere presence in the room while the Tyrant said anything was a punishable transgression. Saddam continued smiling, in a slimy, nasty way, the weariness having been wiped off his face; perhaps he was enjoying toying with us.

I snapped: "Read it!"

'Ali looked at me, horrified. I had broken a spell. I think those were the first words spoken to the Tyrant since the judge had called him "Mr. President." Saddam swiveled toward me, and kept on smiling mysteriously as though he were being entertained.

"No . . . I don't think I will. Not enough room," he said, sweeping his arm to embrace the whole room. "But you look like a brave man," he said, nodding in my direction. "Here, take it. You read it later—you are on duty, after all. Consider it a gift. Pass it on. Sell it if you like; it might make you rich and famous." He was drawling again, savoring his words in an irritating way. He passed the papers to me. I took the speech and put it in my pocket, determined not to say another word. 'Ali was looking sick.

I could not but take a peek at how it started.

In this my Last Will and Testament, I declare that an illegally constituted court, an Occupier's Court, has condemned me to death. Before God you must know that in condemning me, they have in fact condemned you and all your ancestors. For what did I do or teach that all the ancient kings of Sumer, Babylon, Assyria, and after them your Prophet, Peace Be Upon Him, and his successors, did not do and teach before me?

"How dare you!" I shouted, forgetting I was not going to speak again. "Comparing yourself to the Prophet!"

"This is neither the time nor the place for modesty," he said quietly, evidently pleased at having drawn me into conversation. Then he leaned forward, pointing to the wristwatch on my arm indicating the proximity of the time of his execution.

"Know that I am the distillation of five thousand years of your history."

I took to fumbling with my Kalashnikov, astounded at his brazenness, mumbling something like "You had your moment in court and did not deny your crimes."

Staring at me again with those unblinking eyes, he said, "Was that your court, or America's? The only justice I recognize comes from you."

"From me?"

"Yes, you . . . and him," he replied, nodding in Ali's direction. "And the people of Iraq.

"This so-called court exists," he went on, "because I stood up to America and America occupied us. It is not your court; it is designed to set us against one another, Sunni against Shi'i, Kurd against Arab. I never recognized it."

"No outsider can set Iraqis against one another," I replied. "We are brothers in suffering."

"I don't see you fostering brotherhood other than by mouthing platitudes and looking like a clown with that gun. You won't need it. Don't worry. I want to die onstage, before an audience. A life sacrificed in the right way and at the right time is a life well spent."

"You deserve to die."

"Why?"

"Because you have no regrets, do not apologize for your crimes, and will not ask for forgiveness from your victims."

Saddam snorted, tossing his head back: "Would you forgive me?"

"Certainly not."

"Nonetheless, I am going to ask you to forgive me."

"For what?"

"For letting you down."

"How could you do that?"

"By dying . . . It was not in my destiny to execute the idea that I lived for. And so I let you down."

"Don't let it trouble you. Nothing you can say or do today is going to change my mind."

"A smart one!" he said, amused. "Look, son, why not judge me as one who has been joined at the hip to our people for thirty-five years, longer than you have been on this earth? I am able to teach you things."

"I doubt it."

"He who has learned how to die is free in a way that you are not, even with that gun in your hand. I offer you my freedom. Let it be your first lesson."

"I don't want it."

"Ahh . . . you say that now. But the truth of my dictatorship will survive among you as whisperings," he went on, "late at night, in your living rooms, talking about the latest outrage. It will survive because it is born naturally in the instincts for unity, security, and order. I gave you those things, and now they are gone. The desire to regain them, however, will not go away, and as soon as you feel that desire, know that my spirit is back, walking among you. Death will be my redemption."

An ancient doctrine came to mind that I had seen in one of my father's books. It claimed that the true sovereign had two bodies: one mortal and the other immortal. Why was this arch-manipulative, deceitful, genocidal maniac talking to me about spirits and immortality and redemption? Was it all an act for the benefit of the simpletons he thought 'Ali and me to be?

"Spirits walking among the living . . . what rubbish. Your whole life was a crime against this country. If you lived for anything, it was for the palaces you kept on building while we languished."

"And you, what do you live for?"

"The freedom to be who I am, and serve God."

"Be careful what you wish for. This freedom the Occupier gave you is a license for gangsters. It originates in the idea that all men are born good and have been corrupted by evil institutions such as the ones I put in place. In their place, he has contrived to erect around you new institutions. These he calls 'democracy.' But this great lie he calls democracy, resting on the even greater lie he calls 'freedom,' has existed for less than two hundred out of the five thousand years in which your ancestors have known civilization. His so-called democracy has only ever been enjoyed by a tiny fraction of our race, that very same fraction that occupied, colonized, divided, stole, and ruled at everyone else's expense. His principles and lofty so-called human rights, a doctrine designed to demote the future of a nation over its present, rest on a history of violence far greater than I ever practiced. Is this what you live for?"

"Of course not!"

"Ask yourself then: Is the Occupier's view of human nature convincing? I say not. Men are born weak, and the notion of 'tricking' their weakness through mechanically contrived institutions like democracy is both stupid and foreign to our Arab nature. You and your friend over there," he said, "are supposed to be soldiers. Are you?"

"Of course we are."

"Don't lie to me, son," he drawled. "I don't have the time for it."

"Okay, okay. In a manner of speaking, I am not in the Iraqi Army. My superiors in the Army of the Awaited One asked me to put on this uniform for today."

"I suppose your leaders arranged all this behind the backs of the Americans?"

I didn't answer, and fell silent. My leaders had switched armies on me for one day, the day of the hanging, and dressed me in a New Iraqi Army uniform. I was told not to boast or talk of my temporary membership in the New Army. Previously, I had never been encouraged to look upon the government as anything other than the Occupier's puppet. Now I was a soldier of said government, elected in 2005, even though I never had a day's worth of training in my life, and did not vote for anyone in the elections. In fact, the first man I killed during the fighting in Najaf in 2004 was not an American but a fellow Shi'i from the same New Army whose uniform I was now wearing.

"Our Iraqi nature is more deceitful and meaner than most," Saddam went on in a voice tinged with sadness. "If among the Palestinians, for instance, envy takes the form of trying to educate oneself to be better than the next man, in Iraq, the preference is to denigrate excellence. If a man is rich, the Iraqi will wish him to be poor; if a man is generous, the Iraqi will insist it is for the sake of business. Another's helplessness rarely stimulates compassion; more often it excites ill will. Any threat to self-importance is enough to create a lifelong resentment in a real Iraqi man. The success of my dictatorship relied less on terror than on understanding and working with these vices . . . Add up your current rulers, son, by which I mean all the ones now in government, the ones who were in earlier incarnations of the Occupier's government, along with all their advisors and those buffoons they put in Parliament and their advisors . . . Don't forget them. Roughly, how many people are we talking about?"

"I have no idea."

"Ten thousand or so, I say. Not more. Fair enough? Not counting secretaries, clerks, and the like, of course. Here they are, then, all ten thousand of them, filling important leadership posts in the shiny new democratic institutions the Occupier has provided . . . Now tell me, according to whose view of human nature are these people today behaving, mine or the Occupier's?"

"What are you talking about?"

"Does their behavior in the service of the people who elected them support the view that men are good? I am asking you to tell me if that is the case based on your own experience. Or, do you find support for my view that men are at their core selfish, desirous of enriching themselves at the expense of those they are meant to serve?"

"I don't understand . . ."

"I think you do, son. You don't like where the argument is taking you."

"And where is that?"

"To the truth of my dictatorship, which is grounded in how naturally rapacious and disgusting people are. You see them bleeding your country dry at this very moment in the name of your Occupier's freedom and democracy. Don't deceive yourself, son!"

I didn't want to go on, and he was beginning to look tired. Several awkward minutes later, musing to himself, he appeared to contradict everything he had just said.

"Among the meanest Iraqis I have seen shooting stars of greatness, scintillating moments of kindness. These light up the sky if only for moments before fading away . . . I lived for them, son. Nothing I have said is intended to denigrate my people. It would be wrong of you to understand me that way. You see, I am like you, I am one of you . . . We are one."

"You were never one of us!" I shouted. "You set yourself apart and had us killed in your prisons and never-ending wars."

"The true dictator is a lonely man; he holds back parts of himself that at great personal expense he has to make indifferent to family and friends. He lives a radical kind of loneliness, like a prisoner in one of his own cells, loving no one, and expecting none to love him. The people he trusts the least are always the ones who claim to love him the most. Strange, is it not, how everything in the end is reduced to one form or another of love . . . Do you love Iraq?"

"Like I love my own life. It is why I am carrying this." I lifted my Kalashnikov, pushing it in his face. "It is why I am here."

"Well spoken! Arab Iraq! . . . That is the idea I have lived for and will die by. It seems we do have something in common."

"Not on your life," I said, getting angry again.

"Let us start with the fact that I am your president."

"You are a criminal awaiting execution."

"Never mind. I was your president. And you are my children, whether you like it or not; even those bastards who sat in judgment over me are my children. You may not have loved me, but you knew I was strong and you feared and respected me. Compare me one last time with your current crop of rulers, that class of ten thousand or so individuals we talked about earlier. Notice how desperate they are to enhance their authority. They do so not because I was popular— I never stooped to curry favor, not even from you. They do so because they are so spectacularly unpopular. They desperately want to be seen by you as something they know in their hearts they are not. More people praise me in Baghdad today than praise them. Why? . . . Because not one of them loves an idea bigger than his own self. Of Iraq they are wholly ignorant. Instead they bow before your enemies, sometimes Iran, sometimes Saudi Arabia, and always America . . . Tell me: What is Iraq to you?"

"My country, my nation, the cradle of civilization. We invented writing, law . . . Do you want me to go on?"

"Nicely put. And the essence of every nation is singularity, oneness, is it not? You are of it, or you are not. You are with it or against it. There are no half measures. Agreed?"

"Yes."

"This essence of the nation is just an idea, an idea wrapped in mystery; its origins can be many things: a lie, a myth, or perhaps something inherently unknowable. It does not matter. The point is never to confuse the idea of the nation with the purely mundane. No nation, however great, was founded on something called fact. We always begin with an idea, which, as I said, can even be a lie. The details of the lie serve to differentiate nations from one another; in and of themselves they do not matter."

"So what matters?" I asked, feeling a bit lost.

"Faith in the nation matters: unyielding, unbending, and unthinking faith. Feelings, instincts, and traditions . . . these go into the making of such faith, and come before utility and logic. Love of the nation matters. Blind love. Faith is that all-encompassing, unreasoning blind love. Are you with me?"

"I think so."

"The fountainhead of your love, your faith, is the deep well of our own particular Arab past. That inheritance shapes your hopes and desires; it is who you are. The problem of the Occupier, the stone upon which his rule shall stumble in Iraq, is that it treats these fundamental things like goods that can be bought and sold in the market. The Occupier finds them charming, perhaps, but as a foreigner does a bazaar full of fake antiques. The Occupier is incapable of understanding the innermost core of your singularity, the very fundaments of who you are as a person."

"I think I see what you are driving at."

"Now look at these same things through a different prism: Are you a good Muslim?"

"How dare you . . ."

"Keep your shirt on, boy. I am merely trying to reason together, as it were, step by step; think of it as an exercise. Do you have something better to do?"

"Go on."

"So you are a good Muslim, a man of True Belief. Your faith is the object of your love. Another word for it is Spirit, a Spirit that is to the nation what your soul is to the cells of your body; blood, bones, and organs, these mundane things return to the earth, but your soul has a separate connection to God, whose realm it hopes one day to enter. So it is with the nation, whose physical attributes are separate from its Spirit. Now, this Spirit is a truly remarkable thing; it is capable of outgrowing earlier incarnations; it evolves and changes, perfecting itself over time while essentially remaining the same. And yet those earlier incarnations belong to it; they are still present, so to speak, in the deep well of your patrimony."

"I don't see the point of all this."

"You will. I said the nation is an idea wrapped in mystery, and you agreed. I asked if you were a good Muslim and you said you were. Now I say the living proof of that mystery is what makes you a Muslim."

"Proof?"

"Our Holy Book, the Quran, revealed to us Arabs by God through an Arab Prophet and in our own Arabic tongue. No coincidences or accidents of fate there; just God's will. His proof: the Quran. He chose us Arabs over all the other nations on earth at the time, just as in an earlier manifestation He chose the Jews."

"I don't like where this is going."

"Why? Because I brought up the Jews . . . They didn't do anything by creating Israel that we don't want to do as Arabs and Muslims."

"You are putting Arab victims on the same plane as Jewish victimizers."

"I understand your feelings. My point is that some of our Muslim clerics would have you believe, wrongly, that being an Arab nationalist and being a good Muslim are two different things. They are not; they are one and the same. The Occupier also wants you to forget your umbilical connection with Islam, the essential Spirit of our nation; he calls it separating religion from politics, and his minions are trying to do just that by breaking up that gigantic singular Arab tree called Muslim Iraq into the easily scattered and broken little twigs that you are turning into today."

"But religion is prior to nationalism," I said lamely; "it is more fundamental." No sooner had I said that than Saddam changed course:

"Didn't you say you loved Iraq, son?"

"I am not your son," I snapped back, irritated at my inability to press home an argument.

"Don't be rude," he said, pointedly raising his voice, like an elder admonishing his junior. "Have respect for your traditions. How solid is your love of Iraq? Answer the question!"

"I already did."

"Then which comes first: your love of Iraq or your love of Islam?"

"That is a false choice. I reject the dichotomy."

"Precisely! . . . You have made the point I was looking for," Saddam replied.

"Islamic community in times past is Arab nation in times present," he went on. "These words are cut from the same cloth. But how is God's will carried out? How does the nation come into being? Do you think it is something to be found in nature, sitting out there like ripe fruit hanging on a tree? Of course not! It has to be made, forged into existence."

"By whom?"

"Exceptional men, of course. Exceptional men like our Prophet Muhammad, Peace Be Upon Him. His inner resources gave birth to a Community of Believers, uniting warring tribes and factions into a magnificent fighting force that changed the world. In so doing, our Prophet became the first Arab revolutionary. Only he didn't call what he did an Arab Revolution; he called it an Islamic Revolution."

Flabbergasted, I didn't know what to say. I had never heard someone say that before. Saddam went on.

"It is the same with Israel. Who made it possible? Who created it at our Arab expense? Imperialism, of course, but that was not enough. Never buy into everything your own side says. We say Israel is a creation of imperialism, but we know there is more to it than that. There was a Jewish national idea, analogous to our own Arab national idea, championed by their own exceptional men, prophets in olden times and clever politicians in modern ones; it is they who forged a Jewish state out of that idea—at our expense, of course."

"At Palestinian expense, millions of them! I thought you were never coming around to that."

"So these Jewish leaders nudged, connived, warred, and tricked imperial powers to do what was patently not in their national interest to do. Now I ask you: Aren't your Shi'a leaders trying to trick the Americans into setting up a Shi'a state for them, just like the Jews tricked them into doing the same sixty years ago, supporting the creation of a Jewish state in Palestine? There is no difference."

"Are you telling me our Prophet Muhammad was the first Arab nationalist?"

"Yes, he is the leader of the first Arab revolution. I modeled my life upon his example."

"You call your bloody wars leading the Arab revolution!"

"Don't change the subject! Was our Prophet, Peace Be Upon Him, a leader of *both* the revolution that was Islam and the revolution that is Arabism? Answer the question."

"I need to think about it."

After a short pause, Saddam quietly said: "There are Arabs, incidentally, in whom the Spirit languishes."

"You mean they are not good Muslims?"

"The other way around, son; I mean they are not good Arabs. You Shi'a are a case in point."

"Are you implying that we do not love Iraq?" I replied angrily.

"History shows," he said, ignoring me, "that your elites, your so-called learned clerics, sniff out weak government like rats scurrying about in the garbage. At the outset of our statehood, three of your most influential Ayatollahs issued rulings declaring against Iraq. They boycotted the elections and opposed employment in the state, including the army and all offices of the government; they ruled against Shi'a children attending public schools. King Faisal, our first king, was far too tolerant with them. Still your clerics would not bend. And so, if you ended up with a state disproportionately populated with Sunnis, it is the fault of your clerics."

"How dare you say that? You discriminated against us more than anyone, targeting our clerics, our rituals, and our mosques."

"Only when you did not give Arab Iraq your total, unconditional, and absolute loyalty. Sometimes you did, as in the war with Iran, which we would have lost had you not fought so bravely on behalf of this country. And sometimes you did not, as in 1991, that great page of treachery and betrayal. Then, I cut you down mercilessly, and would do so again."

"You are the arch-sectarian!" I said, my face red with anger. "Your tanks drove into Najaf in 1991 with the slogan 'No More Shi'a After Today' painted on them. And you accuse us of disloyalty!"

"That was not my doing. An overzealous commander painted the slogan on his tank. I had him demoted for that. I despise sectarianism."

"Liar!"

"Why would I lie to you today of all days? . . . All I want is that before we walk out of this room, you accept the essential oneness of three things: being an Iraqi, an Arab, and a Muslim. Unlike your so-called leaders, I never cared two figs how a man prayed, with his hands folded in front of him or straight down by his side! Do you?"

"No."

"I thought as much. Men who play games with the date of the appearance of the crescent moon and the beginning of the Feast of Sacrifice in order to screw their Sunni brothers demean us Iraqis in the eyes of the whole Arab and Muslim world."

"I have had enough."

"Remember me also, son," Saddam went on, ignoring me, "as the one who destroyed Atheism and Disbelief in Iraq, not your clerics."

"What on earth are you talking about?"

"The fight against communism in the 1970s, of course. Do you not know that you Shi'a—I mean your fathers' and grandfathers' generations, before you were born—were all Communists back then? And had been since the 1940s, when your community turned away from those turbaned crows you call clerics and joined the Communist Party. There was no such thing as an Islamic movement in Iraq when I came to power. There were only Communists . . ."

"My grandfather may have been a Communist . . ."

"I see from your face that you do not know your own history. Your clerics were terrified in the 1950s after a handful of them woke up to see hundreds of thousands of their very own marching under Communist banners. But they could do nothing about it. I broke Communist power in Iraq because the nation was under threat from imported ideas like Atheism and subservience to the Soviet Union."

"How did you accomplish that?" I said skeptically.

"Ruthlessly."

"Yes, but how?"

"I turned them against one another."

"How can you claim to love and be so cruel at the same time?"

"Do we judge God by the same rules we judge ourselves? Does He not kill mercilessly when He has to? Did He not prefer Abel to Cain and create the first murderer, whom He then turned into an outcast? We love Him for these things. He sowed the seeds of violence in us, and we love Him for so doing. Similarly, the selfless leader kills for Justice. He too cannot be hedged about by private morality. Unlike God, however, a leader cannot expect to be loved for killing. He is alone and never knows whether he is loved or not; it is wiser therefore to assume he is not. If Iraqis hate me today, they do so because true Justice is for the most part a cruel business. I long ago accepted that I would pay the price of my people's hatred for the work I did on their behalf."

"You say you turned one Iraqi against the other?"

"The secret is to hold every individual personally accountable for all the difficult decisions that have to be made, however unpleasant. Every Iraqi, including women and children. If a man is about to betray his country, one must teach his wife and children to inform on him, or punish them until he desists. Complicity in the workings of the state forges ties that cut across all differences. It irons out all blood or ethnic ties, which belong to a more barbarous age, in order to fashion modern citizens. I am not saying it is easy; I am saying it is necessary; it is the ideal toward which one must strive. Teach, but when necessary force, your citizens to get their hands dirty. Do this long enough and your citizens will become as desirous of their state's continuing success as you are. That is my legacy. Remember me for it, son. Now I am tired of talking. I want to rest."

I often think about that bizarre conversation. Not a week passes without my rereading the piece of paper I slipped into my back pocket that day. I served the Sayyid for four years; it turned out he had killed my father's best friend, and the Tyrant had killed my father. How do the words and the killings fit together? Perhaps they don't. If I were Sayyid Majid's son, not my father's son, would I see things differently? Who is Saddam? Who is the Sayyid? I mean who are these two men really, deep down under the surface of things? Are they different from one another?

Would either Uncle or the Sayyid be able to separate the words on the pages of text Saddam gave me that day from the person of the Tyrant who wrote them? Suppose I lied and told them I had written the speech; would they fault it? I think not. Uncle would say: "Bravo, son! I like it; I really like it!" And the Sayyid? What would he say? He would approve as well but add that I was being too harsh on the Shi'a. True, our clerics said those things all those years ago, but they belonged to a different era. True, communism is the devil incarnate, but we Shi'a would have dealt with the Communists in our midst. "Better not wash dirty laundry in public, son," he would have said. "Take those passages on the Shi'a out." But, to hell with what the Sayyid thought, and what Uncle might say. What did I think about my conversation with the great Tyrant?

We were due a rotation, which couldn't come fast enough as far as poor 'Ali was concerned. He left the room. I stayed on, missing my tea break. For a short while the Tyrant and I were completely alone in the room, and he initiated our last and perhaps most extraordinary exchange of words. No amount of time will erase their freshness in my memory.

"You seem to have a little education," Saddam suddenly said in a conversational tone. "What is your name, boy?" We had been alone in the room for a few minutes. An instinct made me tell him.

"Hmm . . . Do I know your father?"

"You had him killed in the camp at Radwaniyya in 1991."

"So he was one of those."

"What do you mean, 'one of those'?"

"One who carried arms against the Motherland during that black page of treachery and betrayal in 1991 you call an Uprising."

"My father had no arms on him when your security men caught him."

"In Najaf, wasn't it? They caught him in a basement, in a house next door to one belonging to the old Ayatollah who died in 1992, Khoei, shortly after we put him on television."

I was dumbstruck. How did he know?

"You are wondering how I remember. Decades of making it my business, son, go into a memory like mine; I try to know every family in this land; their nearest relations, their children, how and to whom they married, into and out of which tribe, the mental abilities of their sons, when and under whom did they serve in my armies, what prizes or honors had they received, whom did they hate and love, and why—always I want to know why men do things—their inner motivation, if you will. Do they become members of the Ba'th Party for convenience or out of conviction? It doesn't matter to me; I am not going to punish them, but I need to know. I used to keep index cards with names, not the tens of millions of files that those buffoons in my intelligence services keep, and from which they can never find anything when you need it. I would construct family trees in my head, forming patterns of human connections, which I could visualize. Eventually, I needed them less and less. Of course I remember the case of your father."

"What do you remember?"

"Why we put him in Radwaniyya, and what happened."

"How did he die?"

"I trusted such details to my cousin; he handled all that; I only remember things I need to remember. Nature has its limits, you know. But rest assured, your father died well."

"Why do you say that? What do you mean?"

"I seem to recall he was a man of principle, like Sayyid Muhammad Baqir of the House of Sadr. He had fought very bravely in the war against that treacherous son of a bitch Khomeini. I am getting old and a bit rusty, but I remember giving him a medal. He held the line in Fao, when higher-ranking officers from my own hometown were fleeing in fear from the numbers of heaven-seeking Iranian teenagers being flung at them. Incidentally, I had them all shot for that, even though they were from Tikrit."

"One of those officers from your hometown you did not shoot," I said.

"How do you know?"

"Because he served under your cousin in Radwaniyya, and smuggled a letter to my mother from my father."

"How interesting. I did not know that," he said with the faintest hint of a smile curling like a wisp of smoke around his lips.

He gave a little laugh and said: "Perhaps he did not flee the battle, and there was no need to shoot him. But your father was a Shi'a, a son of Najaf no less; I wanted him decorated, and I wanted his compatriots to see that I had decorated him."

"Why decorate a junior officer who was repeatedly denied promotion because he was a Shi'a?"

"Ahh . . . with you Shi'a I have to be very cautious, and dole out honors selectively, and in proper doses. I chose to single him out in 1988 for bravery above the call of duty because it suited the country's needs at that time. Anyway, he was brave. Tell me, what was in that letter?"

"He thought he had been betrayed, but didn't know by whom."

"Of course he was betrayed! Those savages you call revolutionaries were slitting the throats of their neighbors, settling accounts, and denouncing all and sundry! How could I find anybody in that madhouse without an informer?"

"Who?" I asked, barely able to breathe with anticipation. "Who told you where Father was?"

Saddam Hussein paused and looked hard into my face before speaking; you could see he was choosing his words carefully.

"There were two other men with your father that day; they were our main target, not your father. One of them was also an officer in the Great War with Iran; I never discovered his real name until afterward, when he surfaced in London. He was there as protection for a third man, who was our main target, a man your father greatly admired."

"His name, what was his name?"

"Majid, the son of the Grand Ayatollah Khoei. The three of them were planning to break through our lines to ask the Americans for help; American troops were only a kilometer or two away, sitting on a huge arms depot that the traitors were desperate to get their hands on. Majid and this ex-officer made it out, but your father stayed behind, I think to cover their tracks and destroy incriminating documents—that is when we caught him. Just ten minutes earlier, and we might have got all three. Anyway, that which I was unable to accomplish in 1991, you and your friends did for me in 2003."

"What on earth are you talking about? And who gave you the location?"

"I am talking about the murder in the Great Shrine of the Imam in Najaf, on April 10, the day I decided to make a tactical retreat from Baghdad to lead an insurgency against the Occupier. I was reliably informed that his own people shredded his body to pieces, your Sayyid and his men, as a matter of fact. You might say they did our work for us, even if it came thirteen years too late."

"Who betrayed my father? Please, sir! Tell me his name."

That "sir" just slipped out. I could have kicked myself, and shudder with shame when I think about it—not that I was thinking about what I was doing at the time.

"Why, your uncle, of course. He had been working with us for years."

Saddam must have read the expression on my face.

"Ahh . . . I see," he said softly, the faintest shadow of a smile again forming around a face that looked puffy and was slowly turning grotesque.

"I thought you knew, son . . . especially after you joined the Say-yid's army."

BAGHDAD TODAY

The Tyrant's ideas opened the doors, and we walked right through. The Tyrant fell, and we became addicted to his legacy: betrayal.

Endless betrayals . . . of whole communities, and within them, of victims, of victimizers, of the one become the other, of exiles plotting against one another, of all plotting against the country, of friends stabbing one another in the back, of most learned and esteemed Houses scheming against equally learned and equally esteemed Houses, of brother selling out brother.

Was it the fault of the Tyrant? Or were we all to blame?

We Shi'a of Iraq were born in betrayal when we abandoned Husain son of 'Ali, cousin of the Prophet, God bless him, to the armies of the pretenders. Annually since, for one thousand years, we have beaten our chests, whipped our backs, and passed swords across our shaven scalps in atonement.

Did we choose to betray? Perhaps we were forced into it, against our better natures. Perhaps it was written into the war that changed everyone's life. So many wars . . . which one? It has to be the last, the war that so easily might never have been—the Tyrant who might still be there; the exiled men from London who would yet be bickering in their conference halls, living on the charity of host governments; the Sayyid who would still be hunkered down in his murdered father's house in Najaf, knowing the *killer of his father and two brothers, knowing and silent, a silence only broken when he cut to ribbons the scion of another great House of the Shi'a in Najaf: the Ayatollah's son, the one who did not keep silent . . . who did not betray.*

But I betrayed him, my father's friend. All of us betrayed him. And as we betrayed him, we betrayed ourselves. God have mercy on our souls. Forgive me for serving the House that cut him down. Ignorance is no excuse. Not when betraying him sits at the very heart of all the other betrayals, defining the very meaning of the word for us Shi'a of Iraq.

Uncle, was it really you? You held the Sayyid in the palm of your hand, and before him his father, whose organization you built to oversee the Holy City's reconstruction after the Great Uprising. Who paid for it? Who oversaw it from Baghdad? Who wanted it to happen so that long after he was dead he could pull the strings behind the scenes? Uncle, you were there. Always capable: everybody's right hand.

I know there are ambiguities. The world that the Tyrant built changed what betrayal is. I know that is what you will say. When everyone is a betrayer, then perhaps no one is. I know you will say that. You must say that.

But the Tyrant is gone. Now it is our world, not his. We alone occupy it. We cannot go on blaming him forever. He is not responsible any longer. His sins are our sins now. So who is responsible? Are we condemned to build a country in which no one is responsible? Is such a thing even imaginable?

Everything changed on the day of the hanging. Insecurity and uncertainty shaped the days and months and years afterward, and go on doing so. Even the unborn in this accursed land enter it too soon to understand the pain they will have to endure. Daily, it seems, little by little, I crawl toward the places that hurt the most; it is as though I need to go there and cannot stop myself. The expectations of others joined hands with my own unease, pulling me into an abyss that I still struggle to climb out of. If this was the darkness that I fell into after the hanging, the whole land has fallen into another, much darker than mine.

What happened that day? I did not know then, but I do now: Doubt happened. Radical doubt—the kind that admits that not everything can be understood, that even facts no longer speak for themselves. Doubt of this sort is hard for a defender of the faith, a soldier in the Army of the Awaited One, a Shiʿa Muslim, and a male Believer. We Believers are, after all, sworn to submit to God's will. Submission is the mark the Prophet left upon the face of this earth. Is there room for doubt in total submission?

Our father, the Prophet Abraham, God's friend, did not experience doubt when God commanded him to sacrifice his son—so great was his Belief. I used to think that Abraham's noblest quality was this act of total submission. I am no longer sure. Today, I wish that this Prince of Faith had been touched by doubt; I want to know the hand holding the knife trembled in the air, hesitated, before He stopped it from plunging into his son's breast. But the Good Book tells us that did not happen. Abraham didn't flinch. He didn't doubt. Tell me I am wrong, God, please! Don't condemn me to live suspended in the gap between what Abraham did and what I wish he had not been able to do.

I am being told the Barbarians are knocking at the gates. Is it possible? Can I afford to wallow in doubt with Barbarians at the door? Should I be wasting my time on pencil and paper and storytelling? Shame on me! They are saying Baghdad will not hold. The city will fall; all around me cities are falling. Whole chunks of territory are acquiring new names. Baghdad is surrounded. They are in Abu Ghraib. They have taken Mosul. Iraq is no more, they are saying. Clerics are issuing a call to arms. "Protect the Holy Places!" they shout from the rooftops. "Pick up your guns!"

The politicians still argue, still jostle against one another for a seat at the table, still give speeches and appear on television, still make statements and strike deals, still promise, still bribe and take bribes. Why aren't they picking up their guns and rushing to the front lines?

But where are the front lines? And where are they, those Barbarians? How can I tell who they are? They look like me. Certainly they are outside the city. I hear the sounds of their artillery. Perhaps they are already inside.

Car bombs are exploding everywhere. So they are inside. And they are out-side. Where are they? Who are they?

There are no walls that can protect us from ourselves, no barricades to man, no front lines to defend in the dark corners of our souls. I will need my old Kalashnikov, sitting over there in the corner. No doubt about that. They will come for me. Of that I can be certain.

Acknowledgments

In *Republic of Fear,* published in 1989, I acknowledged being indebted to Iraqis who could not be named for obvious reasons. Sadly, three decades later, I am obliged to do the same. People who do not wish to be named gave generously of their time, trusting me with sensitive information without in any way being responsible for the uses I put their trust to. I am solely and wholly responsible for what is in this book.

Among those whom I can thank by name are Ma'ad Fayadh, Kamran Qaradaghi, Salem Chalabi, Ahmed Naji, Mustafa al-Kazimi, Hassan Mneimneh, Harith Hassan, Azzurra Carpo, Laura Gross, Alan and Pamela Berger, Lawrence Weschler, Naghmeh Sohrabi, Cyrus Schayegh, Emmanuel Farjoun, and Roger Owen.

I have made use of a number of nonfiction works that must be mentioned. I owe the "feel" of wartime conditions in Najaf during August 2004, and the stories that go into the chapter "War in Najaf," to discussions with Dexter Filkins and Warzer Jaff, who were there. See Dexter Filkins's compelling accounts in the *New York Times,* August 29, 2004. I am also indebted to him for the scene with Muqtada slipping furtively out of Sistani's house, and the dead donkey and its owner, shot by snipers, which both Filkins and Jaff witnessed and was retold by Filkins in one of the finest books of frontline reporting that I have read: *The Forever War* (Alfred A. Knopf, 2008). Other nonfiction works I relied upon are the excruciatingly honest insider account by Hamed al-Khaffaf, a senior aide to Ayatollah Sistani, *Al Rihla Al Ilajiyya Li Samahat Al Sayyid Al Sistani Wa Azmat al-Najaf* (The Curative Journey of H. E. Al Sayyid Al Sistani and the Crisis of Najaf), 5th ed. (Beirut: Dar al-Mua'rikh al-'Arabi, 2012). I could not have written the chapter "Names of Things" without the extensive classificatory research into the armed militias operating inside Iraq during 2006 by Sayyid 'Ali al-Husayni, published online as *Kharitat al-Tandhimaat al-Musalaha fi al-'Iraq* (The Map of Armed Groups in Iraq), published originally in 2005 and reissued online in the fall of 2007 at iraker.dk/v/50.html.

On the apocalyptic ideas of 1990s Iraqi Shi'ism associated with Sayyid Muhammad Sadiq al-Sadr, I am grateful for the comments of Roy Mottahedeh and the in-depth discussions and e-mail exchanges with Hassan Mneimneh and 'Ali Mamouri.

In ways too numerous to mention, Judith Shklar's seminal essay "Ambiguities of Betrayal," published in *Ordinary Vices* (Harvard University Press, 1984), helped me think through the many quandaries of the phenomenon. More generally, Part Three of this book, the conversation between Saddam and my narrator, is indebted to great precedents such as Dostoevsky's "The Grand Inquisitor" and George Steiner's strange *The Portage to San Cristobal of A.H.* (Faber & Faber, 1981), in which Hitler implicates Western civilization in his emergence, much as I have Saddam do for Arab Muslim civilization.

Cormac McCarthy's inimitable darkness is a balm I seek when I am thinking about Iraq; likewise, Seamus Deane's weave of family grief and politics in *Reading in the Dark* (Alfred A. Knopf, 1997) and Vasily Grossman's telling of the Battle of Stalingrad in *Life and Fate* (New York Review Books, 2006). I don't know why this should be so, other than that it is uplifting to find beauty while one is groping to describe darkness. The same can be said of the poetry of Nâzim Hikmet, Osip Mandelstam, and Zbigniew Herbert, whose sensibility haunts this book. Lawrence Weschler, whose own books are always an inspiration, first introduced me to Herbert and Polish postwar poetry, with its deep insight into societies that have been traumatized by nationalism, war, and totalitarianism.

A different kind of gratitude, finally, must go to my editor, Dan Frank. He not only believed in this book from early on, but he always knew how to separate the essence of what I wanted to say from the words that I dumped on his desk. And he did it, time and again, with such grace. This is a far better book because of him.

A Personal Note

I lived in Iraq for most of the time between 2003 and 2006, the period covered by the events in this book. They were momentous years, which abruptly changed the course of a nation and ultimately foreshadowed upheaval in the whole region. As time passed I stopped asking myself whether the ugliness of the fallout from the tyrant's overthrow and U.S. occupation could have been avoided. To be sure, the occupation was brainless, and made worse by the fact that the regime it replaced had rotted during the 1990s. The Ba'thi state of 2003 was not the Republic of Fear I wrote about in the 1980s. But even that does not explain the scale of what went wrong.

The snowballing of the catastrophe that is post-2003 Iraq transfixed me: the speed of it, the underlying passions, the strange new ideas that suddenly possessed people like demons, but above all, as I witnessed it, the self-destructing Iraqi agency behind it all. That agency is what I had to write about.

Iraqis, not Americans, were the prime drivers of what went wrong after 2003, not only the ones who had suffered and lived through the regime of the Ba'th between 1968 and 2003, but also Iraqis who rode in from abroad, as my narrator observes, "on the tanks of the Occupier."

Necessarily my attention was drawn to society's fate, or what the characters sometimes refer to as the "idea" of Iraq, an idea that was up for grabs, and instantly discarded the moment the American occupying authority appointed the "Iraqi Governing Council." But it was not Americans who did the discarding; it was the Iraqis they had empowered, the nucleus of the new governing elite that still dominates politics in Baghdad today.

I, like many others, knew that "Iraq" was an idea bound to be challenged after more than thirty years of a dictatorship that was never comfortable with the borders of post-Ottoman Iraq and that launched two wars of expansion to change them. What did it mean to be an Iraqi once the great dictator was gone? Was it possible to cobble together a new kind of Iraqi identity, not based on the bombast of "the cradle of civilizations" or the supposed glories of the Abbasid era? No one knew; Iraq had "turned into a question for itself," as the narrator's uncle in my story puts it.

However, no one predicted the speed with which the new Iraqi Arab political elite would abandon an idea nearly a century in the making, and which they had spent decades in opposition claiming to defend. When an idea such as Iraq is abandoned, the country is sure to follow, as it is doing as of this writing. In this book, set long before there was something called ISIS capturing great big chunks of Iraqi territory, I try to explore not the causes (much too difficult) but the way the abandonment happened, its human and felt side. Even that I know I have not done justice to. There is much more painfully critical research and writing to be carried out.

Ideas by their very nature are general; people are not. The conflict is as irresolvable as the fate of "Iraq" is today unknowable. I have tried to imagine the two bouncing off one another through the experiences of my characters. This is not a polemic directed at others, as some of my other books have been; it is an exercise in self-examination, an attempt to show, if only by way of reminding myself, what happened to Iraq during those three crucial years.

My characters are not real people; they are composites, sometimes exaggerated, assembled mosaic-like in search of underlying truths that might illuminate how Iraqis, especially Shi'a Iraqis like myself, so abysmally failed not only the whole country after 2003, but also their own community. I hoped to exploit the close-up view I was granted by virtue of my previous work examining tyranny in Ba'thi Iraq, to imagine how perfectly competent, well-educated, and intelligent individuals drove the country into an abyss, and, perhaps more generally, what that says about what counts in the politics of great historical turning points in the lives of nations.

Friends and colleagues urged me to write a different kind of book. I owed it to those who went along with my justifications for the 2003 war to critically examine my previous support for the war, they said, or the fact that I never wrote about Abu Ghraib (of which I am ashamed). Was it all worth it in the end? Would I in retrospect still say the things I said before 2003? Did I not owe it to the memory of all those who died to apologize, perhaps, for the disgraceful way Iraqis treated what the United States did for them by toppling their very own homegrown tyrant? And then, of course, there was the delusion I propagated of building democracy in a country that almost immediately descended into the worst kind of civil war imaginable.

These are legitimate questions that need to be addressed not only by me, but by anyone who argued for the 2003 war. Whether they are good reasons to write a book is moot; the point is, that is not what this book is about. The fact is for years I couldn't write, because had I done so it would have been in anger and bitterness, in a work filled with recrimination and wallowing in guilt. I did not want that. Perhaps I couldn't write, period. I don't know. At any rate, I shunned all opportunities to comment or write about the deteriorating situation in Iraq. Perhaps I was too close to events, or had too many scars in the failed attempt to make a better job of the opportunity the United States, for its own post-9/11 reasons, offered the people of Iraq—I still think that is what it was—and which we Iraqis so abysmally failed to take advantage of.

In my defense, I want to say that while I always thought of

democracy as a *possible* and unquestionably desirable outcome, in my heart of hearts I never believed it was *necessarily* the path that a post-Saddam order would take. I conceded, when pushed by Bill Moyers on his program *NOW* in February 2003, that the chances for a successful transition to democracy were very slim—the bleakness of all my previous books is evidence of that. Nonetheless, I argued on the program that even if the chances of a successful democratic transition were extremely low, they were still worth fighting for from an Iraqi point of view (I make no such claim from an American point of view; there is a difference between the two, as difficult as that may be for a believer in the universality of human rights, like myself, to swallow). The most important changes in politics are by definition unpredictable and happen at the very outer limits of what is possible—they are not a function of the lowest common denominator of a society as abused as Iraq's had been for thirty years. At any rate, democracy is not as important as the cessation of abuse. On those grounds alone, I still stand firmly with the war of 2003. The terrible thing, of course, is that egregious abuse did not end in 2003; it began all over again, as victims turned into victimizers and vice versa. Could it have been otherwise? I believe so.

Mine was the politics of hope, as some have called it, of daring to believe that the unimaginable before 2003 was possible after 2003. Of that I am guilty. But in that respect, I am no more guilty than the brave young Arab activists of 2011, who also took issue with the odds and lost; the only difference being many of them died for what they believed, while I returned to live in the West; a big difference to be sure, but not a political one.

Two would not return: my friend Ammar Shabandar, who was killed by a car bomb on Saturday, May 2, 2015, in the Karrada district of Baghdad. And Mustafa al-Kazimi, who washed and buried him in Najaf, and to whom I always knew I was going to dedicate this book, long before dear Ammar was killed. Exemplary journalists, but more important exceptional human beings, they covered abuse and war on a daily basis, delving deep into the pain of ordinary Iraqi men and women (and children in Ammar's case), while almost everyone else looked out only for themselves.

The two are also, like myself, "Foreigner Iraqis," the unfriendly term I coin in this book for all of us who returned to build a New Jerusalem in Iraq. Both returned from exile in Sweden to serve. In the flurry of e-mail exchanges following the shock of Ammar's death, we friends of his—Hassan, Rend, Mustafa, and I—worried about Mustafa, still in Iraq, fighting the good fight against all the odds. Hassan in heart-wrenching words urged Mustafa to leave Iraq. I have been doing the same for years. He won't; I know. Our entreaties fall on deaf ears because Mustafa, like Ammar, is that rare kind of soul who is still able to bestow on that tired and abused word "patriot" a good meaning. I bring this up for a larger reason. Criticism, of the sort I try to practice in this book, is not worthy of the name if it is not born in love.

We Arabs who took issue with the abuses of our regimes, and acted upon it, and especially I who was up there in the limelight calling for the toppling of the dictator, have an obligation to answer for the sectarian turmoil that ensued, symbolized by the disgraceful way in which Saddam was executed in 2006. You knew it was over when that particular circus was concluded. The mountain of Iraqi dead since 2003, most of whom were killed by other Iraqis, compares in its scale to the worst excesses of the Saddam era. I acknowledge I have a responsibility to them, to Ammar, and to the living who still believe and who refuse to leave the front lines, like Mustafa. This book, scathing as it is toward the men who created the politics that gave rise to all the killing, all friends of mine, is all I know how to do by way of atonement.

Iraq, it turns out, was the dress rehearsal for what befell an entire region. In fact, the main event did not end up being an Iraqi one; it is an all-Arab rolling affair, today being played out in Bahrain, Syria, Libya, and Yemen; tomorrow somewhere else. To describe it as a "crisis" is grotesque; it is a civilizational breakdown that began half a century ago, when it gave us the tyrants activists such as Ammar and Mustafa so much wanted to rid us of. Then followed all the wars, and the civil wars, and the intifadas, and the al-Qaedas, and the Hizbollahs . . . until finally we come to the failed states and the ISISs of our own time. Yes, it was ISIS that killed Ammar, but it might as well have been the Cabal of Thirteen, or the entire class of Iraq's Shi'a politicians who between 2003 and 2006 created the politics upon which ISIS thrives.

It all began in Iraq; perhaps the Lebanese Civil War (1975–1989) was a foreshadowing. But Iraqi-style sectarianism was more lethal. And it was not invented as a way of doing politics because America chose to get rid of Saddam Hussein in 2003; it is infantile to think that, although many in the region still do. The rot goes much deeper. For the sake of all those Iraqi dead, such as Ammar, and for the sake of the living, such as Mustafa, I had to tell the story of how we made our own failure in Iraq, and why we own it, not the great big bogeyman of the West.

Iraq is also the arena that best shows why our failure is an all-Arab and all-Muslim one, neither merely Sunni nor merely Shi'i. The failure is too big, too deeply rooted in what has been happening in the interstices of Arab culture for so many decades now, to dress it all up with labels such as "made in the USA." Far too many otherwise intelligent men and women continue to say such things, some of them leaders empowered by Western action in 2003. They look you in the eye and say: ISIS is an American or a Saudi or an Iranian creation. You know the irrational is supreme when you see American warplanes pummel ISIS in Tikrit, and Iraqi Shi'a leaders, who would otherwise be rotting in Saddam's jails, making such statements even as the bombing is being aired on television.

The triumph of the irrational, however, is not a permanent or a lasting state of affairs, written into the genes of who we are as a culture. Mustafa and Ammar know this. One day, a new generation of activists acting in the spirit of the defeated democratic activism of 2003 and 2011, people like Ammar and Mustafa and not like the Cabal of Thirteen, or the Governing Council, will morph the darkness into light, into a new beginning for Arab Muslims, returning them to the fold of civilization.

My realization, in late 2004, that Iraq was sliding toward civil war was a turning point in my life. The whole edifice of hopes that had clung to that slim possibility of a different kind of transition from dictatorship crumbled. Self-doubt began to eat away at the optimism that had sustained me since 1991.

Strangely, I recall precisely the moment when it began. I was having dinner in the summer of 2004 at a good friend's house in an upscale district of Baghdad. Another friend, then a minister in government, was present. The three of us, all graduates of the same elite American university, spent the evening discussing politics. The host talked as if he had all along predicted a Shi'i-Sunni breakdown. He spoke with a kind of certitude, and self-assurance, which I found troubling. We both began to raise our voices and lose our tempers, something that had never happened before. What bothered me was the feeling that he was looking forward to a final showdown with those "Sunnis," who, he predicted, would be crushed. And Muqtada's uprising, with his ragtag "Army of the Awaited One," made up of deadbeats and thugs—I chose only the best to populate my story: Haider, Muntassir, and the narrator—had just proved they could fight the Americans in Najaf. Both friends were excited and upbeat about that fight, going so far as to see in Muqtada al-Sadr the leader of a second intifada (the first being in 1991). Here were the shock troops in the Armageddon against Sunni Arabs that was being prophesied. I experienced that evening something I had not seen in either of my friends before. Cynics say it was there all along. I don't know. We all changed in 2003. Through the eyes of close Lebanese friends who had experienced the carnage of the Lebanese Civil War, I had seen how that kind of violence was the ultimate political evil that could descend upon a country, worse even than Saddam's tyranny, and that the only point of anyone's politics ought to be how to avoid going there.

·   ·   ·

With the exception of Saddam Hussein and Muqtada al-Sadr, I knew all the politicians alluded to in the book. Many of them I worked with in the course of meetings of the Iraqi opposition during the 1990s in Iraqi Kurdistan, London, or the United States. I knew the real people, I hasten to add, not the sculpted versions of them that appear in the novel. Among them was Sayyid Majid al-Khoei; he was in fact murdered on April 10, 2003. I did not make that up. I interviewed him at length in London in the early 1990s, shortly after his escape from Najaf. The interview appeared in my 1993 book *Cruelty and Silence*. Sayyid Majid requested at the time that I conceal his identity, because he risked being misunderstood, having saved the life of a wounded Ba'thi officer, slated to be killed just like poor Hasan al-Najafi, whose fate, a true story, is told by my narrator's grandfather.

The narrator and his grandfather, along with his mother, father, and uncle, bear no resemblance to any Iraqi living or dead. I know or met people like them and like Haider, Abu Haider, and Najmaldin, but they are composites. Colleagues at the Iraq Memory Foundation and I, for instance, helped one man who had been an Iraqi pilot flying search and rescue missions during the Iraq-Iran War and who became terrified at one point because, he believed, Iranian agents were hunting his fellow pilots and gunning them down at night, just as I describe in "An Intimate Killing." I cannot confirm that the man's fears were legitimate; I can only confirm that they, and similar apprehensions, abounded after 2003. There was much settling of accounts in the first year. Many people were killed silently outside of the political limelight. Eventually we arranged for our colleague at the Memory Foundation to work abroad for a year. If a deeper resemblance to real persons crosses the reader's mind, it is purely accidental.

The stories my fictional characters tell are by and large based on real events. The conditions in Radwaniyya Prison during 1991, as described in a letter the narrator's father smuggles out to his wife, are taken almost verbatim from the testimony of Qassim Breysam of Basra, who was interviewed in 2005 by Mustafa al-Kazimi, then of the Iraq Memory Foundation (an interview, along with hundreds of others conducted by Mustafa, that was aired repeatedly on Iraqi television).

The U.S. Army did wipe out a harmless group known as Soldiers of Heaven, *Jund al-Samaa'*, as described by Haider and my narrator, and as reported online in *The Times* of London on January 29, 2007. Separately, I had access to a detailed Iraqi police report written in the immediate aftermath of the attack, replete with pictures, smuggled to me by an Iraqi security officer who was one of the first to visit the devastated area after the event. I do not know if the Americans knew what they were doing, and I am inclined to agree with Iraqis on the ground who told me they were tricked into it by Shi'a enemies of *Jund al-Samaa'*.

Events in this work of fiction follow the real history of what happened (the murder of Sayyid Majid, the siege Muqtada imposed on Ayatollah Sistani's house, the formation of the Governing Council, the wars between the Houses of Hakim and Sadr, the arrest of Saddam Hussein, the negotiations over the "suspension" of the arrest warrant for Sayyid Muqtada, the war in Najaf, the Sadrist alliance with jihadi Sunni groups,* the deal that Ayatollah Sistani brokered, the blowing up of the shrine in Samarra, the civil war across Baghdad, the hanging of Saddam Hussein).

There was an arrest warrant for Muqtada al-Sadr for the murder of Sayyid Majid issued by the American Occupying Authority based on an original investigation by a judge from Najaf, an investigation neither instigated by the Americans nor conducted with any American involvement.† The warrant was "suspended" following a secret deal struck between the House of the Shi'a (the literal translation of

---

* Sheikh Ahmed al-Kubaisi is one of the Sunni jihadis who bussed insurgents to Najaf and Karbala from Fallujah and other areas in the Sunni triangle, according to Paul Bremer. The first public statement of Hamas in support of the Mahdi Army dates to August 12, 2004; it focused on condemning "the barbarian American aggression against Iraq" and Najaf, in particular, and solidarity with the Iraqi people. The second statement, dated August 19, 2004, was much more specific, mentioning solidarity with Muqtada al-Sadr in particular.

† See Patrick Cockburn's account in *Muqtada al-Sadr and the Fall of Iraq* (London: Faber & Faber, 2008), 196–97.

Al-Bayt al-Shi'i, the name they gave themselves in 2003) and the occupying authorities. After the election of the first Shi'a-led government in the history of Iraq in April 2005, the original investigation was annulled and replaced with a new, phony one that found no one guilty of the murder and released two previously convicted direct perpetrators of the crime who had been arrested and imprisoned on the basis of their own confessions. The prime minister at the time was Ibrahim al-Ja'fari, a senior member of the Da'wa Party (the Party of the Call in the novel), and currently the minister of foreign affairs.

The stories related in the chapter entitled "The Second Conversation" concerning Sayyid Majid's role during the Uprising of 1991 accord with what eyewitnesses I interviewed in the early 1990s said, material I incorporated in *Cruelty and Silence*. There was a little boy of eight, Ahmed, whom Sayyid Majid saved just as one of my characters says he did. The Ba'thi officer whom Sayyid Majid rescued, a local man from Najaf, had asked for Sayyid Majid's "protection" in exactly the same cultural sense that Sayyid Majid employed when he asked Sayyid Muqtada al-Sadr for his house's "protection," only to have it denied and his murder authorized, as the novel recounts.

The contrast between the behavior of these two men, twelve years apart, the one who gave protection in 1991 and the other who denied it in 2003, both Sayyids from the most eminent religious families of the Shi'a world, is another reason I chose fiction as the form in which to tell my story. This is a book about character in politics, as well as ideas. In his wartime writings, Camus makes the point that character is rare in politics, unlike intelligence, which can be found everywhere. The narrator's uncle, an exceptionally intelligent man, exemplifies that insight. A lot of politics need have nothing or very little to do with character or the moral failings of individuals. But trust is a judgment made on the basis of character, and there are watershed moments in the lives of nations, such as 2003 in Iraq, when character, not intelligence, becomes all-determining, when one's actions routinely turn into commitments, and when there is a heavy human price to be paid for virtually every choice that one makes.

I observed innumerable instances of murky moral behavior among the returning community of Foreigner Iraqis, especially those who went on to occupy high positions in government, and who I saw steal and betray without batting an eye. The sheer scale of the corruption was a shock, far exceeding anything experienced under the Ba'th. Some of that was to be expected; perhaps, even, it was unavoidable at a time when Iraq had regressed to a cash economy—no banks, no credit cards, just circulating bags of cash. Of course there was corruption. What even is corruption under circumstances such as those of Iraq immediately after the tyrant's fall? And by what standards, and whose laws, dare we judge people? For these reasons, I can find it in my heart to excuse corruption, but not murder.

Among the nonfiction works that inform this work of fiction, I must mention Ma'ad Fayadh's firsthand account of the murder of Sayyid Majid, *Dhaheera Saakhina Jidaan* (A Very Heated Afternoon) (Beirut, 2007), published originally as a series of articles in *Asharq al-Awsat* shortly after the murder. Fayadh accompanied Sayyid Majid on his return to Najaf in 2003 and was with him in the shrine when the rabble-rousing started. He was captured and bound by Muqtada's men along with Sayyid Majid, but later released. My account of the murder does not rely solely on Ma'ad Fayadh, however. After years of trying and digging, I managed to corroborate Fayadh's account, add considerable detail, and carry the story forward by obtaining access to the original file that first the House of the Shi'a in the Governing Council in 2004, then the Governing Council, then the Ja'fari government of 2005, and finally the Maliki government of 2006–2014 worked hard to suppress and supplant with the whitewashed Sadrist version of events.

The story of the cover-up of Sayyid Majid's murder is in many ways more telling than the murder itself. All the members of the House of the Shi'a, whom the narrator's uncle refers to as the Cabal of Thirteen, were implicated. They either orchestrated the cover-up or knew about it and acquiesced. And most of them were personal friends of Sayyid Majid who worked with him closely during the 1990s.*

In fact, the secret concealed by the cover-up was not really a secret at all. I doubt there was anyone in the entire class of leading Shiʻa politicians of post-2003 Iraq—a class of several thousand people—who would not tell you in the privacy of their homes that they believed Sayyid Muqtada ordered Sayyid Majid's murder. But they all thought that it was not in the interests of the Shiʻa as a community (or their own intra-Shiʻa alliances and political future) to admit to the fact; hence the enormous success of the cover-up.

I, of course, think the exact opposite is true: the cover-up lies at the core of the Shiʻa elite's failure after 2003. Hence Sayyid Majid al-Khoei's murder is the intellectual and moral backbone of this book.

A cover-up of this magnitude works only when many people are directly or indirectly implicated; Saddam knew this well, having mastered the art over thirty years, to the point of rewriting history and successfully telling Iraqis what, when, and how to think, on any subject under the sun. The public was never entirely unaware of what was going on, conferring bad character traits upon the whole class of returning exiles, unfairly in some cases, because of the trickery and

---

* Evidence for the cover-up can now be adduced from documents released by WikiLeaks. See wikileaks.org/cable/2004/07/04BAGHDAD119.html. An article drawing the same conclusions by Aymenn Jawad al-Tamimi appeared in the Lebanese *Daily Star*. See www .dailystar.com.lb/Opinion/Commentary/2011/Sep-20/149186-iraqs-politicians-hover -above-the-law.ashx#axzz21GNFbOP8. The House of the Shiʻa was desperate to keep the cover-up a secret, which is why they took the extraordinary step of not allowing the Coalition Provisional Authority to make a copy of the letter, as noted in the WikiLeaks documents. The same was true of Prime Minister Nuri al-Maliki, who in a letter dated January 14, 2007, smuggled out of his office, advised the senior leadership of the Mahdi Army and their fighters, including some of the men personally involved in Sayyid Majid's murder, to withdraw from Baghdad so as to "retain our [Shiʻa] great gains" and not get caught up in the American-led surge, which would then target only Sunni militias. The letter stresses this would be "temporary," lasting for the duration of the American military surge. Were the Americans, Maliki's big backers at the time, aware of this ploy? I wouldn't be surprised.

deceit it now began to associate with the House of the Shi'a and the governing class.

Incidentally, the word "cabal," which is used in the novel to describe the leading group of thirteen Shi'a members of the Bremer-appointed Governing Council, the individuals most directly involved in the cover-up, captures the contempt that Muqtada himself, and the Sadrist movement generally—and, therefore, my narrator and his uncle—had for the House of the Shi'a between 2003 and 2006. A strange psychological dynamic was at work, in that the more the Foreigner Iraqis, or the House of the Shi'a, or more generally the stream of carpetbaggers and would-be politicians returning from exile after 2003, tried to curry favor with Sayyid Muqtada, the greater was the contempt he held them in during those crucial first years after 2003. That sentiment, of course, did not extend to Sayyid Majid, whom he did not hold in contempt as much as he hated and, probably rightly, feared.

The original Iraqi government file that I rely upon in my novel was almost certainly destroyed by the April 2005 Ja'fari government, around the time that two men who had confessed to the actual stabbing in the original investigation, Mustafa al-Ya'koubi and Riyadh al-Nouri, both senior followers of Muqtada al-Sadr, were pardoned and released from jail following the Shi'a-led whitewash. Only the U.S. government retains copies of the original investigation, buried by now deep in the bowels of its National Security Archive.

In December 2002, at the conference of the Iraqi opposition in London attended by around one thousand people, Sayyid Majid and I informally headed two competing groups of "independents" (Iraqis unaffiliated by choice with any of the traditional parties represented in the conference, all of whom ended up in the Governing Council the following year). The details are unimportant, but we were caucusing during a break in the main conference and the vote was going against me (we are both great talkers, but he had the better argument). At that point some of my so-called friends in the Iraqi National Congress pulled a trick to avoid a vote being taken. They came rushing in to announce the main conference was reconvening, and we all had to dash back into the main hall because an important vote was about to be taken. The meeting of the independents broke up, and my "friends" had a big laugh about it afterward. I was embarrassed, but they had thwarted Sayyid Majid, and that was the point. I think Sayyid Majid knew all along what was going on, but I was famously naive and didn't guess right away.

Two or three weeks after that episode, my father and I and a few other guests of Diwan al-Kufa in London were having lunch at an Iranian restaurant on Westbourne Grove.* There were several bottles of wine standing prominently on the table. When it came time to pay, the waiter indicated that another customer sitting by himself in the corner of the room, whom I had not noticed before, had already paid for the meal; it was Sayyid Majid, always the gentleman.

Sayyid Majid's father was Grand Ayatollah Abu'l Qassim al-Khoei, widely considered to be the most respected "Source of Emulation" in the Shi'a world since 1970, the year of the death of his predecessor, Sayyid Muhsin al-Hakim. The Ayatollah who replaced Sayyid Abu'l Qassim al-Khoei following his death in 1992 was his brightest student, Sayyid 'Ali al-Sistani, a "quietist" cleric cast in the mold of his teacher and mentor. He was named successor in Khoei's will and accepted as such by the entire clerical establishment of Najaf. Sistani remains until today the most respected source of religious authority in the Shi'a world. I was granted the privilege of meeting him in 2004. Sistani, incidentally, unlike my fictional counterpart, disapproves of the title "Grand Ayatollah" (the first Ayatollah to do so) and has expressly requested on his website that his followers not use it any longer.

---

* Diwan al-Kufa was a London-based Iraqi cultural center established by my father, Muhammad Makiya, and named after the first private Shi'a University, which he tried to establish in southern Iraq until the Ba'th shut it down in 1970, expropriating all its privately donated assets.

Ayatollah Sistani hates getting involved in politics, and will do so only when the situation is dire because of the bungling of the governing Shi'a elite, toward whom he feels responsible. It was he who stood up to Iran and would not have another Iranian stooge as prime minister, which is how Haider al-Abadi, the first decent Iraqi politician since 2003, came to replace Maliki. The odds against Abadi succeeding are enormous; sharks beholden to Iran surround him, and sectarian criteria determine whom he can appoint. How strange that Sistani, a ninety-year-old recluse born in Qum, should be the last Iraqi patriot standing with anything like genuine authority in today's Iraq.

The third of the "Three Houses" that have a role in this book, and the most important from the viewpoint of Sayyid Majid's murder, is the House of Sadr. It owes its eminence in the second half of the twentieth century to Muhammad Baqir al-Sadr, a leading Shi'a scholar of the 1970s, also a student of Khoei's, and a founding member of the Da'wa Party around 1960 (the exact date is disputed). Sayyid Mohammad Baqir, and his activist sister, Bint al-Huda, died gruesomely at the hands of Saddam Hussein's intelligence services in April 1980, five months before Saddam launched his war against Iran. The timing, no coincidence, only confirmed the regime's fear of Sayyid Muhammad Baqir al-Sadr as potentially Iraq's future Khomeini. In any event, he was an implacable, charismatic, and exceptionally intelligent foe of the Ba'th who also had the scholarly credentials to succeed Khoei as Grand Ayatollah had he lived. Saddam knew that. In the novel, Saddam Hussein's description of what he did to Sayyid Mohammad Baqir and his sister in 1980, and why, is of course fiction, but not of the kind that any Sadrist or expert in the politics of the period would object to.

Sayyid Muhammad Baqir al-Sadr's cousin Muhammad Sadiq al-Sadr (referred to in the novel as Sayyid Sadiq) was Muqtada's father. He had spent much of the 1980s bitter and resentful, not of the Ba'th regime, which had killed his cousin, but of Ayatollah Khoei, Sayyid Majid's father, and the clerical establishment he represented, for supposedly snubbing him and not giving him his rightful place in the clerical hierarchy of Najaf. In a famous interview known as the *al-Hannana* interview, Sadiq al-Sadr went on record claiming that Ayatollah Abu'l-Qassism al-Khoei collaborated with the regime of Saddam to keep him at bay.

By the end of the Uprising of 1991, Najaf was a wasteland, with huge swathes of the city leveled, its great libraries burned, its clerical class, many thousands strong, either dead or in exile. The regime needed someone to oversee its reconstruction. They also wanted an Arab who was known for his hatred of Iran (Sayyid Sadiq's feelings were not unconnected with the fact that Khoei and Sistani are of Iranian origin), and on this basis the Iraqi regime indirectly supported Sayyid Sadiq's claim to be the Grand Ayatollah with money and the power to grant or deny residency permits to clerics from overseas—from Iran, Afghanistan, and India predominantly—who wanted to reside and study in Najaf. According to the International Crisis Group, which gained remarkable access to the Sadrist movement, conducting important interviews with Sadrists in Iraq during 2005 and 2006, the Ba'th regime exempted Sayyid Sadiq's sons and a number of his students from military service, and authorized him in 1996 "to launch his own publication, *Huda*—a striking gesture in a country whose press was tightly controlled."*

The establishment clerical class backed by the wealthier merchants and upper middle class of Najaf rallied around Sistani, Ayatollah Khoei's nominee. Sayyid Sadiq seethed with resentment because he had again been denied his rightful place under the sun,

---

* From International Crisis Group, *Iraq's Muqtada Al-Sadr: Spoiler or Stabiliser?* (Middle East Report no. 55, July 11, 2006), 3. This report includes interviews with Sadrists from the leadership and the rank and file. Clearly compiled by Iraqis working for the ICG, it includes background on Sayyid Sadiq and his conflict with Sayyid Sistani. See also International Crisis Group, *Shiite Politics in Iraq: The Role of the Supreme Council* (Middle East Report no. 70, November 15, 2007), which covers the war between the Houses of Hakim and Sadr. On the *al-Hannana* interview, see Loulouwa al-Rachid, "Du bon usage du chiisme irakien," *Politique Internationale* 101 (Autumn 2003). I have also benefited from the book by Harith al-Qarawee entitled *Imagining the Nation: Nationalism, Sectarianism and Socio-Political Conflict in Iraq* (Bacup, UK: Rossendale Books, 2012).

notwithstanding all the money he could dispose of to bribe students away from their traditional mentors. Armed with the authority to deny residency permits to students or scholars of theology he did not like, he launched an intensive anti-quietist crusade, accusing the traditional Shi'a clerical establishment of remaining silent, or "quiet," after his cousin's execution and distancing themselves from the very poor and the very young by their preoccupation with abstruse and outmoded religious questions. Soon the establishment clerics found themselves the target of a smear campaign, one that insulted them personally, something previously unheard-of in conservative Najaf, where respect for the clerical class was a matter of honor. Vulgar leaflets and cheap cartoons and posters started to appear denigrating the quietist Ayatollahs and telling them to go back to Iran. In 2003, at the time of the murder, Sadrist activists surrounded the homes of Ayatollahs 'Ali al-Sistani, Bashir al-Najafi, and Muhammad 'Ishaq al-Fayadh; Ayatollah Sistani was forced to call upon local tribes to drive Muqtada's men away.

This rising tide of nastiness would culminate in the murder of Sayyid Majid. Sayyid Sadiq, Muqtada's father, had coined the notion of the "vocal" cleric and proceeded to use the monies flowing in to him not only to gain students and followers, but also to set up "popular bases" in anticipation of the long-awaited return of the twelfth Imam of the Ithna 'Ashariya branch of Shi'ism (the Twelfthists), the dominant branch in Iraq. The twelfth Imam, named al-Mahdi (literally "the Rightly Guided One"), had supposedly gone into Occultation and would return at the end of time as the last divinely chosen Imam. In accordance with his father's writings on the imminence of the twelfth Imam's return, Muqtada al-Sadr appropriated his father's notion of the "vocal" or activist cleric and named his militia the Mahdi Army—or, as I have rendered it in English to give a sense of its wider meaning, the Army of the Awaited One.

Sayyid Sadiq was no longer content to challenge just the quietist establishment, but Iran (by proclaiming his authority over the Shi'a of Iraq and denying Khamenei's claim to pan-Shi'a leadership) and the Ba'thi regime itself. The latter was one enemy too many. By the late 1990s he seems to have become carried away with his own rhetoric about the imminent return of the Mahdi to the point of going about wearing a shroud, looking to become a martyr, which the regime duly obliged him with when it gunned him down along with Muqtada's two older brothers in February 1999. From the date of that killing, the organization Sayyid Sadiq built went into hibernation, from which it emerged only after the last remaining son of Sayyid Sadiq, Muqtada, sanctioned the murder of Sayyid Majid on April 10, 2003, the event that sits at the heart of the novel and the seed from which sprung in that same year the gigantic tree of the Sadrist movement in Iraq.

Opinions differ as to the precise date of the fall of Saddam Hussein, with the American media and U.S. government insisting on April 9, 2003, because that is when the pictures of the statue in Firdaws Square being toppled were taken and aired all over the world. Many Iraqis, myself included, have settled on April 10, 2003, as the day of the tyrant's fall, because Saddam Hussein was seen praying in the Mosque of Abu Hanifa and walking about in 'Adhamiyah on that day. He fled Baghdad shortly afterward. April 10 is also the day of Sayyid Majid's murder.

I carried this union of liberation and murder with me for ten years, not knowing what to do with it. I felt it had to lie at the heart of anything I wrote about what went wrong in post-2003 Iraq. But how best to capture the enormity of the conjunction?

The literary resolution of the nexus of liberation and murder takes place in the novel through the person, or character, of Saddam Hussein, standing in as he so obviously does for that long legacy of abuse—he was the past that would not go away because Iraqis had hanged him (the United States, it was my understanding at the time, was against the hanging, not in principle but because of the timing). One evil quickly replaced another, worse than the first, civil war, and the furies of killing and destruction are not over yet.

Saddam Hussein understood the unwritten rules of Iraqi governance and statehood that were so effortlessly imbibed by those who followed him. In the first part of the book, which sticks closely to the known facts about the hanging, Saddam says very little. But the little he does say is factual. I chose to adhere as closely as possible to the known facts concerning how he died.* I did not witness the hanging myself, but worked to re-create the context and scene from innumerable sources. The story of "The Rope," for example, comes from one of those sources, a young aide to the prime minister attending the execution who had lost a close relative to Saddam.

The Saddam who reappears on the other side of Sayyid Majid's murder in the third part of the book is, on the other hand, a completely fictional construct, as brutal as the historical Saddam but far smarter and better read. And he likes to talk, lecturing the narrator regarding "the truth of my dictatorship."

In the world that he built, Saddam explains, betrayal was everywhere. To betray was to survive and was therefore morally justifiable, or at least morally ambiguous, and difficult for outsiders to condemn. Betrayal was the place where character and politics met for the duration of his rule. No one understood betrayal, and used it as a political tool, better than Saddam. He made the rules of this terrible world; he knew best how to manipulate its sources and passions. That is why in the fictionalized portrait I have created of him in Part Three it is he who best understands the failings of Iraq's new crop of leaders. They are all, he points out, "my children," including, needless to say, those who lived for decades in London, Washington, and Tehran.

---

* The chanting and the opening of the trapdoor before Saddam had finished reciting the Shahada were captured on a smart phone belonging to an Iraqi government official and are available on the Internet. A photograph of Saddam on the platform showing the pulley and the three men in ski masks was published in an article in the Kuwaiti newspaper *Al-Anbaa* on February 9, 2011. See also the report in *The Advertiser*, December 20, 2005. The scene of Saddam's body being exhibited in front of the prime minister's office, with the chanting crowd, and the shroud being lifted from his face, can be seen on YouTube: www.youtube.com/watch?v=lO037ky6TtI. See also another clip with voice-over from Iraq's Biladi TV station, owned by Ibrahim al-Ja'fari: www.youtube.com/watch?v=lgJ4CPy7zeE.

Why did betrayal persist and live on, even flourish, after the tyrant was gone? And why did Foreigner Iraqis, men who had lived abroad for so many years, betray more than Iraqis who knew no better, who could not be expected to shed overnight the mistrust and cautionary habits of a lifetime? I don't know, and dare not hazard a guess. I only try to show in this book how it did.

In a simplistic view of sectarian behavior, it is assumed that if leaders betray, at least they don't betray members of their own sect. This may be true in a zero-sum world, but that was not the world of post-2003 Iraq. The long-suffering community of the Shi'a are the greatest victims of their leaders' sectarian politics.

Which brings me to the challenge of this book: the argument that the failure of post-2003 Iraq is one of leadership, and of Shi'a Iraqi leadership in particular; it is a "subjective" failing, not one explicable by the brutal facts of tyranny alone or by a disastrous occupation. Failure of the kind I am writing about cannot be predicted; it was not a foregone conclusion before the war. People made it so. Civil war and a complete breakdown in Sunni-Shi'a relations were not inevitable consequences of war and occupation; Iraqi leaders knowingly or unknowingly willed them into existence. Individuals with weight, who would not cater to the basest sentiments, might have made a difference. Others have convincingly portrayed the many failures of the American occupation. There is no point rehashing those here. But the deeper failure, the one that this book is about, was always an Iraqi one.

Since one could not expect Kurds or Sunni Arabs—both fearful and prickly minorities, always on guard and on the defensive—to be the driving forces of a new Iraq, the failure I am referring to has to be laid at the door of the Shi'a leaders who emerged and who were knowingly handpicked by the Americans to become the dominant force of the governing elite in Iraq.

They had the most to lose by failure; they represented a majority that had potentially an entire country to gain. No one would have benefited from success as much as ordinary Iraqi Shi'a; that was the promise that the Americans held out and that Shi'a leaders failed to deliver; they played instead the game of competing over who had suffered the most, and scheming to make Sunni Arabs, or former Ba'this (which was virtually everybody), pay for the decades of abuse, maliciously now attributed to them as an entire community.

De-Ba'thification in Iraq, which to my shame I defended before the war, was in practice witch-hunting or de-Sunnification. Nothing else. The same is true of the Commission of Public Integrity, perhaps the most corrupt and sectarian institution of the post-2003 state. The Shi'a elite fought for these institutions, administered them, and implemented their provisions, even as they failed in everything else (providing electricity, repairing the shambles that is Baghdad, building infrastructure, expanding and modernizing the country's oil production and refining capabilities). Americans had very little to do with de-Ba'thification beyond authorizing it. De-Ba'thification went along with, among other things, rewriting Iraqi history to claim that the state had always been a sectarian Sunni enterprise, a politics belied by the facts and doomed to bring out the worst in the very people they needed to win over the most. Much of Western academia and the media followed suit in a quest to find simple, pseudoscientific "causes," supposedly rooted in "age-old" hatreds, for what were in fact crass political tactics, and choices of the worst sort. Those choices amounted to the invention and the institutionalization of the new politics of our times: sectarianism.

The Iraqi state created by the British in 1932 was no more intrinsically sectarian than the American republic was intrinsically racist. To be sure, Iraqi society was sectarian, perhaps profoundly so, as profoundly as American society was racist. But I am referring in both cases to the state, not to society. Politicians, parties, leaders, and intellectuals could choose to work against racism (Lincoln, Martin Luther King, Kennedy, Johnson in the United States), or they could go along with it, to the point, in Iraq, of promoting and instituting sectarianism into the body politic, as the Shi'a political class has been doing since 2003. Neither racism nor sectarianism is easy to eradicate, but at least racism was pushed back in the United States (where it flares up from time to time, as it did in Baltimore and Ferguson in 2014). In Iraq, however, driven from the political top down into the social and cultural base, it had to become the be-all and end-all of politics; it is now very hard to eradicate. And, of course, the rest of the Middle East is following suit, adding to and embellishing the contribution of Iraq's Arab Shi'a leaders to civilizational breakdown in the Muslim and Arab world.

Sayyid Majid's murder, and its cover-up, showed from the outset that no one in the country had that intangible mix of foresight and generosity of spirit to rise to the great historical occasion of the tyrant's downfall. It may be fortuitous that he was murdered on the same day as the Ba'thi state collapsed. But there was nothing fortuitous about the cover-up that ensued. And this, of course, is the price that sectarianism, like racism, always exacts: it dehumanizes the sectarian and the racist, even as it violates and punishes his victim. Society as a whole is debased.

An anecdote may be helpful here. In the 1990s I engaged in a standard sort of argument with my friend Barham Saleh (former deputy prime minister of Iraq) concerning the possibility of Kurdish secession from a post-Saddam Iraq. The argument would play itself out with Barham talking about how "artificial" the Iraqi state was, and how logical a Kurdish state was, and, while agreeing, I would defend the idea of Iraq, saying something like "Don't throw the baby out with the bathwater," meaning Kurdish secession could end up being more costly to the Kurdish people than staying in a new federal Iraq (something that may no longer be true, as the Kurdish leadership is starting to realize).

The irony is that in the end it was the Kurds who stayed, providing the more responsible ministers to successive Iraqi governments, and it was the Iraqi Arab Shi'a leadership who threw the Iraqi baby out with the bathwater, and gave us ISIS.

It is extremely painful for me personally that Sayyid Majid al-Khoei was Iraqi Shi'a sectarianism's first victim; here is yet another variation on the story of Cain and Abel: a murder between first brothers, at the dawn of a new world, unleashing mayhem onto their race. Thus are laid the seeds of continuing and ever-escalating violence as we heirs of Cain try to be who we are at someone else's expense.

I am not religious; I knew Majid only, as others did, as a good and ordinary man, the first of many hundreds of thousands of good and ordinary Iraqis to be murdered by their fellow Iraqis out of hatred or revenge. But he was also the son of Grand Ayatollah Abu'l-Qassism al-Khoei. There is nothing ordinary about that. His murder, and its cover-up, should have sounded a warning to the whole community into which I was born. It didn't. What does that tell us? It tells us that when Sayyid Majid died, something in all of us died with him. Perhaps it was dead already on the day that Saddam fell. As my narrator realizes at the very end of his quest: Sayyid Majid is an ordinary man, but he is also everyman; he is "us."

He is Ammar. He is Mustafa. He is my cousin Sa'ad, who was shot dead in his car by Sunni jihadis intent on driving him out of his neighborhood. He is the Sunni Arabs who were evicted from their homes in Baghdad and Diyala, or those who had holes drilled through their skulls by the likes of Haider during the first civil war of 2005–2006. He is the Iraqi Christians today being driven out of homes that belonged to them centuries before Islam even existed. He is the little Yazidi girls sold into slavery by ISIS.

Yes, Sayyid Majid is every Iraqi who allowed his patrimony to be betrayed by men (and they were always men) claiming to be acting in the name of that new chimera of post-2003 Iraq: "Shi'a rule."

ABOUT THE AUTHOR

Kanan Makiya was born in Baghdad. He is the author of several books, including the best-selling *Republic of Fear, The Monument, The Rock,* and the award-winning *Cruelty and Silence.* He is currently the Sylvia K. Hassenfeld Professor of Islamic and Middle Eastern Studies at Brandeis University. He lives in Cambridge, Massachusetts.